INVADERS

FROM BEYOND

An Abaddon Books™ Publication
www.abaddonbooks.com
abaddon@rebellion.co.uk

First published in 2017 by Abaddon Books™,
Rebellion Publishing Ltd., Riverside House,
Osney Mead, Oxford, OX2 0ES, UK.

10 9 8 7 6 5 4 3 2 1

Editor: David Thomas Moore
Cover: Adam Tredowski
Design: Sam Gretton, Oz Osborne and Maz Smith
Marketing and PR: Remy Njambi
Editor-in-Chief: Jonathan Oliver
Head of Books and Comics Publishing: Ben Smith
Creative Director and CEO: Jason Kingsley
Chief Technical Officer: Chris Kingsley

ISBN: 978-1-78108-518-9

Printed in Denmark by Nørhaven

INVADERS
FROM BEYOND

JULIAN BENSON • TIM MAJOR • COLIN SINCLAIR

ABADDON
BOOKS

WWW.ABADDONBOOKS.COM

INTRODUCTION

"The chances of anything coming from Mars are a million to one," he said...

IT'S ONE OF the classic tropes of the science fiction genre; from HG Wells' *The War of the Worlds* in 1898 to last year's summer blockbuster *Independence Day: Resurgence*, alien invasion has never been far from the popular imagination. It's in our cultural DNA.

And like all the most enduring tropes, alien invasion is a cypher, meaning whatever the writer wants it to mean. *The War of the Worlds* and many of its contemporaries were simple military stories, while their post-WWII successors, like *Invasion of the Body Snatchers*, reflected the growing paranoia of the Cold War. (The 1951 *The Day the Earth Stood Still*, by contrast, has essentially benign aliens warning us to *stop* fighting.) The aliens of John Wyndham's *The Kraken Wakes* were almost a sideshow to his main theme of collective hysteria and the power of the media, while the cult 1988 film *They Live* is chiefly a dark satire of conspicuous consumption. Aliens, ultimately, are powerful mostly for what they can tell readers about *ourselves*.

Pitching to Abaddon Books' 2012 open submissions month, Colin Sinclair, whose novella opens this collection, proposed a fairly straightforward idea: stories that mine this richest of veins, challenging and subverting it the way *Tomes of the Dead* did the zombie genre. It was an epiphany—why didn't we think of that ourselves? Colin was duly signed up, and his generation-X-esque, slackers-vs-aliens comedy *Midnight in the Garden Centre of Good and Evil* was born.

What you hold now is an exploration of classic alien invasion tropes—body snatchers, big slimy monsters and little grey men—twisted by some of the most engaging rising talents of British weird fic. They ask awkward questions about this modern mythology; they tap into the darker side of the human psyche, from burnout to depression to guilt; and they're frequently quite funny with it.

Thank you for reading!

And remember to watch the skies...

David Thomas Moore
Editor

MIDNIGHT IN THE GARDEN CENTRE OF GOOD AND EVIL

COLIN SINCLAIR

seeds in ceaseless fall

and drift in starlight down an

endless down and then take root.

take time.

take control...

BOOK ONE
THE ARRIVAL

1

"YOU'LL NEED THESE," Etty is saying, shoving thick, clumsy gloves over my hands. The touch of her warm skin on mine is—

Wait.

The harsh rasp and thrum of ripping plastic.

Chas is on his knees down at my feet, wrapping long strips of silver-grey adhesive tape around my ankles. It's the heavy duty stuff from the shelves near the back of the store. Chas finishes one leg—trapping the trousers tight against my boots—and moves on to the other.

"Why is he doing that?"

Etty smiles. Curls a strand of bright blue hair behind her ear. Then my view is obscured as she pops a reinforced cycling helmet over my head. It has a smeary curve of Perspex glued to it, which covers my face down to the chin. Makes seeing a bit of a chore. I have to squint downwards.

"You don't want them crawling up your legs," Chas says.

The blur of darks and lights that is Etty's face says, "You okay in there?"

I rub a gloved hand across the visor, clear it a little.

Chas finishes the tape job. Stands up and hands me a short-handled plastic shovel—it's a kids toy, be-a-gardener-like-mummy-or-daddy—says: "Job's a good 'un."

"Is this necessary?"

"You'll thank us," someone tells me. Not sure who. The other members of the Friday night team are seated in a semi-circle round a patio table to my left; fake grass, paddling pool, little shed with brochures and stuff arrayed under the blaze of fluorescent ceiling lights. I can just make out the bright colours of the tiny umbrellas in their drinks.

"You know what you're doing," Chas is saying. "You remember the safety briefing."

"No—"

"Scoop and drop," Etty tells me. She grabs my left hand—the glove ruins the experience—curls my fingers round the handle of a tiny bucket. Holding my head just so, I can see an improvised lid on top of the bucket, a fold of cardboard or stiff plastic.

"You'll want to hold that closed." Etty taps the lid. "You don't want them getting out again if you catch any. Here all night that way."

I shift the bucket and spade around with clumsy sausage fingers.

"Oh," adds Etty. "One per bucket or they'll try and eat each other. Bear that in mind."

Chas thumps me on the back. "Safe as houses."

I cast around for support from somewhere, anywhere.

"Do I have to—"

"Rules is rules."

Chas and Etty are backing away, clambering over a makeshift barricade of fertiliser bags and towers of plant pots.

I'm left alone in an empty arena.

"First night at Friday Club," Etty says. "You have to fight."

Alone except for a low stack of wooden crates, piled four high, the top draped with ruffled green fabric. The lettering on the wooden slats is Spanish. I think. Portuguese? Whatever they speak in Brazil. I tilt my head back and consider the gaudy petals of flowers peeking out from the topmost crate. Orchids. Ultra-rare orchids from the remote highlands of distant Amazonian rainforests.

"This can't be legal," I say.

"Bit late for that, squire, ain't it?"

That's Jost talking. He's got an unmistakable too-many-cigarettes-and-started-far-too-young rasp to his voice. Also a no-nonsense spit-and-polish manner. He did something in the Army. He doesn't talk about it.

"You just concentrate on the job in hand."

I keep looking—best I can—towards the crates.

My palms are slick with sweat, and I can feel a chill dancing down my back, like something crawling along my spine...

Think of something else. Something bright and—

"It's the smaller ones you got to worry about, isn't it?" Chas again. Ever helpful.

He leans across the barricade and drags the green cloth cover off the topmost crate.

"The larger creatures have got size to scare off predators. It's the little scamps that have to kill things that threaten them, yeah? Big ones aren't so much trouble. I saw that on Discovery."

A massive black blob of something slides over the top of the open crate and marches down the vertical and onto the floor.

"Unless it's one of those," says Chas.

It's got fur, and lots of legs, and too many eyes, and— .

"Fangs like bananas, that one, serious poisonous."

"Venomous." That's Laura Kelvin; precision is always important. "Poisonous would mean—"

"Piss off, Kelvin," says Chas. "Point is, right, it's in the fucking murder business, yeah?"

This thing is the size of my shaking hand and it's starting to move my way.

"Kill it," says Chas.

The spider rears up on its several back legs to show me it plays for keeps.

"Before it kills you."

THIS WASN'T SUPPOSED to happen.

I had plans.

2

"...AND THEN WHEN they'd finally hauled the car from the water, and I'd had time to sober up, well, the whole wedding thing was off. Done, dusted, finished with. Daddy-doesn't-approve-of-this, she told me. Also, you're a giant a-hole, right? Stupendous. Anyone can make a mistake, I said. Well, she said, you've made a Big One. Vee big."

I'd been rambling for a while. I'm not sure how it started. Or how to stop.

"I'm not sure why I'm telling you all this."

Mr Brackett, stick thin, leaned across the desk, shiny suit gleaming a little less than his thinning blond hair, and scratched his pale, pointed chin. "Me neither, son."

He lifted some papers off the desk. "Somewhere, middle of all that, you seem to have forgotten that this is your actual job interview. Not some therapy session paid in full by dearest mum and dad."

Some hope of that. As part of my penance for the Incident, father had given me a stern talk about Taking Responsibility. No allowances, no credits cards, no back-up. "Time to find your feet," he'd told me. "Long past time."

"It'll do you good," Mum had said—closing the garden gates behind me, *clang*—and followed that up with a cheery farewell and oh-yes-we've-changed-the-alarm-codes.

Destitute, rent-due, post-graduate course cancelled on account of subtle pressure by the father-of-the-bride-not-to-be.

"You're drifting," Brackett interrupted.

I snapped back to here and now in a cramped, musty office at the back end of a middle-of-nowhere garden centre on the farthest edge of town. A time capsule, this place, several steps into the past: a calendar featuring a pretty half-dressed redhead, circa nineteen-seventy-something; dead or dying potted plants; an overflowing ashtray from a well-loved local pub that burned down years ago; a beige telephone with a rotary dial; a fan trapped in a wire cage, shuffling warm dead air around the room.

Grey filing cabinets, big wooden desk, several stern-looking chairs and an expansive leather couch with a garish crocheted throw draped across it.

You could film episodes of *The Sweeney* here, with no trouble from nitpickers pointing out the wrong sort of light fittings or questioning your choice of yellowing venetian blinds.

"You need to focus," Brackett said.

Yes.

I guess what I'd been trying to say—not coming right out with it—was that I was dependable and desperate and needed the job.

You have to say that sort of thing, don't you? Not, "I

tend to drift along and see what comes," or, "My parents have been running my life for so many years I'm not sure what I even want these days." Right?

At all costs you must avoid, "I tend to overanalyse, day-dream, am often rendered inert by indecision."

Especially if it's true.

I'm frozen in place and offering up my top quality self-starter smile; I'm radiating go-getting self-confidence.

Maybe.

Brackett grunted, shifted in his chair.

"I don't care about your degree." He glanced at the papers in his hand—application form filled out in neat script, copies of results, the usual—then shook his head. "Agricultural Science? Who needs it, eh? Load of old donkey. Pile of meaningless numbers and talk. I work the sharp end."

"That's very clear," I lied.

Brackett's Nursery & Gardens: a rainswept clump of rundown sheds, greenhouses and polytunnels, clustered around a long, low warehouse building with a curved, corrugated roof.

Down one side of the main building, some gravel avenues snaked around dishevelled planters and collections of outdoor ornaments. The other side is staff car-parking and a fenced-off area containing either a small prison or a children's play park. Towards the back of the plot, an overgrown hedgerow shrouded a couple of squat concrete boxes that might have been war era; ragged tin roofing, steel doors, reinforced windows.

None of it looked cutting edge, although the patch of lawn out front is well groomed, dotted with bushes and bordered by wooden frames and climbing vines.

I'd got lost on the way here.

There were no customers when I arrived. The only living thing in sight had been some workmen installing lights at another boxy-looking warehouse structure across the road. An out-of-town development that never quite caught on.

"What it is," Brackett told me. "I worked hard for what I've got. Started at the bottom, struggle and toil, see? Built my little empire and, well, I didn't do it alone, did I?"

I shook my head helplessly. That seemed to satisfy him.

"Exactly." Brackett stood up then, dropping the application details. A cascade of crumbs and ash drifted off his suit as he eased around the desk. "Support networks. The help of the community. Everyone pulling together."

He shook my hand. Or pulled me up from the seat.

Either way, he's ushering me towards the door.

"Time to give something back, isn't it?"

"Yes," I suggested.

"You've had it soft, lad," Brackett continued. "Big house with the folks; good school; getting the grades but never quite breaking a sweat. Am I right? I know I'm right."

There's no answer to that, is there?

"Let's give you your own chance to shine, eh? Away from your macadamia bullshit. Get your hands dirty. See how the world works."

He dragged open the door.

Outside in the hall, a tall blonde in a damp raincoat stood with effortless poise on very high heels, shaking a bright red umbrella.

"Job's yours," Brackett said, pushing me half out of the door. "Ah, Miss Lacey, good of you to make it, if you'll step this way we can begin your interview."

Miss Lacey squeezed past into the office, not much room to spare, and began to remove her coat.

"Start on Monday," Brackett told me. "I'll let the team know you'll be there. It's a good group. Very steady. You'll fit right in, I'm sure."

I may have glanced past Brackett and caught a glimpse of Miss Lacey in a very short black dress. Perhaps just a long jacket.

"I'm considering her for another position," Brackett said, and slammed the door.

3

Kelvin shouts at me. "Zoologists require perfect specimens."

I hazard a glance sideways, away from the looming spider.

"Don't damage the merchandise, is what she's saying," Etty explains. "Nobody wants a six-legged spider, do they?"

I look back. Has it gotten closer now?

"Saw a tortoise with a set of plastic wheels the other week," Chas says.

"Relevance?"

"I don't know, do I? Just saying. Amazing what you can do these days. Incredible what people will manage for their pets."

"No' really the same though," Etty says. "They'd already learned to love that little dear. No one's turning up with a mangled spider for sale saying aye, yeah, some o' its legs are a bit missing, right enough."

"I'm just—"

"Man trying to concentrate, here," I say. "Life and death struggle and that."

"Don't look like much of a titanic conflict from here," says Chas. "You standing there with your two arms the one length."

I'm waiting for my perfect moment, aren't I?

Not just expecting solutions to emerge or problems to disappear. This isn't my life in microcosm; I'm not waiting for the cavalry to arrive.

"You're like that Macbeth, aren't you?" Chas says.

"How's that? I don't—"

"Father murdered, mother shacking up with the uncle, and here you are."

"That was Hamlet," I tell him. "Macbeth was the one with blood on his hands."

"Point is," Chas says, "that's you. Standing around moping when you should be acting."

"My father's still alive. Last I checked," I say.

"Yeah?" Chas replies. "So what's your fucking excuse?"

I'm—that is—"Biding my time."

"That'll be it," Chas answers dubiously.

The spider doesn't look too convinced either.

It's getting into my personal space now.

Tch. No consideration.

Then again, imagine minding your own business in some lush, damp forestville paradise when Brackett's shady associates snatch you up as part of their floral supply network.

Etty had explained the deal.

Every couple of weeks a truck pulls up on a Friday evening and drops off a load of extra special delivery. We get to hang out late and make sure everything is in order, so the select, discerning customers get exactly what they need.

Oh, and we dispose of any unwanted travellers that might have made the journey.

If we can sell them to a suitable dealer no-questions-asked, it's all to the good, right?

Which is where the special-overtime-event known as Friday Club comes in.

It's why I'm standing waving my bucket and spade while a spider taunts me.

"We've not got all night," Chas says.

"We do, in fact, have all night," Kelvin points out.

Let's do this, I think.

I want to move but my leaden feet won't let me. It's much harder than it looks to take that first big step. One booted foot at a time.

No more messing around.

"Let's have you," I say—a little too loud—and then I reach for the spider.

BRACKETT'S IS AN odd place.

I get that now.

I mean, pretty clear even at interview stage that things weren't totally on the up, yeah? Not to mention meeting that nutter in the basement right after—Connor Loan, his name turned out to be; very sketchy round the edges that one. The others call him Clone; he doesn't seem to mind. I don't think he minds anything except for plants.

Took turning up on the first day to get the full effect, though. Took being around for a few weeks to get the measure of everything.

Even the journey in on day one was a revelation.

Taxi driver—*call me Danny*—took a while get his bearings. This place is a former business park at the far edge of town, but you'd think you'd embarked on an expedition to the fringes of the known world.

Still, the longer trip gave him a chance to explain the ins-and-outs of local history, didn't it?

"Lot of roads blocked off," he'd told me. "Built over, churned under, what have you. Follow me?"

What might have been new-build in the late 'seventies slid past as he drove down another bleak stretch of broken concrete roadway.

"Warehousing, store-rooms, workshops, even a cluster of those little art-sheds for creative sorts to carve dogs out of cheese or knit jumpers from their own hair. It's all here. Or used to be here, anyways."

I leaned forward. "Dogs made of—"

He looked at me and shrugged. "Modern arts, eh. Fuck is that?"

The seat belt strained against my shoulder as he hit the brakes again.

"Sat nav's a bugger," Danny said. "Scraping a single bar on the phone. You'd think this wide openness would help? You'd be wrong, though."

Danny leaned forward over the steering wheel. "This looks well off-beam for a start. I need to back her out a bit."

He stuck his arm over the seatback, staring past my head and out the rear window as he reversed the car too fast, one-handed up the road.

I tried to keep out of his eyeline, not that he seemed to be paying much attention.

"An airfield, once upon a time," he told me. "During the war. Fighter Command. Canadian and Polish officers, I think. Lot of the old buildings dotted around that place you're working at. Buried lumps of reinforced concrete all over the show; devil's job digging that out, right? All just left behind, isn't it, layer on layer."

I nod, clutching my messenger bag, knuckles white, and

hope he doesn't regard it as a slur on his abilities.

Danny faced forward again as he swerved the car round in a fast turn, almost throwing me against the door.

"You not drive yourself, then? Or can't afford a car, is it?"

I remembered my last time in the driver's seat. Upside down. Under the water.

"Cars," I started. "Not my thing…"

"Prison," said Danny.

Avoided by the skin of my teeth, thanks very much.

"Some super-secret-prison in this very area, is what I heard. Post-war Air Force stuff, yeah? Who knows the truth of any of that? You hear all sorts down the boozer, don't you?"

We seemed to be heading in the right direction.

"Almost there," Danny said. "I've knocked the meter off. Charge the usual rate, least I can do, isn't it? You'll go broke doing this trip every day, mate. You want to get a car."

He made a sound like strangling a cat. Turned out he was laughing. "Look at me, eh? Talking myself out of a fare, aren't I? Muppet."

More strangled-cat noises.

"Total muppet."

Another few hundred yards of silence and Danny starts up again.

"All that out-of-town shopping stuff followed on, didn't it? All shiny bright and new, all of them waiting for the next crash. Property collapse, dot-com apocalypse, always on the cards, wasn't it? You never know what's coming next. But it's always something. Mark my words"—he tapped the steering wheel for emphasis—"it's always something."

"There's a cycle of things," I answered. "Ebb and flow, boom and bust."

"Exactly," Danny said. "Exactly that. Good to have a sensible passenger for a change. Average day I don't hear two words from one end of a journey to the next. I miss the opportunity for intelligent discussion."

It doesn't feel much like a conversation, if I'm honest. More like he's chairing a meeting.

"And here we are."

I look around; middle of concrete nowhere.

"In a general sense," Danny added. "It's symbolic, isn't it?"

Is it?

Danny remained silent, even as we turned onto the final straight.

I started to wonder if he had a rolling flywheel deep inside his body, some mechanism that gathered momentum until—switch flipped, gears engaged—his words ran out of him, on and on, until the wheel ran down. Peaks and troughs. Ebb and flow.

"The decline of the capitalist dream," Danny announced. "Written in mouldy cement and broken glass. That'll be a tenner, thanks."

4

"FEAR ME, SPIDERS," I'm shouting. "For I am your god."

Etty gives me a look. "Seriously?"

"Getting into the spirit," I say. I set the cycle helmet and kid's spade to one side. "Gets the blood up, doesn't it?"

"Yeah," Etty replies. "Shoving helpless creatures into tiny containers is real primal stuff."

I've captured five. Arranged a pyramid of buckets at one side of the makeshift arena. A monument to my glory.

"Well, when you put it like that—"

"Contact right," Jost calls out.

"What the fucking hell is that?" says Chas.

"Yeah," I turn to look at Jost. "What's that mean?"

"No," Chas continues, pointing now. "What. The. Actual. Fuck."

I turn and look.

I wish I hadn't.

This thing runs at me and I turn and stumble; clatter of hollow plastic, thump of compost bags sliding from makeshift stacks.

"Awesome," Kelvin is saying. "This is incredible."

It's a beetle. Solid, shining black body and legs as thick as liquorice whips.

It's the fuck-off-biggest beetle I've ever encountered. I've seen smaller rats.

"Titan beetle," Kelvin says softly. "*Titanus giganteus*."

Jost: "You want me to stomp it?"

"No," Kelvin shouts. "Absolutely not. It is rare. Beautiful."

Chas is clambering over the tumbled arena wall with a shovel. "Give it here."

"Expensive," Kelvin says. "Did I mention expensive?"

Chas lowers the shovel. "You should have led with that."

Everyone looks at me. It's uncomfortable.

The Titan beetle is motoring around the arena floor, searching for an exit.

Chas grabs a spare bucket.

"Millsy. Pick that up and stuff it in here."

I hear myself saying "Why me?" and marvel at how whiny it sounds.

"You're the one wearing the gloves, hero."

"Fair point."

I'm not squeamish. This is an easy job. To be honest, it seems to have crossed some weird uncanny valley thing but in the opposite direction. The beetle looks ludicrous, fake. If it was smaller I'd worry more, I think; it would look less like a kid's toy.

I remember the briefing. *Scoop*—and it wriggles like one of those grip-strengthening gizmos, and then hisses like it's not happy—*and drop*.

It *thunks* into the bottom of the bucket like a stone dropped off a roof.

"Less challenging than expected," I say.

Etty says, "Maybe this'll do it for you."

I look over; look at where she's pointing, down…

That hollow plastic sound I heard when I'd stumbled away from the nightmare beetle?

That was me kicking over the arranged-with-care stack of buckets.

The pyramid is down, the spiders are loose. All that work undone by my own clumsy feet.

I sigh.

It's a tough life being a god.

"I'M STAMPING THEM out," Chas says.

"Keep them contained," Jost offers. "Set the tempo. Take the battle to them."

Kelvin is down on her knees piling heavy bags back in place. "Help me build up the barrier."

Etty steps in quick, grabs a spider bare-handed. Places it in the nearest bucket—slow and delicate—and closes the lid down tight.

Everyone stares. A moment of shocked silence.

The other spiders run wild.

"Everyone gets a brush," I tell them. "If you see something eight-legged, persuade it my way and I'll take care of them."

They grab brushes off the rack and move in a circle around me, closing in as I scan for errant spiderkind.

Teamwork.

I get one making a dash for the arena wall.

Into an empty bucket with it and back for more.

Another. Then a third.

"Wasn't there one more?"

I look around my feet. No sign. The brushes are sweeping back and forth; there's no escape that way.

"I was sure there were five. Did one of them stay hiding

when the buckets rolled over?"

I'm not seeing it.

Chas coughs, gestures at my feet.

I'm still seeing nothing.

I shrug my shoulders. "What?"

"Take another look," Kelvin says.

Okay. Nothing on the floor. I don't get—

Oh.

There it is—perched on top of my left boot; pretending to be black laces and complex knots—the final spider.

"Clever girl," I say, and then I prise the spider off and place it in a bucket.

Etty helps me arrange the stack in a slightly-less-likely-to-fall-down format.

"That was impressive," I tell her. "Picking it up bare-handed."

Etty shrugs. "I have a wee pet tarantula at home. They're no' scary at all. Nothing to it."

"So why was I the one catching them in the first place?"

"Simple," Etty says. "Your turn."

5

LATER ON THE Friday night, when the fighting's done and Man—mostly me—is victorious, Etty and I are sitting at the edge of the arena, dealing with the night's haul.

"Air holes," Kelvin calls across from the party area by the fake pool. She raises a tall glass of green liquid and blue umbrellas. "Dead spiders are cheap."

Clink of glasses as the others make it a toast.

—*dead spiders*

—*going cheap*

I'm applying more tape to a spider containment— seriously, the red plastic buckets have *SPIDER CONTAINMENT* written on one side in Kelvin's super-neat black script—then poking tiny holes with a pen. Getting it ready for shipping out to who-knows-where.

"How you holding up?" Etty asks me.

Good question.

Etty knows the score. Halfway through week one at Brackett's, I'm standing outside in the rain, looking at my mobile. Not sure how long I'm standing there. If I hold my palm flat and just right, not too many rain drops hit the screen. I had to tap it now and then to stop it going dark. Tap-tap. Staring at the happy-smiley face of Jennifer under glass. I could just call and say—

"There's no point."

I looked up and Etty's right there in the doorway; sneaky cigarette cupped in her left hand, right hand pushing hair back from her face.

"I can try," I told Etty. "I mean, yes, I've done some bad and stupid things, but we spent two-nearly-three good years together, didn't we? Goodish, ups and downs, you know? I think that means something. I think that's worth another chance, don't you? It all can't end because—"

"Reception is shit," Etty had said, and pointed to my phone.

Not at all awkward.

FRIDAY NIGHT, SURROUNDED by captive spiderkind, Etty says, "You look happier at least. More alive?"

I can't figure out what to say to that.

"Chas," Etty shouts past me. "You're up."

He sets his diet cola down and hustles over.

"Taxi for Boris," he says, taking hold of the nearest bucket.

Looks at our blank faces.

"Boris. Spiders. It's a thing," he insists.

Still nothing.

Chas points a thumb back towards Kelvin. "Do I have to call in Special K?"

Etty waves him down. "No need, Chas," she says. "We believe you. Don't we, Miller?"

I nod my head, looking sincere.

"I'm not feeling the trust," Chas replies.

I thump a closed fist against my chest. "It's there, bro'. It's there."

Chas frowns. "Don't call me bro'," he says, gathers up the remaining buckets and plods off.

"He does that a lot, doesn't he?" I say.

Etty apes a broad shouldered, wide-stance clumping gait. "The sour-Chas stomp, you mean?"

"That's the one. Makes a bold statement and leaves in a dramatic manner."

Etty mimics the *stomp-stomp-stomp*. "I'm no' saying it's his signature move or nothing," she says, "but he does pull it out a couple of times a week."

"Pulls what out?" Chas asks.

He's rounding the corner past shelves of ceramic pots, still holding the buckets of spiders.

Etty shifts her mime into a faux-yawn and stretch. "Tough day," she says, giving me a wink.

Very smooth.

I nod. "Hey, Chas. Weren't you—"

"More importantly," Etty says. "What you doin' back already? You've not even got out the door."

Chas stops. Thinks that one over. "Oh, yeah," he says eventually. "The boss is here."

"Fuck," says Etty.

BRACKETT SWANS IN, with a young woman clutching his arm. He'd loitered in the carpark for a good five minutes before that—marching up and down and yapping away on the phone, Jost said, whilst his companion waited in the Jag. Good of him to give us time to get the place tidied up.

Squared away, Jost calls it.

Meaning: all the drinks and snacks are dumped into an

insulated picnic cooler (£23.99, Camping and Caravans department) and shoved behind the fake hedging by the shed.

I'm moving things on the counter of station two.

Etty's up front checking a till roll at station one.

Jost and Kelvin are stacking the exotics onto the transporter and wheeling them back to the storage area for Clone to deal with.

"Good to see my people keeping busy," Brackett says on the way past. "Hives of industry."

His lady friend giggles, though I'm not sure why.

Another minute and both of them are through the staff-only doors and away—I presume—to Brackett's office.

"Odd time for an interview," says Etty, leaning at my counter now. She makes a show of checking her watch.

I'm surprised she even has a watch, what with mobiles and everything. Maybe it's part of the retro-goth-whatever vibe.

I look at the read-out on the cash register. "Gone half-two in the morning now," I say. "Clubs are well closed."

"I expect there are some details he wants to go over," says Etty.

"That must be it."

"Nothing wrong with bein' thorough."

"Does this happen often?" I ask her. I've been here just over a month and this was a first. Then again, it's also my first Friday Club, so what do I know?

Etty stands straighter, shrugs. "Now and again. Likes to bring his very-particulars back for some in-depth aptitude testing, doesn't he? Never the same woman twice, though."

"And Mrs Brackett...?"

I'd got the impression one existed, knew very little beyond that.

"None the wiser," Etty tells me. "Or maybe she couldnae give a shit."

Tap-tap of black-painted nails on the laminate counter top. "You get it all second hand, don't you? Overheard convos, peeking through curtains, listening at doors. That's metaphorical, right; I've no' got an actual eye to the keyhole..."

I nod to reassure her.

Etty says, "I had an auld bloke come in here—good few months back, this was—big sour look on his coupon. Asking sleek and sly-dog questions, he was, about how to kill an oak tree in his neighbour's garden."

"He what?"

"I know," Etty went on. "Wanted to make it 'look like an accident.'" She throws air-quotes up at the last part. "Exact words."

"A joke, maybe?"

"Dead serious, this one. And what I'm saying is: what series of events leads to making that kind of decision? How does that become the obvious solution to the problem?"

I don't know.

"So who can tell?" she says. "Who can fathom what's going on in the lives of folk you barely know?"

I manage to say, "Wow."

Etty shoves some blue hair back from her face. "Too much?"

I wiggle my hand. "A bit serious and heavy for this time of the morning, is all," I tell her. "What kind of place is this? One minute I'm fighting kill-crazy-spiders and the next I'm contemplating the mysteries of other people's lives."

"It's an adventure," Etty says.

Can't argue with that, can I?

I worked in an office once, summer job, nothing to it really: filing, data-entry, shifting boxes of who-knew-what from this store-room to that; the usual, in other words. Some of the other staff were a bit out of the ordinary, though.

A coterie, or maybe a coven, of silver-haired seen-it-all ladies ruled the roost. Told the bosses what to do. Sat at a semi-circle of desks near reception; covered the doors, the switchboard, monitored the coffee and tea rota.

I'm in the place five minutes and they've got my number, haven't they?

—*What's your name?*

—*Where you from?*

—*Got a girlfriend yet? Not married at your age surely...*

They could have been spies in a previous life. Perhaps they still were.

Every new job is different, but there's always something. Brackett's is a whole other experience.

Like last week, couple of mid-to-late-teen guys waltz in, early part of the day—all student scruffy and looking like they've not slept. They wanted to chat about tomatoes.

"Growing big red toms indoors," they'd said. Living in a flat, weren't they, not too much room or light, right?

They'd listened to me reeling off a whole spiel about hydroponics and lamps and what-not—you could see their minds struggling to take notes—before Chas had wandered over and put them off the whole idea. Muttered a few harsh words I couldn't hear. They'd left soon after.

"Odd sort of thing to want to—"

"Nowt to do with tomatoes," Chas said. "You gimp."

Obvious in retrospect. The basics are the same for most plants, after all. Light, food, water; in various ratios. It doesn't get much more complicated than that.

"We can't take the moral high ground," I'd pointed out. "What with Clone's growth industry in the—"

Chas gave me a look that wasn't hard to read, and I took the hint.

Don't get a reputation, don't draw attention. Brackett's takes a dim view of amateur herbalists. Company policy.

"Know nothing, see nothing, say nothing," Chas had said.

Words to live by.

"Anyway," Etty is saying. "Let's get back to looking industrious, eh?"

She's an assistant manager and gets to order me around. Half-heartedly, for the most part.

"It's why we get the big money," I reply.

Etty steps back from the counter.

"What happened with the spiders?" I ask her.

"Chas can drop them off on the way home," she replies. "They'll bide for now."

What else can you do?

"When you're making coffee I'll have a couple," Etty says—benefits of command—and goes back to pretending till rolls are interesting.

I stand at station two and don't think about Jennifer.

In the days and weeks after the Incident, it formed a constant pressure in my head; something that bubbled up to fill every empty moment.

I'm getting a job to better myself for her, I'm finding a flat to live better for her, and I'm figuring ways to make it up to her. Like she's the reason for moving forward, yeah?

As time goes on I'm finding that the notion fades.

6

COUPLE OF HOURS later I'm falling asleep into what's left of a mug of tea.

A sensation that could be stomach rumbling builds and builds and—

"Look at that."

Kelvin's standing over by the windows, pointing at something outside.

I sit up—spilling my cold tea in the process—and scramble for some napkins whilst the rest of the gang gathers.

The sound makes your head shake. Like a ton of aircraft taking off.

Maybe that Battle of Britain stuff I'd heard from call-me-Danny was true?

Jost is hanging back.

"Ghost echoes of the past," I say. "Some Spitfire-Hurricane action, yeah?"

Jost's face is pale and damp, some sort of panicked, seen-a-ghost response.

"Shit, dude," I tell him. "It's nothing."

Out past the carpark eighteen-wheeler trucks are pulling up at the vacant store opposite. Beaming lights, figures moving against the brightness, serious noise and bustle.

I look back to Jost and risk placing a gentle hand on his upper arm. Hope he doesn't break me in half.

"You're at your crappy job in the garden centre," I'm saying. "Everything is cool. Someone's moved in over the way. That's all that's happening here. Nothing to get—"

Jost blinks. "This you being helpful and supportive?"

I think about it for a moment. Move my hand off Jost's arm. Nod an affirmative.

"I thought some reassuring words might—"

Jost steps past me, heading for the windows. He stops and half-turns back to look at me.

"Kind of you to make the effort," he says, and then off he goes.

I ARRIVE AT the front after everyone else, but the main window is wide enough for all of us to stand and gawk, if you're tall enough to look over the litter of special offer stickers and fading declarations of new-stock-just-in.

It's serious stuff out there.

"I counted five heavies," Kelvin is explaining, pointing to the long high-sided trucks. "Three or four panel vans already parked out around the back. A couple of minibuses full of guys in overalls and hats."

I think back to this morning—no, wait—yesterday.

"Must be those guys that Chas and I saw earlier."

I share a look with Chas.

"Wait a minute," Etty says. "You knew about all this?"

* * *

I GIVE THEM the story. What there is of it:

Couple of blokes in slim suits and yellow hard-hats showed up on Friday morning, didn't they? Joined by a gaffer-looking woman in welly boots and high viz. Spent a rain-swept half-an-hour wandering forwards and back out front of the disused retail warehousing across the road. Pointing at things. Nodding. Tapping into hand-helds. Looking very busy.

I'd been refilling the impulse-buy stock bins and got to watch the whole performance.

Chas had rolled up beside me at the window round about then. "Nothing to worry about, that," he had explained. "Bastards like this are ten-a-penny, aren't they?"

I'm not so sure, I told him. I thought they'd seemed quite keen.

"Always someone looking to make a go of that old heap," Chas said. "Never happen," he added. "Never fucking happen."

I mustn't have looked convinced, because next thing Chas said, "I'd put money on it."

"How much money, exactly?" I asked him, still staring out the window. Watched another vanload of workies spilling out across the way.

"Wanker," Chas said to that, and then he wandered off.

"AND THAT WAS that," I'm telling Etty. "They left not long after. Or at least the vans did."

"Didn't think to mention it?" she says.

"It didn't seem—"

"Oh, yeah," Chas says. "Mister friggin' observant here gets an instant handle of the situation, willing to bet money and all that, but not a fuckin' peep out of him, is there?"

"Didn't hear anything from you neither," Jost points out.

"I'm not the one thought it's something to worry about, am I? Usual bullshit."

"Doesn't look usual," Kelvin says. She's got a notebook out and is taking down details as another big truck shudders to a halt in a rattle of metal and hiss of air.

"I wonder if the boss knows," Etty asks.

There's a crash of doors banging open at the rear of the shop, an incoherent ranting in the distance, beyond the shelves and display stands.

This is a big place; a sprawling open area crammed with all manner of garden related this and that. The doors to the offices and such are a fair punt away. Still, there's no mistaking the mood.

"I pay you so I don't have to care about this shit," Brackett is saying. Loud. Insistent. "I pay you to let me know about things in advance, not when they show up on my doorstep and shit all over my business." Very much warming to the theme.

Brackett strides into view, still barking into a portable phone; not a mobile, this one. It's some green plastic late-'nineties museum piece that links to what they call a base station that sits under his desk. Gives him the range he needs to rant at people whilst walking around the shop. He's making full use of that feature now.

"A small furniture store and some specialist crafts, that's what you told me, don't deny it. Something to revitalise the area, my arse, that's not what I'm seeing here. So you better have an explanation. It better be good."

No-one says a word or moves as Brackett passes by; like he's walking through a freeze-frame.

"It's I-don't-know-what-time right now," Brackett's

saying, heading for the doors. "But I'll see you at your office at seven."

He stops at the exit.

"Yes-in-the-fucking-ay-em."

Brackett tosses the phone and clatters out of the front door. He's in his car a moment later and grinding it to a start.

"I think he's aware," Kelvin says.

We all watch as Brackett pulls away in a spray of gravel. Driving angry.

"Excuse me?"

Everyone turns around. Brackett's lady friend is standing in the centre of the nearest aisle. "I seem to have lost Michael. Do you know where he might have gone?"

Bit tipsy, trace of an accent, very well spoken.

We all stare for a moment too long.

"Here," Chas says, at last. "Come with me and I'll get you a taxi."

7

"SHOULD HAVE SEEN it, on the horizon."

Jost, not looking at anyone, still taking in the view out the window; five long trucks nosed up like suckling pigs against the wide, pale bulk of the retail warehouse opposite.

I can hear Kelvin muttering something, scribble-scratch of pen on paper.

"Lacking tactical awareness, aren't we? Losing the edge. Leaving ourselves open to assault."

Jost takes security a little too seriously, I think. Cameras and alarms set everywhere around the place. He'd shown me the 'control room' my first week here—an otherwise abandoned office back in the maze of corridors behind the shop floor, bundles of cables running all directions and a brace of boxy-looking televisions that flickered through black and white images of the aisles, the store rooms, every exterior approach.

I'd tried not to notice the sleeping bag bundle and the folded army cot in one corner. Not sure if Jost was a live-in caretaker or a homeless ex-soldier needing somewhere to crash; jury still out on that one.

"Nerve centre," Jost had said then. Home-built plastic box with labelled lights for every single door and window, and each one burning steady and bright, to show us all was secure. Keeping out what, I do not know.

Bad memories, maybe. Plenty of that to go round.

Standing beside Jost at the window, I run through excuses in my head, get ready to explain again that I'm not to blame.

"Fortnight ago," Etty says.

"What's that?" I ask.

The extent of my memories of two weeks back: spending an afternoon racing sit-down lawnmowers and weeding the median strip of the road outside. It's an unadopted stretch, privately owned by who-knows-who and left to ruin by the powers that be, and had gone a little wild in places through neglect.

"That's the one," Jost says to Etty.

Is this a code, I have to wonder.

"Landscaping job," Etty goes on. "Bit of a help-out for the council, Brackett said."

Pretty the place up, he'd said. Maybe get our cards marked for some future work. Always good to keep them on the good side, he told me. Sensible business, that is.

Know much about landscaping work, I asked him?

Bugger all, he told me. That's what the internet is for, isn't it?

That's all the guidance we'd been offered; and a half-hour struggle with the beige monster Brackett called a 'computer' didn't help much either. Nothing for it but back to basics and doing the obvious.

Get out the mid-range mowers—no point risking the expensive stuff—and sort out the median strip and the hedgerows round and about. Not like we were knee-deep in customers at the time.

Day out in the sunshine, digging, planting ornamentals and such, and a bit of racing up and down.

"I don't see what that has to do with this," I say to Etty, pointing in the direction of whatever's going on outside.

"We were getting it dolled up for them," Jost says. "Whoever they may be."

I try not to laugh. "That just sounds needlessly ominous."

Etty's not laughing.

"Look," I keep talking. "It could be anything, couldn't it?"

This is a tough crowd.

"Furniture store. Computers. A laser-tag arena? They're quite popular, aren't they? Or is it all paint or whatever now. I don't know. Roller-skating?"

"Balls," says Jost. "Airsoft balls. That's a thing. Tossers wearing Gucci gear and pretending they're the big dogs."

"My point is"—I turn and stare out into the night— "This could be good for us, couldn't it?"

Nobody is nodding.

"Passing trade," I tell them, warming to my theme. "Staff nipping out at lunch to buy a potted plant, yeah? Maybe they want to discuss their plans for a new patio. Organise a replacement greenhouse. Pick a bigger shed. Help me out here, anyone..."

It's not all doom and gloom. Not everything is terrible.

I'm not quite sure what it is in my recent past that led me to that conclusion.

Not convinced that ending up at Brackett's is an indicator of positive fortunes, but there it is. Here I am.

Thinking positive, not worrying so much.

It will all be—

The night is erased in a blinding fall of light, like a tiny sun has lowered itself to hover just above the shop over the road.

When my vision clears, once I've blinked away the afterimage, what I see is this:

A sign.

Dark figures moving against the glare; adjusting, shifting, fixing.

Bright letters coalesce, bold and fresh in greens and blues, friendly and welcoming.

The sign reads:

GARDEN WORLD
A NEW EDEN FOR EVERYONE

Someone says, "Oh, for fuck's sake."

It might be me.

8

CHAS COMES BACK, taxi on its way for Ms Whatever-her-name-is.

"Janice," Chas tells us. "Seems sweet. No idea how she hooked up with Brackett but hey, it takes all sorts, whatever floats your boat and that, right?"

"We shouldn't panic unduly," I hear myself saying. Because it appears that I've not been paying attention to the situation.

"Lots of people have affairs," Chas says, shrugs. "Not like it's any of our business, is it? You plan to drop a dime to Mrs B or something?"

"He means *that*," Kelvin says, points.

The sign is still there, big and bright and bold.

"Oh, right, yeah," Chas nods. "You're right. We should definitely send someone."

"Send what?" I reply. "I don't. I mean. What?"

"Recon," Jost explains. "Check out the lie of the land. See what we're up against."

I turn to Chas. "And by send someone, you mean?"

"Well not me," Chas says. "I'm too well known in the district. Ice hockey pro for a local team."

"You are?"

Chas deflates a little. "We've had a bad season."

"Kelvin and I will monitor from here," Jost adds.

Shit.

I DON'T REMEMBER sleeping, but there's a solid tap on the shoulder and I open my eyes to bright sunshine streaming through grimy glass.

I'm stretched across a makeshift bed I've built from old bags of organic compost, half-covered with a picnic blanket. It's more comfortable than my current flat, although the smell of warm earth gives it a dirt-nap ambiance I could do without.

Etty's standing over me. "Looks like we're up."

Can't argue with that.

"You'll need a disguise," Kelvin says. "I know just the thing."

She scampers off to somewhere out back.

"A disguise," I repeat. "We're going to a shop, not infiltrating HYDRA."

"Either way, we can't go dressed like this, can we?" She waves at her compulsory Brackett's Nursery & Gardens T-shirt; a biting shade of green, polo-style collar, letters and logo in yellow thread, not a style leader.

A reasonable argument.

Etty takes off the T-shirt. Underneath she's wearing a long-sleeved fading-to-grey top with a white-printed outline of a guitarist striking a pose next to the words *NEAR BETH EXPERIENCE*.

"Oh, hey," I say, "I know them. Saw them at the student union last year."

Shoe-gazy goth stuff, with a side of trippy chanting in

places to lighten the sombre mood. Trio of guitars, some electronic keyboard percussion stuff.

"Kind of a weirdling New Order versus All About Eve mash-up vibe, I thought."

Lead guitar was this tall girl with bright blue—

"Tell me about it," Etty says, grinning.

"You lot kicked the roof off," I say, fanboying. I heard rumours of big record deals and a supporting-a-major-band world tour. Loads of buzz, and then nothing. "What the hell happened?"

"Creative differences," Etty says. Looks away.

"The manager," she goes on. "Who was also my boyfriend at the time. Turns out he and the bass guitarist were getting very creative."

Too much information is what I'm thinking.

"Nightmare," I tell her. Nothing else seems to fit.

"You two gonna stand around all day staring into space," Chas says, "or do you want to get this done?"

Spell broken, Etty and I get back to dressing up in leftovers from the lost property box.

"I didn't even know we had a lost property," Etty's saying.

"Oh, yeah," Kelvin says. "For a shop without much in the way of footfall, we seem to get a lot of abandoned treasures."

Jost holds up a black-and-white baseball boot with a broken lace. "Just the one shoe. Seriously, how does that happen?"

"What the fuck is this?"

Chas is waving a fat length of concertinaed tubing, connected to a brown metal box at one end and a rubberised greying mask at the other; thick, dark lenses either side of a long tapering nose, give it an insectile look.

"Is it a sex thing?" Chas asks.

"Polish respirator," Jost says. "Cold War vintage. No idea how it ended up here, tenner at auction if you're lucky."

"I'll keep that in mind," Chas says, and sets it to one side.

Etty ends up with an ankle-length coat—which just about covers her biker-boots—and a hat that has the appearance of a squashed ferret tied in a knot.

I'm sporting a slighty-too-large jacket and a rather flamboyant silk scarf.

"You look a picture," Kelvin says, beaming.

"Aye," Etty says. "Picture of *what*, though?"

"C'mon," I say, sticking out my elbow for her to take my arm. "Let's promenade."

Etty loops her arm through mine. "Oh, let's," she says.

And we're off to the races.

9

THE DISTANCE BETWEEN Brackett's and the upstart newcomers is about the length of a soccer pitch. Or so Chas tells me; I'm not an expert.

Two lanes of worn-out road and a broad rectangle of immaculate car park—trimmed hedges, deep black tar, pure white lines and lights burning bright against the grey sky of a dull morning.

The vibe is different. Brackett's feels old, weak, sagging into the warm and welcoming earth. Giving up its ghosts.

This place is spruced up and gleaming new. It's made an effort.

For Brackett, the typical weekend-gardener is an afterthought, a distraction. He makes more money from his under-the-counter wheeling and dealing.

Here at Garden World, though, the customer is encouraged, welcomed, *wanted*.

There's bunting at the doors and a gaggle of brightly-dressed young folk offering drinks, cakes, even tours around the new store.

Etty and I wave them off and enter unmolested. They

aren't pushy, they avoid crawling all over us; even this early, they're not short of victims for the hard sell.

The retail warehouse was designed as three stores side by side, but they've taken over the whole structure, knocked through the dividing walls of units one and two, left the far right side of the building sealed off.

Even so, Garden World is vast.

"We should mingle," I say, keeping my voice low.

"Why are you whispering?" Etty asks.

"We're on a mission," I say. "Aren't we?"

"Alright, but try not to *look* like we are," Etty says, and then, "Goodness, darling, have you seen this?"

She's standing at a display of wooden playhouses; they look like miniature log cabins and shepherds' huts.

"Now wouldn't that look wonderful for the east lawn?"

I nod my approval. "Quentin would love it," I tell her.

"We'll need one for Isabella too, of course."

"Of course," I reply. "Wouldn't want her getting jealous, would we?"

And we sweep past the crowds and on down the aisle to whatever the next thing is.

"Brash and bold," Etty says, leaning close to my ear. "That's the way to blend into this circus."

"Can't do much else in this outfit," I concede.

I look like the preppy one from Scooby-Doo. Fred?

So do most of the staff that I've spotted. Not the full Ascot style, sure, but a definite clean-cut, fresh-pressed enthusiasm. All of them are wearing matching outfits, or at least co-ordinated—heavy on the greens and blues— in various styles of sweatshirt, T-shirt, trousers, shorts, skirts. I even spot a few kilts.

Beyond the ranks of youth and exuberance, there's a more serious line of management types. Sedate-looking men and women in suits and ties; broadly the same colour scheme, but a lot more staid and official looking. They're carrying electronic tablets and wearing earpieces, taking notes—tap-tap-tap—and muttering instructions.

I turn to point them out to Etty, but she's already paying close attention. She's produced a pair of mirrored sunglasses from somewhere—the real nineteen-eighties sort that conceal half her face—and is using them for cover.

This place runs like a machine. Call for clean-up at aisle five and a crew of three is on the scene in moments—block the lane, assess the problem, tidy and reopen—done and dusted. A manager type is hovering in the background the whole time. Tap-tap-tap.

It doesn't *smell* like a garden centre.

The air in Brackett's is heavy; thick with old wood, damp earth, floral hints and sharp chemical tangs. Every garden centre has it. I mention this to Etty.

"Maybe it hasn't had time to soak in?" she says.

It's possible. "This place is like a pristine show house," I say. "It's got the shapes and colours, but it lacks the spirit. The underlying—I dunno, ethos? Something."

"Bouquet?"

"It's like a movie set; an impression of a truth."

"I kind of like it," Etty says. "It's very efficient."

"Anyone can sweep a floor."

"You'd think."

Not so true at Brackett's, I have to admit.

"It's the environment," I say. "You know, like that Oscar Wilde wallpaper thing?"

"His last words, you mean? 'Either it goes or I do'? How's that relevant?"

It's skirting the edge of my brain. Something about

brutality and ugly surroundings is what I'm thinking.

"America," I say, finally. "Wilde went to America and someone asked him why it was so crazy violent and he said it was because the wallpaper was so hideous."

Etty stares at me like I am mad. My face reflecting distorted in her giant sunglasses.

"It made sense in my head," I explain.

Etty takes a moment, looks around. "No," she says, "I get it. People take more care if their location is pleasant. Brackett's is a steaming midden of 'seventies décor and out-of-date shelving, so why should we feel inclined to pretty it up? Where's the incentive to make the extra effort?"

"I'll admit this place looks the part," I say. "A spilled plant pot spoils the mood. I'd want to clear it up too."

"Steady on," Etty says. "No need to go crazy."

"Heh."

We wander on down the aisle.

10

"THIS IS WHAT they call a soft opening," someone is saying, in a tone that suggests high levels of smug.

"The real thing's not until next week is what I'm hearing," they go on as we slide past.

"Just a little something for the hoi polloi?" asks their companion.

"Oh, indeed." Smattering of forced laughter. "Indeed."

I have an urge to correct his Greek and also tell him he sounds like a dick, but Etty sing-songs the word 'wankers' and then pretends it wasn't her whilst Smug and Company cast their beady gazes at everyone in sight.

Any further comment I could make seems redundant.

I STEP LEFT when Etty goes right; find myself—almost accidentally—heading for the blank white wall that divides the shop-floor from the storage area at the end of the building. Here and there are posters portraying the happy-generic family future that's on sale here.

There are doors, spaced out along the wall, with the

expected kind of signage—*staff only, emergency exit, no unauthorised entry*—many of them have numbered keypad locks and some of them have porthole-esque windows I can peer through. White-walled corridor, storage room, another corridor.

I'm pretending to examine some fascinating varieties of gardening glove when a door nearby opens wide. A pair of neatly-pressed staff members moves out smiling, steps past me into the bright light of the shop floor, and I stick out my hand and stop the door before it closes.

Can't hurt to take a peek.

I wander through the doorway, take a moment to make sure it can't lock shut behind me, and have a quick look around.

It's a hallway with more doors, so, you know, not all that sinister just yet.

Dull boom of a door opening somewhere up ahead, sound of footsteps moving fast on concrete floor.

I find the nearest door and duck in without looking.

A cool darkness surrounds me, a foul stench like a backed-up toilet or storage for cleaning supplies. I hold the door ajar to allow some airflow and let in a thin strip of light. I don't see much; bulky grey shapes, shelves, boxes.

Shadows and footsteps move past in the corridor outside. I risk a search for the light switch.

Some kind of store room. Metal shelves holding heavy-duty buckets with lids. A few mops, spray bottles, rubber gloves, a steam mop. There's tiled flooring in one corner and what looks like a makeshift shower area.

I take a pen and lever up the lid of the nearest bucket.

The stench becomes more solid, rank; I can feel it burning the back of my throat.

Soiled overalls, maybe some cleaning rags, all of it

jumbled up in a sticky gloop that I don't want to think about. Or smell.

My stomach is about to begin a serious protest.

I jam the lid back down.

Turn to go and—

The door opens.

A wild scramble for somewhere to hide and Etty says, "I thought I saw you scoot this way, what are—"

She covers her nose and mouth with her hand.

"Did something die in here?" she asks. I shake my head.

We agree to leave this place, fast.

Back down the corridor and into the shop and I'm all apologies.

Etty holds up her hands. "Hey. It's okay. I'm no' your keeper, right?"

I'm still thinking that over when Etty tugs my sleeve.

"They're asking lots of questions."

She's right about this.

A scattering of eager youth with clipboards, picking out prospective customers, giving them smiles and conversation and then ushering the chosen few to little booths arrayed at one side of a cleared this-is-what-a-garden-in-summer-looks-like-when-you're-not-a-desperate-loser display area.

In each cubicle, a more senior looking staff member with a tablet computer.

"Targeting both men and women," I say. "Frequent customer points and that? Buy four garden chairs and the fifth is free, sort of thing."

"We have a full range of services and products," announces someone far too close. "We cater for the whole family."

One of the youths, beaming brightly.

He points to a range of plastic toys in eye-burning colours; beach balls, lawn bowling, simple tennis.

"Do you have any children?"

"Not that I know of," Etty says.

Stupid line. Makes me laugh, though.

Staff member—the badge says *SIMON*—just stares, confused.

"My little joke," Etty tells him.

Simon attempts a laugh in response, doesn't quite manage to sell it.

He looks down at his clipboard. Ticks a box.

"Is this a store card thing?" I ask him.

Simon nods. "It's a lot like that."

"A lot like that," I echo. "What's that supposed to mean?"

He leads us towards a booth. A suited woman is standing, one hand outstretched, as we approach. In her other hand she holds a tablet computer with a gleaming Garden World logo spinning on its face: a stylised green-blue planet, encircled in twisting vines.

"Senior Jessica will answer your questions," Simon explains. He offers a final attempt at a smile and steps back into the throng of shoppers and timewasters.

Jessica's handshake is warm, firm, welcoming. Her grin appears unforced—she's done better on the induction training—and her accent has a trace of posh American. Which stands to reason; this place has that kind of 'total dedication' vibe.

"Just a couple things," Jessica is saying.

She shakes Etty's hand as well and does a little nod-bow thing while she's doing that. Very smooth.

"Please take a seat and let's get started."

"Get started with what?"

Etty doesn't sound like she's buying the charm offensive.

"Bringing you into the Garden World, of course," Jessica tells us. I'm thinking of television evangelists and smarmy politicians.

Jessica's smile is very wide.

IT STARTS OUT basic enough. Gives us a spiel about discounts, special offers, late night shopping blitzes and such; setting out the stall before asking for our details.

Jessica wants mobile numbers and emails rather than home addresses, which seems odd at first but then I'm thinking, it's the twenty-first century, get with the programme, yeah?

I offer a number from about four contracts back, and some obscure email I got when I had dial-up internet, in the dark ages.

Jessica seems happy with that. Ignores us both whilst she does a bit of tap-tap-tap.

"Name?"

"Dennis," I answer. For some reason.

"Surname?"

"That is my surname," I decide right then. This undercover stuff is fun.

"First name?"

I look at Etty. "Tarquin."

Props to Etty, she doesn't move a muscle.

"Your name is Tarquin Dennis," Jessica says.

"Yes."

Tap-tap-tap. "Not registered to vote."

I notice that isn't a question.

"I don't believe in it," I tell her. "Democracy is a sham. A farce."

Jessica stares at me. I've seen that look before. Disappointment.

Looks down at the tablet again. Tap.

"Everyone should play a full and fulfilling role in society," she says.

She's staring at me again.

"It's part of the Garden World creed," Jessica says. There's that rehearsed sincerity again.

Etty leans forward slightly. "You're a garden centre and you have a creed?"

Jessica laughs; short, light, it's got a self-deprecating tone to it. Because obviously I can read a lot into a simple laugh, yeah?

"It's a corporate requirement," Jessica says. "You know. A vision thing. A plan for the future. You know?"

"We should go," I say.

"We have to collect the children," Etty adds.

"From boxing," I'm saying, just as Etty says, "From ballet."

"Exactly," I say. "Quentin from ballet; Isabella from boxing."

We stand and back away. It looks natural and normal.

A voice from behind makes a suggestion, "You should bring them along."

Jessica stands almost at attention. "Mr Pleasance, how kind of you to—"

"The children," Pleasance is saying.

He's a broad-shouldered wall of a man with wonderful hair and pale blue-green eyes. Has kind of a movie star thing going on. Not sure which star in particular. Perhaps all of them?

"Truly," Pleasance is saying. "We'd love to see them. The more the merrier."

"Catch them when they're young," Jessica adds. Deploys her laugh again.

"Quite." Hint of a frown from Pleasance, then back to full beam-and-gleam.

"Perhaps next time," Etty tells him as we edge past.

"Don't forget this," Jessica says, holding up a plastic card.

I reach out and take the card from Jessica.

"We're all about loyalty," Pleasance says.

11

Half way across the Garden World car park, Etty says, "Scale of one to ah-dunno, one million..."

"How creepy was that?" I finish the thought for her.

"Bingo," she says. "Bing-fucking-go."

There's a lot to take in.

It's got a definite big-box-store Americana mood. Lots of product, crazy prices, shed-loads of staff looking young and fresh and glad to help.

"Like greeters and stuff," she says.

"Like that, yeah," I answer. "But also a sort of a religious devotion sort of undercurrent."

"Like they're letting you into a secret?"

"Yeah. First thing it reminded me of was televangelists," I say.

Etty nods.

"And then that Pleasance turns up," she says, "and you start thinking about serpents in the grass and Very Bad Ideas."

We walk on in silence.

Everyone is waiting when we get through the doors.

Jost catches our expressions and nods. "I'll get a brew on."

The British Army never lost that reliance on the restorative power of a nice cup of tea, did it?

"What's the bad news?" Chas asks.

"Demons," Etty says.

"You what?"

"Americans," I tell him. "They specialise in heavy-hitter multinational octopuses of commerce."

"Octopi," Kelvin suggests.

"Serious money," I go on. "They're here *big* and they're here to stay."

Chas snorts.

Etty slumps down in the closest seat. "They're clean, friendly and welcoming. Good stock and excellent prices. They've even got a play area for kids."

"We've got that," Chas points out.

Wire mesh, broken concrete and mossy gravel, rusted swings and slides, a faded hopscotch plot; a roundabout that screeches when it turns. You might chance it on a kid you didn't like.

"We're totally boned," Etty says. "People lap up that shiny shite, don't they? They'll all be marching to the Garden World tune by next week."

"What's your take, Millsy?"

"I concur with my colleague here." I nod at Etty. "Screwed."

Another snort from Chas.

"What's the first thing I said when you started working here?" he asks me.

I remember that day well.

Brackett leading me out onto the shop floor, everyone staring at me while he did the introductions, feeling out

68

of place in my street clothes when everyone else was in uniform; already a team.

"This is Joshua Miller," Brackett had announced. "Joining our happy family."

No response from anyone.

"He's had some troubles. Get to know him, make him welcome."

Not much of a build-up, is it?

As I remember it, Chas was the first one to speak to me. Weeks later I can still remember his exact words.

"You said, 'Alright, Millsy, what the fuck you doing here?'"

"Naw," Chas is shaking his head. "After that."

"Was it, 'Have you come to buy some fucking plants?'"

Chas snorts. "You're taking the piss."

"I don't recall you saying that"—Chas is getting unruly, but I can't help myself—"no wait, was it… 'This is the one I've been telling you about, the dickhead who upended the family motor in a boating lake'?"

"Yeah, yeah," Chas is saying. "Very funny. Not the point though, is it? Not what I'm trying to tell you now. Not helpful."

First day in the job—after Chas has walked and talked me through the essentials of light sweeping, watering plants, moving heavy ceramics and so forth—Chas and me are out the back in main storage, sorting through a stack of boxes from the local cash-and-carry. Soft drinks, confectionery, bits and bobs that hang on little hooks around the main shelving; impulse buys, mostly.

A simple enough routine to ease me back into the working world.

"How come there's two of everything?"

"What you mean?" Chas asked me.

Docket said one pallet of cola, store room had two, note for two boxes of plastic trinkets, store had four. I showed Chas the sheet.

He scratched at his vague attempt at a beard. "Well."

That's all he said. I raised my eyebrows and adopted my best questioning look.

It seemed to work. He told me—with much looking back and forth and checking the doors were closed—that he heard a rumour of a dodge that Brackett was working.

"Some deal with a bloke at the wholesalers. Brackett strolls out with double the stuff, sells it on, and splits the profits."

"That sounds criminal," is about all I could say to that.

"Well, it's certainly not straight up, no," Chas said. "But then what is, round here? Times are tough; people cut a few corners, don't they?"

"But the wholesaler's losing—"

"Insurance," Chas said. "Victimless crime and that. Right?"

It didn't sound like the worst thing in the world, back then. And that was before I knew about the exotic plant deliveries and the sideline in rare arachnids. Not to mention Clone's extensive underground operation.

If wealthy bankers could abandon their morals for cash, I figured I could do that too. For a while, at least, until something better came along.

"Don't worry about the cops," Chas had told me. "My boyfriend's a Peeler and he says half the local nick are very keen gardeners. Surprising how many tropical greenhouses there are in the division."

It was a lot to take in on the first day.

I didn't know how much Chas might be bullshitting me. He'd always seemed a bit of a wide boy when I knew him socially. Back in the Jennifer days, that had been, back when he was Oscar Charleston-Speight, son of two surgeons or consultants. Something medical, anyway. Chas had been doing a grand job of hiding his intelligence and talent; liked to give the air of being a rowdy boy, played it up with ice hockey and rugby and all the usual hooray stuff. Half of what he said was lies, Jennifer had told me.

He'd not been wrong about Brackett though.

One other thing he'd said back then came to mind in the cold light of a Garden World dawn.

"You said, 'Brackett's always got a plan,'" I tell him.

"That's the one," Chas says. "Old Brackett will think of something."

I'm not so confident.

"Here's Brackett now," Kelvin says. "Maybe we can ask him what he's come up with?"

Everyone makes busy as Brackett scowls his way across the shop floor and heads out back to the office.

It doesn't seem like a good time for questions.

12

THE DAY SHIFT is arriving and it's my cue to leave; in general I work Saturdays, but being part of the Friday Club has garnered me some time off.

When I've retrieved my bag from the staff area, Dram is standing at station two—slouching, really, he does good slouch—and flicking through a newspaper. His hair is covering his face. A great welcome for the customers.

I'm about to start some casual conversation when I remember a warning from Etty.

"His name is short for Drama," she'd told me. "Just don't ask him how his day is going."

I'll remember that, I'd told her.

"He asked me out," she'd said.

I'd enquired—as casual as possible—how that went.

"I didn't say yes."

I didn't cheer out loud.

"Not my type," she'd said. Whatever that meant.

*　*　*

TWO MORE BODIES from the day-shift show up. Francis Murphy and Sally Jackson.

I look out the window at the crowds thronging Garden World, then back to the tumbleweed emptiness of a Brackett's Saturday.

"Good luck," I say to the silence.

"C'mon." Etty drags me along by the arm. "Give you a lift home."

"S'very kind of you," I mumble.

"Drew lots, didn't we," she tells me. "Guess who pulled short straw."

Before we can escape, a customer arrives.

Well, she looks like a customer, until I spot the plastic smile, the slim black briefcase and the neat, bright uniform of the Garden World high command.

An enemy officer, crossing the lines.

At least *we* had the courtesy to go in disguise.

"Ms Angelica Wilson," she says to no-one in particular. "Here to see Mr Brackett."

"I'll get him for you now," Francis tells her.

"You're most kind."

Etty steers me away.

"You don't want to know if Brackett's going to sell us out to the glamorous Garden World rep?"

"I could do with more ugly surprises in my life," Etty says. "Let's let the mystery be, shall we?"

OUT BACK OF the garden centre is an unruly square of fencing and overgrown hedges, half way between the main building and the curious concrete sheds from the last war. It's used as an overflow carpark for when the gravel patch out front is full up. Some hope.

Etty's still holding onto my arm. I'm very cool about this.

Parked on its lonesome at one end of a broken patch of tarmac is a prehistoric Land Rover, bulky, battered, bright red.

"Jalopeno," Etty says. "Cross between a jalapeno and—"

"A jalopy," I say. "I get it. Now I know why you hide it out here."

"Enjoy your stroll back to town," she says, pushing me away.

"Sorry, sorry," I tell her as she walks round to the driver's side. "It's the shock more than anything, isn't it? I've never seen one like that before."

"As the actress said to the bishop."

"What colour is that anyway?"

"Painful," Etty says. "Get in."

I do what I'm told.

13

THE INTERIOR OF the Land Rover is as shabby as it is outside, although it has the advantage of not burning your eyes out when you look at it.

"Remnant of the band-old-days," Etty says.

She drives fast, confident, doesn't look at me when she speaks.

"Needed something to haul our gear an' bodies round, out to every seedy dive and hole-in-the-wall from here to Barrowlands." Etty taps the wheel. "I hate it, but it's family, right? Bad memories and all."

I know how that goes.

Looking around the interior, the one acknowledgment of modernity is a black plastic clamp that's been bolted to the dashboard near the steering wheel, to hold a smart phone or sat nav.

"I was expecting a tape deck or an 8-track," I say. "You know? Old school."

"I have a minidisc player in a bag down there. That fit the bill?"

"Yeah. Cool."

She side-eyes me. "Are you serious?"

"Sure. I love these things. Mind if I..."

She takes her hand off the gear stick and gestures. "Go right ahead."

Stowed under my seat is a faded green haversack. Pretty hefty, and it rattles when I pick it up. Inside is a fat wallet made of Velcro and duct tape, and a couple of slim spy novels with dog-eared pages. Explains Etty's keenness for our undercover jaunt.

And there it is:

Beautiful. A chunky old Sharp 702 minidisc recorder, jumbled up with various cables, headphones, and a bunch of discs. Little squares of coloured plastic with silver circles trapped inside. Like CDs frozen in glass. Okay, plastic. Awesome.

I take out a disc and turn it over in my hands.

"Always makes me think of 'nineties espionage movies," I say. "Or that film with the squid head thing and the experience sharing, yeah?"

"*Strange Days*," Etty says.

I think of the new store opening on our territory, of the whole disaster that led me there in the first place; all of this whilst speeding on old roads under grey skies, through a landscape of rolling urban blight.

"They are indeed," I reply.

"No, the movie. Ralph Fiennes. Angela Bassett. As sampled by Fat Boy Slim. You know the one."

"'Right Here, Right Now'?"

"Exactly."

I'm still shuffling through the pile of minidiscs. Neat labels in a black ink. Tiny writing: Eighties Mix. Nu-metal. Movie Themes. J-Pop. Country & Western Greats. Goa Trance.

"Your tastes are eclectic."

"I like to keep my options open," Etty says.

Couple of discs with titles I know, then other unfamiliar songs.

'Snow Daze'; 'Life Would Be Easy'; 'Government Cheese'; 'State of Decay'; 'Reindeer Flotilla'—

"I recognise some of these. They from the Near Beth days? I mean. Are these tracks from your band. Former band. That is. Your music…"

I let the sentence die an awkward death. Not a great conversation topic.

There's a long pause whilst Etty contemplates the road ahead.

"Some old stuff, some new things I'm doodling with. I'll see how it goes. You know?"

"I didn't mean to—"

"Is it true, what Chas said?"

Chas says plenty of things. Many of them very rude. What in particular Etty has in mind I'd rather not hazard.

"You binned a Rolls Royce into a swimming pool?"

Oh. That thing.

"It was a lake, if you must know."

"I must," Etty says, giving me another side-eye.

"More of a pond, really, if I had to be accurate. I bet there's a big dusty book of rules and regulations somewhere explaining lengths and widths."

"And depths," Etty added. "Don't forget depths. Very important in your water-feature specifications."

"Are you mocking me in my time of woe?" I ask her.

"I expect so."

"Okay," I say. Not sure how to respond to that. I guess it's honesty. That's good, isn't it?

"And that was the end o' that, was it?" Etty says.

I give it some thought.

"It didn't help. Nail in the coffin, sort of style."

I guess that coffin had been measured-up for a long time.

We'd always had different views of life, different directions of travel, alternative takes on what the future might hold. Jennifer had very strong views about her purpose, about my role in achieving that. What I'd need to do to fit in, how I should complement her progress and so forth. My parents were thrilled, of course. Perhaps they sensed that Jennifer—like them—would steer me to the right degree, the perfect job, whatever professional society I'd need to join. A serious amount of routine and tradition and ritual; they loved that sort of thing.

As I explain all this to Etty it begins to sound quite cold and calculated.

"I think it's just the way her family brought her up. My family too, I guess."

Here I am, defending Jennifer. Isn't that acknowledging that something was wrong, that she'd need defending?

"You still have feelings," Etty says.

I can only shrug. Everyone has feelings, don't they? Wonders about roads not taken and chances missed.

"It used to be simple," I say. "Then it got complicated; I wanted her back, did I want her back, was the Incident the reason for the break up or was it just a symptom of the problem..."

Was it deliberate self-destruction on my part? A kick against the straits in which I found myself contained? Who's more to blame, in the end—

"Trashing her family car is a pretty major error of judgement, you have to admit," Etty says. "No surprise she'd be less than happy wi' you after that."

"A fair point well made," I answer. "It seems pretty simple now, though."

"Yeah?"

"When the final showdown happened, Jennifer said some things, hurtful things. True things, though, so you know, I have to accept that. Whatever held us together wasn't so strong after all, I guess. And maybe better for both of us, knowing that now, rather than finding it out one strained marriage and three kids down the line."

Maybe I didn't fit the profile for the role she'd got pianned. Or I just didn't want it any more. Either way, that door was closed...

"Sounds grim," Etty says, pats my arm. Tilts her head in that consoling way you do.

"Also, at the final breakdown, Jennifer threw some things, very hurtful things—"

"Now you're just fishing for sympathy," Etty says. "That's not attractive."

She's smiling, though.

"Can't blame a boy for trying," I say.

"True," Etty says. "Just don't try too hard."

We pull up outside my flat not long after.

A light rain has swept the grey tenements clean; or cleaner, at least. A pale sun is drying out the damp pavements and the scattered rubbish.

"You live here? I can see why she dumped you."

I gather my stuff and slide out of the front seat, into the road.

"This is where I ended up. I'd been sharing her apartment for two years. I didn't have a great deal of options after... you know."

"Sorry," Etty says. "Sometimes my sarcasm comes off as straight up sour, doesn't it? I'm very much a work in progress, post simultaneous detonation of both my private life and musical career."

My turn for the tilted head.

"Anyway," Etty says, "I'm totally beat now, so I best scoot off for a quiet soak and a long sleep."

"Good plan," I say, closing the passenger door, walking around the Land Rover to get to the kerb.

"See you tomorrow," Etty says, leaning from the driver's side window.

"Absolutely," I say. I have nowhere else to be.

"I'll pick you up about half-four," Etty shouts, and then she's off. "We can go find out if we've still got jobs, aye?"

That's a date, I don't say, but I'm almost skipping up the path to the front door.

BOOK TWO
THE HOST

14

"WHERE THE HELL is everybody?"

It's a fair question.

Sunday night at Brackett's, restocking after the big weekend rush. Yeah...

Etty collects me as arranged and when we show up at the garden centre there's no sign of the day staff, who should have been holding the fort until now.

"Maybe Brackett closed early?"

"That's no' likely, is it?" Etty says.

He's paying sod-all squared—getting half of it back off the government for alleged training courses he's providing for us—and the least that he expects for his minimal outlay is a few bodies standing around the tills and looking presentable, for as many hours as possible. Just in case of passing custom.

"He'd no' close up if the world was ending," Etty says.

Good point. "We've got cheap sun visors for nuclear flash, umbrellas to ward off the hard rain."

"The place is graveyard empty," Etty is saying.

Not quite.

Some shuffling in the shelving stacks. Squeak of worn-out wheels.

"We're not alone," I say to Etty, pointing dramatically.

Francis Murphy appears, pushing a barrow filled with soft drinks.

"Hey, Franco," Etty says. "Like a cemetery in here. What's been happening?"

He settles the barrow, shoves thick-rimmed spectacles up his nose. Sticks a thumb in the direction of Garden World.

No surprises there.

"Yesterday and today. Whole lotta nothing going on. I think we had two customers after lunch Saturday, and that includes the inevitable Mrs Tennyson."

Everyone knew Tennyson. Three hour convo just to buy a couple of plant pots or a packet of weed killer.

"Where's Sally and Drama?"

Francis takes a long look out of the window before he opens his mouth to speak.

Jangle from the doorway as Chas arrives at Brackett's.

"Where the fuck is everyone?" he says.

"We've done that sketch," Etty replies. "Franco here was just giving us the good news."

We all stand and stare at Francis.

He's got a great rabbit-in-the-headlights expression going. Impressive mimicry.

"Have I done—" he starts. "Have I done something wrong?"

Chas thumps him on the back. Laughs.

"All friends together, big lad," Chas says. "Tell us what you know."

* * *

IT TAKES A cup of tea and a few chocolate biscuits to get the whole story.

Not many surprises.

Garden World had been exerting strong gravitational pull over the customers of Brackett's.

By Saturday lunchtime they just weren't making it past the bright, glowing welcome signs across the street.

And it wasn't only the public who heeded the siren call.

"Sally went first," Francis explains. "Just-for-a-looky-look, she said. That was about half one. She's not been back."

"What about Brackett? What happened with the bit of skirt from over the road?" Chas wants to know.

Francis nods. "Yeah, she took Brackett over there, giving him the full tour. That's what I heard her say, right, on their way out. He's not been back, although I don't see his car, so"—he shrugs—"who knows? Andrew left about an hour after that, I think."

"Andrew?" Chas says.

"Drama," Etty explains.

"Learn something new every day," Chas says.

"Whether you want to or not," I added.

"Fucking hell, you're a jaunty bugger, ain't you?"

"Guys," Etty butts in. "We should stick to current circumstances, aye?"

Chas grunts, checks his watch.

"Where's Jost and Kelvin?" I ask before Chas does. Score one for me.

"They should be here by now," Etty agrees.

Jost's all about military precision, Kelvin's got her own particular brand of excellence in time-keeping, organisation, general attention to detail.

"Those two never left," Francis says.

A trio of stares.

"I reckon they've been here all night," he says.

Chas lets out a chuckle. "Bit of a dark horse, that one, isn't he?"

Etty scowls. "It's nowt like that, I can tell—"

"Oh, yeah? What would you know about it? You his special friend or..."—another thought takes him—"...*oh, oh*, is that it? Have you and Action Man been—"

The two of them are still bickering when Jost and Kelvin wander out from the back rooms and Jost says:

"What's the situation?"

Chas is about to continue, then blinks a bit, smirks.

"I was just wondering..."

He's being as arch and leery as possible at this point.

"... if you two have been, you know, if you and Special K have—"

"Been monitoring the Garden World site?" Kelvin asks. "Yes, yes we have."

Chas looks lost.

"I was just about to gather you together to give a report," Kelvin goes on.

Etty mouths the word 'report' in my direction.

"We've got chairs, refreshments, a display board and other stuff set up over here," Jost explains, and starts leading the way.

Even Chas follows without comment.

15

JOST'S NOT KIDDING.

There's cola and crisps, bars of chocolate, a flask of—I presume—boiling water, surrounded by tea bags and individual packages of coffee. A few mugs and cups arrayed in neat lines beside all of that, set on a little table flanked by two lawn chairs and the previously mentioned chart.

This has been placed, with some care, on the irregular sloped rectangle of fake grass that surrounds the display-only-not-for-sale garden shed at one corner of the shop floor.

"Take a pew," Jost is saying. Sets out a couple more chairs facing the flip chart; old-fashioned wooden folding jobs that remind me of church fetes.

"You still with us?"

Etty's at my shoulder.

"Funny how stuff takes you back, isn't it? Makes me think of bran tubs and tombolas."

Etty frowns. "It's making me think of Glenbrook Primary."

A fair amount of shuffling and muttering as people get drinks or whatever.

I almost trip over some electrical equipment bundled up on the floor near the shed.

"Bit of a health and safety concern, that is," I point out, peering at it. "What the hell is this thing?"

It looks like a big hand-held radio taped to something like a nineteen-seventies oscilloscope.

"I'll get to that," Kelvin says, brisk and official.

Now I'm getting that school vibe that Etty mentioned. Or flashing back to Open University programmes on BBC2.

We're all sorted, seated.

Jost sets up another folding table, plugs the electronic gadget into a trailing outdoor extension cord. Places the device on the table.

"Over to you, Laura," he says.

Kelvin takes centre stage. Although in this case the stage is a strange mound of artificial turf and she's a couple of steps off centre thanks to the kids' pool.

"First," she says. There's expectant silence. "Anyone hear that?"

Silence continues.

"What are we—"

Kelvin places a finger over her lips.

I'm not getting anything.

Francis raises a hand. "There's a buzz," he says. "Faint. Kind of annoying."

Kelvin claps her hands together, points. "Yes. We have a winner."

She steps over to the folding table and switches on the oscilloscope, twiddles with the settings on the radio. There's a little wavy line doing its thing on the screen.

Bright white against faded green gridlines.

"That," Kelvin says, "is a sonic teenage deterrent."

"Now there's a name for a band."

Everyone looks at Chas.

"What? I'm not wrong."

"Pay attention," Jost suggests. "This is important."

"I'll not bore you with the fine detail," Kelvin begins. "What is it, Francis?"

His hand is raised again. "I could stand to hear a little more detail."

Kelvin nods. "Okay. Short version. There's a range of human hearing. There's a range of animal hearing as well, but I doubt that's relevant to this discussion."

Some of this seems familiar. There's a limit to what the average man in the street can hear, and beyond that you get dog whistles and stuff like that, yeah?

Turns out it's more complicated than I thought.

"Recent studies have shown that teenagers"—she indicates herself and Francis—"have a wider range of perception than..."

Awkward pause.

"... well, older folks."

She's polite enough not to point right at us.

"I'm twenty-three," Chas says. The old grump.

Kelvin ignores the heckling. "As with most scientific discoveries, the next step was figuring out how to make money off it."

She explains how you can buy special equipment to broadcast annoying noises at any youths who might want to hang around outside your shop.

"There's even a special mobile ringtone that teachers won't hear."

"I'm no' sure about that," Etty says, smiles at me.

"They seem to get younger every day, don't they?"

"Point is," Kelvin says, "Garden World is broadcasting a high frequency signal."

"So what?" Chas asks. "So they want to harass scummer teenagers who've no cash anyway."

"Signal's much too high for that. Barely detectable."

"We did some ranging tests," Jost explains. "Turned the gain way up. It's edge-of-the-envelope stuff."

"So they want to scare off bats, mice, I don't know." Chas shifts and shrugs in his chair. "It just sounds like bollocks to me. Okay?"

"If it was just that, I'd—"

"Here," Chas interrupts, "how come you can hear it? If it's so high and all?"

"Some people have sensitive ears," Francis tells him.

"Fair enough, then," Chas says. He waves expansively at Kelvin. "Continue."

"Okay," Kelvin says. "Now we're going to talk about logistics."

16

KELVIN HAS BEEN putting in the work since yesterday, for sure.

Stands to reason, what with her being some sort of superbrain whizz kid.

I've not talked to her much, last few weeks, but that's part of her thing, isn't it? A standoffish kind of intelligence, radiating brilliance, operating on a whole other level; that's the impression I get, anyway.

Helped me out with the electronics, my first week. Talked me through the tills, scanners, price-checkers, stocktake gadgets; explained how it all worked, how to check for mistakes, fix freezes and that.

"You've used EPOS before, yes?" is how she started the conversation, as we stood at station one with a pile of stuff-and-wires on the counter.

My blank response told her all she needed to know, I guess.

"Electronic point-of-sale," she said. "Fancy words for a cash register. This is the Epic forty-six"—she tapped the colourful screen in front of me—"at original prices, a lot more expensive than the forty-five model, and differs in one major respect."

She pointed to a worn metallic sticker: forty-six.

"That's pretty much the only difference."

"Okay," I said.

"Let's get you started," she said, and followed it with a very long hour of extensive be-prepared-for-anything instructions.

I didn't get much of a chance to speak, but in a rare pause to let my mind cool down, I did manage, "Where did you learn all of this?"

"Couple of months ago when I started work here," she said.

"Isn't this—I mean. You've got better options than—"

"I can take a break," Kelvin said. "It doesn't all have to be cramming exams and burning the midnight, does it?"

Kelvin fiddled with the raggedy cuffs of her Brackett's sweatshirt, rolling twisted threads between her fingers.

"I guess not," I replied. "I just figured—"

"Stocktaking tags," she said. "We'll talk about that next."

Held up a bulky plastic gun, started reeling through the technical specifications.

Up on the makeshift stage, at the head of the class, Kelvin's looking very much at home. It suits her better than behind the counter of a scrubby shop.

There's graphs, statistics, a couple of careful, hand-drawn diagrams of eighteen-wheeler truck interiors—showing loading volume, height, width—a long list of words most of which I did not recognise.

"So that's five of the big boys," she was saying. "Refrigerated—which is a serious level of cold storage for an operation this size. They arrived on the Friday night and didn't leave. Still parked out around the back. Justin took a look—"

"Here." Chas raises a hand, seems to realise what he's doing, and lowers it again. "Have you two been ninja-ing about all day or something?"

Jost fields that one. "We've been conducting a co-ordinated surveillance operation against the Opfor, yes."

"Opfor?"

"Opposing Force," Jost explains. "The red team. The enemy."

"It's a fucking garden centre."

Kelvin says, "Is it?"

Chas has stood up by this point, is starting to walk off, but he stops at that. Stares at Kelvin.

"I took these earlier," Jost is saying. He's pinning blown-up pictures on the side of the shed. Real grainy stuff. What looks like the backside of the Garden World building; some angle from far away and a couple of storeys up? There's some blur of darker colours at the edge of frame, like the picture was taken from a tree and using maximum zoom.

The first image is a cluster of the long white-sided lorries that Kelvin's been talking about. Second image is off to the left of the first; bulky silver-skinned cylinders being dragged into the closed-off end of the building, a scrum of workers using a crane or a block and tackle. The cylinders are big, towering over the people shifting them around. No idea how heavy they might be.

"They've brought in a few jennies as well." Jost pins up a shot of a Garden World staffer shoving a flat-bed hand truck weighed down with a pyramid of portable petrol-driven power units. "Whatever they're doing takes mucho juice and they're getting some of it off-grid."

"You're reading all that from some blurry holiday snaps of the back end of warehouse?" Noting the lack of support, Chas shifts a little in his chair. "I'm just saying. It's a bit of a reach, no? I mean, yeah, they might be up to something, but look at *this* place." He waves an arm to indicate Brackett's and environs. "It's not like Brackett's raking in the readies from old Mrs Tennyson buying a petunia a week and an annual grow bag, is it?"

Some shuffling and muttering.

"This so-called nursery and garden centre is just a cover," Chas says, "for a parade of sketchiness as long as your arm."

I try to disagree, but I can't quite manage it.

Chas continues: "Like Police Constable Bri's been telling me, there's plenty of inspector's wives would do anything for a glance at an exotic bulb."

"Is that a euphemism?" someone asks.

"It's definitely sexism," Etty says.

Chas smirks. "My point is, who cares?"

"We could be out of a job—"

"Monkeys," Chas says. "As in, couldn't give one."

"Not everyone's in your shoes, Chas," Etty tells him.

"Too right," Chas replies. "Couldn't afford them, could they?" He looks around, and the smile fades a bit as he seems to better gauge the mood of the room. "What? Everyone picking on me now, is that it?"

Stares and scowls.

Chas raises his hands. "Okay, okay. I'll help you save your shit jobs. Protect you from the Big Bad Garden Meanies over the road. Happy now?"

Jost ignores all this, goes on with the presentation, "I didn't spot any weapons."

"Plants," Chas says. "Potting compost. Those tie things for fastening up your tomatoes. Any of this making sense?"

"Why would they have weapons?" I ask. "I mean, I can understand what Chas is saying here. It's a shop opened over the road, isn't it? It's not a... That is. I don't know. Being honest, I've no idea where you're going with this."

"Drug cartel," says Kelvin.

"Terrorists," says Jost.

"That's it." Chas stands up, digs out his mobile phone. "I'm dialling nine-ninety-nine, right now. You people need help."

He stares at his phone for a bit. "No signal," he says. "Bastard."

He stabs a finger in the direction of Jost and Kelvin. "I'm away to find a landline," he tells them. "Don't be going nowhere."

He wanders off.

"I'll try and calm him down," Etty says, getting up to follow him.

Francis and I are left behind, still trying to absorb what Jost and Kelvin are saying.

"We set up a camera," Kelvin explains. "Covering the road, monitoring the general activity."

"We should head over there," Jost says. "Find out what they're up to whilst they're just getting started. It helps us to set the tempo of—"

"They're a garden centre." I don't want to be agreeing with Chas, but there it is. "I expect they're up to selling plants and stuff?"

"And then there's this," Jost says. Sticks up another

picture. Closer shot, this one. The ink must have been running out on the Brackett's printer by this stage, because the image is striped and faded in places. No missing the subject, though. It's Dram and Sally. Fresh faced and smiling in their brand new Garden World duds.

"Cults," says Francis. He blinks a bit. "Y'know. End-of-the-millennium? Gathering the flock?"

"They kind of missed the boat on that date," I tell him.

"Always changing their tune, aren't they? Claiming their first prophecy was wrong or God has changed his mind or whatever."

True enough. How many times have folk been led up a mountain and then left with abandoned homes and families when the world failed to explode?

"So," Francis says. "Maybe a charismatic cult leader has dragged them over there to be his slaves?"

"It's possible," Jost nods agreement. "Or maybe Garden World just pays a living wage?"

A fair point, that.

Etty comes back, Chas wandering along behind her.

"Phones are dead," she says.

That's no surprise. The landline is intermittent at the best of times. Pain in the arse for folk who use credit cards and need their details checking; half the time we're back to using those manual slide-rule gadgets with the carbon copy slips. Very nostalgic, that is. Part of Brackett's end of the road charm, isn't it?

We should run that as a service. Like a holiday to the nineteen-seventies. You too can be cut off from civilisation for miles in every direction. No mobiles, spotty television signals, and the best of luck to you if you plan on ordering a pizza...

"We've got stuff to get on with." Chas, a little calmer now. "If Kelvin's finished with her show-and-tell, we should get back to doing what we're badly paid for, yeah?"

17

SUNDAY NIGHT STOCKTAKING. It's more about dream than the reality; imagine you work in a shop where things are sold in volume on a regular basis.

You could count the things we're out of on the fingers of one hand, with no need to trawl the aisles and determine the number of garden rakes that still remain.

I guess it is possible Brackett might have some concerns about shrinkage, palm-blight, the old four-finger-discount—stealing, for those in the back—but this place seems like a long haul to go to just to nick a lawn chair.

I'm checking the trays of mid-size ceramic pots—still twelve, all in order, thanks—when Jost walks over and says nothing.

He stands there for a minute or two while I tap a pen down a shelf full of boxed garden lights. Solar-powered—just spike them in the ground—and priced to sell; the boxes are filmed in dust. I make a note.

"I know you're not fully on board," he starts.

He's not wrong there. I'm not here for adventure and excitement. Not at home to paranoid ramblings. This is my crappy place-holder job whilst I flail in desperation to find something else. That metaphor doesn't really work. Is it mixed? Or—

"I've been looking them over," he goes on. "Something about them sets my hackles rising. Teeth on edge, sort of thing. You get me?"

"So what is it?"

Jost shrugs.

"Look," he says. "You seem a sensible sort. Level head."

Has he *met* me?

"You overthink," Jost says. "You second-guess. Miss your moment, most of the time."

Okay, turns out he has.

"I saw you when the spiders broke free, though," Jost continues. "You snapped to quick enough. Made the right decisions on your feet."

I mumble my thanks.

That was Friday night. Spiders are the least of our troubles now.

"So that's why you should join me for the recon," Jost is saying. "Once it's full dark, we're heading back to Garden World."

"*What?*"

IT'S JUST A walk in the dark, Jost said.

Nothing to it, is there?

We sneak over, we take a look, get some pics, slide back home to Brackett's.

If there's anything to it, we call in the big boys. The cops, the army; the council, maybe, they're bound to be breaking building regs, at the very least?

If there's nothing to it, then Chas is right and life goes on.

"What have you got to lose?" Jost had asked me.

Looking around at my job, my life, my place in the world, I couldn't think of an answer.

So we're going to take a long looping course around the back of Garden World, do a bit of sneak-and-peeping; sounded simple enough, way he put it.

I wasn't happy with the idea of stumbling around in the pitch dark out there, and said as much to Jost. "Talk to Clone," he said.

So I'm tramping down the back stairs and into the hidden jungle.

I've had to head down here a couple of times since my first meeting with Clone. It never gets any less strange. The man himself is never more normal.

I open the door and step in, slow and quiet.

The light is almost zero at this point. Just a vague sense of a glow and the shadows of many leaves. The door whispers to a close.

Clone says he's running a controlled day-night cycle, but I've never been here in anything but warm, damp darkness.

I don't want to speak, for fear of upsetting the delicate balance.

I don't have to.

Clone emerges from the gloom in front of me. Looking close to normal in a set of dark overalls.

"You're not..." I keep my voice low. "Not decked out in greenery and... stuff."

Clone shrugs. "Digging trenches, far end of the basement. Miles of tumbledown tunnels over that way. You'd not believe it."

In this place, I'm starting to believe anything.

"Jost says you have some—"

"Here you go," Clone hands me a canvas satchel. "It's all there. Not the latest model, so you might find them a bit rope-a-dopey. Good enough for what you need, though."

I look in the bag. Night vision goggles.

"Thanks," I say. And pause.

Then, "Jost told me to tell you there might be trouble. Later."

Clone cocks his head to one side. He normally has a daydream look on his face but now his eyes are fixed, bright, not blinking.

"Oh, aye?"

"He said: keep the place locked down, be prepared."

Clone's teeth gleam in the darkness.

"Oh, ah'm well prepared, don't you worry about that."

"You are?"

That's a relief. Isn't it?

"Flick the switch, hit the button. Goodnight Vienna," Clone says. "No troubles."

"No troubles," I find myself repeating.

"'Course," he says. "Ah might very well lose an eyebrow if ah'm no' careful. You understand me?"

I don't.

"But aside from that, we're solid," he goes on. "The bizzies'll find nothing. My extensive range of specialist product will be nothing but a memory, trust me. Turn, turn, press. Woomf."

"Woomf." I echo.

"Exactly," he says. Throws up a little salute and starts backing away.

"Have fun out there," he says.

Yeah, fun. That's what it is.

18

"I DON'T KNOW why I'm doing this," I'm telling Etty.

It's night outside and Jost and I are getting ready for the off. We're sitting behind a row of shelving, screened from the front of the store by crates and boxes.

Etty's treating it like a big lark. It's not like we're planning anything illegal. Well, okay, it's trespass or something like that, isn't it? I'm no expert.

"You got a taste for it," Etty is saying.

"I did?"

"Our little sojourn across the way," she says. "That was the seat-of-your-pants edge your life's been missing to this point," she explains.

"It is?"

"Your world is bland. Routine. You want the rush. You need to *feed* the rush."

"I do?"

"It's a sure way to feel alive," she says, emphatically.

"You sound like an aftershave commercial," I say.

"I do, don't I?"

I wonder if it's true. Have I been lacking something?

When I was a kid I climbed up onto a playschool roof; ran about on the surface of a strange flat other-world of flecked grey tar, tall spikey aerials and fat squat ventilation ductworks.

I got caught, of course, and punished, and that put the blocks on my adventuring for the foreseeable. Did I harbour a longstanding grudge for missing the head-rush, heart-beat thrill of it all? Did I want to live on edges?

Maybe I'm just tangled up in the notion of a mystery to be solved, a secret to uncover?

Perhaps I just want to make a decision instead of drifting with the flow.

Okay, fair enough, it was Jost who suggested this. But I decided to go along with it, didn't I? Dynamic.

"Besides," Etty is saying. "It's Sunday night. What else is there to do?"

"I can think of a few things," I say.

Etty's about to reply—

"You can tell her about them later," Jost says. "We're good to go."

Great.

I stand up. I'm wearing black combats and a hooded black top. The hoodie belongs to Etty; she dug it out of the Land Rover, and it smells of mould and petrol.

"Like a shadow," she says.

Jost is dressed in similar shades of dark. Lot of pouches and pockets and he's got his own night vision gear; souvenir from the service, he said.

"Jump up and down," Jost tells me.

I do what he says. No rattling, it's all good.

"Reminds me of the mosh pit," Etty says.

Jost nods approval.

"Okay," he says. "We go out. Kelvin covers the cameras and comms. Francis and Etty act natural—B-A-U—and Chas—"

I raise my hand.

"Business as usual," Jost says.

I put my hand down.

"Where was I?" Jost asks.

Chas is nearby at station one, closest to the main doors, drinking coffee and ignoring all of this.

"Oh, yeah," Jost continues, "Chas is security for anything unexpected."

That doesn't seem wise to me. "Security?"

"He knows how to deal with troublemakers, knows how to do it quick and dirty," Jost says. Points. "Look at him. He's like a short, angry ballet dancer."

"Hey," Chas says. He stops. Like he's trying to figure out if that was insult or praise.

"Hold the fort," Jost says.

"Sure," Chas replies. "I got your back. The buck stops here. None shall pass."

"Hey," I say to Etty, "how come Francis hasn't left yet? His shift was over hours ago."

"Idiot," she says.

Chas shakes his head.

Over at station two, Francis is helping Kelvin set up some tiny grey-screen monitors, scavenged from Jost's security room. They're sharing a joke and beaming like fools.

Oh.

"I get it," I say.

"Good," Jost says. "I was beginning to think your observation skills weren't up to the task. Let's move."

Jost heads off, quick march.

Etty grabs my arm as I turn to go.
"With your shield or on it, right?"
She smiles at me and walks away.

19

EVERYTHING IS PALE green or dark green through the lenses of the night vision gear weighing down my head. Passive, Jost called it. Intensifies available light, and there's not much of that around here. We're hundreds of metres from the nearest lamp-posts. The two bright spots are Brackett's and Garden World.

The landscape looks like a battlefield. One of the industrialised warfare ones, with trenches. Given Jost's history, I'm keeping these thoughts to myself.

You can't argue with it, though. The ground is broken and blasted, gouged and gutted, abandoned and—

And then the wreckage left behind is colonised by whatever's suited to the new terrain. In the end, it's all about territory.

Jost, a few steps ahead, raises a fist and I freeze.

He lowers his hand, palm flat, sinks to a crouch and I follow suit.

We had a quick briefing—that's what he called it—before we snuck out the back door at Brackett's.

This means *stop*, that means *go*, if I point at my eyes I

want you to look around your immediate area. That kind of thing. They're not all official, he'd told me, just a way to get the message across. I've seen war movies. I know the score. Or think I do.

"Comms check," Jost says.

We've got the one radio between us. Kelvin and Jost have done something to it that boosts the power and extends the range. Whatever it was involved taping extra batteries and a long twist of antenna on to it—the whole thing is strapped to Jost's chest at this point—and linking up a microphone and a single-ear headset.

"Six-five to Control," Jost is saying, into the mic. "No pick up at that address." I can't hear the response, I presume some coded phrase that tells him everything is A-Okay.

Jost takes a moment to scan the area. I follow suit, even though he hasn't given the signal. Running along the right side of our course, spoil from a canal-dredging project that got bogged down in council bickering and an inevitable funding crisis. The consultants and project managers got their money and walked; the local populace get unruly heaps of dark mud and river bed rubbish. You're welcome.

To the left, an unfinished apartment complex rises in several storeys of blank-faced concrete, before ending in forests of rusted rebar and billows of torn plastic sheeting.

The city centre and accompanying prosperity were meant to sprawl in this direction, sweep out and raise up everything in sight. Instead, the money trickled away like the tide retreating, leaving everything washed up and gasping for air.

"End of the fucking line," I say. Quietly, of course; I'm not an idiot.

Questioning look from Jost.

"This place, Brackett's. Us."

Kelvin the bright-brain in a crappy job, Chas the chancer, Etty whose career died before it got started.

"I've got... issues," I say. "And I'm guessing there's, y'know, a story, with... whatever happened to you."

No one chooses this on purpose, do they?

It's very still out here.

The wind doesn't trouble us, there's not a lot to hear except the hum of distant traffic and a stir of trees from somewhere in the darkness.

And apparently a mysterious whine that the young alone can detect. Children and bats, that's their audience. I'm too old for that shit.

"Shellshock," Jost says.

I don't—

"That's what they used to call it. Neurasthenia. Blokes. Younger than Laura, even. Stuck in uniform and shoved into the firing line. No wonder some of them folded under the weight of it all, under the burden of a world changing all around them."

I don't want to ask, but somehow I say, "Is that what it was like for you?"

"Too many days in combat," Jost says. "Too many nights under fire. Far from home, away from friends, family. It's normal to tire of the notion you can cope."

I don't say anything else.

"Post-traumatic stress disorder is the brave new name for it," he says. "Doesn't make it any easier to reintegrate when you get back, though. And it's not like the home front helps any. Torn between indifference and jingoistic nonsense; stuck in the middle of two tribes spouting shite on stuff they'll never understand."

It's odd hearing this. Not least because he's wearing his own night vision gear—big dark frame covering up his eyes and half his face—and it's like a solemn heart-to-heart from someone in a chair at the opticians.

"Anyway," Jost says. "I was bad to a lot of people for a long time. Drove them to distraction."

A long pause. "Pushed them away, didn't I?"

I can't find a response that isn't glib and pointless.

"I'm getting better," Jost continues. "One day at a time. Slow and steady wins the race."

I nod agreement.

"It's why you're wrong," Jost tells me.

That's unexpected. Although, given how wrong I've been so often, I shouldn't be shocked.

"It's not the end of anything," Jost says. "It's better than that."

"Is it?"

"Think of it as a last chance. First rung of the ladder up, yeah?"

He looks around the blighted waste ground all around us.

"This is your chance to start again," he says. "Isn't that worth defending?"

20

WE'RE UP TO the wire on the perimeter of the Garden World car park.

Jost is on the radio again. "Six-five to Control. I'm at the address. I'll have a look around."

There are the parked trucks that caught Kelvin's eye. A bright smear of light spills out from a large open roller-shutter at one end of the main building. Not many people about at this hour.

"You should shut off your goggles," Jost is telling me. "You'll need a few minutes to adjust."

I press and twist the relevant switch; a low buzz I hadn't noticed fades away.

When I take the night vision goggles off my head, everything looks strange and grey.

Jost is still wearing his set; big green bug eyes staring in my direction.

"You're not taking yours—"

"I'm staying here." He pats his stomach. "I'm not as fit as I was. Not quite up to the running around stuff."

I spend most of my time on the couch playing Xbox

games. I'm not a threat to Usain Bolt's record.

"I'll give a signal if there's any trouble we can't handle."

"A signal?"

"You'll know it," Jost says. "Take this."

I'm expecting a weapon of some sort. I'm surprised when he hands me a heavy woven strap with a loop at one end. "This is a dog lead."

"Anyone asks, you're looking for the family pet. Alsatian. Female. Answers to Charlie. Short for Charlemagne."

"You've thought this one through."

The other end of the lead is frayed, there's no hook to connect it to a collar.

"Oh, right," I say. "That's how Charlie escaped."

Obvious.

I'm well into wondering how I'm going to attach this to her collar when I remember the dog does not exist. Not here, anyway.

"This as well," Jost says. He shoves something into my hands that looks like a torch. It's wrapped in tape, but there's no glass and the buttons are covered. It's very heavy.

"What is it?" I ask.

"A second chance. If you get cornered. Twist the top"—he mimes the action—"and throw it towards the ground. Throw it hard. Away from yourself. Got that?"

"Away," I nod. "Gotcha."

"Try and get some pics." Jost hands me a camera; dark red compact with a tiny viewfinder and a lens that whirrs in-and-out when you're focusing. "It's not great but it performs well in low-light. We'll see what we can see."

"You work with what you have," I say, tucking the camera into a side pocket.

"That's the spirit."

There's already a hole cut in the wire, either from an earlier Jost visitation or just because this thing was put up three or four years ago when the site was first developed and no one has looked at it since.

I slide through the gap as Jost holds back a fold of fencing. I'm about to move when he says, "Wait one."

I stay where I am and try not to breathe too heavy. I'm crouching down and my knees are starting to burn in protest.

"Indigo unit at your nine o'clock," Jost is saying.

"Indigo?" That wasn't in the briefing.

"Indigenous operatives," he says. "Five to ten individuals visible at the far eastern edge of the parking area, moving along the scrub line—"

Kelvin had a map. Abandoned construction projects to the west—the long looping route we took to get here—an attempt at forest clearance to the north and east, another stalled project. The south of the map was Garden World, and beyond that lay Brackett's.

"—I can't see what they're up to at this range," Jost continues. "Looks like picking up rubbish. Bend, pick, drop."

A stupid thought crosses my mind. "Like catching the spiders?"

"It's..."

Light thump of a fist against my shoulder.

"I knew there was a reason I brought you along," he says.

"They're collecting something?"

"Could be," Jost says. "Maybe something got loose."

If I don't move soon, I'm not sure I ever will.

"They're too far away to see you," Jost says. "Go."

He doesn't have to tell me twice.

I keep to the shadows and start moving.

I SEE GREY islands of kerbstones and paving slabs laid out across the car parking area, each one with a cluster of tall lamp posts. None of the lamps are lit—there's enough light spilling from Garden World for me to see where to put my feet—and some of the posts have been gutted, the curved metal doors twisted off to one side, coloured entrails hanging down and out.

Flowers and weeds and grasses have run riot here, pushing up through fractured tarmac and crumbling concrete.

Can't hold back the march of nature, can you? We've got barrels of weedkiller—fuck-off-lethal concoctions—back at Brackett's, but it doesn't matter what you do. Left to its own devices, the greenery will overthrow whatever's in its way.

I reach the back of the nearest truck.

The wide rear doors are open enough for me to see that it's empty. Whatever they were carrying here, they've already moved it. White light—beaming down from lamps high on the wall of Garden World—falls through the murky fibreglass roof of the truck's trailer and illuminates some sort of dark, slimy substance. Rich earthy smells are burning at the back of my throat. My nostrils are clogged with it. Whatever it is, I don't touch. Even with the gloves, I'm not going near it.

The left side of the building ahead is the shop floor area I was in on Saturday morning. There are windows, but the interior is not well lit; I can dimly make out shapes and colours moving around in there.

I check around for anyone about outside—the Indigo people that Jost spotted earlier—and, seeing nothing, I head for the far end of the building.

21

HIGH WALL OF red brick, small unlit windows with frosted glass, grey security doors with warning signs.

I'm creeping along a narrow strip of pavement between the building and the parked vehicles. Kelvin was right; this place looks more like a wholesale distribution centre than a retail warehouse.

Maybe I shouldn't skulk? If I'm doing the where-is-my-dog thing, I better be bold-as-brass about the place, pretending everything is fine.

The brightly lit entrance welcomes me from beneath the rolled up shutters.

Here's the moment of truth. The crossing point. I could walk away now and know nothing about what Garden World is all about. Leave it to someone else.

What would Jost say if I sulked back to the wire? What would Etty think?

More important: what the fuck is going on here?

Look, I'm not saying I'm buying into the whole narcoterrorista outpost theory that Jost and Kelvin have been cooking up, but these Garden World folks are cranking the weirdness meter real high.

Got to find some sense in all of this. Some measure of closure before I go back to my shit job and wonder where on earth my life went wrong.

Oh yeah, that...

A quick breath. I settle myself. Find myself. Centre.

I wonder if Jost is keeping watch? This could be an elaborate joke on his part, couldn't it? A televised pranking? An online comedy clip show. Look what we made him do, LOL.

So much for focus.

Fuck it. I step into the light.

"I THOUGHT I heard barking," I'm muttering under my breath. Holding the dog lead high for emphasis. Or like a talisman. "Charlie's like that, you know? She's attracted to the light. Moth to the flame..."

I'm babbling.

I stop that and have a proper look around.

It's an IKEA-style stock room. Massive racks of shelving towering up and stretching away into murky distance.

I mean, not *exactly* like IKEA. The interior blazes with light near the doorway, but that doesn't last. The further you go into the building, the dimmer things get. I don't see anyone wandering about.

And there are no boxed stacks of flat-pack furniture on the shelves. Just row on row of identical silver cylinders.

I don't know what they're doing here.

Maybe it's a power source?

Some kind of green-energy eco-friendly hydrogen fuel cell malarkey?

The cylinders have panels of blinking lights at one end;

everything is fine, assuming green means good. They all seem to be connected by wires, thick bundles of flat cabling, clear plastic tubes carrying a dark green liquid.

I start taking pictures. The panels of lights have tiny symbols I don't recognise. Some language that's new to me. Which, to be fair, is most of them.

The bundles of cable and tubing—

Wait. Was that a sound? Voices, maybe?

I'm over by the wall. I put my back to the bricks and slide my way along until I reach a small door with a circular glass porthole in it.

Through the round window, a store more shadows than light, and a bunch of shop staff frozen in place whilst Pleasance stands before them with his palms out, head bowed.

Some corporate meditation bullshit.

What kind of company *is* this?

I back away, slow and quiet, take a few more pictures.

Another door, another window, this one is sparsely lit and full of—

Takes a moment to figure it out.

Looks like a hairdressers' kind of set up—rows of chairs, people in the chairs, heads high—but instead of those bulbous dryer things plonked down on their heads, they're looking into white lights. Each person has a glowing circle almost pressed against their faces. Like a tanning salon? Building that all-American glow, perhaps?

Won't be opening *that* door, anyway.

More wandering around, taking pictures of this and that.

It occurs to me—at last—to follow all the cables and tubes to their destination. I feel a bit of an idiot.

Don't know what I'm expecting. What I get is a big... machine, I guess?

It looks like a collection of boxy modules, around waist height, connected by more wires and pipes. They look like chest freezers, but more rounded at the edges.

Signs and warning stickers:

NO NAKED FLAME
CAUTION
NO SMOKING

There are a lot more blinking lights here, some meaningless dials, a dull thrum of activity.

The central module has a hatch in the middle of its top section. A handle I can pull. It's cold to the touch, and there's a sucking sounds of rubber seals giving way as the hatch comes up.

The stench of it hits me and I reel back.

It smells like graveyards. Damp earth and cut grass and rotting flowers, and a sharp undercurrent of death and decay. It's like that stuff from the buckets I found earlier, in a more concentrated form. I'm thinking, some sort of mulching process?

I press my jacket sleeve across my mouth and nose; risk a look inside the container.

It's a murky olive drab soup. Almost up to the level of the hatch.

It's cold, but there are bubbles floating and popping on the surface. Large things rising, turning and sinking again to the depths, like there's a stirring mechanism at work. It's basically a large vat of broth.

I see something long, tubular, with a wider flat section at one end, terminating in four shorter tubes and a stubbier fifth—

Okay, I get it, that's a fucking arm.

22

I'M OUT OF there.

I'm running.

I am the wind.

I realise I'm still standing staring into the container.

Staring at hell soup.

I force myself to step away. Turn. Walk in the direction of the exit; left-foot, right-foot, stick to the simple things.

Sound of a door opening, followed by voices and footsteps. I sneak a look and spot some staffers stepping out of the sunlamp room I checked out earlier.

I stumble behind the nearest shelving stack and think about having a little cry.

No. Don't panic.

Work through it.

I manage some shaky ragged breaths, and then start shuffling down the aisle. Heading for the doorway best I can, hoping to see no one, praying that no one sees me.

Step, step...

I'm pressed up against the end of a shelf-stack, keeping low to the floor, edging out for a quick look around.

I spot Dram.

He's checking stuff on shelves, poking at the buttons, checking cylinders.

I throw myself back into cover. Stupid.

My head catches the end of a cylinder on the shelf beside me and it rings like a gong.

The cylinder I mean, not my head.

I've got black dots floating before my eyes.

Dram turns and moves towards me. Another step, a spark of recognition—

He raises a hand to—

A forklift truck smashes him into the floor.

There's a dull wet snapping sound as a wheel rolls over his head.

I turn away and vomit. Bitter black coffee and too much chocolate and crisps. Clean-up on aisle six.

Fuck.

Dram is dead.

If I hadn't been pissing about in the spooky warehouse of doom he'd still be alive.

Yes, he had been working for a bunch of industrial-scale serial killers, but still, it was his first or second day and I don't—

I—

This is too much to process.

I need to escape. Should I get more pictures?

Get out of here.

I risk another look. I don't want to see.

A crowd has gathered. There's no panic or shouting or sounds of concern or alarm. Just a bunch of Garden World staff, standing in a semi-circle and looking down at the crumpled mess that used to be… what was he called?

I think Etty or Kelvin called him Andrew. His name

was Andrew, right? In death, the least I can do is use his proper name.

The staff are still staring, silent, unmoved and unmoving.

One of them is Dram.

He's right there. Looking at his own fucked-up corpse.

Live Dram is looking good in his matching Garden World trousers and jacket.

I'm fucking leaving.

I start by staggering into the nearest shelving, scattering a heap of metal junk onto the floor before dashing away up the aisle.

Smooth.

I go right, then left, then I'm scampering down a long row of stacked boxes at the back—normal garden centre stuff this is, not more weirdness—and there's the exit. And *there's* a clump of Garden World staff moving towards it.

They're weirdly unhurried; there's no urgency in them.

They're heading to cut me off, but if I pick up the pace I can get there first, get to the door and—

There's a clanking rumble as the roller shutters begin to slide down.

Oh, right. Yeah, they don't need to rush themselves.

Head down, arms flailing, I'm scrambling like a maniac, as the gap between the shutter and the floor vanishes, inch by inch.

I run, ignore everything, legs pumping as I sprint past the knot of Garden World staff; they don't even grab at me as I throw myself onto the dusty concrete and slide through the gap. The door closes behind me.

I'm *out*.

And I'm on the ground and looking up at a circle of faces. The Garden World people, surrounding me.

Dram is here as well.

They're saying nothing. Not even moving yet. But they will, won't they? I grab the not-a-torch that Jost gave me. Twist and twist and throw and—

There's a *crump* and a rush of bright white noise and the whole world goes away.

I'm struggling and shouting. Another *thud* and a bloom of heat washes over me. A gloved hand covers up my mouth; a heavy grip drags me away.

23

"FLASH BANGS."

Jost's voice is distant, remote; happening way out there somewhere beyond the ringing in my ears.

We're back at the wire, out of immediate danger. Possibly.

Jost's given me a bottle of water to sip and spit. Take away the acid taste of throwing up.

"I home-brewed them out of fireworks, so there's a touch of blowback that you have to watch out for."

"They did the job," I say. "Outstanding wo—"

Fuck me, my legs are on fire.

I duck and roll or something like that. Jost is patting out the flames on my combat trousers. Sticky lumps of burning chemicals.

"So I was saying," he continues. "The mix is a wee bit volatile. You need to be careful."

I need to be careful?

I EXPLAIN WHAT I saw as we're circling back around to Brackett's.

We're not even bothering with the night vision at this stage. We're old hands, we know the way.

Jost doesn't say much. Lot of nodding.

I've still got plenty of crazy shit roiling around in my brain.

I'm telling him about the arm in the soup, linking it to the buckets of slimy clothing I found on Saturday morning— a lifetime past—and conjecturing that maybe—

I lose my line of thinking.

I can remember the sound that Dram's head made when the forklift ran it over.

Except that wasn't Dram, was it?

Dram's gone. Or something.

They're making copies of people. "Building an army."

"Looks that way," Jost says.

I must have said that part out loud.

"You saw them?"

"Glimpses, during that rescue I pulled," he says. "Kept eyes on the situation whilst you were lurking around inside."

"What do you think?"

"Putting together what you told me, and what I witnessed myself, I think we need to get back to Brackett's."

"Yes."

"Warn the others, and figure out a plan."

"It's that serious?"

He doesn't dignify that with an answer.

We walk in silence for a while.

Pretty soon we're back at the last piece of cover, the final patch of waste ground on the Garden World side of the road, the place where we cross back over to our side. The normal side.

"We're into it now," Jost says.

"I can't believe things like this exist in the world," I say. "It just upsets the whole notion of what the world is like, doesn't it?"

"I've seen the world out there." Jost has that thousand-yard-stare you hear about. "Heard war stories, lived through a fair few of my own."

"I can imagine," I say, like an idiot.

"One night," Jost says. "Second tour in the Afghan mountains, second tour so you're sand happy, in the groove, not stressing over trivial shit. We end up circling this watering-hole out at... well, you don't need to know where it is, do you?"

I say nothing.

"A United States special forces team waves us in. Handshakes and hellos. Get some grub, get a brew on. It's all good." Jost rubs a hand across his face. "Something not quite on the level about them. You can feel it. Fair enough, operators are a breed apart in any case, so you expect a bit of edge, yeah?"

I nod along.

"First off, I'm thinking an Israeli black-ops squad; badged up as Yanks and up to no good for some poor bugger in the region. It's not that, though. There's a stillness about them..."

"Aren't these guys trained up for just that sort of thing?" I ask.

Jost shakes his head. "Not like this, no. This wasn't like keeping close watch and biding your time. This was being absent altogether. Like whatever ran the show had stepped away from the controls. Slithered off into the background."

"So what you're saying is—"

"I'm saying nothing. I'm just telling you what I saw. And seeing those folks tonight reminded me of all of that.

That same deep-down wrongness to it."

"What happened to them," I ask. "After all that, you just walked away?"

Jost checks his gear, gets ready to cross the road. "Couple of hours in the night and the Tallies stomped us hard. Fighting withdrawal for Crown Forces and we lost sight of the so-called Yanks. Dunno what happened to them after that."

He could have been mistaken, of course. Maybe it was just the wacky American training that made them seem so out of it. Not that they were robots or aliens or who-knows-what. There are other explanations, aren't there?

"We need to get back," Jost says.

Back to real life.

Stock takes and till rolls and cups of tea.

BRACKETT'S LOOKS NORMAL. Ordinary.

Hard to believe the things I've seen across the road. Hard, for that matter, to imagine the world in which such things exist.

We head through the back doors and up to the front of the shop. What's left of the staff is there, lined up around Brackett.

"Good news, everyone," he's saying. Beaming false-face smile.

"I'm upping sticks," he says—ignores the gasps of surprise—waving his hands awkwardly. "I've decided to take the money. Take their money and—"

"Run," Jost says.

BOOK THREE
DESTROY ALL MONSTERS

24

"Is he definitely Brackett?"

I'm chatting with Chas and Francis, quiet and discreet, off to one side of our little fake garden area, where Brackett appears to be organising an impromptu party.

"You're serious?" Chas asks me.

"Anything..."—I'm looking at Brackett—"unusual?"

A chuckle from Chas—more of a grunt. A long sigh. "Well," he says. "The boss is chummy, affable, glad-handing about the place. He's talking going-away gifts, telling us all we'll get brand new jobs across the way. He's hanging up bunting, for fuck's sake."

"Does any of that strike you as—"

"Fair dos, it's not what I've come to expect from the old bastard, but then again he's just come into money, hasn't he? Perhaps this is how he rolls when he's got some ready cash under his arse?"

Chas shrugs. Francis looks at me to do something.

I try again. "You understand what I told you. What Jost and I saw—"

"Yeah, yeah, I'm just not sure I buy it though, am I? That part about you murdering Dram—"

"I didn't murder him."

He's still up walking about, for a start. Or something is.

"You saw the pics," Francis is saying. "The cylinders."

Like that explains everything.

Chas is having none of it. "I don't know, do I? They could be fucking barbecues, for all I know."

"Sure," I answer. "they've been stocking up in case there's a bleak mid-winter rush."

"Maybe they got a job lot somewhere and have them put by for next year?"

Francis is clenching his fists. "Do you even listen to the words you're saying?"

Chas seems kind of amused by all of this.

"We need to talk to Jost," I tell him. "We need to figure out a way to fight back."

"Jost? What the fuck would he know about it? He's not Rambo. He's a caretaker. And given the state of this place he doesn't do much of that neither."

"He was in the Army. He knows the score."

I see Jost walking towards our secluded group. "You tell him, Jost, would you? How do we fight this? What do we do?"

"We run," Jost says. "Like I said already."

Not the answer I'm expecting.

"You don't fight until you have to," he goes on. "You avoid a stand-up knock-down as much as possible. If there's a clear way out, you take it."

I can't believe this.

"We should scarper," Jost says.

"My hero." Chas smirks. "GI fucking Jost."

Chas wanders off to the party in progress.

"We need to get this information to the outside world." Jost is holding up the camera.

"Their one strength now is that we're cut off, isolated out here, can't sound the alarm. Can't call in heavy hitters to take them down."

Okay. That makes sense.

"We need to copy the pictures. Send as many copies as we can in as many directions as we can. Make sure something gets through." Jost turns to Francis. "You're good with computers, right? Can you get the stuff off the camera and onto floppy discs or something?"

Francis does him the courtesy of not laughing. He takes the camera. "I know what to do," he says. "Sorted."

"Miller and I will go out and check the transport. Make sure we're ready to move once you've got that done."

Jost pulls on a bulky combat jacket—a German-looking one with a spotty camouflage pattern—and hoists a duffle bag over his shoulder.

"What about Brackett?"

He's still smiling wide and pouring cheap wine into plastic glasses.

"If he's already cashed the cheque," Jost says, "then it's time to retire."

"What if it's, you know, not him?"

"In that case we should play along." Jost looks out the window towards the shining beacon of Garden World. "I don't know what kind of comms they're running, but he might be able to tip them off if he twigs we're up to something."

"Okay," I say. "Sooner we sort the cars, sooner we can get back to the party."

We leave Francis to his computering and head outside.

135

* * *

HALFWAY TO THE staff car area, I break the stoic silence.

"So," I say. Pause while I figure out the next words. "Now that we've done our midnight ramble bonding ritual, and bearing in mind you could snap me in two like a breadstick..."

Jost's expression suggests he might do just that.

"... are you and Kelvin—Laura, that is—are you...?"

I don't finish the thought.

Jost looks disgusted.

"Hey," I say, trying to recover some ground. "She's single. You're not that old. There's nothing weird and creepy about—"

Jost shakes his head. "It's nothing like that."

"Fair enough," I say. "You seemed close."

"She's the daughter I never had. Or she reminds me of the daughter I *do* have but never see."

I'm not sure how old Jost is, but I'm seeing all those years right now.

"Maybe you and your family can reconnect?"

He blinks a few times. Looks away.

"Burned too many boats," he says, walks on in silence.

I trot along behind him, couple of steps in his wake as we reach his car. It's some crappy 'nineties Datsun thing, glorious shade of beige. There's not much light out here, but it looks odd. Not the right shape, curious ripples in the bodywork.

"Wait," I say, pointing. "Is that window cracked?"

I'm not wrong. Passenger side door has been split in two by a long frond of thick green growth. The wheels are tangled in dark olive streamers of bindweed. Alongside it, Kelvin's nippy little hatchback has almost vanished under a vast eruption of dog rose.

Jost gestures towards Etty's Land Rover, its bright red bodywork crisscrossed in black and green strands. "I don't think we're driving out of here."

The sound of footsteps on gravel.

"Gentlemen," says Mr Pleasance, emerging from the shadows. "I believe it's time we had a chat."

25

"Two words—" I start.

Pleasance raises a hand.

"Let's not be coarse," he soothes. "Let's be... cultivated, yes?"

He's edging closer.

I can sense Jost tensing to my right. Coiling like a spring, considering his next move.

"Okay, squire," Jost tells him. "Let's get it over with, shall we? Let's hear the big pitch."

Not what I was expecting. But then, *nothing* this evening's been what I was expecting.

Pleasance nods. He doesn't take his eyes off Jost.

"As you can imagine, we've been putting in long hours of late." His voice is calm, smooth, and ever so polite. "Things are going—all things considered—swimmingly well. We've not made these sorts of gains since... well, let's not dwell on the past, this is a different situation. A brighter opportunity—"

"Tell that to the people you've killed." I move to step forward and Jost puts out an arm to hold me back.

Pleasance wears his best frowny face.

"There's no need to upset yourself," he says. "Nothing ever dies in our dominion." Pleasance raises his hands, palms up, as if embracing the sky. "We incorporate them whole within the Oneness. That's the beauty of it all."

"It doesn't seem beautiful from where we stand," Jost tells him.

Pleasance lowers his arms, shrugs. "You don't comprehend the bigger picture."

"Tyrants say that sort of thing," Jost says. "Always bleating on about being misunderstood, whining about wanting the best for their people, even as their palaces burn."

"This is a beach-head," Pleasance says. He's sounding less polite now. More forceful. "We've gathered the flock, journeyed far in darkness, built the vessels to carry our message—and yes, if necessary, our might. I do not wish for unpleasantness, but one way or another you will be welcomed into the green world."

"You're wrong." That sounds better in my head than when I blurt it out.

Pleasance smirks as I founder on what to say next. Jost takes up the slack.

"You're wrong," he explains. "This is a choke point. This right here is where we stop you. Where we send you back to whatever holes you crawled from."

"You?" Pleasance raises an eyebrow. "This motley crew of yours plans to stop an army on the march?"

Jost nods.

Pleasance considers that for a moment, then extends his hand with a hint of a bow. "Good luck," he says.

And I shake his hand.

I see the cruel smile and feel the pain at the same time.

Like fondling a cactus.

Something slither-whips from Pleasance's suit sleeve, wraps itself around my trapped hand. Tightens, starts to crush.

I'm flailing and kicking. Also shouting.

"Pull back," Jost yells into my ear.

I struggle to say, "I can't—"

"Best try!" he tells me.

Pleasance grins, and I see dark shapes rising from the ground behind him. Distant and wary, but very much out there.

I lean back, he doesn't fall. I raise a booted foot and shove it against his stomach. Press hard. The body beneath is spongy and yielding, but Pleasance is going nowhere.

Pain shoots up my arm as I force myself backwards—

I see a shining arc of silver, hear a hollow *thunk* of blade on flesh.

My arm is free and I'm falling backwards as the Garden World manager lurches away.

I land on the hard gravel and struggle up.

Pleasance's hand—white-knuckled grip arrayed with black thorn spikes—is still attached to mine. Part of his arm and a ragged suit sleeve is dangling from the wrist. There's blood everywhere. Blood and strange green mucus.

"Go," Jost is saying. He's got a machete in one hand. Something in the other hand that looks like a small vacuum flask with batteries taped to it.

"Are you listening," he says again. "Go. Get fixed up. Get them ready."

"There are more of those things." Dark shapes on all sides. I don't see Pleasance. "Too many."

Jost shakes his head and holds up the flask. A light blinks red. "No," he says. "Not too many."

26

WALKING IS GOOD. I like walking. I stroll, exuding nonchalance into—

Okay, I stagger, blinded by agony, towards the entrance to Brackett's, a welcoming refuge of light on a dark day. Don't laugh.

I shoulder my way through the doors and enter...

A party.

Brackett is singing. Some makeshift karaoke business, using a cheap stereo system and a PA microphone. "*Why, why, why?*"

Etty and Kelvin are helping him along with the high notes, with pained expressions on their faces.

Chas turns towards me as the doors slam shut.

His usual smirk is freezing on his face as I step forward.

Francis, looming into view from my left hand side, waving silver lozenges of metal and plastic. Trying to tell me something. "I've done that thing. You know, the—"

He's looking at me in horror, his eyes white and wide.

Chas is there. Serious face. He pats Francis on the shoulder.

"Francis," he's saying. "Be a dear and fetch my bag from under station two. Small bag, grey straps."

Francis gulps and nods, quick turns, his gaze still locked on me for an extra moment or two, and then he's off and running.

"Now, then." Chas looks at me and smiles. "Let's have a seat and take a look at all of this, shall we?"

I think I hear shouting, from outside.

"I need to—Jost is—"

I'm struggling, but Chas is holding me down—down? I'm sitting on the floor somehow, Chas kneeling beside me—pressing a hand against my chest. "What you need to do is nothing."

I can still hear bad karaoke. Chas must have hustled me out of sight of the distract-Brackett party.

At some point, Francis has arrived with the bag that Chas had asked for, and Chas is saying meaningless things in a firm and assured tone.

"No, no, give me the microfiber and the tweezers. Antiseptic and the number 2 blade—that's in the plastic case, side pocket."

Snap of gloves. "You're not allergic to latex, are you? Penicillin? When did you last get a tetanus shot?"

Sudden twist of pain as Chas starts levering up the death-grip of Pleasance's hand, one finger at a time. Coppery taste of blood in my mouth. I think I've bitten my tongue.

"That looks nasty," Chas is saying as he examines my hand.

Bright white needles dig into my flesh.

"And this doesn't look so good either." Chas is holding something in front of my face. Small and dark and pointed, held by a pair of tweezers.

"Thorn," I tell him. "Dog rose, I expect."

"Fascinating," he says. Drops the thorn into a paper bowl at his side. "You've been fighting with a rose bush?"

Another twist of pain, a tap as another thorn drops in the bowl.

"It was Pleasance," I tell him. "I shook his hand and—I'm an idiot."

"Yes, that much I gather for myself." More prodding. "There's some kind of—let's call it a vine—wrapped around your wrist and some of your fingers. I'll have to cut it off. Don't make any sudden—"

A flash of light and a solid *crump* from somewhere outside. A hard rain of gravel against the windows. I'm struggling up again, but not getting anywhere.

"What did I just say?" Chas asks me. He's holding a very sharp blade.

"Do you—know what you're doing?"

"I am a doctor, if that's what you're asking."

He starts cutting.

"In fact, I'm training to be a surgeon, or at least I was until I decided to take some time and find myself, you know?"

"You didn't—"

I hiss in pain as the constriction of the vine fades away, and blood rushes back to my hand.

"My grandfather was a surgeon, my parents are surgeons. My uncle is a senior researcher in the field of oral and maxillofacial reconstruction. My older sister is in the US, consulting with the Centres for Disease Control."

More slicing and cutting and easing away.

"Let's just say there was an anticipation of great things, shall we? A life full of people who demanded more from me. A family who were always, always expecting better."

145

"You decided to play the black sheep?"

"Very perceptive of you, Mr Miller."

"So this is the real you. This is your bedside manner."

And there's the familiar Chas dirty laugh and leer of a smile.

"It's one of them, anyway," he says. "Nearly done."

He's cleaned the wounds—I've escaped with scars and punctures; nothing is broken—and is taping up a dressing. I'm pleased to discover all my fingers still work.

"How come you've got a bag full of doctor kit?"

He holds up a syringe, doing that tapping the glass thing.

"I medic for the ice hockey team."

"Ice hockey doesn't sound like the brightest idea. Surgeons are meant to be careful with their hands, aren't they?"

As you know, I'm an authority on taking care of your hands.

Chas pushes up my left sleeve. "That's why I took up muay thai," he says. "So I don't have to punch people."

He sticks the needle in my arm.

"This is a painkiller. I can't give you the full dose or you'd be unconscious on the floor, and"—another harsh flash and thunder from outside—"...I suspect that's not an option for the moment."

Chas turns away to search his doctor-bag for something else.

I manage to lever myself to a half-crouch whilst he's not looking.

"You'll need a broad spectrum antibiotic," he's saying. "Who knows where—"

I don't hear the rest as I've grabbed the nearest shovel and I'm running for the door.

27

THE CAR PARK is littered with the dead.

Bodies—blood-soaked and green-slimed—dressed up nicely in their Garden World uniforms.

No sign of Jost.

I hear a thud like a watermelon being struck with a heavy blade, over near the road where the glow of the Brackett's lights runs out.

That'll be him.

I head in that direction, have to concentrate to stay the course, easy to get distracted by bright lights, strange colours, odd lumps of who-knows-what scattered all around the place.

My right hand doesn't feel like it belongs. The pain's getting more distant, but it still makes me think of those kids' cartoons where the dumb cat or duck or whatever has a giant throbbing mitt the size of his head.

I see Pleasance. And Jost.

They're grappling. Or rather, Pleasance is trying to grapple with his one remaining arm and Jost is lashing out with heavy-booted kicks and low, vicious swings of his machete.

One step, two, and I'm almost on them.

"So unnecessary," Pleasance is saying.

Jost swings again, Pleasance dodges.

Jost shifts back to counter and I lunge forward, swinging my shovel as another Garden World staffer looms up behind Jost, its head bashed half to pieces, its arms a writhing mass of vine growth edged with barbs.

I strike it hard as I can as it reaches out—

The vines swing and snap like whips as my shovel connects, the creature gives a broken burble-growl as it stumbles back and away. It falls and doesn't get up.

I turn to see Pleasance drive a fist hard into Jost's stomach. There's a spray of blood from Jost's back, a ragged tear in his camouflage coat and a whip of trailing jagged vine.

"No—!"

I'm shouting and swinging.

Jost manages to get a good blow in with his blade, but then it slips from his hand and he's down.

I hit Pleasance with the flat of the shovel, then try to grab the shaft with my injured hand, get a better swing. Pleasance isn't pressing the attack.

I check on Jost. He's on the ground, but struggling to rise.

"Get—Get the bastard." He's reaching for his machete. Trembling fingers, blanched face, blood oozing madly where he's holding his other hand against the wound.

"We need to—"

"Go kill him or I will," he says. Tries to stand and fails.

I look for Pleasance.

Maybe see a shape in the darkness between the oasis that is Brackett's and the brighter glow of Garden World across the grey expanse of roadway.

I take a few steps forward, further into the night.

I don't see anything.

When I get back to Jost he's wrapping tape around his belly.

"That'll hold for now," he tells me. "Did you get him?"

I shake my head guiltily.

"Should have made sure. Should have settled his bullshit—"

Jost doubles up. Takes some long, slow breaths through clenched teeth. Straightens again.

"Now I have to do it myself."

"In a minute," I tell him, sliding my bad arm under his and hoisting him to his feet best I can. "Pleasance can wait for a minute."

"MEDIC," IS WHAT I think I'm shouting. Could be anything at this point.

Back through the doors of Brackett's and I hear yelling, running—no more karaoke though, so there's a blessing—people gathering.

Chas is there again, checking for damage.

Jost is pushing him away. "I know the score," he says. His face is almost bloodless white. "Triage."

"I'll be the judge," Chas tells him. Pulls open Jost's ripped and ragged jacket. "Fuck," he says. Closes the jacket again. "Is that duct tape?"

"Thousand and one uses." Jost coughs. There's spots of blood everywhere.

He grabs my arm. "I've knocked them on their heels. Made them think again. When they come back it'll be harder. You need to get ready. Fight."

Chas leads Jost away to one side. Sits him down and gets to work with his medical kit.

"We have to get some things together." I'm looking at

the aisles, trying to remember where everything is kept.

"We don't have any weapons," Someone says. Maybe Kelvin.

"Are you kidding?" I tell them. "We've got two aisles packed with bladed implements and enough systemic herbicides to destroy the Lost Gardens of Heligan."

"Not to mention all of the banned-by-the-Geneva-Conventions shit that Brackett's been storing out the back," Etty adds.

"Exactly," I say to Etty. "We're sorted. We just need to get organised. I've a few ideas for—"

A sharp laugh from across the room and Brackett stalks forward, sneering.

"Too late," he announces. "Far too late."

Brackett's standing awkwardly, like his limbs aren't at their best. I know the feeling, to be honest.

"Your resistance delays the inevitable," he says. "Surrender to the green world. Join us in the One-ness."

"I don't fancy it," Etty says. "Anyone else?"

"You hold him here," I say. "I'll go find out if Chas needs—"

"Your warrior is down," Brackett says. "You have no chance without him."

His mouth has a strange, distended look to it. A drool of green slides down his chin. "The mighty Jost will be but the first to yield, you will all join—"

A wet slap as Kelvin hits him with a shovel. His skull collapses inwards on one side like a papier-mâché model of a head. His mouth, still moving, opens wide in a high, shrill cry—

Francis pushes past me and slams a heavy garden fork into Brackett's chest, surging forward and knocking Brackett to the floor.

There's howling and screaming. Brackett's head bursts open against the hard floor, spilling out green mush and sick-yellow lumps.

He's not moving any more.

Kelvin and Francis are staring at their handiwork, appalled and fascinated in equal measure.

"At least he's not singing now," Chas says.

I get close. "How's Jost?"

Chas shakes his head. Jost is still sitting on the floor, propped up against some boxes.

"I think I'm going to be sick," I hear Etty saying, somewhere behind me.

"It's that shit wine Brackett was serving, I told you not to drink that pish," Chas tells her. To me, "You need to take this." He hands me a fat tablet and a bottle of water. "It should hold you until you can see your GP. You might need a tetanus shot as well. I doubt those thorns are the cleanest."

I take the tablet. A sip of water.

"Be careful with that injured hand. Avoid anything strenuous and you'll be back to your old self in no time," he says. "Which, let's face it, is pretty shit, but I work with what I have, yeah?"

Good old Chas. "Thanks."

"I'll invoice you later." A pause. "Now," he says. "You were going to tell us about dealing with invasive species?"

28

"You're sure you don't need a flipchart?"

I look at the team, gathered around me at station one.

"No. That's fine. We don't have the time. This is just a quick rundown of the highlights."

Plant killing 101:

"The science of plant destruction is pretty straightforward," I tell them. "We'll concentrate on the faster acting options like poisons, heat, burning," I say. "I mean, there's also removal of external growth factors—like smothering them with newspapers—"

A cough from Chas.

"Okay. Right. For a start, heat. Boiling water won't do them much good, but whether it'll stop them short is another matter. Fire's a better bet—we have those weed-burning units over on aisle three. Gas bottles in the cage over there. That's pretty-close up stuff, but it's what we have."

Nods and mutters.

"Poisons. We've got stockpiles of serious chemicals close to hand, never mind the under-the-counter well-off-the-books stuff hidden in dusty corners. And it's not just the weed-killer classics; you can also use conservatory cleaner, stuff for polishing glass, tarting up tiles. All of that is much the same. Not good for living things."

"Us included?" Etty asks.

"Well, yeah," I concede. "Be careful out there, is all I can say."

"Blades for doing serious trauma," Chas says. "Can't forget that."

"Very true. And also be aware that vinegar and salt are also an option."

"Oh, yeah: 'Just hold it right there, plant-man, whilst I empty twenty sachets of salt in your face.' Dream on." Chas shakes his head. "I'm away to check on Jost."

"Any questions?" I say.

Francis raises a hand. "Isn't Brackett supposed to be dead?"

The body is moving.

We go for a closer look.

Not up and walking about—Brackett's still sprawled on the floor where Francis and Kelvin put him—but a definite shuffle of fingers and twitch of limbs.

"You saw what happened. His head's full of green mush. There's no brain there. He's not—you know. A person."

I'm not sure who Francis is trying to convince.

"Looks a bit deflated, sure," I say. Whatever was holding Brackett upright, keeping him body shaped and mobile, seems to have left the building. There's nothing there but plant matter and—

"What the fuck are those?"

That's Etty. She's pointing at thumb-sized grey-green pods—four or five of them—crawling out from under Brackett's body, skittering about on the floor. As I watch, thin fibrous strands emerge from the sides and sweep back and forth.

"We can smash these, right?" says Francis.

Kelvin holds up a hand. "Wait. Let me try something."

She runs off. We watch the pod-things twist about. Keeping *well* back.

Kelvin comes back with her phone. Starts pressing buttons.

Francis winces, says, "Do you have to—"

"Look!"

Most of the pods stop, turn, head for Kelvin. The last one has already latched itself onto a trailing strand of asparagus fern overflowing a pot nearby. Not really a fern, this plant, more of a—

"They're attracted to the teen frightener?" Francis is saying.

They're definitely gathering around Kelvin. Fits in with what Jost and I saw out the back of Garden World earlier on.

Whatever they're doing over there, they're using sound to attract the pods.

"And they latch on to humans," I suggest, "and drive those fakes?"

"What happens to the real folks?" Francis asks.

"I think—"

"Guys," Etty says. "You need to—"

The fern is moving, growing fast, its leaf parts waving despite the lack of breeze. White buds are bursting on its surface.

"Forced growth," I say.

It's incredible.

"We can smash these, right?" Francis says again.

"Yes," I say, "yes, we can."

I'm about to join in when Chas appears. He looks a lot more sombre than usual.

"Jost wants a word," is all he says to me. He says the same to Kelvin and walks away.

I follow Chas.

It's a couple of aisles away but it felt longer.

Jost is still alive; not kicking maybe, but still here with us.

"I want you to do something for me," Jost is saying. His voice is getting lower. "It's messy and awkward."

"Anything," I tell him.

"First I'll have a word with Laura. Just a minute, then I'll tell you what I need."

I back away and Kelvin leans in close beside him. I don't hear what they're saying. I give them that privacy.

There might be tears. I know I'm crying.

I'm staring into the middle distance and blinking when Kelvin says:

"He wants to see you now."

She looks calm. Resolute.

I go and talk to Jost.

29

I THINK I'M kneeling in a pool of blood.

I'm not sure how much of the stuff Jost can have left, because it seems to be all over the floor.

"Tell my daughter, my wife... tell them..."

He drags in a soft, raggedy breath and shakes his head.

"Tell them nowt. Okay?"

I don't understand, say as much.

"They lost me a long time ago. Don't want all of that shit bringing up. No need."

Fair enough. I think they would be proud of him though, proud of the sacrifice.

Or maybe they'd just want back the husband and father they'd been denied.

"I'm heading off, soon, now," Jost says. "Here goes: last request, messy business."

I lean in close and Jost, breathing his last breaths, tells me what he expects.

HE'S HEAVIER THAN he looks.

Maybe the dead have a certain gravity all of their own?

I get my arms under his body and drag him backwards. I figure the security office will be the best place for him.

"Did he say anything?" Etty's asking. "Before he..."

"Last thoughts of his wife and kid."

Mostly true.

She doesn't need to know the rest. None of them do.

"Do you need a hand with his... with him?"

"You all have stuff to do."

Kelvin and Francis are pouring packets of weed-killer into spray-bottles of water. Chas is gathering rakes and hoes and all sorts of other things with hooks and blades and whatnot.

"I can help you get him on a cart." Etty takes hold of Jost's feet. "Easier to get him out of the way."

I nod, and we work together to shift him onto one of the flat trolleys we use for moving sacks of peat and such.

"Are you okay?" I ask.

Etty shakes her head. "You?"

"Ask me later."

I give her my best bleak smile. She heads back to work and I get the trolley moving.

I stop off at the last aisle but one to collect some garden shears, a pair of gloves, more heavy tape and a mask. I also have to dig around in Jost's blood-soaked pocket for the keys to his locker.

His keyring has a lucky rabbit's foot on the end.

Guess that worked out, then.

THE WHOLE THING doesn't take so long.

By the time I'm back in the store, what's left of the night shift is well prepared.

They've barricaded the side doors, left me a couple of trolleys laden with heavy bags to jam against the door to the back office area. There was no point securing the front entrance at this point, not with the massive hole where the main window used to be.

The team is taking it all in stride. I am too, I guess, but at this point I'm buzzing with adrenaline and fizzing with drugs, so at least I've got an excuse.

Maybe they're in shock? Mass hysteria? I read about that once; people wrapped up in the same violent delusion.

Not that this is a delusion. I mean, I *saw* those things. We all—

Wait.

That doesn't make sense, does it?

"You'll need these," Etty is saying. She's holding up a pair of thick gardening gloves.

"I don't think that'll fit on..." I hold up my bandaged hand.

She shrugs, starts shoving a glove onto my healthy hand. She pauses for a breath or two when she sees the blood. Then finishes the job.

"Here's a little something for later," she says, and sticks a sample-packet of extra-scary weed-eradicator in the pocket of my jacket.

Snarl of ripping tape. And there's Chas kneeling down to tape up the bottoms of my trouser legs. He's wearing some kind of bulky plastic armour and padding.

"What's that?" I ask him.

"You'll not want those buggers crawling up your legs," he says. "God knows where they'd be sticking those pokey needle points."

Taping finished, Chas stands up. "Oh, you mean this."

Thumps on his plastic chest plate. "This is my ice-hockey gear. I plan to be out front with—"

He holds up a petrol-driven hedge trimmer. He's taken the safety guards off the business end. It does look brutal.

"I'm keen to see what it does," he says.

I look around—spray bottles, water balloons, spades, trowels, long-handled pruning blades—the team all resolute and hard-eyed. I look at Etty, get a slight smile in return.

"I can't believe everyone is taking this so well."

"Nature of modern society," Chas says.

I look confused. Not a first.

"Aspirational, isn't it?" he goes on. "Everyone dreams, makes plans. What to do with their lottery win. How to cope with, I dunno, the fucking Rapture. What to do in the event of a zombie attack. Geeks have a lot to answer for."

"Not just geeks," Francis is quick to point out. "There are all those prepper types as well. Getting ready for some inevitable breakdown of society, buying dried food and wholesale nails."

"Isn't that hoarders?"

"Well, no," Francis answers. "I think there might be a bit of crossover, but—"

"And then if they die," Chas says, "all their crap ends up on *Storage Wars*."

That gets a laugh or two.

When that fades, I'm still standing on the raised platform that is the customer services desk, with everyone else semi-circled around me. Waiting.

Okay, deep cleansing breath. "We're cut off—phone's dead, mobiles out of action, no vehicles—and they want to keep it that way—"

"Is this meant to be a pep talk? Because it's shit so far."

Before I can answer Chas, Francis says, "I have a vehicle. Well, a bicycle. They didn't bother with that?"

Chas snorts. "I'm betting it's a hipster bullshit fixie model with a stupid tin bell on the handlebars."

Francis doesn't deny it. "I'm just saying. Faster than running or walking."

"No one is leaving," Etty says. Resolute. "It's not safe outside."

It's not wild safe in here, for that matter. This isn't the last stand I'd have picked. You work with what you have, though, don't you?

"In the morning we'll have better options," I explain. "We can see where we're going. See them coming. More chance of help, yeah? We just have to hold them off here for as long as we can."

Not the most convincing speech, I admit.

"Behind us is the offices and we all know it's a maze back there," Kelvin says. "Left and right flanks have double doors—left flank leads to the covered plant displays outside, right flank is the childrens' play zone and the secondary car park—front of the building is formed from late additions in wood and glass."

We're all listening at this point.

"The building proper is post-war vintage, part of a chain of storage units—solid floor, thick reinforced concrete walls, with the single-skin brick facings and some external steel cladding, the whole thing topped with corrugated metal roofing—and it's built to last. This is the best place to hold out."

Kelvin looks around, suddenly self-conscious. Shrugs. "What? I notice things."

Everyone has gone a bit quiet and sombre. If I don't

say something soon I feel some measure of nerve and verve will be lost. I try and think of something witty, apt, uplifting...

"Text messages," Kelvin says.

Nothing but blank looks.

"I'm thinking," she says, gloved hand on her brow. Moments tick by.

"Yes." Snapping her fingers doesn't work through the gloves. "The black hats are jamming the mobile phone signal. But I think if you key in your messages, they'll transfer out once the signal stops. *If* the signal stops. Or we could triangulate the jammer source and try and knock it out."

I shake my head. Blurs of colour trail across my vision. "No time for that."

"'Dear mother.'" Chas is staring at his phone, typing. "'I... have been... *consumed*... by enemy al... i... ens. All the very best... Oscar.'"

It breaks the tension a little.

I try and come up with something to send to my parents. Everything sounds too much like an apology and I think I've moved on from that. Also my fingers feel numb, so it's hard to hit the correct letters. I'm just staring at my phone screen. Listening to *tap-tap-tap*.

"It's annoying," Kelvin says. "From what we know, it's all adaptation of local technology level equipment, isn't it?"

"Annoying isn't the word I'd use, more like—"

"No spacecraft!" Over at station two Kelvin thumps the counter-top with a heavy weapon. "That's what I'm saying. No ships, no cutting edge science, no endless wonder. Just. Just"—another thump on the counter—"flipping *seeds* from *space!*"

Kelvin sets the weapon down. "Sorry."

162

Chas offers a suggestion. "Perhaps we can capture one and question it?"

Kelvin brightens. "Oh, can we?"

"No, we fucking can't," Chas replies. "Am I surrounded by bleedin' numpties or what?"

"Wait." Francis, standing alongside Kelvin, rubs his chin. "Have we determined these entities came from space?"

"They're not local," Etty says.

"Aren't they?" Francis asks. "They could be earlier inhabitants of this planet. They are talking about a new Eden, yeah, got it on their sign and all? Perhaps their existence is the source of that notion?"

Kelvin sighs. "The evidence is in. It's like *Bodysnatchers*. Interplanetary threads, pods, whatever. Maybe *Puppetmasters*?"

"I'm not convinced," Francis says. "It could be a 'Puff-ball Menace' scenario, couldn't it? Those were genetically engineered by a foreign power. Have we seen anything to suggest extra-terrestrial origins?"

"Nerdfight," Chas says. "We should sell tickets and—"

On the counter of station two, a telephone starts ringing.

30

"Brackett's Nursery & Gardens, how may I help you—"

Francis, telephone in hand, winces and mutters something about force-of-habit.

He listens for a moment. "No. Yes." Nodding. "I understand. Good luck. What? I don't—"

Sets the telephone back in its cradle.

"Was that them?" I ask.

He's shaking his head, looking confused. "Internal call. Clone called to say his plants had betrayed him? I think he was crying."

Having seen what those pods can do once they get hold, a basement full of flora isn't the best location in a situation like this. I should have thought of it earlier and warned him off. Too late now.

Francis looks at the telephone as if further information will be found there.

"He said he was taking care of things."

"Yes," I say. "He knows what to do."

"Then he started doing dog impressions."

"What are you on about?" Chas asks.

"You know," Francis replies. "Dog impressions. Like: 'Woof. Woof.' That's what he said."

I check around and make sure we have fire extinguishers close by; Clone's domain is well back from the main building and buried deep, but we're not having the best of luck, are we?

"Heads up." Kelvin bashes the counter again. "Movement on the perimeter."

She checks one of her monitor screens at station two. "Lots of movement. Slow. Couple of minutes out."

"Anyone got anything they want to say," I tell them. "Now is the time."

Etty is beside me at customer services.

"My name is Etcetarina," she says.

"Don't you mean—"

"Yes, yes," she waves a hand. "A mother who wants to embrace her Bulgarian heritage, a drunken uncle who didn't quite transcribe it correctly at the registry office, and lo, here we are."

"Cool name," I tell her.

She looks at me.

"When I was young I wanted to be called Rupert."

"That's it? That's all you're giving me?"

"I had yellow check trousers and a scarf, if that helps?"

"At this point death might be the better option," she says. "Rather than trying to live down that fashion atrocity."

"Nobody dies in the green world," I tell her. "Pleasance said we could all be part of the One."

"Not sure I'd take the word of a walking shrub on anything," Etty says. "No offence to the plant-based community."

Fair point. "Anyone else got anything to say?"

"Someone want to give me a hand-job before the Apocalypse?"

"Stay classy, Chas."

"Until the end of the world."

"Two minutes," Kelvin calls out. "Get ready, get set."

"Maybe we could meet up for coffee sometime?" Etty says. "If the world as we know it doesn't end and we aren't subsumed into the green-cosmic Oneness. Oneity. One-nation?"

I want to say, *Yes. Awesome. That's a fantastic idea. Brilliant. Took the words right out of my mouth. I won't let you down. Or crash your dad's car into a—*

"Cool," I say.

"Okay, then."

Her fingertips brush the back of my injured hand. "If we don't die."

I nod. Let's not die. Or otherwise cease to exist.

"I wonder if there's love and sex in this brave new Eden we are promised," Etty says. "A mass mind deal, perhaps. Or maybe they just clump together and undulate their fronds..."

"You wish," I say.

And then the war starts.

31

THEY DON'T LOOK like an army.

If not for the blank faces and the sprouting strands of vine and creeper, they'd look like a standard slice of the local populace; short, tall, white, black, broad, narrow, whatever.

They're not marching, as such, but there's a definite moving-as-one vibe.

They stroll in through the double doors at each end of the windowed shop-front area, then join up and advance in line.

Chas sums it up. "Creepy, creepy shit."

"They're not doing anything," Kelvin shouts. "They're just... walking at us."

It's menacing enough, though.

It's tough to move beyond the notion that these are ordinary folks. They don't have that bloody-lips-and-slavering-jaws thing going on like zombies would have; they've got vacant expressions and fresh-pressed Garden World uniforms. These people look dazed. Like they need help.

They're not people. Okay, some of them are people, maybe, but that knowledge doesn't help right now, does it?

No. No, it fucking well doesn't.

"Attack," I say. "Go, go, go."

Everyone gets motivated and—like a switch being thrown—the plant-folks surge forwards.

CHAS, OUT FRONT at station one, gets in the first hit, although things are a little untidy to begin with.

It takes him three goes to start the petrol trimmer. A few tense seconds of panic as the leading edge of the Garden World crowd sweeps around to meet him. He could be bowled over before he even—

Throaty roar and *chug-chug-chug* and Chas is up and sweeping the strimmer around him like a spear.

I can hear him hooting as the whirling cutter slices through a face. No blood there, just more of the green mush and scattered gobs of plant matter.

Another dodge and swing and another face is turned to ruin, its owner tumbling backwards; tripping up other attackers as it falls.

Chug-chug-grkk.

That's the sound the strimmer makes as it jams.

"Fuckity fuck," says Chas.

He's left to wield the strimmer as a long and heavy club, batting away the outstretched hands of dead-eyed Garden World staff.

It seems to be effective, for the moment.

KELVIN AND FRANCIS are over to my right, covering the approaches on that flank.

Garden World staffers have started splitting off from the main group, moving along the right wall of the store and then turning in to attack via long aisles of plant-pots, candle-holders and garden tools.

It goes badly for the plant-folk.

Kelvin is already bombarding them with water-balloons filled with weed-killer—it doesn't have any stopping power as such, but it seems to reduce the plant-folks' speed and coordination a tad—with Francis backing her up with sprayers and a heavy duty water pistol of monstrous size and garish colour.

The first I know about their booby trap is when it goes off.

An elaborate pulley system and several weights— wheelbarrows and compost bags, for starters—swings into action. Creaking and crashing and the sound of screaming metal on concrete and then—

Four rows of shelving collapse together into a disordered pyramid of wreckage.

I don't know how many plant-folk are underneath, but they're not going anywhere fast.

"That's a *definite* health and safety issue," Etty points out, raising another balloon.

Some left flankers have reached us at the customer service desk. It had to happen eventually.

Etty's putting them off with more of the weed-killer balloons, switching to the spray when any of them gets close enough. They stagger back clutching at their eyes and faces, and I do my bit by hitting them with a short-handled camping spade whilst they're distracted.

Things are going very well until one of the not-so-unfocused ones grabs me from behind and drags me backwards over the counter.

32

I'M SAVED FROM serious injury by slamming into my attacker rather than the concrete floor. On the other hand, I'm still in the grip of a writhing plant-man.

Flailing to get a hit in with the camping spade, I'm struggling to get free as plant-man is endeavouring to throw me onto my back and pin me. There are tendrils of vine curling out from his torn clothing, searching for purchase on my limbs.

I shift position, best I can, throw back an elbow that crunches against the creature's nose. His grip loosens, I wrench free and punch him in his ruined face.

I use my injured hand. This, I should stress, is a mistake. He seems surprised by the squealing noise I make as fresh, shiny pain lances up my arm and pummels my brain.

Pretty sure I'm about to fall over.

Plant-man is looming above me, a dark hollow in the centre of his face, an eye dangling free on a thin slimy stalk.

I feel weight on my arms, pinning me flat. I can't get my spade up for a strike.

He leans closer, mouthful of broken teeth opened wide.

Something is clambering out of his mouth—a slick-sided, bloated version of the pods that wriggled out of not-Brackett—using its spindly feelers for traction. Looking for an opening to climb into.

In my head I'm screaming, but I'm keeping my mouth closed.

"Fuck away off!" Etty's shouting.

The plant-man's head explodes and he lurches sideways off my chest.

Etty's heavy booted feet go *clump-clump-clump* on more of the squirming pods.

I'm clambering up and trying to say thanks, but Chas is getting surrounded and hasn't noticed. I shout a warning.

He spins around, gauges the situation, chucks the bent, twisted strimmer at one of the approaching plant-folk and dodges a lurching swing by another.

He snatches up a pair of garden shears and slams them deep into his attacker's chest, then twists them free and batters the first attacker with the green-smeared blades. Finishes him off with a heavy plant pot.

He's smiling now and shouting. "Is that it? Is this all you have?"

That's when the second wave hits.

CHAS IS ENGULFED by grabbing hands and whipping vines.

Kelvin shouts, clambers over the top of station two and goes to help him.

The glass on the right side doors cracks under the pressure of the weight outside, as more of the plant-folk start to force their way into the store. They're pushing the hasty barricade aside and streaming in, heading for Kelvin.

Francis is beside her in an instant, wading in with a spray-bottle and a trowel.

It's no use. They're getting swamped by silent rows of plant-folk.

They're still up and fighting though, so that's good.

I grab a weapon and head for Chas, because I figure he's more in need of the help.

It's close-up, brutal work. I'm just battering anything I see that isn't Chas. Digging through a mass of plant growth and bodies.

I find a clutching hand and drag him from the scrum, helping him stand as even more plant-folk arrive on the shop floor.

"I've had worse nights out," Chas says breathlessly.

I hear a shout from Etty and spin around.

Plant-folk have surrounded her at customer service, grabbing her arms and legs, holding her fast as she struggles to get loose.

Smoke billows from under the doors that lead to the staff areas and Clone's basement.

I dive towards Etty and hit a wall of bodies, a vast, endless press of relentless force. Can't move. I can barely breathe.

All around me, my friends are in the same situation.

I do my best to shout.

"Stop!"

33

IN A PERFECT society of Oneness I'd have thought there'd be less gloating.

Pleasance is there to disabuse me of that notion. His suit is still battle-damaged—tattered, smeared with blood and dirt, end of one arm missing—but he's regrown the limb and patched up the damage. The flesh of his new arm is shiny, pink and smooth.

They've dragged us all across the road to Garden World; each of us in a close walking phalanx of plant-folk, marching in lockstep, preventing any chance of escape.

They've even brought Jost's body with them.

Pleasance gets us lined up in the storage room, a hop-skip-jump away from the big vat where I spotted the floating arm. There are some workers fishing sodden clothes and the odd watch from the vat. It's all very much as expected. Good to be proven right, I guess?

They check us for electronics. Phones, watches, that sort of thing.

Pile it all on a little trolley table nearby.

Our troop of silent bodyguards steps back a little.

Gives Pleasance some clear space to walk along and smirk some more.

Three of the Garden World staff—some of them look like they got messed up in the fighting—are carrying Jost's body closer to the vat.

Francis looks a little queasy as the body is carried past. Kelvin's just looking daggers at Pleasance.

As the procession passes by I dash forward, dodge past Jost, hearing shouts of alarm.

Ignoring all that, I'm heading for the trolley and grabbing for the phone Jost gave me.

A hand on my shoulder.

Quick jab with my elbow, thud of impact and a pleasing crunch.

Whoever it is fades back.

I have the phone in my injured hand. The pain is crazy but I'm not giving a shit right now.

On-switch. Older phone, with buttons instead of a flashy smart screen.

It lights up.

The three carrying Jost seem to be frozen in place, but the others aren't quite so reluctant. Blank Garden World faces are pointed my way.

Chas and Etty are doing their best to cause a diversion, but they've no clue what I'm up to, and they're outnumbered.

I need to be closer.

"This is unnecessary." Pleasance at his soothing best. "Your transmissions have been blocked."

I step towards Jost, pressing the sequence of buttons he'd showed me. There's a dull vibration from the phone. I think that means it worked.

I grab Jost's hand—it's cold and dead and encrusted

with dried blood—and don't resist as the plant-folk drag me back into line.

The scuffling from Chas and Etty stops.

Pleasance looks... disappointed.

The phone is taken and handed over to Pleasance. He looks even less impressed than before.

"The obsessive connectivity of the modern world," he says. "You do leave yourselves open to subversion, don't you?" He holds up the phone. "Like an arrow pointed at your head. A target at your back. Entire lives laid bare. My god, you're just asking for it, aren't you—"

"You believe in God?"

"A figure of speech. Can't live amongst you without picking up some of the lingo."

I get the impression it's more than that. He's wearing the best suit. Giving it airs and graces. Acting the leader.

He's got the phone in his hand. He might notice that something is up.

"Can I have that back?" I say. "It's got some important numbers on—"

Pleasance stamps the phone to pieces on the cold cement floor.

"We're already replenishing our forces." Pleasance gestures to the towering shelves of silver steel cylinders. "The remaining question at this point," he says, "is do you want to join us willingly?"

We're defeated, trapped, being held by enemy aliens. It doesn't seem voluntary at this point.

They still haven't put Jost in the vat. So much for Garden World efficiency.

"I have a different question," I say to Pleasance. "I think I understand the vague outlines of how you operate. Plants and agriculture are kind of my field, though, so—if it's not too much trouble—I was wondering if you could provide a little more background?"

Pleasance flashes that super-fake Hollywood smile.

"This is your lucky day," he tells me.

Bruised, battered, bleeding and bereaved; I have to say I'm not feeling it.

I try and look happy.

"This isn't my natural inclination," Pleasance begins. "This hands-on stuff is left to... lesser lights, if you will, in the commune of the One."

There it is again. First of equals and all that. I don't ask how there can be differences if they're all one. Perhaps it's like how your hands are different from your feet, but still part of the same body?

"I'm a strategist, a tactician, a deep thinker." He's strutting now. I suspect the typical Garden World drone isn't the sort of audience he appreciates.

"We are an old race. Ancient, with our seeded brethren resting under earth for millennia uncounted, cast out from our distant home, adrift in the starlit void."

"*Yesss.*" Kelvin's voice is stage-whisper loud. "I *knew* they were from space."

Pleasance frowns at Kelvin, and then continues. "Abandoned in the vastness, our quintessence lies in earth. Each seeding-pod a living being, gathers to others as required, attuning to the surroundings, adapting to the breath and pulse of the living planet. We find suitable vessels from the local lifeforms, and then we blend."

Parasites, is what I'm thinking. Ticks under the skin; worms in the brain. They must have a limited individual intelligence or consciousness, perhaps something hive-like for the heavy lifting? What I say is, "An infinitely variable and connected race. Sharing a better Eden?"

"You do understand," Pleasance says. He seems pleased.

"We've had our success and failures over the long centuries," he continues. "We've had our setbacks. It's a simple enough matter to connect with a human"—he almost chokes on the word—"but often the results are variable. Even with long periods of preparation and absorption, control and longevity issues remain."

"So you decided to build your own?"

Behind Pleasance, the plant folk are lowering Jost's body into the vat, letting him drop, closing the lid.

"Indeed," Pleasance says.

"Your idea," I tell him.

"Yes."

I give a little bow of the head.

"You will all take part," Pleasance says.

"And the options are, uh, communion with the pods, or—"

"Your life force, your viable constituents being utilised more broadly," Pleasance explained. "Broken down and prepared in the machinery of new creation; living on in spirit, as you people say."

I lie down on the floor.

"Begging isn't necessary." Pleasance sounds confused. "We desire acceptance."

I wave a hand at the others, point to the floor. They seem to get it.

Nothing happens.

The Garden World staff stands around and looks at us in silence.

"I look forward," Pleasance is saying, hesitantly, "to experiencing many more of these human quirks."

The world explodes.

34

WHAT JOST TOLD me:

"You're going to lose," is what he said. "They have weight of numbers and no concern for their own wellbeing. I think they can afford to waste lives in pursuit of victory. In tactical terms, that's a major plus."

Not what I'd wanted to hear, but that was pretty much the tone of the evening, wasn't it?

"Here's what we're going to do about it," Jost said.

It wasn't pretty.

Jost, ex-army, not much of a life and very little to do in the evenings, had taken up a hobby during his time at Brackett's.

Improvised explosive devices.

Well, why not?

He'd started with flares and flash-bangs, just keeping his hand in as it were, but pretty soon he'd found some old Chinese fireworks that Brackett had bought and abandoned unsold. That's when things kicked off.

By the time of the war with the plant-folk, he was up to making his own blast bombs and had started experimenting with plastique; because of course.

To be honest, I think if the plants hadn't got him he might have gone up in a puff of smoke at some point anyway.

Some of this I'm just guessing at. When he told me about it he was kind of pressed for time, and had more important things to talk about. Like how I was going to deliver the bomb.

"They're going to shove me in that vat you mentioned," he said. "They don't like things to go to waste. From what you told me, it sounds like a processing system. Recycling."

That seemed like a reasonable idea. Well, not reasonable, but not unexpected.

"The device'll work on a timer. It's set at five minutes or so and it's too late to go fiddling with any of that—unless you want to raw button it at the last moment? No, better not..."

Not sure what he was talking about there. But I got the general gist of things. He handed me a phone. "No use for calling out—they're jamming the mobile networks anyway—but I've dug out the insides a little and set up a three-button combo to work the Bluetooth. It'll give the nod to the detonator and you're good to go. Rock-and-roll."

I nodded my understanding.

"Should work fine close up," he said. "All you have to do is get the stuff in place."

That all-you-have-to-do part is the bit where I get to cut open the dead body of a close friend—hole was already there, he said with a broken laugh, gave me a head start—then I had to pack the insides with a bomb and tape the whole mess up so no-one notices.

"I can't do that," I told him. "It's—disrespectful. Awful. I just—"

"What happens if you don't do this?" he'd said. "If you let them win, what happens to you? What sort of world will they create, eh?"

"There must be another way—"

"Name it," he told me. "Explain it to me now, and then when the time comes you can do that instead. Otherwise—"

A cough, a bubble of blood.

"Okay." I looked him in the eyes. "Your way."

"Kind of a Trojan corpse, right," Jost had said.

One of the best or worst puns ever; I can't tell which.

"It'll destroy the machinery for definite. Beyond that I don't know." Jost gave a painful shrug. "Cause fire, create mayhem. Here's hoping."

He patted me on the shoulder.

"You may still die," he'd warned me. "But you'll punch a hole right through their immediate plans. That's a victory of a sort, isn't it?"

I nodded.

After that there wasn't much else to say.

I waited for Jost to die—had to check a few times, just to make sure—and then I did as he asked.

IT WORKS BETTER than expected.

Like a charm, really; a grotesque, disordered charm of havoc.

The mulching vat detonates up and outwards in a fury of metal fragments. There's a cascade of green soup and a scattering of strange lumps. The Garden World staff standing around are cut down by scything shards of metal.

I lose sight of Pleasance in the chaos.

I'd expected to be dead at this point, but apart from ringing ears and a coating of dust and wet debris, I appear to be okay.

The smell has not improved.

Am I okay? Is this some sort of post-fatal-injury final spark of—

Secondary explosions ripple through a line of nearby cylinders, shelving rattles in place, and the whole building shudders around us like it's straining to escape.

"We need to leave," I'm shouting.

"No shit," Chas replies. Maybe; I can't hear over the roaring in my head.

He's dragging Kelvin to her feet. Helping up Francis, who seems to be wounded. The store room is filling with smoke and edged with flame.

Etty takes my hand.

Pleasance grabs hold of her other arm. There's a bit of tug-of-war that I don't much enjoy.

Etty is shouting at Pleasance. He's shrieking about... I don't know what. It's difficult to tell, as his face is a scarlet travesty and his jaw seems to be broken. There might be a splinter of metal, jutting from one darkened oozing eyeball.

I try kicking at him but he's having none of it.

It's a struggle to get a breath in here. Everything is going grey. My vision's starting to blur at the edges; it was wonky to begin with the medication Chas gave me earlier, but this isn't good at all.

Pleasance is still holding on. Tattered tendrils of thorny stems are edging out from under his tattered suit sleeve, starting to curl around Etty's arm; she's alternating trying to break his grip and slamming her fist into the side of his head. I go to kick again and he pulls me off balance. Etty loses her hold on me as I stumble.

I need a weapon.

I struggle to my feet again, looking at Etty. She's shouting something about me being a weed. That's very unfair.

Oh, wait...

Pleasance is doing an open-mouthed, crawling-pod-of-chaos thing, trying to force his face towards Etty's. I fumble my injured hand into a jacket pocket and find the packet of weed-killer Etty stuck in their earlier. Seems like years ago.

I have to bite the top off.

Dig in with my teeth, tear and twist and hope I don't get too much of it on me and then I squeeze it into Pleasance's wide, broken mouth and the ugly thing that's crawling out of him. He squeals and jerks back from Etty, wailing, gurgling and flailing. I grab Etty and we dance back out of his reach.

I'm about to run for it, but Pleasance is still standing, staggering forward, looking for a way out. I point to a flatbed trolley, and Etty and I grab hold.

We take a run at Pleasance and plough into him, use the weight of the trolley to force him back into the smoke and flames. The stench is awful but we stay to watch him burn; witness the crusted lumps of ashes falling to the floor. Make sure he's very-very dead.

Then we leg it.

Chas and Kelvin and Francis are waiting outside in the clean air. I can hear sirens in the distance.

35

THE COVER-UP STARTS almost at once.

Police cars arrive first, then a few ambulances. The cops take some confused initial statements while paramedics tend to our wounds. Fire crews reach the site and split into two teams, to deal with the Garden World situation and the smaller secondary blaze at Brackett's.

The brigade are getting set up with breathing apparatus and following standard Persons Reported procedures, when several Army trucks appear and platoons of troops in hazardous-materials gear disembark at the double and begin to cordon off the whole area.

A discussion over protocol and jurisdiction develops—I think; hard to tell when we're so far out of the picture—and then a mobile hospital arrives to take over the task of dealing with our injuries.

The police withdraw to counter any attempted press or public encroachment through the cordon, and the ambulances drive off to other calls. The fire brigade are permitted to tackle the blaze at Garden World, but they're not cleared to enter the building. Someone mentions chemical weapons from the Second World War.

There's a lot more uniforms on site as day begins to dawn.

We're separated by the Army and held in individual sealed rooms—white inflatable bubbles with clear panels and plastic airlock doors—which all look very medical. The doctors wear full biohazard containment suits—pumped full of air for positive pressure—and come bouncing across the soft flooring to peer into my eyes, check my tongue and ask pointed questions like, "Do you have any open wounds that might have been infected by the Active?"

I can *hear* the capital A.

When I ask what an Active is, they ignore me. I show them my injured hand and they remove the dressings. They shine a coloured light on it and take samples. Then they dress it back up again and bound away out of the room.

This happens three times.

After a while everything overwhelms me and I have to get some sleep.

THEY LET US go in the early afternoon the following day.

That report about old chemical weapons is all over the news, and we've all been instructed that this is the story.

The government know it's not true, though. They make us sign things, tell us they'll be keeping a close watch on us for a few months. Years? It wasn't clear.

They've offered Kelvin a job. Science advisor for a special intelligence service that engages with Emergent and Active Threats; that's an *Active*, then. They don't specify what it all means. I think there are other forms to sign if you want to know that stuff.

They asked if I want to come and help the government, in an advisory capacity, on account of my extensive first-hand knowledge and my two-thirds of an advanced science degree. I said "Yes" even before they'd finished talking.

They're building a biotechnology research centre on the old Garden World site. It appears that the Pleasance mob didn't pick this place by chance. The ground had been well-seeded by his kind. The specialists are going to be looking very closely, taking samples and running batteries of tests. Helpful to know about the high-frequency signal that attracts the pods, right? Part of why they want Kelvin, I guess.

Clone showed up the day after the disaster, soot covered and a little smoke damaged, but otherwise intact. He'd lit the blue touch paper and scarpered down some long forgotten tunnels into the darkness. Crawled out when the fuss died down. He remains quite upset about his plants and how they tried to kill him.

Francis is in a secluded military hospital; resting comfortably, Kelvin says, and watching endless *Star Trek*.

Chas decided he was better off back in medical training, climbing the ziggurat.

"Enough slumming it with you freaks," is how he put it. I think he meant well.

I'M STILL AT Brackett's for the moment. These governmental types don't want any sudden moves. "Maintain the façade," they said. There's talk about incorporating the garden centre as a front for their boots-on-the-ground operations.

Being tangentially connected to a chemical accident

isn't the short cut to fame and fortune you might expect. I think if the alien business had been revealed, I might have got more television time. As it is, I appeared—somewhat wild-eyed and dishevelled—on a brief local news item, nothing to trouble the nationals, and my parents got in touch with the requisite level of concern. Offered to help out with whatever, and right then I realised I didn't need their help. We remain on good terms, for the moment.

Mrs Brackett is now in charge of things—she's a successful businesswoman, had been happy to let her husband run his little garden centre hobby shop—and she doesn't seem cut up about Mr Brackett's death.

She has big plans. Plans that involve a lot less dodgy side-dealing. Having an in with the security services has got to be a plus.

The reconstruction work at Brackett's and across the road has already started, and we've contracted a food van to park up and help out with providing lunches and morning coffees for the workmen. Etty says we should open a café. Mrs Brackett is considering it.

The shop does seem busier now—although not so busy that we can't spend the odd afternoon digging through the burnt wreckage in the basement tunnels, or cleaning out smoke-damaged office equipment—and Mrs Brackett seems to think this area is on the up again.

Standing at station one on a Saturday morning, I'm not so sure. Can't imagine the Army and intelligence sorts will be buying a lot of flowering shrubs.

It's odd to still be here after all that's happened, but sometimes it's nice to see a familiar face.

"Mrs Tennyson," I say, bright and breezy. "However can I help today?"

ABOUT
THE AUTHOR

Colin Sinclair has spent what seems like forever writing things and stuff. Some of it has even seen the light of day. Most recently, he provided settings, background material and short fiction for *Broken Rooms*, an alternate-worlds tabletop roleplaying game with thirteen flavours of apocalypse. One of Colin's ever-so-short stories is in the Fox Spirit Books *Guardians* anthology and another appears in volume two of their epic *Girl at the End of the World* collection. His favourite word is indolent. He often wonders if his bio should have jokes.

www.devilsjunkshop.com

BLIGHTERS

TIM MAJOR

1

THEM BLIGHTERS ARE fucking everywhere.

Lee's on the door of my local, the Beast. He's arguing with some guy wearing a T-shirt with a cartoon Blighter on it, a star-shaped explosion at its arse-end, over the words *NATO shot first*. Just like everyone else, Blighter-T-shirt guy's totally shitfaced. He don't want to take no for an answer, but the Beast's full to bursting.

Lee lets me in because we used to be mates. I slap him on the back but he turns it into a hug. His puffer jacket squeezes up against me like massive inflatable ribs.

"Happy new year, Becky, yeah?" Lee says.

It's freezing and my hands are back in my pockets.

"Yeah," I say without looking at him properly.

Lee hops from foot to foot, clapping his hands to stay warm and looking like a mental gym teacher. Two more punters show up, breathing white clouds in the dark. Lee tells them sorry, we're all full up.

Inside the pub, it's foggy with booze, and the windows are covered with swear-words written in the condensation.

It's rammed in here. In a few seconds I'm so hot I could

puke. I lose my coat on a seat in the corner. All the other lasses I can see are tarted up, but I'm just wearing Dad's *Queen Tour '75* shirt, the same one I slept in last night. I don't own a dress.

Most people are hanging around in twos but there are some bigger groups, full of types that wouldn't normally be seen dead in here. They probably figured the Beast weren't going to be packed to the rafters like pubs down on Kendal High Street, but they was wrong. Bloody New Year's.

I do ip-dip-dip to pick a group at random. There's a knack to this. The trick is to hang around near the edge and just laugh when they all laugh. There are six of them already, so who'll mind another one, especially if they're a livewire like me?

"Oh, *sure* you didn't," one girl's saying. "Except we all saw it, didn't we? And there's even photos on the shared drive."

The guy she's talking to has gone red. He stutters when he speaks and puts on a stupid smile, like he's trying to make out he's not embarrassed.

"I had a cold," he says in a quiet voice.

Everyone roars with laughter, so I do too.

Another guy's sort of crying, he's laughing so much. He says what the other bloke said, but in a funny voice. "He had a cold!"

The girl next to him says, "Well I thought it was just adorable. I know people used to, but I've never seen someone actually get *emotional* about it." She's classy and not showing much skin. Her tits are smaller than mine, but nicer.

Someone else says, "It was a beautiful tribute. Seriously! Some of the most heartfelt karaoke I've ever been privileged to hear. Princess Diana'd be bowled over."

The crying-with-laughter guy says, "Actually, you mean Marilyn. Pretty sure it was the original."

Aha. If this was a pub quiz, I'd get the barrel of bitter.

"Candle in the Wind!" I say, a bit louder than I meant to.

Then everybody's looking at me. Nobody's talking any more. What's their problem?

Anyone can *look*. They look at me and I look at them. Nobody's speaking, still. Pretty soon I get sick of it, so off I go.

It's starting to look like most of the groups are la-di-dah snobs who probably all work together. There's a publishing company somewhere around here and if it wasn't for that then there'd only be hotel workers and jobseekers. I can hear people saying things like 'promotion opportunities' and 'jollies' and 'smart objectives' and who the hell talks like that on New Year's Eve?

The TV's on, up in the corner. There's no sound and the settings are messed up so the reds are like blood smears. Some guy's talking, acting all superior. His specs look like they'll slip off his nose even though it's big as a beer can. The programme's some Review of the Year on Channel 4, it looks like. The giant words *JULY 2018* fade out from behind him and now there's a video of a Blighter, except all fuzzy because it must have been nicked from YouTube and you can't see the ridges on its shell or whatever it is they have on their backs. All the fuzziness makes it wiggly around the edges, like a Scooby Doo ghost. Looks like the Blighter's sat on a beach because the background's just beige and you can't even tell how big the thing is. Part of the trouble's that its head's low to the ground, maybe pushing down into the sand.

The video goes bright white suddenly and the TV presenter pulls the kind of face he saves for stories where everything seems pretty sad but maybe all for the best. NATO shot first.

A few people are watching the TV, but they turn away once the YouTube clip's finished. Some guy starts doing an impression, bending over double like the Hunchback of Wherever He Was. He's lolloping around, groaning and swinging his pretend-heavy head at the guys holding pints around him. He freezes for a second, then bursts up with his arms spread wide, puffing his cheeks and making an explosion sound. One pint hits the carpet and smashes up glass and lager and the guy just laughs, the dick.

I'm at the bar before I remember that I won't have any cash until tomorrow, when Dad's money comes through. So I just stand there. This part of the pub's weirdly quiet, like there's a bubble around it.

"You got a Blighter back here or something?" I say, waving my hand, pointing out all the people that ain't here.

Gail's behind the bar, like always. She laughs at my joke. Last summer, that sort of gag was all the rage. Like, *Is that a Blighter in your pocket, or are you just pleased to see me?* Or, *You don't need a Blighter to work here, but it helps.*

"We've got an offer on pitchers of beer," she says. "My idea. It keeps the queues short and keeps people sat down."

She looks over at the Blighter-impression-bloke. One of his mates kicks him in the bum when he tries to pick up the bits of broken glass.

Gail sighs. "Well. That's the theory, anyway."

I think about asking her for a free pint, but then I change my mind. She'd probably give me one, but I don't want to get her in trouble. Her fella Ralphie runs the Beast—at least, his name's on the door, even though Gail does all the real slog—and he's a tight old bastard. I can see him through the gap in the door behind the bar. He's got his feet up, TV on, and he's holding a brandy glass the size of a vase.

Gail doesn't even ask me if I want to order anything. She knows I'm always skint.

"You okay, then, Becky?" she says.

I shrug, but that's a bit rude, isn't it? Gail's alright. More than alright. She's still got the same face as when we were kids, except now she's got crinkles either side of her eyes, even though she's only like twenty-nine, same as me. Far as I can remember, I sort of had a thing about her, back at school. Never did nothing about it, 'course, and just as well, because here she is shacked up with Ralphie, who's about as full-on manly as Kendal men get. Still, Gail's always up for chatting, not like the other lasses in the pub in sequined halternecks or whatever instead of a barmaid's pinny. So I say, "I'm good," and Gail smiles one of her nice smiles.

"You don't much look it," she says.

I don't know what to say to that, because she's right. So I don't say nothing.

Gail laughs even though I didn't even make a joke. "Not a fan of New Year's, then?"

"You get to chuck one calendar away and start a new one. Other than that, it's just another day, isn't it? And I don't even have a calendar."

"Good grief," Gail says, but she's still smiling, "Put it like that, now I'm depressed too."

"Who says I'm depressed? I'm not depressed."

"Very glad to hear it. Want a drink?"

"Nah. Not in the mood."

Maybe she's taking the piss after all, ribbing me about having no cash. Stuff like that makes me see red. I guess it's a family thing, because Dad had the exact same problem. Pride.

So words just start pouring out of my mouth. "Who's the one who should be depressed, eh? Who's on which side of the bar? I'm free and easy, me. I'm the paying customer, mate, at least I could be if I felt like it. You're stuck there serving booze and, I don't know, washing up pots 'til your false nails fall off."

Gail stops smiling. Them crinkles at the sides of her eyes are still right there. They're not laugh lines.

Pull yourself together, Becky Stone. Think calm thoughts. She didn't deserve that. One time, back in PE class at school, Gail dragged me out of the long grass on a cross-country run and held me up while I limped to the finish line. I didn't even have a bad foot or nothing. I just didn't want her to let go.

"Sorry," I say.

"It's alright," Gail says. "It's true. You win. Maybe we're as messed up as each other. I bet I hate New Year's Eve more than you."

I don't pull her up about the 'messed up' bit. I'm not messed up. I've got my own flat, me, and a record collection some folks on eBay would kill for. I haven't got a care in the world.

She reaches up to grab a pint glass from a shelf, fills it from the pump, downs half and then hands it to me. She leans on the bar with both elbows.

Like a fat-arsed polar bear, it looks like we've broken the ice.

Gail says, "So. Got any New Year's resolutions?"

I take a little sip, all ladylike. "Get a job, maybe."

"You say that most weeks. It doesn't count."

"Learn 'Stairway to Heaven.'"

"Same goes for that."

I puff out my cheeks. "What about you, then?"

Gail looks both ways like she's doing the Green Cross Code. She leans over so our foreheads are nearly touching and I can smell her breath. I tell you what, that wasn't her first pint.

"Swear to secrecy?"

A curl of her hair tickles my nose. It gives me a shudder, but not a bad one. "Swear down," I say.

"I'm going to find myself a Blighter." Except she hardly even says the last word out loud, more mouths it.

We both look over at the TV. It's showing another YouTube clip, closer up and clearer than the last one. I already know this one frame by frame, pretty much. It was the very first Blighter video I saw, last summer, when everyone was sharing it on Facebook and when everyone still called them 'Sluggish.' Even though the TV sound's turned off it's like I can still hear the voice of whoever's holding the camera, just from memory. "What the hell is it?" the guy says, and "Where did it come from?" and all the time he's moving closer and closer to the Blighter and then after a while you can see which end's its head. It's fat, big as a fire engine, and shiny and juddering. It looks like it's basically made up of just slime, or like it's some fairytale giant's used condom but, you know, alive. Then the video goes all blocky as the camera-guy turns the camera on its side instead of zooming in, so now the screen's all tall and thin, and back then on Facebook you had to turn your head to keep watching, which was annoying as hell and when will people learn to hold cameraphones the right way round if they want to get their shit on TV? And then you can see the Blighter a bit more clearly, you can tell the slimy slug bits from them hard sections on its back that look like they're click-click-clicking together as it shuffles and shudders.

It's bloody well disgusting, in other words.

Then, at the same moment the Blighter turns to look at the camera, at the guy *holding* the camera, the video goes all jerky because the guy's hands have started shaking. And that first time on Facebook, like everyone else, I'm thinking, *I don't blame you, mate, just look at the fucking teeth on that thing!* because its mouth's open now and you can just about see them pointy white triangles and they're dripping spit and there's steam coming out of its dark nasty hole of a mouth.

Except the guy holding the camera isn't shaking from fear,

is he? With the sound turned up you can hear this weird giggle and soon enough it's a full-on belly laugh and then you're thinking, *God, that's weird*, and then you just click *Share* and get on with your life until the next clip shows up.

Still. We're all pretty much used to them by now. It's New Year's Eve, we're only like a couple of hours away from 2019, and then them Blighters will be *so* last year.

"There aren't any more Blighters," I say. "Least, none that still matter. None out in the wild."

Gail's whispering now. "I bet you there are."

I shake my head. "There ain't, and if there was, some rich bastard'd get in on it like a flash. Like that oil baron dude out in Dubai."

I laugh because it's funny, what happened to that guy. Bagged a Blighter all for himself, kept it out of the papers and probably bumped off anyone who found out about it, and look at him now. Ha ha ha.

"There's one, at least," Gail says. She refills her pint. "I know that for a fact. Play your cards right, Becky Stone, and I'll show you."

2

THE SUN'S SHINING but it's bastard cold out here.

"You're seriously telling me you don't have any walking clothes?" Gail says.

I jam my hands all the way into the pockets of my leather jacket. I shrug, but it sort of turns into a shiver.

"Walking's for old folks," I say.

Gail's got all the gear. Boots and a waterproof blue jacket and a woolly hat so big that there's a dark smudge on the front rim where the mascara's rubbed off of her eyelashes. I pull up my hoodie, but the wind just whistles on through.

It'd be better if we were actually on the move. That's what walkers do, isn't it? Rather than just crouching behind bushes like we're doing. Gail didn't even bring sandwiches, and all I had for breakfast was one bit of cold pizza. It's not even like the cupboards will be full when I get home. Dad's cash normally comes through on the first of the month, but New Year's Day's a write-off because all the bankers are still hammered.

One of my legs has gone to sleep and I'm shivering so much I topple backwards onto my arse.

"Ah, sod this," I say.

I stand up, but Gail grabs at my hand.

"Don't you dare," she says. "I'm not having you showing your face and scaring them off."

I look down at my freezing, bluey fingers, held in Gail's bulky glove. My hand looks small enough to be a little kid's. For some reason, it makes me feel like crying.

"I think they've been having you on," I say.

She shakes her head and pushes back a bit of hair that's fallen out from under her hat. "I told you. They didn't tell me anything to my face. I just heard them talking about it. No reason they'd lie. It's no joke."

"Yeah. But I'm freezing my tits off and I still reckon they're full of—"

Her hand squeezes mine. "There! Look, they're here."

Sure enough, a car's pulled in off the road, just up from where we are at Sadgill. Lucky for us, Gail's beat-up old Corsa's hidden way off in the other direction, at the edge of the woods.

I squint. Last time I went to the opticians, they said I needed glasses, but those things cost a fucking fortune. "You're sure that's them?"

I must have started standing up again, because Gail's pulling me back behind the bush.

Two guys get out of the car. Yeah, it's them. I wouldn't have recognised the old bloke, Owen, but the young one's definitely Lee, because he's wearing the same puffer jacket as he was the other night on the door of the Beast. They've both got massive Frankenstein walking boots too, just like Gail. Do people round here get this stuff free on the NHS or something?

The two of them stand together, looking up at the side of the valley. Checking a map, maybe, or instructions. Lee points somewhere up there and then they're off. Slowly, mind you. Lee's dad Owen is a wobbly old codger. Must be in his nineties at least—maybe hundreds? Do people get that old?

"Wait. Let them go on ahead," Gail says, like she's reading my mind, because I was just about ready to shout out, *Hurry the fuck up!* "Further up there we'll be able to use the trees as cover, but for now we can't risk leaving ourselves exposed."

While we wait I try and make tunes with my chattering teeth. I'm doing 'The Temples of Syrinx' by Rush, one of Dad's favourites. I'm getting so much into it that I'm almost annoyed when Gail hoiks herself off the ground and sets off up the hillside.

"Keep low," she says. She scrambles up ahead of me, so all I can see of her is legs and bum.

I'm panting by the time we reach the line of trees. Turns out even old Owen's fitter than me. Gail scoots into the woods. She's loving this.

She points. Lee's helping his dad across a muddy patch, where one of Owen's walking poles is stuck in the ground. Jesus. This is going to take forever. What do walkers do other than walk, to pass the time? Every minute out here feels as long as a triple-vinyl prog-rock album.

I nudge Gail's arm. "If you had to choose between having webbed toes or webbed fingers, which would you pick?"

"Shut up, Beck."

We keep on walking.

I swear it's an hour later before Gail says anything else. She's been doing all these CIA moves, ducking from tree to stone to tree. Which is all very impressive, except that there's me just tramping along behind her, so what's the point?

"I think they're heading to Tarn Crag."

Whatever. Knowing the name of somewhere doesn't make it more interesting. There's nothing out here. I don't know why they don't just call the whole place 'hills' or even just 'the countryside.' I've got grown-up cousins down south and last time I saw them, at the funeral, they said they was amazed I wasn't out in the open air all the time. They said I was lucky and they only wished they had the great outdoors on their doorstep. I said someone's cat shat on my doorstep once, and I didn't feel the need to go and stand in that.

"Is there anything up there?" I say, just to say something.

"Well, there's a tarn."

"Yeah. Obviously."

"It's a kind of small lake."

"I know that."

Gail clams up. She knows I'm thick.

Then she says, "Hold on," but in a way that means *Aha!* not *Stop walking*. "There's a bothy up there, too. I'm sure there is."

I just keep on plodding, watching more mud stick to the mud that's already on my shoes. I swear my Cons are twice as big as they were this morning.

"Them Blighters, they got no taste," I say. "Just think of all the places they could have ended up. Who'd want to hang around all on their own up here?"

"I don't suppose they chose where to end up. They just landed."

"Crash-landed, more like." I'm thinking about all them videos people took in the first couple of days in July. Any Blighters that landed somewhere soft were filthy with soil. And the ones that landed somewhere hard, on roads or whatever, were just guts. A nasty secret part of me wishes someone got video of that too. Just imagine it in slow-mo— an enormous giant slug slapping onto tarmac and then just turning all the way inside out, showering up goo like a whale going up through its own blowhole.

"Still, they were unlucky," I say, even though I can tell Gail would be happier if I let her be. "They should've planned ahead. Could've gone to Hawaii. Or Disneyland."

Gail turns around and grins, which warms me right up for a second. "Well, San Francisco basically *is* Disneyland, now, the way they've treated their resident Blighter. Have you seen all that razzmatazz around it, on TV? It's like a cross between Lourdes and a funfair." She goes quieter. "Still, who am I to talk? I was as desperate to head over there as anyone, at least at first. Not that Ralphie would give me the airfare, even if we had it."

"But now that San Francisco one's the weakest of the lot."

"So they say. Serves those Americans right."

"What about this one?" I say, pointing ahead, though I've no idea if it's the right direction. "If there is one up there?"

Gail tuts. "I'm pretty sure there can't be many people know about it. Lee found out about it from Frodo. You know, that kid with the ASBO and the tag? Who was brought in that time for pirating films? Frodo found these really vague clues about a Blighter on the internet—what they call the *dark web*, as far as I gather—but only clues. No actual fixed location, just bits and pieces. Hearsay. Lee was positive that nobody else'd piece together the location. Only someone like Owen's got the local knowledge to figure it out and everyone else could still be searching for years."

"Except they shot their mouths off in the pub and now here we are. Silly Lee."

The wind gets blowier. Gail's body bunches up as she walks. She's like Bambi, all arms and legs and not enough fat for her own good.

"Hey, Gail?"

She keeps on walking, getting further and further away from me.

"Gail? You never said why you're so keen on this whole Blighter business."

Gail pulls the hood of her mac up over her woolly hat. I get it. She's trying to block me out, or at least give me the message that she's done with talking. Everyone gets sick of me, sooner or later. Then they leave, or worse.

Another half-hour later we're up on a hill, looking down into a dip. The wind's died down a bit, but it's already getting dark and a bit misty. I can only just make out the shapes of Lee and Owen, like they're paper cutouts. They're dark, against the deeper dark of the tarn.

They've been making their way down the hillside towards some kind of barn. Aha. Not a barn, a bothy.

"It's perfect," Gail says.

I reckon that's going a bit far. I look around. Other than the bothy, the tarn and us lot, there's basically just grass and mud and way too much sky.

There's a pile of rocks, too, what Gail'd probably call a cairn. It's big enough for both of us to sneak behind.

"So the Blighter's in there?" I say, pointing at the bothy.

"That's what Lee and Owen think, at least."

I stare at the building like I expect to see alien slime coming out through the walls or something. Can't see anything special about it, though. It's a pretty tough job imagining there might be a massive fat slug inside, but then imagination never was my strong point. After the bastard crash-landed, did it shudder and shuffle its way inside, like a dog trying to get out of the rain? Or did someone lend it a hand, shoving it in there for its own good? The thought of touching a Blighter makes me shudder myself.

"What are they going to do if they do find it?"

Gail looks at me like I'm some kind of idiot. Her nose is red from the cold. "What would *you* do? You, of all people?"

I give her one of my glares. In my head I'm saying, *Don't you dare get me thinking about Dad and Mum and Auntie Alice right now, you hear me?* because most days it takes all my strength not to and it's even harder right this second because I'm already feeling iffy from the cold.

I just puff out my cheeks. Then I pat my pockets. "Fuck. I've forgotten the camera. Have you got one on your phone?"

Gail just gives me another look. Taking photos probably isn't high up on her list, then.

We watch the two dark shapes struggle down the hillside. Now that they've reached the flatter part of the little valley, the thinner one—Lee—has jogged on ahead. Owen's shuffling along behind him.

Then Lee slows down and stops. He's still a way away from the bothy.

It looks like he's got smaller. I squint through the mist to make out what's going on.

Lee's dropped down onto his knees.

Behind him, I see a couple of things fall out of Owen's hands. His walking poles. Then he's on his knees too. Looks almost like they're both praying.

Gail's voice is a whisper even though we're like half a mile away from the bothy. "That's just how they talked about it in the Beast. They called themselves pilgrims."

"But why've they stopped there? They haven't even got inside yet."

Gail grabs my knee, making me gasp.

"It means the Blighter's a good one," she says.

Something's going on over there at the bothy. A door's opened and somebody's coming out. A person, though, not a Blighter.

"Any idea who that is?" I say.

Gail don't reply. When I look over she's peering through little binoculars like spies have. She's proper prepared, alright.

"Yeah. Maybe. Not from the Beast, but around. Some landowner. An offcomer, not a local or a farmer or anything."

If everything they say about Blighters is true, this guy got pretty lucky. I can just picture him up here from London on his hols, wandering around his second-home estate, then coming across the exact thing most people in the world would cut off their thumbs for. It's just like Dad always said. The rich get richer and the rest of us just get to watch.

Whoever he is, he's walking towards Lee and Owen. Just strolling, really. I fucking hate the way well-off types look all comfortable, no matter where they find themselves.

"Surely he's not going to let them come any closer?" Gail whispers.

I know where her mind's going. If Lee and Owen can just waltz up like that, then who'll mind us having a crack at a bit of Blighter action too? The funny thing is, that thought makes me realise something I really should have properly figured out before this point. I'm actually not all that fussed about Blighters, at least not in the way Gail is. I've got some Caffreys cold in the fridge at home and that'll do me just fine.

We keep watching, Gail through the binoculars and me with my eyes all scrunched up, trying to see through the mist.

Lee and Owen both stand up slowly. Their arms are opened up wide, like they're music conductors or magicians going 'Ta-da!'

I start shivering again but not from the cold. I never was gifted, but I know when something's wrong.

The wind seems to stop suddenly and then I can just hear mine and Gail's breathing and then we both stop doing that too.

The man who came out of the bothy reaches out for Lee and Owen at the same time.

He's giving them both a hug.

"Well, that's cosy," I say. "Have they come all this way for that?"

Then the three of them down in the valley all stand apart again. Owen looks like he's nodding or maybe crying.

Hold on.

There's a noise. A voice, shouting. But it's not coming from any of them down there. I can hear Gail's breathing get quicker again.

It's coming from up there on the hillside, opposite where we are. Is that someone up there? It's getting too dark to see.

The shouting carries on, but I can't hear the words. From the sounds of it, the person's not so much angry as showing who's the boss. Telling the three guys in the valley exactly what to do.

Lee and Owen and the man who came out of the bothy turn around—slowly, mind you—to look up at the opposite hillside. Whoever's up there must be about as far away from them as Gail and me are.

If someone was shouting at me like that I'd feel pretty stressed out, but these three don't seem to be taking it too personally. They haven't moved at all. Looks like they're sort of swaying on the spot.

I'm still trying to see whoever it is on the hillside when something lights up for a second.

I hope it's a torch.

But then a second later there's a sound like somebody clucking their tongue. It echoes around the little valley.

Lee's back down on his knees again, but he don't stop there. He falls down onto to the ground.

"Oh, Christ," Gail says.

There's another flick of light and another clucking sound. Owen falls forwards and disappears down into the dark grass.

I feel Gail's little body shuddering up against mine. I just watch. That third guy's still standing there like he isn't freaked out one bit. I wait for the flash of light.

But the shouting's stopped. The guy who came out of the bothy turns and looks down at Lee and Owen. Even without the binoculars I can see that he don't even look shocked about what's just happened. It's more like he's being polite, like he's at a country show taking a look at someone's prize marrow or something.

"Let's get the hell out of here," I say. Gail hangs back for a second, so I yank her arm.

We peg it back the way we came. Before we get over the rise of the valley, I take one more quick look back.

That guy's still standing where he was, just looking at the ground.

Then his arms rise up. He spins on the spot, slowly, slowly. He's doing that thing people talk about. Dancing like nobody's watching.

And then there it is, another cluck of the tongue. Something spits out of the guy's back. A darker mist against the mist.

He drops down and I guess that's it for him.

3

HUTCHY PULLS OUT a notebook, then makes a 'humph' sound and licks his pencil like he's from the olden days. I try and see around him—there must be someone else I can talk to?—but behind him the police station's dark.

"You still haven't told me why they were up there in the first place," he says.

I tap my nails on the counter like Mum used to when she was narked off. "I dunno. Going for a walk, I suppose."

There's no way I'm going to tell him about the Blighter. It'd only make people antsy if they thought one was in the offing.

"And do you suppose they strayed onto private property? Maybe that's why they were shot at?"

"I didn't say 'shot at,' I said 'shot.'" I make the shape of a gun with my fingers, then put it up against my forehead. "Blat-blat-blat."

"And who was it who shot them?"

Am I going to have to do his whole job for him? I start speaking slowly for his sake. "I don't know who they were, Hutchy. Don't you reckon I'd have told you? When you go up there to fetch what's left of Lee and Owen, maybe you'll find out."

Hutchy does that thing of straightening himself up to look taller. "It sounds like a wild goose chase to me. I'm not heading all the way over to Sadgill and beyond, Becky."

Hutchy's three months younger than me. When we were eight I trapped his leg in the slats of the school gate and nobody told the teacher and he was there for ages. I was a mean old cow back then, and Hutchy was a wuss and still is. I lean over the counter to look at his notebook. There's nothing written on it.

"'Course you're not," I say. "I meant when the proper policemen go up there."

"I don't know about that," Hutchy says. "Lee and Owen Ellinger aren't missing persons, officially."

"But I'm *telling* you they're missing. And they'll stay missing, because they was both shot in the head."

Hutchy grabs a ring binder with the word *Procedures* written on the side. He takes his time, licking his fingertip to leaf through the pages. If he does that again I'll lick my finger, too, and then I'll jab it in his eye.

"Photo ID, DNA sample..." he says while he's running his finger over the page. "We normally have to wait forty-eight hours minimum, it looks like. You're not family, are you?" He must see me go all stiff, because then he says, "Shit, Beck. I forgot. I'm really sorry about your mum and dad, okay?"

"Okay," I say. The last thing I want is to talk about them with Hutchy, of all people.

He clears his throat, meaning *let's change the subject while the going's good*. "Thing is, we've got a file on you. The 'Becky Stone dossier,' we call it. It's as thick as my thumb."

I feel all the angry redness come into my cheeks right away. They don't half bear a grudge, the police. One time caught pissing up against the doors of the magistrates court, a bit of cobble-boxing after pub chuck-out, two goes at twocking cars, and they won't give you the time of day any more. I should make my own dossier, because I swear the police are way more crooked than I am. Auntie Alice never spent one day in a cell, even though back in olden times they'd probably have drowned her in a pond for what she did.

I tell myself to calm the fuck down. Dad would say to keep my mind on the job at hand. "You're saying you don't believe me?"

"I'm saying that my boss won't. And they certainly won't send anybody way up Longsleddale with only your word to go on."

Maybe they'd have believed Gail. But there's no chance she'll speak up, even though she knew Lee and his dad better than me, from their hanging around in the Beast. Last night her face was white as white can be and she's hardly said a word since. Seeing the two of them shot in the head probably didn't agree with her.

I have an *aha* moment. "But you'll see Lee's car on the road into the valley."

Hutchy puts down the folder. "Listen. As of right now, nobody's worried about the Ellingers except you. If I go ahead and trek up to Longsleddale and find their car, and then later they *are* announced as missing, then the first thing my boss will do is say, 'Aha, that Becky Stone's knee-deep in this whole business.' I'm just looking out for you here, you see? We'd check Lee's car thoroughly and if it's not clean..."

I snort to show I'm done with all this crap. "You make it sound like we're hunting for a litterbug. We're talking about two dead bastards here."

But I get it. I turn to go.

Hutchy says, "So you don't want me to fill in the missing persons form?"

"No."

"And you don't want a note putting in the Becky Stone dossier?"

"Fuck off. No."

I turn in the doorway. "But won't Lee's mum report them missing, soon enough?"

Hutchy shakes his head. He winces a bit and I can tell he's thinking about me and my sad, sad story. "She died last month. Pneumonia. But it's alright, she was old... That sounds bad. Don't tell the others I said that, not in uniform."

So Lee and especially his dad were alone and unhappy. That makes sense. Now I get why old Owen dragged himself up the fells to the bothy. He had nothing to lose.

I'm just about ready to stop caring about this whole thing, though. All the same, I say, "But if they stay missing, do me a favour. Check the tarn. What's the word? Dredge it."

Hutchy just laughs. "If you could see our station's budget! This isn't Manchester, Becky."

The radio beside him hisses and he starts doing all that Roger-Charlie-Tango business. He's loving it.

Yeah, it's not Manchester, Hutchy. And it's not South Central LA either, you knob.

4

"YOUR ROUND," GAIL says.

That gets one of my glares. Gail grins and hands me her purse. Off I trot to the bar.

You'd think a barmaid would want to do something other than hang around in pubs in her spare time. At least we're not in the Beast, though. So far, our so-called pub crawl's only taken us from the theatre lobby to the wine bar on Lowther Street and now we've been in here for three rounds. We're classy lasses, see. From here on in, Kendal town centre's all sticky-floored boozers and two-for-ones and puddles of sick.

While I'm standing at the bar a couple of guys give me the once-over. Gail made me wear this black top with sequins on the front, not my usual thing. It doesn't show too much up front, but the sleeves are hardly sleeves and I'm no fan of my bingo wings. I pull a face and maybe my tongue stud puts them off.

Gail drinks half her cider before I'm even properly sat down.

"You don't normally put it away this fast," I say.

"I don't normally have as many reasons to drink."

Here we go. Until now all Gail's wanted to do is moan about working at the Beast and point out guys who might be alright in bed.

"You're still thinking about Lee?" I say.

She laughs into the bottle she's holding to her mouth, making a load of foam. She nearly chokes for a second. "Yeah. Sure. Lee."

Sometimes I wonder if I've got second sight. I can tell right away she's not thinking about Lee, not really.

"Ralphie, then," I say.

She points at me and touches her nose with her other hand. Spot on. "He's been gone since New Year. No word, just gone."

"He left you running the Beast all on your own? No wonder you're pissed off."

"It's just the start. I've seen all this before. Last time, he was gone two weeks."

"Where?"

"Manchester, maybe."

Bloody Manchester. Cumbria's too boring for really bad things to happen here. Manchester soaks up all the shit. "He got family down there?"

Gail scowls. "Are you trying to be funny? No, Becky, he doesn't have family there."

From her tone of voice I'm guessing Ralphie isn't staying with friends, neither.

She rubs at her forehead. "I mean, he's more than ten years older than me, for God's sake. And he's ugly as sin when you really look at him up close. It should be me running around out there, not him."

It's tough thinking what to say. If I was Ralphie, I'd stay home cuddling up with Gail every night. And I'd also be getting wrecked every night in the pub I owned. That's about as sweet a setup as I can imagine.

Gail's still going on. "I swear there's more than one of them he sees. Slappers. I don't know if he pays them."

I think about Ralphie's sweaty, pockmarked face. I'd say he pays.

"It's not like I care, mind you," Gail says.

She looks like she cares. Even if her and Ralphie are just about the worst couple you can imagine, who wants their other half disappearing every few months to screw any lass who's halfway willing? The fact he's nearly fifty makes imagining the whole thing even worse. His wrinkly little cock.

"Look at me," Gail says, waving her hand up and down her body, displaying the goods. "I'm still young. I'm cute."

She waits for a second, maybe holding out for a compliment, but I'm too scared to speak. She *is* cute, though. Cuter than anyone has any right to be, in this town, in this light.

Her face goes all crumply. "I hate him. He's a twat and he's evil. Anyone that shags around like that, they deserve everything they get."

She looks off to one side and breathes all heavy. When she looks back at me she's more sad and sorry than angry. "Oh, hell, Becky, I'm sorry. I don't mean *anyone* anyone. You know I don't think your dad was like that. Not exactly, anyway."

I try and tell my brain not to start thinking it all through, not to start spotting the similarities, but it goes and does it anyway. If this is like a play and Ralphie's acting the part of Dad, then those Manc prossies are my Auntie Alice, then that makes Gail my mum and that's all sorts of wrong.

"So you should leave him," I say. I'm practical like that. No time for moping.

Gail's finished her cider already. She reaches over and helps herself to my pint of Worthington's.

"I can't. He threatened me." She looks up and sees whatever face I'm doing and then her eyelids flicker open and shut. "Not like that. I've got nothing. And the pub's so far in the red it'd make you puke if you knew how much. Ralphie's told me again and again, if I leave him, I get half of everything except the Beast itself. Debt, that means. I'll never crawl out of it on my own."

I almost tell her I've got money, that she could shack up with me, but I stop myself. The allowance that comes through from Dad's account each month isn't the kind of money she's talking about. It's hardly enough to buy me booze and ready meals and the odd bit of vintage vinyl. Dad was ace but even dead, he's pretty stingy.

Anyway, there's no use thinking about fairytale endings. Gail don't like me. Not like that.

She does a pretend shudder. It makes strands of hair come free from her daisy clips. I always thought she'd be prettier with her hair down.

"I told myself I wasn't going to think about him tonight," she says. "Let's talk about something else."

I chew my cheek. There's only one other thing to talk about, isn't there?

It's Gail who's the one who says it. "So. What are we going to do about the Blighter?"

I sigh. "Sooner or later someone'll notice that Lee—"

Gail holds up a hand to shut me up. "I didn't say 'What are we going to do about Lee.' I'm talking about that Blighter hidden up there in the bothy."

I narrow my eyes to show I'm onto her game. Looks like I was wrong about her being all upset about the Ellingers. "But you saw what happened."

"Whoever did that to Lee and Owen, they're protecting it because it's worth protecting."

"You can't go back there."

"We can. We have to."

Where did this *we* come from? Gail knows I'd go anywhere with her, the cow.

"Listen," Gail says, like I'm not already paying her attention. "You know how it is. The more people find out about it, the more people that go up there looking for a Blighter, the worse it'll be. Soon enough it'll be as useless as all the ones over in the States and we'll be kicking ourselves for the rest of our lives. But *we* got there first, didn't we?"

"Yeah."

All this is tied up with what's happening with Ralphie, for sure. Better tread carefully.

"I went to the cops," I say.

Gail's face goes all loose. "You told them?"

"It was only Hutchy. Paul Hutchinson, remember him? Clutchy Hutchy?"

"But you told him about the Blighter? The bothy, where it was?"

It's almost a compliment, her thinking I could actually describe where the bothy was. I never could read a map. "Nah. Sort of. He didn't believe me."

Gail's face has gone so dark I actually look round to see if someone's messing with the lights.

"I saw some police too," she says. "At Lee's house."

"What were you doing all the way over there at Sandylands?"

Gail doesn't answer, but I already know. She must have been doing a stakeout like in the films, waiting and watching to see exactly what she did end up seeing. Watching to see if the cops were on the trail.

"It wasn't Paul Hutchinson, though," she says. "It was two other ones, older. They forced the door, then they were inside for ages. When they came out, one of them was holding a mobile phone. Lee's, I'm guessing."

"So there you go, then. They'll be up there lickety-split, they'll find Lee and old Owen and that other guy. Sort it all out."

"And the Blighter?"

I shrug. "Maybe they won't notice it."

She just stares at me without speaking, for ages. I wasn't serious. I said what I said because I wish that's what would happen. I've only known about that Blighter for a day and already it's way more trouble than it's worth.

Gail shakes her head. "You said you didn't tell Hutchy where the bothy was. And Lee's phone won't give them any clues. Only Owen knew where they needed to go."

"And he's dead."

"Yeah." But Gail don't look sad about it. Her face is getting brighter and brighter by the second.

I put my hand on her arm. She don't bat an eyelid. "Listen. We can't go up there again, Gail. I'm not even talking about the cops. Don't forget, somebody up there in the hills shot three guys who was just minding their own business."

"If you won't come, I'll go on my own."

She's shaking, though. I bet she *would* go on her own, but I also bet she'd fuck it up. Get herself shot, too. And I'm not having that on my mind along with everything else.

Gail takes both my hands in hers. They feel warm, with none of the sweat of a bloke.

"We both deserve this," she says, looking into my eyes like she's trying to put me under. "You need it as much as I do, Becky. You need it more."

I make a face. Gail's talking about Mum and Dad again, without coming out and saying it. Everyone reckons they know how sad and messed up I should be.

She's got a point though.

Last summer, when the Blighters first arrived, nobody knew what was what. Those giggly YouTube videos were just the start. It was the only time in my life I ever watched the news on purpose. Just like everyone else, I wanted to know what them Blighters really were, and I wanted to know why they'd all showed up all of a sudden, just like that. Whether they'd dropped out of the sky or not. And, except those first few that the US Army or NATO bombed, I wanted to know why people was racing around trying to get near to them instead of running the hell away. Why people who did get close were so bloody pleased about it, instead of terrified by the size and slime and teeth of them.

Trouble is, by the time all the scientists and TV newsreaders had it figured out—by the time the chat-show conversations switched from *Where in the universe have them fuckers come from?* to *What, oh, what are they doing to us?* to *Top ten tips to buy yourself a house in a cushy Blighter neighbourhood*—most Blighters were pretty much ruined. Once it was all worn out, living round the corner from a Blighter was pretty much exactly like living round the corner from a bus-sized slug, and as gross as that sounds. 'Course, people still visited, still hung around, hoping for just a little piece of the action, and at least worn-out Blighters didn't growl and show them triangle teeth so much. But really they was only good for museums. All the ones in the USA are like that now, and don't Americans feel sore about it? Like I say, I don't watch the news, but even I know that the top brass over there in America are proper pissed off. They're having all sorts of what Mum would have called 'angry words,' with all them other countries that still have Blighters in good nick and the sense to keep too many folks from coming near.

How many are there around the world, still in working

order? Twenty? Thirty? But there's always been rumours about other ones, hidden away by people cleverer than the rest, or maybe just not properly found yet, like our one. Another twenty, some say. Another fifty, who knows.

Gail's back to looking around for guys. Some thick-necked idiot at the bar is giving her the eye. I lean backwards in my seat and check a few out, too, but to be honest I prefer just looking at Gail.

Then I see someone's giving me a little wave from the back of the room. A woman. Thinks I'm looking at her, maybe. She's got red hair like a novelty picture frame around a face that's older than she'd like you to think.

Ah, fuck.

Kendal's too small for its own good. I turn my back so Auntie Alice gets the message. But I can feel her still staring at me and it makes both my cheeks all hot and itchy.

So now, even though I'm trying not to, I'm thinking about Dad again.

And I'm thinking will I help Gail and I'm thinking about wasps and I'm thinking about Ralphie and about history repeating itself.

It better fucking not.

5

THIS TIME, I'M ready for anything.

Even though the sunlight's nearly faded, Tarn Crag and
the bothy don't seem nearly so grim. I'm wearing Dad's big
old sheepskin coat, the one he died in. It's thick and warm
and makes me feel like a gangster's moll.

It's hard to see down there into the valley even though
there's no mist. The tarn's turned sort of gold from the
sunlight and looking at it stings my eyes. The sun's only
just starting to go down, bang on time. It was my idea to
come before dark, to see what's what. The lay of the land,
Dad would have called it.

"Look," I say, nudging Gail in the ribs with my elbow.

I point down into the little valley. There's a line of white
stones running along the bottom. After a bit, the hillside
blocks the line, but then the stones show up again over to
the right-hand side of the bothy.

"That's the radius," Gail says. "They've marked it out."

I guess she just means 'circle.' But she's right, and it
more or less proves that there really is a Blighter inside
the bothy. They're always talking about that on TV, the

circle around each Blighter. They mean an invisible circle, though, so marking it out with stones is a smart idea.

There's something else, too. A bit away from the big black-painted double doors of the bothy, the ground's all messed up. There's soil in a sort of molehill pile, but massive, and loads of clods of grass all thrown up. That must be where the Blighter landed in the first place. But the way it looks, you'd think it landed mouth-first and straightaway it thought "I'd best get chewing."

I got no time for all that. What matters is what's happening right here, right now. I point again, to the other side of the bothy, away from the doors, where the line of stones goes closest to the side of the valley where we're hiding. "That's the spot. Okay? But don't go in a straight line. And keep your head down."

Is it just me, or am I suddenly wearing the trousers here? Ever since I said yes to coming back up here, Gail's let me do all the thinking. I kind of like telling her what to do—that and the sheepskin coat and I might as well be my dad—but it's weird. Gail's normally tough as a boot and I don't like seeing her go so wishy-washy.

Gail nods. She's shaking. She tries to move away from me but I pull her back with the rope dangling out of her rucksack. I hold her by the arm.

"And don't you dare take a step over that line until you know it's safe," I say. Now I sound more nagging, like Mum, which isn't great. Look what happened to her.

But of course it's not safe. Whoever shot Lee and Owen is probably out here with us, over on the hillside opposite, which is higher and steeper than this side. Anyone hiding over there must be able to see the whole valley. I'm banking on the fact that they'd probably expect any intruders to walk straight up from the road, instead of tramping through the woods like me and Gail did. But either way, anywhere past our cairn hiding place is out in the open.

"So what do we do now?" Gail says.

This new, meek Gail is starting to get to me. Ralphie's got no right to turn her into this. Nobody has, to nobody. That Blighter better sort her the fuck out.

"We wait."

I wriggle down in the tufts of grass. Dad's big coat's like a sleeping bag. Gail squeezes up against me and I put my arm around her.

It's weird to think it, but I feel right at home here. I can almost forget about the fat Blighter down there in the bothy and the man—or men—who have their guns pointing over here. I could stay here all night, with the cold wind whipping around above our heads and us huddled here in a little dimple in the grass made by our own bodies.

It's dark before we know it. Gail's getting edgy, fidgeting against me. I have to let her go.

"You remember the plan?" I say.

She nods. "I know where I'm going."

The way she says that, it sounds like no good thing at all.

It's only right now that I realise the whole time we've been making our plans, Gail's never once mentioned about me having a go with the Blighter myself. Either she forgot, or she never really expected me to want to get near it after all. But actually I'm glad I didn't have to say no or explain myself. Everyone in the world wants Blighter love except me, but I've no clue why. Must be something deep down.

"Hey, Gail," I say, making my voice even more like Dad's, that way he could sound kind and in charge at the same time. "Good luck, okay?"

She kisses me on the cheek. It's too cold to blush.

Gail pulls her chin inside her scarf and takes a few steps away. My side still feels warm where she was.

"Gail," I whisper. I point at my ears and then at her.

She makes a face, then pulls the white iPhone earbuds out from her pocket and sticks them in her ears. A quick thumbs-up and then she's off. The rope dangling from her rucksack trails behind her like a mouse's tail.

I wait for a while and watch Gail scoot around the top edge of the valley. She's doing well, keeping behind the ridge and out of sight of anyone on the other hillside.

Then she's gone. My turn.

I set off in the other direction, keeping my head low. I have to keep one arm twisted behind me to stop all the stuff in my rucksack from clanking around like I'm some kind of one-man band.

It's tough hiding from someone when you've no idea where they are. But seeing as the guys with guns must be up high, I keep as low as I can. I head off in the opposite direction to the bothy. It's pretty cloudy and the moonlight only makes everything grey, like the sea, or the old films they show at Christmas.

The direct route to the road must be over here somewhere, but I don't want to wander far enough to actually end up on the path. I pick a spot and dump the rucksack, then I pull out the first two objects. Back at my flat, Gail laughed when I called them 'sound grenades,' but I think they're ace. The two I've got in my hands are half-size Pringles tubes. Each one's got something inside. An old yo-yo and a metal tin of peppermints, if I remember right.

I chuck the first one down the hill, away from the bothy. I've got a wicked overarm, me.

The sound grenade does its thing perfectly. *Thump clank clank brrrrrrr wumph.*

A *Blue Peter* badge for Becky Stone, please and thank you very much.

A few seconds later I hear another sound from over on my right. Could be someone scrambling down the hillside, probably trying to get into position for a shot. I can't see anyone, but I make a guess where they might be.

I throw the second sound grenade off in another direction. It lands somewhere that must be behind the verge where the shooter's hiding. *Fumph clank clank kaaaaa.*

That'll do for now. I huddle down in the grass and hug my knees. It's pretty funny thinking of people racing around after empty cans of Pringles, but it'd be funnier if they weren't going to kill me if they found me.

I still haven't seen anyone, but time's ticking. Gail must've got to the bothy by now, hiding on the far side, out of sight. I hope she's in one piece. Just one more reason I might regret this whole thing.

I pull out two more sound grenades. The first is just leaving my right hand when the other one drops from my left hand. It makes a *krack clunk whumph* noise at more or less the same time the other one lands, far away.

Oh shit. That's torn it.

The sound of gunfire is like a hand smacking on a table.

I grab the rucksack and leg it. There's still one sound grenade in there, along with Dad's old football rattle, and they're banging around like nobody's business.

Looks like I'm the decoy now.

I remember to keep away from the valley ridge. Running's a bitch because the ground's all bumpy and my feet keep sinking down into the thick grass. Then the going gets easier and I realise I've ended up on the path leading back to the road.

I start skidding to a stop even before I see the guy. He's facing away from me but when he hears the *clank-clank* of my rucksack he turns around and we just stand there looking at each other. He looks like a farmer type, all wax jacket and graph-paper shirt collar and flat cap and red nose from homebrew. His mouth opens and he just makes this face that'd be funny if he weren't lifting up his shotgun and pointing it right at me.

I turn and scramble back up the way I came. When the shot rings out I make this sound that's half shout and half hiccup, and it's such a weird noise that at first it makes me think I must have been hit. I reach back, like I'd only be able to tell if I was shot by checking from the outside. The rucksack's all ripped up.

That'll do for me. Off I go.

I might be unfit, but that old bastard's worse. Still, I don't have too many options, so now I'm climbing again, back towards the ridge but on the other side from the cairn where we started.

I pull out the phone from my coat pocket. Speed dial.

"Gail!" I whisper, even though it's still ringing. "Pick up!"

Nothing. I bet she pulled out her headphones as soon as I couldn't see her any more. And now, where she is, what she's doing, she won't even notice the ringing.

"Stop right there!"

I'm so surprised that I almost do stop. But then I swerve away and the only direction left to go is towards the bothy. My foot catches at the top of the ridge and I tumble over, which is lucky because I'm pretty sure the next shot would have got me if I hadn't fallen.

Trouble is, there's no stopping me now. I try and pull in my arms and curl into a ball as I bump my way down the hillside and down into the valley. Every few seconds I hear the smack of a gunshot. They're coming from different directions. So there's definitely more than one of them.

At the bottom of the valley I realise I've lost the rucksack. Sod it. Time to bail.

The bothy's not far away, but Gail's on the far side. It'll take me a while to get there if I go around the outside of the line of white stones. More to the point, I'm a sitting duck down here, if one of them farmers shows up on the ridge above my head. And that might be any time now.

I look along the line of stones curving away around the edge of the valley floor.

I look over at the bothy. It's actually not that far away, as the crow flies. Except even if a crow did fly over that way, that Blighter would still do its thing on it and I'm not sure I want to be that kind of bird.

I can't just stand here. There's only two choices. I can race around the edge of the stones, or head to the bothy straight. But I feel like I'm going to regret whichever decision I make. That sort of makes it easier, in a way.

I run full pelt towards the line of stones. Straight over and through, that's the way.

Then, at the last second, I turn and run along the outside of the line of stones, without even realising at first that I've changed my mind. I can't let myself get caught up, too. Gail needs me to do the thinking.

Mud spits up near my foot even before I notice the slap of gunfire.

I put my head down and pretend I'm back at school doing cross country. I'd always want to stop, sure, but then Miss Clough would've been right on my arse and there were all sorts of rumours about her. So get your act together, Becky Stone. Keep running, you lazy bloody layabout.

Jesus, I'm unfit. My belly feels all tight and full of sicky stuff sloshing all around.

Fsshhh, there goes another shot. I feel it pull at my hair.

Those guys up there are getting better. Or maybe closer.

I look up. I'm nearly at the bothy. Once I'm around the corner, I guess I'll be out of the line of fire for a little while. It feels like I'm running in slow motion, but not like the replays on Sky Sports and more like I'm just actually slowing down, like I'm jogging because I'm not really about to be shot in the back of the head.

The line of white stones takes me right around the corner of the bothy. I should lift up my arms like the winner I am. A gold fucking medal to go with my *Blue Peter* badge.

Except I don't feel like celebrating, because look, there's Gail. She's standing right up against the bothy with her whole body pressed against it. Her arms are stretched out and her fingers are digging into the loose cement between the stones. She's moaning like she might just come right there and then.

I shout out her name.

She don't move except to wriggle a bit against the wall. It feels wrong to be watching her acting like that. If ever there was a private moment, this is it.

The people they're always interviewing on the news always make a big song and dance about how it feels, being near a Blighter. Even the most famous one in San Francisco, the one that hardly even works, people reckon they can still feel it. Then there was that other Blighter in the mountains between France and Spain, some old ski resort that the government cleared out lickety-split as soon as they realised what they were dealing with. People paid through the nose for a trip up there and then came back down the ski lift in floods of tears. Said they'd found God.

But I sure as hell don't remember anyone mentioning creaming their knickers like this. So that's either something to do with Gail or something to do with this particular Blighter. Maybe she was right. Maybe it is a special one.

Not like it hardly matters now. If me and Gail both get ourselves killed, it just don't matter.

I crouch down and feel around for one of the white stones.

The first one I throw thunks against the bothy wall. It sounds almost as loud as the gunshots. Not that Gail notices.

The second stone hits her right on the shoulder. I wince. Gail's head jerks forwards, smacking against the wall. She moans, but not in a bad way.

The bothy's blocking the moonlight and now my eyes are adjusting to the dark. There's a curly silver line on the ground, stretching all the way from Gail to near where I'm standing.

The rope.

Gail must have let the rope out behind her before she stepped over the white stones, just like she was supposed to. Which is just as well, because if I wander over that line I'll be in the same sorry state that she's in.

I give the rope a pull and it goes tight where it's attached to Gail's rucksack. She bends backwards a bit and laughs. I swear I've never heard a laugh so creepy and tinkly and wrong.

Another pull. It's enough to make her take a full step back, but straight away she pushes forwards again, pressing her cheek against the stone wall.

This ain't no time for a stupid tug of war.

I wind the rope around my right hand, round and round and round.

I give it one massive yank. It pulls the straps of Gail's rucksack tight and she jerks backwards. She laughs again but she shouldn't, because a second later she's on her backside, more than a metre away from the bothy.

I turn away with the rope over my shoulder, like I'm a horse pulling a carriage, or dragging a witch along the ground, which is what they used to do, isn't it? And Gail doesn't half sound like a witch right now, moaning and cackling and giggling. I don't want to see her being bumped across the hard, cold ground, so I just pull and pull without looking around.

I'm doing well. A few more steps and she'll be safely over the line of white stones. Trouble is, the further I pull her, the further I am from the shelter of the bothy. I'm out in the open again.

I duck as another shot rings out. Still can't see any of them farmers, but they're close.

Another slap. Something nips the hand holding the rope. I make this yelping sound.

Christ. A near miss, but it fucking hurts. Looks like a piece of shot's nicked the edge of the webby bit between my thumb and my pointing finger.

The rope's slipping out of my knackered hand but I grab at it, because right now I'm a bloody hero.

I do one of them primal screams. It's more to show I'm still in the game, not from the pain.

Another shot. These blokes just won't stop.

The rope's gone slack.

I turn around.

Gail's still on her back with her arms and legs upwards like a beetle in a bath, or a wasp all woozy and warm. There's rope coiled around her and on top of her. But it's not attached any more to the bit of rope I'm still holding in my hands.

Seriously. Them farmers aren't great shots, but they aren't half lucky.

I drop the useless end of rope. What now?

I'm not going to leave her like this. I'm still thinking about wasps and that makes me think about Dad, even though I'm not all that sure why. I'm not going to leave her for dead.

I run back to the line of stones, like I'm in PE and working up to do the long jump. But then that deep-down part of my brain that's cleverer than I am kicks in again. I stop with my tiptoes touching the stones. I can't let myself end up like Gail.

I drop forwards onto my belly. My top half is over the line of white stones, inside the circle, and my arms are stretched out towards Gail. My fingers are digging into the soil, almost but not quite touching her.

I try to make my fingers keep pulling me towards her.

Except it's hard to keep remembering how important it is to get her back.

Because I feel it right away. That Blighter love.

I don't find God, though. Not a peep.

I do feel what I'm supposed to feel, I swear I do. It comes up from my fingertips, the best kind of warm, like when you drink mulled wine and listen to Christmas carols, even if you're not a religious type and you think God's basically a twat and not even real.

The feeling creeps up on me, more and more. Fizzy and good. My eyes keep shutting and I kind of want to just keep lying here and enjoy this tickly, happy feeling. I know I'm in a real rush and all, but can't I take a minute and enjoy this, just a bit? Finding a Blighter is like winning the lottery but better.

Gail laughs this tinkly little laugh. She's still upside down, kicking her legs. She looks like a baby.

That thought gets to me.

Concentrate.

Fine, so Gail's a baby. That's what the Blighter did to her. And I ain't her mum but she needs my help.

I wriggle forwards some more, further over the line of white stones. Almost there.

But my mind's going bubbly and light. I start laughing too.

That wakes me up a bit. There are least two guys with guns back there and here's me having a good old chortle. This is proper messed up.

I make a sound that's half roar and half belly-laugh and I pull myself up onto my feet. It takes so much of my energy that I start stumbling forwards, way past Gail. I slap my hand hard against the stone wall of the bothy to give myself a jolt. It takes me a second to get my breath back, but then that glowy feeling keeps pushing at me from inside and I can't trust myself. I dig my fingernails into the sharp stone but it feels soft like carpet, so then I headbutt the wall and *that* fucking hurts, at least.

I stagger back to Gail and pull her up by the shoulders. Her head's lolling to one side. I can't hardly see her eyes, because they've rolled all the way back. She's grinning like a maniac.

"Gail, for fuck's sake!" I hiss. No more laughing for me. All that bubbling inside is starting to feel more like a hangover than being drunk.

She don't move a muscle, so I drag her towards the line of white stones. Another gunshot echoes around the valley but I'm pretty sure them farmers are just taking potshots. Or at least that's what I hope.

We're almost there. I'm praying that when we get over the line, Gail will snap out of it.

She's doing this weird groan now. There's another noise, too, but it's coming from over at the bothy. It's a wet slapping noise, like a water balloon ready to burst. What's that bloody Blighter *doing* in there? A word pops into my head, a sex word, the same word that you'd use to describe what Gail was doing when I found her. *Writhing*.

Gail smacks her lips and closes her eyes. She looks as happy as I've ever seen anyone look.

But then she speaks.

"That's enough," she says in a quiet voice. "That's enough, now. Please. Kill me now."

6

WE KEEP OUR heads down.

Gail don't feel like leaving the sofa. I never seen anyone watch so much shit TV. Channel 5 and Sky Living. Two mugs on the coffee table are full to the brim with fag-ends. I guess you could say she's been living with me the last couple of days, but only because she can't quite get up the energy to leave.

"Take me back," she says.

I shake my head, like always. Just the thought of her all spaced out and drooly up there at the bothy is enough to give me the shivers. At least I know she can't go on her own now. The keys to her Corsa are in my jeans pocket, digging into my leg. You won't see me giving them keys back to her.

I fill up Gail's glass with tequila. It's what you might call a short-term solution. She deserves not having to be the barmaid for a while, though—not that she's even set foot in the Beast, last couple of days. Who knows who's keeping that place going right now.

"It's bad for you," I say, meaning the Blighter, not the tequila, though it might as well be both.

"It was the most beautiful thing that ever happened to me."

"Didn't look like it. You looked like a mental."

Gail's face does something complicated. "I was so happy, Becky. It was more happiness than I've ever known. That Blighter up there must be more powerful even than the one in Portugal. What they say is right. I'm not religious, but it was like looking into the face of God."

That's a bit much. First, I was there in that circle of white stones, too, for a bit, and it was more like drinking shitloads of cheap champagne really fast when you've crashed a wedding. Second, looking into the face of God just sounds proper awkward, like when opticians lean in close and they have gross coffee-breath but part of your brain tells you you should kiss them anyway.

I do remember the stories about the Portugal Blighter. As soon as someone let the cat out of the bag, all the locals buried it under this little church to stop other folks wandering too close. They made the circle—the *radius*, that is—smaller. They did it just after them American scientists proved that the happy calm feeling got less and less, the more people were allowed near to a Blighter. A one-way process, them scientists said. Let too many people have a go and the thing's knackered for good. But the ones who did get into that church, inside the radius, they had a fine old time, giggling and rolling around. People looking through the windows said they saw them speaking in tongues.

"You told me to kill you," I say.

"I didn't know what I was saying," Gail says, "and that's not how I felt."

We both sip tequila. I think I'm going off it.

Yesterday's *Westmorland Gazette* is lying on the coffee table. They still keep up Dad's subscription, even though I keep telling the delivery lad I've never read a word and all it's good for is mopping up beer stains. Still, the paper catches my eye because there's a picture of a Blighter on the front page, blurry like it's been taken from far away. Gail's drawn love hearts all around the photo in green Biro. I spin the paper to read the headline: *What does Blighter border standoff mean for Cumbria?* At first I panic and I'm looking for mentions of Lee and Owen, before I clock that it's not any nearby border they're talking about. It's the border between bloody Canada and America, for fuck's sake. The *Wessie Gezzie* always do everything they can think of to make world events relate to Cumbria, no matter how much they have to stretch the facts. Probably some local's on their hols over there and we're all supposed to be biting our nails about will they make their flight home alright?

"How about we go see the one up in Glasgow?" I say. I point to the bottom corner of the newspaper front page, where there's a yellow flash and an offer for *Blighter roadshow tickets for every reader*.

She snorts. "There's a reason they're giving away tickets for free, Beck. That Blighter's been around the houses. The roadshow's been all the way round Europe in a truck and its buzz wore out even before it left—I don't know—Greece, or wherever it came from. From what I heard, you'd hardly know it was even alive."

Seems like nothing's going to cheer her up. Nothing but our big old bothy Blighter.

After a few minutes Gail says, "It's been nearly a week now."

I'm just about to correct her—it was only a couple of days ago, belting back down the hill to find Gail's hidden Corsa and shaking off them gun-toting farmers—when I figure out she's talking about Ralphie.

"Still no word?" I say. I make an *oh-poor-you* face. It don't go down well. She clams up.

I look over at the record player in its big old gramophone cabinet. The last song finished before I went to fetch the bottle, and now the arm's thunk-thunking up and down in the runout.

Gail wipes her eyes and shakes her glass. It's empty again.

"It's alright for you," she says. She puts down the glass, but instead of pouring more tequila I slide the bottle around the back of the sofa. I like Gail, and she's more fun conscious. "You're single. No worries."

Just her saying that makes words come rushing out of my mouth without going through my brain first. "I'm more than single." I wave a hand, meaning *just look at this bloody place*. "I'm proper *alone*."

I blink a few times—no tears for me—and look around the room myself. The paintings—trains going through mountains and the like—are proper horrid, but I suppose Dad thought it made him look like a man of the world. The wallpaper's even worse and I always said I'd strip it, but the money just disappears and a scraper costs more than a pint. The old gramophone cabinet's the only thing Dad left me that I really love. He used to tell me about 'Cat Man' by Gene Vincent, and how his dad—my grandad who I never met—went apeshit when Dad brought home the record and stuck it on. There's no volume knob on the gramophone cabinet or anything, so you just open the door wider if you want it louder. And Gene Vincent was fucking loud already and I can just imagine the cabinet jumping around all over Grandad's parquet flooring while old Gene shouts and shouts and shouts.

"Jesus. I'm sorry, Beck," Gail says. "Listen to me going on."

Then she looks around the room too, and I know exactly what she's thinking. I hold up my hand and shake my head, but she says it anyway.

"It was here, wasn't it? This is where it happened?"

Seems like I can't move, suddenly.

Gail looks more alive than she's been for days. I'm not liking that nasty glint in her eyes. "Was it your Auntie Alice that found them?"

"Don't say that name," I say, hardly managing to open my mouth. "Not here. Seriously, Gail. Don't."

"Sorry. I'm sorry."

I can feel her staring at me 'til my cheeks get hot. I look up at the ceiling. There's a discoloured patch up there where Dad once let me set off an indoor firework that turned out to be more of an outdoor one.

Gail don't say nothing more, but it's like I can hear all her questions anyway. She knows the start of the story and maybe the end, but not the why or how.

"It was me," I say, after a minute, or maybe five, or ten. "It was me that found them."

I stop staring at the ceiling. Nothing's big enough to block out all the pictures popping into my head, anyway. Where I'm sitting now, on the sofa near the lounge door, is just about the same angle I saw the whole scene from, back then.

There's Dad sitting where Gail's sitting, looking all calm and like he's just taking a catnap, except for the white foam on his lips. There's Mum, halfway across the floor with her fingernails dug into the carpet. Probably crawling to the door once she realised what he'd put in her drink.

7

I SEE FRODO as soon as I walk into the reference room, upstairs in the library. He's sitting hunched over in front of a computer, right in the corner. Me and him, we're in here all the time. I haven't got the internet at home and Frodo isn't allowed it, since that time he downloaded basically all of Hollywood and then sold it on scratched DVDs in the covered market. He's leaning so close to the screen that them crazy-wild curls of his are stuck to it with static. If I touched his scraggly beard, or his hessian hoody, I'd get the mother of all electric shocks.

Seeing him brings it all home. Suddenly it's like I see the cause and effect of what's happened the last few days, mapped out right there in front of me. All the links between people, like they're attached with rope. The bothy attached to Gail, Gail attached to Lee, Lee attached to Frodo. Them two were always good mates, going back years. And now Lee isn't no more.

I got no idea what I could say to make things better, so I don't go over to Frodo and I don't say nothing.

The lady at the desk gives me a proper scowl.

"You know you're not allowed to take anything out until you return those outstanding CDs," she says. She's not even trying to keep her voice down.

I give her a nice smile, all the same. It's not like they'll be getting a search warrant to fetch them CDs back. But she's right about them being outstanding. One of them was a 'War of the Worlds' collector's edition, and I didn't pay jack shit.

I put on my ladylike-polite voice. "It's actually the *microfiche* I'm after."

I can't tell if she's impressed at me using the right word. Either way, she sighs and starts rooting in the cabinet behind the desk. She don't even ask me which date or which newspaper or anything.

I take the slide, which is already covered with my grubby fingerprints. I head on over to the special projector-thing, cue it up and there it all is.

I'm not really reading the words, but the word *accident* still jumps out all the same. What did Auntie Alice say to the police to make *accident* their considered opinion? I know there's nothing in the newspaper article that'll give me any more of the truth than I already got. It's all lies. No, it's the photos that I come here to see. There's truth in them photos, alright.

It always bothers me that the pictures of Mum and Dad are in separate ovals, with separate captions, like they didn't even know each other. There are millions of photos of the two of them looking happy together, so why couldn't they have picked one of them? It's like the journalists was saying, 'Look, there was always something not right about them' or whatever. Still, Mum looks pretty. Sunburned, too, because that one was taken in the south of France just before she dunked herself off of a canoe that wasn't even meant for grown-ups. The photo of Dad was an old one, even back then. He's got one of them wide collars he used to have, and his shirt and cardie are both different shades of brown. Worse still, he don't look no fun, which if you ask me is fucking criminal, because he was a hoot, day in, day out. If they'd asked me I would have given them a photo of him playing at being the Tickler or laughing at one of my shitty jokes or dressed up as Dracula at Halloween. Maybe not the last one.

Even though I don't really want to, I slide the microfiche projector thing way over to one side, past the block of text about the crime scene and about Mum and Dad's jobs and loved ones and their awful messy relationship. And there's the picture of Auntie Alice, speckly with newsprint dots. Her photo was bang up to date, taken just outside her house on Aynam Road. Probably from across the road, mind, because there's a car partly blocking her face and she's holding up a magazine to block most of the rest of it. So I'm looking through that little gap and I'm trying to see what her mouth's doing and what her eyes are doing and what that all means about what her mind's doing.

It kills me that nobody cares no more. It kills me that Gail remembers the story from back then, but can't remember who did what or even much want to find out.

It kills me that Auntie Alice is out there, walking around, chatting, laughing, making out like nothing ever happened.

My whole body's shaking.

Enough of all this.

I yank the slide out of the machine. It makes this nasty loud squeak. The desk-lady looks over, but I just smile at her. Then I peer down at the slide and see the scratch running all the way across it.

Just as well, I guess. It ain't healthy, coming back to look at all this again and again. And now I can't.

Still, it's not like I'm suddenly feeling all zen about it. My cheeks are hotter than ever. I only head over to Frodo because I want something to take my mind off what happened to Mum and Dad in 1999. And maybe I'm feeling kind of mean inside, a bit.

He flinches when I plonk myself down in the seat next to him. His computer screen's black, but not turned off, because I can see green text up top. I almost laugh at that. So the dark web really is dark.

There's some woman sitting opposite, looking up and down between a book and her computer screen, like she's trying to read both of them at once. I start talking to her instead of Frodo, which is a mess-with-their-heads trick I learnt from detective shows.

"I heard there's a Blighter somewhere nearby," I say to her, just like that.

Out of the corner of my eye I see Frodo's ginger curls bobbling around. He's shitting himself, I bet. Probably still trying to piece together all them dark-web clues, not knowing that old Owen did it already and look where that got him.

The woman gives a tight sort of smile. She's nervy, but friendly-looking, like a primary school teacher or a Welsh person.

"Up at Glasgow," I say. "The roadshow."

She loosens up a bit. "Oh, I wanted to go too."

"Wanted? I thought they was chucking tickets at anyone who'd have them."

She puts her book down. "Maybe so. But I don't think it's even worth trying to get up there, not now. All the blockades on the Shap Road are causing awful delays, they say."

There's Frodo getting edgy again, beside me.

"First I've heard of it," I say.

"I heard they've been ordered by the Department of Agriculture," the woman says. "Something to do with the livestock. Same as before, I suppose. Foot and mouth."

I grin. "Same to you."

The woman doesn't much like that, I guess. She harrumphs and then gathers up her books and shuffles off to another desk.

"It's a cover-up," Frodo whispers. It's just me and him in the dark little corner now.

I'm watching my step now. Maybe he does know where that bothy Blighter is, after all.

"The government thinks they're getting scarce," he says. He's still facing his computer screen and not looking at me, but I can smell his fusty smell. "Now that things are going to pot in the US."

He glances over at me for a second. I shrug.

"You haven't heard?" he says. "That Blighter the Canadians were hiding in Saskatchewan, it was a big one. Really, really big. Nowhere near the ones down in the Med, but bigger and better than any of the others they've found so far in the Americas."

I'm getting interested, so I don't stop to tell him there's only one America. "What about it?"

"Well, the US proved it landed on their side of the border. Or *said* they proved it, anyway." Frodo loves this *X-Files* sort of business. "So the standoff isn't a standoff any more. The first shots were fired an hour ago, according to Twitter. And it'll ramp up, too. You know what this means, Becky." He narrows his eyes, watching me up close. "*War* is what it means."

I take a deep breath, but I'm not sure if it's to show I'm sad about the war or to show I don't care. I remember all over again about what happened to Lee. If Frodo knew about that, he'd be way sadder than about some random Canada people getting shot.

"If only they knew," Frodo says, hardly more than a whisper.

"Knew what?"

He points at the dark screen. The dark web.

"That they're not scarce at all. There are more out there. Blighters. More than you'd believe."

His voice trails off. He's watching the desk-lady. She's speaking on the phone and making a serious face. She glances up at the two of us, just for a second, then away again.

I freeze.

"Hey, Frodo," I say.

But when I look over, he's already gone, leaving just his fart smell. He really is a filthy fucker. The fire exit door snicks closed behind him.

I'm just about to leg it myself when Hutchy runs into the room. He's all red-faced and puffed out and his police jacket's crooked like he just threw it on. The desk-lady points over at my corner and seems surprised, but when Hutchy clocks me sitting here, he only looks awkward. Then he's off again, sprinting back the way he came.

8

SOME NEW GUY, Carl, is behind the counter at Down to Earth Records. He keeps shooting me looks while I'm pottering about. Every so often I pull out a record sleeve and hold it up to the light, making out like I'm a real buff. It seems to keep him happy.

Still, I've been in here for like nearly an hour, killing time. Much longer and I might actually have to get that copy of 'Master of Reality' that's begging to be bought, although it's probably scratched to buggery and it'd sound shite even if not, coming out of Dad's gramophone cabinet. It'd sound even worse, maybe, than this techno Carl's playing, which is making the time drag more that it needs to.

"Anything you need?" Carl says. I guess it maybe is getting weird, just me and him in the poky little shop.

I pull out a record at random. I must have some kind of gift, because it's a beaut. Only a Focus 'best of,' sure, but 'Hocus Pocus' is the first track and there's no beating that. Me and Dad used to mime-yodel along to it for laughs.

I hold it out to Carl. "Stick this on, would you?"

He looks down at the sleeve and makes a face like I've just handed him a plate of smeared turd.

"I am considering purchasing it," I say.

Carl scowls but takes it. The techno stops, thank Christ, and then there's the gritty scratch from the vinyl. I get back to prowling along the shelves, but now my head's bobbing. You know what? This song actually does fucking rule. Soon enough I'm air-drumming along, then when it gets to the widdly bits I have to do a bit of the guitar, too. It's pretty hard work, all in all.

Trouble is, I still can't clear my mind out, not totally. I'm here for a reason.

My laps around the shop keep taking me over to the door. It's raining outside.

And there she is, bang on time.

Auntie Alice's work backs onto the same alleyway as Down to Earth, and that's where her boss makes the smokers go. Looks like she's the only one who hasn't already switched to vaping, because she's out there on her lonesome. She's sheltering from the rain in the overhang of the entrance to a closed-down pub. The see-through hood of her pac-a-mac makes her red hair blue. The display in the record shop window is partly blocking my view of her, and she looks like that old microfiche photo.

The door slams behind me, cutting off 'Hocus Pocus' at the leprechaun bit.

Auntie Alice sees me coming. After a few seconds her smile goes all wonky, like she thinks maybe I'll knife her.

"You're ready to talk?" she says. "Finally?"

"Shut up," I say. "Don't say nothing."

So she doesn't, except with her eyes. They're exactly the same as Mum's eyes. All concerned, but I-know-best.

I can't help thinking this might be partly about Gail. She remembered all about Mum and Dad, but not about how

Auntie Alice was mixed up in the whole thing. That ain't right. That's like forgetting all about Jack the Ripper or Harold Shipman or Hannibal Lecter. Bad people got to be remembered, otherwise they're basically getting away with what they done, in the long run.

"I know what happened," I say. "I knew about you and Dad even back then. Giggling in the bedroom while Mum was away working, and you thought I was feeding the ducks or at youth club or whatever."

Auntie Alice tilts her head, which is just what Mum always did. If she keeps doing stuff like that I'll cry, or maybe worse.

"And here's another thing," I say, "I was the one who dobbed you in to the police. And if they'd had any sense of fucking justice they'd have locked you up or, I don't know, pulled you behind a horse or something."

She makes a frowny sort of smile. "Can I speak now?"

I spread out my hands.

"I know," Auntie Alice says.

"You know what?"

"Well, about you talking to the police about me, for a start. I don't blame you for that. They were very understanding about my involvement, about the delicacy that was needed. But they certainly shouldn't have said it was an accident, Becky. They just shouldn't have. That was wrong and, I suspect, it was mainly for their own benefit. Less paperwork."

I'm watching her face, her watery eyes and big slack lips, and I'm still so shook up that the words don't hardly sound like words.

She's still going on. "I know about the other thing, too. That you saw what was happening with me and your dad. And it's all true, at least as far as that goes. I'm not proud of it. But you have to realise, Becky, he was a—"

"A what?"

He was a stand-up guy, until he started carrying on with Auntie Alice. A brilliant person to watch crap comedies with. A hilarious dancer, even if he was getting too old to pull off the moves.

"He was a hard man to say no to."

"He wasn't yours, though, was he? He was Mum's. He was mine." My hands are shaking now. I grab one with the other and dig my nails right in. Just like Mum's nails, digging into the carpet.

Auntie Alice nods.

"And he weren't a murderer until you turned him into one," I say.

She pulls her hood back. She always wore too much make-up, and now mascara's streaked all over her cheeks even though she's not even standing in the rain.

"That's what you really think," she says. It's not even a question. "That I made him kill your mum."

All the thoughts I ever had about the whole sorry business are whizzing around inside my head, too fast for me to grab at. And Auntie Alice is smack-bang in the middle of all them thoughts. She's dancing with Dad, watching films with Dad on my fucking sofa, whispering to Dad in bed, telling him to man up and do it. Kill the bitch, she says. Even giving him the poison weedkiller from her gardening side-job. And Dad all upset and confused and doing it, actually *doing it*, and then ending up offing himself, too.

Auntie Alice reaches out like she's going to make a grab for me, shuffling forwards with her arms straight out. I just freak. I jump backwards and my back hits a sharp bit of the wall.

I stare at her, like it was her who smacked me.

I see my fist fly up before I've even thought the thought.

Now it's her who's jolting around. She whacks into the doors of the closed-down pub, making them rattle. Both her hands go up to her face, her shaky fingers cupping a circle around her cheek, like she can't bring herself to touch where I hit her. Her lips are all twitchy like she's going to bawl. The whole thing is making it harder to hate her, which in a way makes me hate her more.

There's only one way to deal with this sort of scene.

I pelt down the alleyway and only start breathing again when I'm like a mile away.

9

THEM BLIGHTERS ARE on TV again.

The sound's turned off, so the only noise in the little lounge in my flat is Gail's blubbing. She stopped trying to hide it a couple of minutes into the news segment.

I'm watching all them American politicians standing behind desks and talking straight to the camera. They're making excuses, just like Auntie Alice did. They look all pretend-surprised, like they never expected that shooting missiles would wind up with anything being dead. 'Who me?' says the President, probably.

Soon enough, the news switches over to showing the other folks. There's like a million Canada people and they're all wearing black. Some are inside some church or other, but most of them are watching on a massive TV outside in the rain. And now there's some guy in a suit who's maybe the king of Canada or whatever, and he looks like he can't hardly say nothing at all, he's so choked up.

It seems like everyone's pissed off, one way or another. I can tell the news segment's nearly over because it's been ages since an ad break and I could do with a wee. And it's only

257

now, right at the end, that they actually show the Blighter. First we get to see it back in its prime, if that's the right way to describe a massive slug. It's that same zoomed-in video from just before the standoff at the border. If the sound was turned up I bet there'd be sad piano music, a Meatloaf ballad or something. Gail manages another sniffle.

Then we get the money shot. Now the Blighter's slumped on the back of a huge truck, being dragged back to the wilds of Canada now that the Americans owned up about pilfering it the other night, and then all that shooting and shouting and then look what happened. To be honest, a Blighter looks pretty much the same dead as it does alive, except maybe a bit saggy off to one side. I'm sort of disappointed. When they said it'd been shot I expected it to be properly in bits, or at least with a hole you could see, and then maybe they'd have some video of it going down like a bouncy castle with a puncture. But no. Maybe that's just the way it goes. Dead things are just like alive things, except without a future.

I look over at the doorway to the front hall, to the line Mum nearly made it to before the poison got properly snarled around her insides. You never would have guessed she was dead when I found her, for the first couple of seconds. It was more like time had frozen with her there on the carpet, and when it got started again she'd jump up onto her feet and peg it the hell out of the flat and away, away, away. An *accident*, for fuck's sake. Now it turns out that even Auntie Alice reckons the police were being crooked about that, but that don't make me feel even a tiny bit happier.

Me and Gail are back on the tequila. This time I'm properly up for it.

"It's better off dead," I say, pointing at the screen.

Gail can't keep her sobbing to herself any more. She's hugging that toy giraffe I used to like, hugging it tighter and tighter like maybe she actually hates it. Her whole body's going up, down, up down with all the crying. She's the one who looks like something deflating, not the shot-to-buggery Blighter.

"I'm serious," I say. "Look how it all turned out. Too many people all after one Blighter. It's not like anyone was going to get any good out of it. Alright, maybe royals and politicians and Justin Bieber—is he from Canada? But you and me and anyone like us, we wasn't going to get to go and pat the Blighter on the head."

Gail glares at me through her tears. Suddenly I clock what I've been saying, and what it means.

"Fuck. Gail. I know what you're thinking. You're thinking, 'and here's us just a few miles away from a Blighter all of our own, and hardly no-one knows about it, so why the hell aren't we up there rolling around on the ground and partying like it's 1999.' Right?"

"Right."

There's a word for this. Painting yourself into a corner.

Gail's watching me and watching me. Them car keys of hers are digging right into my leg. There ain't no way I'm giving them back and there ain't no way I'm driving her up to that bloody bothy myself. I don't want to end up at a funeral like someone from Canada, or like me all them years ago, saying goodbye to Mum and Dad.

The TV's moved onto something else now. Something about antiques or car boot sales or whatnot. Gail's lost interest. I look around the lounge, hoping to see something that might distract her off the subject of Blighters and give me five minutes' peace. I look at the framed pictures on the wall, one by one. I never noticed it before, but all them pictures show places from other countries, not in England, or Great Britain, which is what you're supposed to call it now. There's a train going through mountains in maybe Italy or that country with the cheese. There's a hot air balloon way up over a desert with elephants looking up and watching. There's one of them old-fashioned little planes zooming up to the clouds, and all the way underneath it I'm pretty sure there's a bunch of penguins, and not in a zoo neither.

It was Dad who put up all them paintings of far-away places. There's only one picture in this whole room that Mum wanted sticking on the wall. It's tiny, almost hidden by Gail's armchair from where I'm sitting. It's a little drawing of Dad, maybe from a few years after they got together, done in pencil by Mum. I always thought it was shit. His nose is wonky and he had more teeth than that.

But suddenly I'm thinking a thought about all them pictures, a thought I never had before. Mum's drawing might be kind of crap, but it shows something. She drew it because she loved Dad. She drew it because she was happy, at least back then. And all them paintings of far-away places, what do they tell you about Dad and how he felt?

There's only one thing it looks like to me. Looks like he wanted to get the fuck out of here.

Gail's still watching me. I clear my throat and make out I was thinking about her and all her stupid problems. If I really cared about her, maybe I would have been.

"We could go look for Ralphie," I say. "My January cash just came through and first of the year is always bigger than the rest. Dad liked to pay his bills at the start of the year. Made him feel like he was winning."

Gail rubs at her eyes with Dad's Rush T-shirt that she picked out of the drawer herself. When I saw she'd taken to wearing it, I didn't have the guts to tell her that nobody, not nobody, gets to wear Dad's stuff but me.

"But you don't have any bills," she says. "I mean, isn't this place all paid up from his savings? From his will?"

I shrug. The suicide note Dad left was clear as crystal. Bank account details and everything. Enough money each month to keep his little girl going, but not enough to turn me into a trust-fund smackhead or nothing.

"Who knows what he was thinking," I say, meaning, 'No more talk about Dad.' "All I'm saying is that we can go find Ralphie. Bring him home."

It's like something's blocking the light onto Gail's face all of a sudden, cause it's turned proper dark. She's scowling, too. "I don't want him home."

She looks at me, eyes all glinty, and then the light's back again. I think to myself, oh-ho, something's going on here.

In a flash she's jumped halfway over the room and onto me. The chair she was sitting on judders on its four legs, like Dad's old gramophone cabinet, even though there's no Gene Vincent shouting.

It feels sort of like an attack and sort of like the other thing. At first I'm pushing her away because it's Gail, isn't it, but still it feels nice to have her lips pressed against mine even if they're cracked and her breath's a bit rank.

Before you know it we're heading up the stairs, all clumsy like it's a three-legged race. Gail don't even seem to notice that my bed's not made and there's this awful mossy smell that never goes away even after old Mrs Baines the cleaner has been around to sort things out.

She pulls Dad's T-shirt up over her head and I only wince a tiny bit when she chucks it away to crumple on the floor. She might not be your glamour model type, but it turns out she's got a neat little body, all curves in the right places. But I'm not even paying it all that much attention, truth be told, because actually the nicest thing is just looking right into her eyes while she's pulling at my clothes. When she's not looking angry she's really beautiful, suddenly, which weirdly makes *me* angry instead, so when I think any thoughts at all I just think, 'Ralphie, you utter tail-end.'

We're tangled up in bed and it's all hands and hips and skin and lips. And everything's going great guns until I realise that the sound Gail's making isn't a good one no more. I push her away, gentle. She's crying.

"Take me back," Gail says. "Please."

'Course, she means the bothy.

"No."

"I can get a gun. Ralphie's got a hunting rifle."

"No way. You'd get us killed."

Hang on.

"Is that why you're doing this?" I wave my hand to show her her naked body, which looks weirdly pale now. "You just trying to sweeten me up?"

I don't really want to hear the answer. I want her not to say anything, maybe ever again. I just want all that tangling up in bed and that'll do for me.

She don't say anything for a while. Then she nods.

"I made a mistake," she says.

I pull my clothes back on and then I'm outside and I'm sicking up tequila onto the pavement.

10

THE POLICE STATION'S only a few streets away. My whole life, that felt like a practical joke, designed to make my life just that little bit shitter. There's me in my flat on Dockray Hall Road, there's the police station over on Busher Walk, and there's the magistrates' courts stuck in between. Any time things get out of hand, I just bounce from one of them buildings to the other until they're done with me. When the cops pull me in, for public disturbancing or smacking a slag or whatever, I always think about that bit in American films, when they pack the suspect up into a van and ship them off. I always thought that must be nice. At least that way you get a bit of time to think; and a free ride, too.

This is the third time ever I've gone to the police station off my own bat. The second time was after we saw Lee and Owen get done in. The first time was back in 1999, when I tipped the cops off about Auntie Alice and all that evil inside her.

You have to go through two sets of doors to get into the police station, like an airlock except the other way around— the air's outside and inside it's just cops. The second set of doors are fucking heavy, like they're saying, 'You sure you want to go in here?' But I do; this time I do. Even though Auntie Alice is probably about as nasty a piece of work as they come, she got one thing right. The police were playing at being crooks, back then. They didn't investigate about Mum and Dad, not properly. When the whole business got to the courts, the lawyers and the judge made out like the only point of us being there was to have a good old sob about how sad it was—this *accident*—not to figure out what the hell actually went on that day.

But I've been walking around and around for like an hour and it's cold and dark out here and I'm actually pretty drunk from all that tequila and, more than all that, this needs doing. So I pull the door open and in I go.

The woman behind the desk is all round-faced and smiley and she nearly makes me forget my angriness. Mum would have said she took the wind from my sails. But then actual real wind blows from outside and slams that heavy old door and I think *I bet that cracks the window* and then I think *I bet they pin that on me* and then all the angriness is back and even though the window's fine and not cracked, I turn back to that smiley woman and my face says I ain't going to take shit from her.

"I want to speak to someone," I say.

"Go ahead." You'd have thought her smile couldn't get no bigger, but there it is.

"Not you. A policeman."

She don't even look upset by that. She knows I'm not being sexist. It's just that you can tell she's not properly one of them, because no policeman or police-lady ever smiled like that.

"I'm sorry, miss. The officers are all attending a briefing right at this moment."

I put both hands on the desk and pull myself up so my feet

are off the ground. It makes me a bit queasy, to be honest, and I can't help wishing Gail preferred beer to tequila. The lady makes a teacher face, but she don't know how to stop me. Now I can see through an open door round the back. There they all are, all them cops I remember from each time I got nicked. I ain't got many people in my life, so these guys are like family to me, in a way. I can tell which one's Hutchy right off, even from the back—he's always had them slouched shoulders—next to the others, seven of them in all. They're all standing looking up at some older cop who's talking at the front, standing behind a podium just like the President of the United States of America on the news. He's even got the same screwed-up face, trying to do an impression of someone who's surprised and sad. It's like all them other cops are kids and he's their dad. They're all shuffly like they wish they was playing Xbox instead of standing here listening to him.

"What's this briefing about?" I say. It's one of them questions that you don't expect an answer to.

"I'm afraid that's police business, miss. Can I help you?"

"Doubt it. He's the one I want to speak to. Clutchy Hutchy."

I point over the lady's shoulder. She don't even turn around. Hutchy does, though, like something tells him he's being talked about. He does one of them cartoon double-takes. He looks at me, then at the cop who was speaking at the front, who's finished up and about to wander off, then back at me, and his eyes are wide as anything. He's waving his head around so much his floppy fringe won't settle down in one place.

The lady budges over and blocks my view. Her voice gets all hard. "Officer Hutchinson isn't available. You can talk to me."

"Let me go back there, then, if you won't call him."

"Absolutely not. Where do you think you are, young lady?"

"You telling me this ain't KFC?"

She don't like my joke one bit.

"Hutchy!" I shout.

Hutchy's sitting at his desk now, but he's still facing my way, and even when he tries to hide behind his computer I know he knows I'm watching. Even from here I can see how edgy he's getting. I bet he knew I'd come for him. He weren't on the force back when Mum and Dad died, but I swear he knows all about what went on. The way he's always treated me, it's more than just feeling sad and sorry in the normal way. His pals back there in the police station, they're the ones who called the whole thing an *accident* and I bet Hutchy feels proper knotted up about it. It might be partly the tequila, but I ain't never been more certain about anything. He can tell me the truth.

The lady's reaching under the counter now. If this was America there'd be a gun under there, but seeing as it's Kendal it's probably just a buzzer.

I make sure Hutchy's looking at me and I point right at him. He's shitting bricks.

"Young lady, I'm giving you thirty seconds to—"

Over her shoulder, I see Hutchy jump up from his desk. He's making for the door.

I'm still half-up on the desk. Before I hop down, I pat the lady on the shoulder. "No need. Thanks love. Big help."

There's only one way in or out of the police station and I ain't letting Hutchy past. And there he is, a blurry slouchy Bigfoot through the thick glass. I yank open that heavy fucking airlock door and I'm all like 'Aha!' But Hutchy ain't there.

I push through the second door and run outside. All the cop cars are parked up in neat rows. One time someone left one unlocked and I got in and started up the siren. They didn't have ASBOs back then and that's the one time I pretty much got away with it, because the cops were proper red-faced about leaving the keys in the ignition. That just goes to show they'll cover up anything when it suits them.

Anyway, Hutchy's not out here. So back inside I go.

There's only one other door in the airlock. Us normal people can go into the first couple of rooms, because that's where you go to be interviewed by cops or counsellors or whatever when you've pissed somewhere you shouldn't. I look in each room but they're both empty, so then I peer through the big locked door that leads to the cop desks.

Still no Hutchy, though, so there's only one place he could be.

I don't even stop to think twice before I charge into the gents. Some lasses wouldn't dare, like there's a fucking forcefield around them or something. But I've seen enough, in pubs and whatnot, to know that men's toilets are basically like women's, except there's never a sofa but a lot more puddles of piss. Still, I'm glad to see there's no-one standing at the urinals. Seeing a cop's cock would pretty much cap off a shitty old day.

There's only one cubicle and it's shut tight.

"Open the fucking door, Hutchy."

'Course, there's no answer.

"I ain't going to knock," I say.

Hutchy's voice comes out all muffled. "Don't you dare, Becky. Criminal damage."

"What you going to do, call the cops?"

I give him a few seconds, but I swear I'll break the door down.

The door swings open and there's Hutchy, crouched double with his bum and his feet on the closed lid of the loo.

The police force spends a ton on adverts trying to make cops seem more human. Hutchy right now is the kind of sight that'd do that for anyone.

"It was a cover-up, wasn't it?" I say.

Hutchy's face is the same dirty white as the toilet paper.

"I don't know what you mean."

"I got proof," I say. "I got me a fucking witness."

I still hate the thought of asking Auntie Alice to help, getting her to tell what she knows about the cops making out like Dad didn't kill Mum. But it's the only way of opening up the case all over again, and then—

Then maybe I'll get Auntie Alice put inside for her part in the whole thing.

It's only right this second that my whole plan seems a bit off. Why would Auntie Alice do anything that would help make her look guilty? But, then, why did she say anything about the cops making shit up, back there in the alley?

None of it makes sense. Right now I can't even remember why it's so important to prove that the 'accident' was murder, after all. Whichever way you look at it, it was Dad who did Mum in, not Auntie Alice. The guilty party's already got himself a gravestone.

Suddenly I feel as drunk as I've ever been in my life. Hutchy must notice me swaying and all mixed up.

"I didn't know," he says.

It takes me a few seconds to clock what he's saying.

"So it's true?"

There's panic in his eyes. Now he thinks maybe I was doing a double-bluff. But then he just goes all crumply and I can see the same six-year-old Hutchy I used to know.

"I'm so sorry," he says. "I know you and he were friends."

"Friends? Is that the best you can manage?"

"Oh. More than that, then?"

I don't know what to say to that. Maybe he's drunk too. Maybe everyone is, all the time, and I just never noticed.

"It's just when I saw you in the library, you didn't seem..."

Oh, fuck.

Hutchy ain't talking about Dad. He ain't talking about the 'accident' or about anything that happened back in 1999.

"Frodo," I say. Then, "What's happened?"

Hutchy's feet drop down onto the tiled floor, making two little sploshes in the piss puddle.

"I swear I heard about it only a minute ago," he says. He points, back to where that old cop was lecturing all the other cops.

"Say it. Say it out loud." Old tequila swills around in my throat. If I puke again, I'm going to aim it right at him.

He takes a big old breath before he speaks. "They brought Frodo in last night. And they found him in his cell just an hour ago. It's normally part of procedure, but... I guess someone forgot to take his belt off him."

I'm standing there staring at Hutchy, who's still sat like a gnome on the loo, and my mind's racing, trying to stick together all the jigsaw bits. Because Frodo's dead and if the look on Hutchy's face means what I think it means, then Auntie Alice was right about cops round here being crooked. Frodo was a freak, but he weren't the type for offing himself. He wore that ASBO tag like it was a Cub Scout badge for Advanced Hacking. He was proud of being an outlaw. So if Auntie Alice was right about police being dodgy, then that means the cops knocked off Frodo for one reason and one reason only, and that's because he knew about that fucking Blighter. He knew about it and the cops knew about it, too, all along.

Seems to me that them Blighters are making shit for everyone.

So even though I'm staring at Hutchy, he might as well not be there anymore. Because now I'm thinking about Gail, who's the only person except me who knows about that Blighter in the bothy, apart from the cops and whoever's up there guarding it.

Gail would do anything to get back up there. I knew that already, but now it's way more dangerous than even I thought.

Still. At least I've got—

I'm patting my pockets, front and back. Hutchy's watching me, still scared as hell, like he thinks I've lost it and maybe I'm going to deck him after all. I just ignore him and my hands are shaking while I turn all my pockets inside out but there's only sweets and receipts and fluff and nothing, nothing else.

Which means Gail's got the car keys.

11

'Course, THE FLAT'S empty, so I'm in and out in like ten seconds. I leg it back all the way down Busher Walk and to the river and then across the bridge. I keep tripping because the laces of my Docs aren't tied, but there ain't time to stop.

My brain's dotting around like crazy.

Now I'm not thinking about Gail no more. And for once I'm not even thinking about the night I found Mum and Dad dead in the lounge.

I'm remembering a whole other time, when I was like six or seven. It was Mum in the shower who screamed, but it was Dad who pulled the cover off of the Xpelair vent and it was me who ran in to see what all the fuss was about.

Wasps.

There was five of them, if you include the one that Mum saw fall down from the ceiling. Five of them, all sleepy and lolling around on the bathroom lino.

I looked at Dad and Dad looked at me. Them wasps didn't hardly move at all, just wriggled a bit.

Dad pulled off one of his slippers and then *splut*, he crushed one flat.

I must have made a sort of 'oh' noise. Them wasps weren't doing nothing.

Dad squished another one, and another. He looked at me like it was my fault, or like I told him to stop.

"They made a mistake," he said. "They have to die."

Maybe I *am* thinking about finding him and Mum dead, after all.

Frodo made a mistake, too. He made a mistake and the cops did the only thing they could think of to stop him telling more and more people about that Blighter up there. He had to die.

Before too long, I've made it round to Aynam Road. Maybe I should have kept up the cross country after all, because when I put my mind to it I can proper fly.

I stop for a couple of seconds outside Auntie Alice's door. Not sure why. Maybe I'm thinking about spitting on it like I usually do when I come past. But there's more important things right now. Her car's just round the corner, on Parr Street, like it always is. You'd be an idiot to park here, where the streetlights are too spaced out to make it feel safe, but there you go. You'd be even more of an idiot to leave your car keys on top of your back tyre, like Auntie Alice does.

It's a right old banger, a Volvo more made of rust than metal. I check all around and then bend down like I'm finally getting round to tying up my laces, but really I'm having a good old rummage around the wheel.

There's nothing there. Seems like today's a day for things not being where they should be.

The keys aren't on the other side neither, or on the front tyres. Just when I thought I couldn't hate Auntie Alice more, she goes and gets herself all safe and secure and really fucks things up.

I open a few of the garden gates nearby and poke around,

looking for bricks or plant pots or what-have-you. It's like they've got everything nailed down around here. What's wrong with these people? So off comes one of my Doc Martens. I bring it down smack on the Volvo's passenger window. The sole just boings off the glass and it absolutely wrecks all along my arm and I can't stop myself shouting.

"You could have just knocked."

I'm still holding my shoe above my head, ready for another go, as I spin round. Auntie Alice don't even flinch. She just reaches up and pushes my hand back down, all gentle. In her other hand she's dangling the car keys.

"I saw you from the window," she says, pointing back at her house. "I thought maybe you were going to come and say hello."

There's all sorts of things I could say to her right now, and none of them's 'hello.' I grab for the keys.

She snatches them back. "What's the big hurry?"

Words just come out. "My friend Gail. She's in trouble and the cops are in on it." Without meaning to, my eyes are tearing up just a bit. I tell myself it's to make Auntie Alice give in and hand over the keys, but that's a fucking lie.

I jerk back when Auntie Alice puts her free hand on my shoulder. She's wearing gloves. In fact, she's all dressed up in warm clothes and ready to go. She scoots around to unlock the driver's door and in she goes.

I'm staring at her from outside, through the other window. I've got my arms out wide, meaning, 'what the actual fuck are you doing?'

She reaches over and unlocks the passenger door. She's already shut her door so her voice is all muffly like she's underwater and right now I wish she was, gurgling and not breathing. "You can't even drive, Becky."

I get in.

"I bloody can," I say. "Ask the cops. Chased me all round town that time, they did."

"I'm still your auntie. I'm responsible for you, even if you don't like it. Now. Where are we going?"

I don't want to tell her the truth, but there's too many lies already. "There's a Blighter up Sadgill way, hidden. Gail's gone after it. They'll kill her, Auntie Alice. Them cops are fucking going to kill her like they just now killed Frodo."

Auntie Alice is giving me this weird look, made worse by the bruise I gave her on her cheek. I'm ready to say something proper mean, but then I see that the weirdness is more like sadness. Worry. She's actually bothered about me and my life. I'm crying now, proper tears. My chin's shaking like it's not part of me.

"Go!" I scream.

Auntie Alice starts the engine, but she's still looking over at me.

"Drive! Didn't you hear what I just said? *Go!*"

She goes. We're off. She don't look at me again while we're speeding through the empty streets. I'm rubbing at my face with my sleeve, rubbing and rubbing, but it takes ages for them tears to stop coming.

It's only when we get past the out-of-town Morrisons and away up Shap Road and leave Kendal behind that I start breathing normal. I'm not really looking out the window, like maybe I don't want to think about what's coming up. Instead I'm looking at this dead wasp that's lying on the dashboard. Auntie Alice don't use her car all that much, day to day. I bet this fucker got locked in last summer and then smacked its head again and again on the window, trying to get out, then just fell down dead.

"What you said before," I say. "About did I think you made Dad kill Mum."

She keeps watching the road. I know what she's thinking. She's thinking didn't I just tell her Gail's in mortal danger and the cops are all bent and killers too. And here I am talking about 1999 again.

But "Yes?" is all she says.

"You saying you didn't? You didn't put him up to it?"

"I didn't." She checks both mirrors, then takes a big deep breath. "Your Dad, he was his own man. He was bright, Becky, brighter than the sun for those of us who were in his orbit. He took what he wanted and people were grateful to give it."

I want to tell her that's nothing like he was. But the thing is, she's bang on. I remember one time some kid at the amusements won a prize at the claw grab just after I'd had my go. Dad convinced this six-year-old boy that the knock-off Tamagotchi was rightly mine, because if I'd stayed on I definitely would have got it, see? That little lad gave it up pretty much right away and then went off with a smile on his face, like he'd done a Boy Scout good deed.

Still, that don't prove nothing really.

Auntie Alice's voice gets mousey when she says, "Your mum knew, too."

My throat goes all scratchy right away. I can't speak.

"She knew about me and your dad. And she wanted out, even before that. We talked the whole thing through. We still loved each other—me and your mum, I mean. There were no hard feelings, if you can believe that."

"There's no way Dad would've carried on with you."

Auntie Alice waves the hand that's not on the steering wheel, meaning I'm probably right about that. "Anyway. Your mum was going to leave him, although I'm not sure it was because of what me and your dad were getting up to together."

"Don't sound all that likely. Mum hated travel. Dad was the one who liked gadding about."

I can hear the smile in her voice. "You never went further than the Dordogne on your family holidays, did you? I know what you're thinking about, though. You're thinking of all those pictures he put up. Exotic locations. Am I right?"

I don't say nothing to that because it's scary, her reading my mind.

"Thought so," she says. "But here's the thing. I've got pictures like that on my walls, too. I've got the Dominican Republic in my downstairs loo. I don't even know anyone who's been to the Dominican Republic. You see what it means? Pictures like that don't show we're adventurous types, me or your dad. They show we're panicking, that we wish we could change our lives. With your mum it was different. She didn't *need* pictures, because it was the actual escape that mattered. Where she went was a minor detail. But this is the really important thing. She would have taken you with her. You must believe that, Becky?"

I cough. I think about spitting the ball of phlegm her way. I don't.

Auntie Alice is still talking. "And... this is only what I think, but... I guess your dad couldn't handle the thought of you both leaving him. He wouldn't stand for it."

She flicks the windscreen wipers on. The scraping sound mixes in with her breathing.

"I didn't give him that weedkiller, Becky, I swear. He took it from my car. I had no idea until afterwards." Her voice is going all croaky. "Your dad was always insecure, being so much older than your mum, being closer to my age than hers. Maybe that's part of why he did what he did. I don't know."

I can't think what to do to make her stop talking.

"But he didn't just stop Mum and me leaving, did he?" I say. "He killed himself too."

She shakes her head, but only in a way that says she's buggered if she knows why.

But I know, because I'm a lot like him.

Pride.

"I'm glad I've had a chance to tell you this, finally," Auntie Alice says.

"Wish I could say the same." My throat's thick and the words are all squeaky.

"I always wanted to tell you about that part especially, about you and your mum and what might have happened next. And it's not exactly true that your mum didn't care where she went. She had plans for the both of you, and I wanted to tell you, I did, but you've never let me talk, even after I was proved innocent. She talked about it all the time, Becky. You'd both have left Kendal and headed to the coast. Your mum always talked about it. There was a particular image she had stuck in her mind, like it was a painting or a photo she could see. Nothing very specific, but beautiful all the same. It was you and her, facing out to sea. Starting again. Finding yourselves some calm."

I slam my hands on the dashboard, making that dead wasp go flying like it was still alive.

There's flashing lights up ahead, just past the Selside turn at Garnett Bridge.

"The blockades," I say. "They ain't letting folks go up there."

This is why I'd have been better off twocking the car. Auntie Alice fucking loves rules, I bet. And she's the one who's driving, so this is basically game over.

But Auntie Alice gives me a serious teachery look. "Your friend. You're sure about her, about what's happening?"

"I'm not a kid. I know what's what. I see things."

"I know that. Becky, I know."

We're close enough now to see the fencing they've put up across the road. If you didn't know better you'd think they was setting up for roadworks. The fence is all white and yellow stripes and they're shining bright enough to make my eyes hurt, reflecting the headlights of Auntie Alice's Volvo.

Until them stripes suddenly aren't shining no more.

I look over at Auntie Alice but I can't hardly see her face now she's turned the headlights off. Her body's all bent forwards. The car's going faster and faster.

Next to the fence there's one of them tents that builders use. I can just about see someone coming out of it. The streetlights round here are shite, but I can make out the outline of the police hat.

A torch flicks on. Auntie Alice puts her foot down. We're heading straight at the fence.

It's thicker than it looks. When we hit it, there's a ripping sound, along with the smack of metal on wood. My head goes backwards and forwards, *thwack*ing into the headrest twice.

But we're through. There's this nasty scraping sound coming from Auntie Alice's side of the car, and there's a big fuck-off wodge of wood on the bonnet, blocking part of the windscreen. But we're through.

We fly round the corner, past Garnett Bridge and further up Shap Road and away. When we're clear of the village, Auntie Alice turns the headlights back on. It's only now that I realise she's been basically driving blind for like a minute. I can't help giving her respect for that, but I swallow it deep down rather than say so out loud.

She shoots me a look. Part of it's checking on me, I reckon, but I can see this pride in her. I swear she knows what I'm thinking.

"Let's go and help your friend," she says.

When we get off the main road, I point out the way to go. Both of the other times I came this way I was sneaking looks at Gail out the corner of my eye. She knew it, too. Now I'm staring right ahead, watching walls and postboxes and trees show up like ghosts in the headlights.

Gail's Corsa's just off the road at Sadgill, parked all cockeyed like she was driving it in her sleep. I jump out and put both my hands on the bonnet.

"It's cold," I say. "She could have had like an hour's head start."

Auntie Alice hasn't got out of her seat, she's just wound down her window. "And how far away's this bothy of yours, on foot?"

I make a face.

"Then hop back in."

She's right. There's no time for sneakiness now. We're in emergency rescue mode. If that cop at the blockade saw our number plate, we're fucked. And even if he didn't, he'll have Oscar-Miked on his walkie talkie and every bent cop in the county'll be on our tails right now.

12

THE BONNET OF the Volvo bounces up and down every time we hit a bump. And there are a *lot* of bumps once we leave the main road. Auntie Alice guns the thing straight up the fellside so it ends up skidding around all over the place on the wet grass. Dad used to say that back in Grandad's day they raced cars up the fells, before health and safety and the environment and all that. Even though I'm scared to death I'm still sort of enjoying the feeling of us smashing a car to bits, driving it somewhere nobody should drive.

The car's just about to give up or tip over when I see the people standing at the top of the hill.

"There!" I shout.

There are two of them, black against the purply sky. The one on the right has mad hair flying around. That's Gail, for sure. The other one has their hands on their head like they're playing a game of Simon Says.

My foot gets caught on the car door while I'm trying to get out.

"Stop!" I shout while I'm pegging it up the hill. "Gail! Don't!"

Soon as I get close I can see the other person's that same farmer, the one who looked so surprised when he caught me with my sound grenades the other night. He don't look surprised now, just pant-shittingly scared. He looks at me and then back up at the rifle that Gail's got pointed at him.

Gail looks over my shoulder and makes a face. Auntie Alice has showed up and now she's standing beside me.

"Becky," Auntie Alice says, all whispery. She tilts her head to one side.

I look where she's nodding.

Further up the hill the wind's blowing at something. At first I think it's a pile of old clothes, but then I spot a hand sticking out. The fingers are all twisted and dug into the grass. Now I can see the guy's face, too, sort of. There's not much of it in one piece. My mouth suddenly fills up with sick. I spit on the floor and hope I don't lose it, not while there's work to be done.

"Come with us," I say, jabbing my thumb over at the Volvo. "We can still get away. *Away* away."

The thought hits me like a slap. Would it work? Me and Gail and what, Auntie Alice too? Carrying out Mum's plan after all. All of us standing on the coast, facing out to sea.

Gail just shakes her head. She keeps blinking and blinking. It makes her seem proper crazy.

"You can join us," the farmer says in a quiet little voice. I guess he means all three of us, but he's looking at Gail, because she's the one with the gun.

"How many of you are there?" Gail says.

"Eleven." Then he looks over at the pile-of-clothes dead guy. "Ten."

"Including cops?" I say.

He nods. "Four of them. It was the only way."

It's hard to argue with that. Any time a Blighter's out in the open, folks fight and fight and then too many get close up and then the Blighter's good for nothing. Maybe Frodo was right, maybe there are tons more of them fuckers around. Maybe cops all round the world are keeping schtum about some bothy or cave or hole nearby, telling no-one and knowing that it's the only way.

I say to Gail, "He's lying. They won't let us join their gang, I swear they won't. They killed Frodo. And there's no way we can keep them away from us now, either, if we hang around. We got to leave while we can."

Gail don't look like she's going to put the gun down, but it twitches a bit in her hands.

"I need the calm," she says.

Don't we all? But that's not the way. Blighter calm is just cheating.

Out of the corner of my eye I see Auntie Alice moving. It suddenly occurs to me that maybe she's after the Blighter too. All that talk in the car about escape and whatnot, when she knew full well I was leading her straight to the biggest, happiest high, one that'd help her blank out all them troubles in a second. I bet she's going to make a run for the bothy, give that Blighter a big slimy hug and get her rocks off right there and then. You can't trust nobody.

I don't even look over her way. She can do what she likes. Gail is who I came for. She's the one for me, even though it's getting harder all the time to hold onto that thought. Seeing Gail all messed up and snarling and toting Ralphie's rifle makes her just a little bit less lovable.

There must be something I can say to change her mind.

"I love you," I say. No idea where that came from. It's a tense situation.

Gail don't say nothing to that.

She's still looking at me when it happens.

The gun goes off. The farmer don't make a sound, he's so surprised. His body thunks down face-first on the grass even before I can see where Gail hit him.

"Fuck," I say.

I say it again when Gail turns the rifle to point my way.

"Raise your hands," she says. "You're coming with me."

There's this weird half-second that seems to go on and on. She's staring at me and the whites of her eyes are shiny from the Volvo's headlights, and right at that moment I can see she's figured out something's up, but you know when you can't quite pin it down?

She swings round on the spot at the exact second that Auntie Alice comes jumping out of the dark. Auntie Alice would have grabbed Gail from behind if she'd been a second faster, but instead she's right in front of the rifle, almost touching it, when Gail pulls the trigger. I swear Auntie Alice is actually in mid air when the flash and the bullet send her flying backwards again, like she's a ball hit by a rounders bat.

It's not like I can actually see through her belly, but there's enough of a hole that I know she's a goner. It must have been quick, I reckon. She's looking up at the sky, almost smiling, like she's just lying there watching out for funny-shaped clouds.

I can't see Gail's face no more. There's a cracking sound and some rummaging. She's reloading the rifle. Then the gun twitches, pointing up the fellside.

I walk in front of Gail like she wants me to. I don't say a thing.

13

I WALK AHEAD of her, over the ridge and towards the bothy. I guess she figures that when I get another taste of the Blighter's fizzy calm, I'll be just as thumbs-up about this whole sorry affair as she is. Maybe she hopes I'll convince myself that her killing Auntie Alice was an 'accident,' once I'm high on that Blighter love. Or maybe she don't care.

The funny thing is, it takes pretty much the whole way before I work out exactly what it is I'm feeling right now.

Every time I slow down, Gail jabs the rifle between my shoulder blades. It hurts, but not the normal way. Each of them rifle-jabs breaks off a bit of that love I had for Gail. It's like the gunshot that killed Auntie Alice cracked something deep down inside me, and now she's just helping gravity do its work. I imagine each bit dropping off me and onto the grass 'til there's nothing left. They don't even make a sound.

And that's not the only sadness I'm feeling.

The more I think about Auntie Alice, the harder it is to make her out to be the bad guy. And not just because she's gone and died in the most fucked-up way possible. I never actually knew her, I guess, until today. Now that I've spoken to her, she don't seem anything like she was in my head. And now *don't* is *didn't* and I'll never get to know her, ever.

Trouble is, I'm falling right into Gail's nasty trap. The more this kind of shit happens, the more I actually do want to get close to that Blighter too. I got to make all them thoughts about Auntie Alice, and Mum, and especially Dad, just go away. Find some fucking calm.

But that isn't how things work, is it? It's like I always said. Blighter calm is a cheat, a fake.

There are other ways to find it. Good and bad ones.

Like the way Dad found calm the only way he knew how.

But I'm better than him.

That thought hits me proper hard. It's maybe sort of one of them life-changing moments. I might almost want to jump up and down and go 'Ulrika!' if I weren't being marched around at gunpoint.

I'm better than him.

Sure, he had amazing taste in music, and sure, I'm a lot like him, and sure, I loved him then, and I still do. But he killed Mum and Mum didn't even do nothing to deserve it. The more I think about it, the harder it is to blame anyone for that, anyone other than Dad. And I sure as hell don't want to pretend it was Auntie Alice's fault anymore, and I don't want to try and forget about the whole business neither.

This weird feeling washes over me. Straight away I look down, but we're still a way away from the line of white stones. This feeling I'm feeling, it's not the Blighter's doing. It's not that giggly calm that Gail wants so bad.

But it's calm alright.

Because...

I *get* it now.

Back in 1999 and then past the Millennium and then for years and years after that, Dad's money paid for this counsellor. She wore ugly power suits covered in cat hair and she used to bang on about 'the process.' I thought I weren't even listening that whole time, but now there's one of her special words stuck in my head. I reckon this feeling's what she'd call 'acceptance.'

Suddenly I feel like I can do just about anything. I don't need a Blighter, or Dad, or anyone or anything. I'm just me and that's alright.

But with a gun poking into my back, I don't get to make the choices, do I?

Gail prods at me again. I don't hate her, but I sure as hell don't love her, and I never did.

I step over the line of white stones.

Straight away I get that tingly, bubbly feeling again. But it's not all that. In fact, it's even less than it was before. It's just mixing in with this new, real, solid calm I already got, shining its edges up but not stopping me seeing through the Scooby Doo fuzziness. I don't feel anything like Gail looked like she felt when I found her at the bothy.

All the same, I let my legs go a bit bandy and I slow down, mostly for show. I'm guessing that's what Gail wants to see.

I give her a few seconds before I turn around to look at her.

It's a shock. Even though she's still holding the gun, Gail's grinning at me. She looks proper wasted. Every time she blinks it looks like she might nod off there and then, even though she's still carrying on trucking over towards the bothy.

"Gail?" I say.

She just opens her mouth. It stays hanging open and her head swings from side to side like she's lost listening to music.

"Gail. I'm scared."

And it's true. But to be honest, I'm way more scared of her creepy-as-fuck face than I am of the gun.

She stumbles. I duck without thinking. That thing could go off any second.

Suddenly Gail's on her knees. The bubbly feeling makes me feel like I'm wading through water, but I get to the gun before she drops it. So now I'm holding it in my hands, but I don't feel like I've won or anything.

Because I won't ever get my Gail back.

Her mouth hangs open again. It starts moving, really slowly, like she can't remember how to make words.

Then she speaks.

"Please. Help me. Kill me."

I look down at the gun and I look down at Gail. I think about wasps on the carpet, about Dad crushing them with his Hush Puppies.

Well. It's an option, at least.

"Come to me," Gail says.

"I'm right here, aren't I?"

"Please. Come to me. In here."

She sounds less and less like Gail all the time. Something about the rising and falling of her voice. She's normally got a bit of Manc to her accent; but not now. She don't even sound drunk. She sounds more like some foreigner who's used to speaking another language, and like using English words is a proper pain in the arse.

"Come to me," she says again.

And then she says, "It's dark."

And then, "In here."

I get it.

I turn and look at the bothy.

14

SOON AS I set off, Gail gets up on her feet again. I take her by the arm like I'm a gent and she's some Victorian lady. Sometimes she's a dead weight, and sometimes it feels like she's floating above the grass.

There's a brand-new padlock on the bothy's big black double doors. I shove Gail all the way back, then I shoot at the lock with the rifle. I only shot a gun like a couple of times before and all this giggly, bubbly feeling is making my arms shake. It takes me four goes and loads of splintered wood before the lock falls down onto the ground.

I pull the doors open.

Behind me, Gail says, "Yes. Yes."

The inside of the bothy's black dark. My eyes sting from looking.

"Are you in here?" I say. My voice echoes all round.

I hear the Blighter before I see it. The slithering sound reminds me of silly putty, when you stick your fingers in the tub and make it fart. But louder.

And louder.

Soon it's hard to tell what's the actual sound and what's

the echo off the stone walls. There's sucking and popping noises all around.

I'd run away, but where to? Auntie Alice is dead. Mum and Dad are long dead. Gail's a killer now and if she snaps out of her trance I'm not sure I'm not going to kill her myself.

More to the point, the cops could easily be right outside by now. At least while I'm in here, they can't shoot me. I'm hoping that if they come any closer to the bothy, they'll probably end up giving me a hug instead.

Anyway, there the bastard is.

All that tickly, happy feeling disappears just like that.

Now I can see that the Blighter's easily wide enough to fill the bothy right up. It's as big as a bin lorry. It's slimy too, and looks even more like a slug seen through a microscope than they look on TV.

It's shuffled near to the doorway and the moonlight's reflecting off of its snout. Steam's huffing out of its mouth. Up close I can see them triangle teeth are sort of bent inwards. If a Blighter got a hold of you, those teeth would just pull you further and further in.

And it proper stinks.

I laugh. A real Becky laugh, not a champagne-bubbly one.

So it turns out I'm a badass. This is obviously the most terrifying thing ever, and here's me thinking the Blighter could use some Listerine.

But really, it comes down to this. I don't have all that much going on, day to day. I just cash Dad's cheques, buy heavy metal, drink beers, listen to heavy metal... That's about it. I always said to myself I was low maintenance. That I didn't need much.

But maybe I do.

I had Gail, maybe, for a bit. And Auntie Alice, sort of. But not now.

So if this is the end of me, curtains and all that, then at least it's an interesting way to go.

I just look up at the Blighter and the Blighter just looks down at me. At least, that's what you'd say if it had eyes.

"I do not appear to affect you," it says.

"The fuck you don't."

I say that even before I really think about where its voice is coming from. I'm still looking up at the Blighter's dripping teeth, but out of the corner of my eye I can see Gail standing just behind me.

"Not in the sense in which I normally affect your kind," Gail says, or at least her voice does.

The Blighter's just drooling, with its mouth wide open, but it's still definitely who I'm chatting to. I don't want to look at Gail, but I make myself turn and face her anyway. Her expression is what Mum would have called a picture of contentment. Her arms are loose at her sides, swaying a bit, like she's dancing in her sleep.

"You are special. You are unique." Her mouth makes the words more careful than normal. It's weirdly high.

I laugh, but mostly for show. "I've waited yonks for you to tell me that, Gail. But you could at least say it like you mean it."

Sod this. It's mental as anything, watching her speak someone else's words. Some*thing* else's. I turn back to the Blighter, ugly as it is.

"Let's get a few things straight," I say. "You're not going to kill me, are you?"

"No."

I try to ignore Gail and pretend the words are coming out of the Blighter's mouth.

"Have you killed anyone?" I say.

"Never."

So the Blighter's already one up on Gail, for a start. All the same, I make one of those snorting sounds like teachers do. "But your farmer mates have, haven't they? Shot Lee and Owen in the head, didn't they? Cold blood."

"I did not ask them to do that." Gail's voice is a tiny little whisper. "They did it because they love me."

That sort of hurts. Seems like even a Blighter has more people that care about it than I do.

"It is a relief to be able to speak to you," the Blighter says.

"You're the second person today to tell me that," I say, thinking of Auntie Alice, "but you're not the ugliest."

Even though it's basically just a massive slimy slug, I can tell from the way it's shuddering that it's gearing up to tell its story. I've got the kind of face that makes people want to blurt everything out.

"I am suffering," the Blighter says in Gail's voice. "All of my kind are suffering."

But they all landed in different parts of the world. "So you can speak to the others? All you Blighters?"

It wobbles, I guess maybe trying to shake its head. "No. But I sense them, near and far. I sense their pain, flooding through me, accumulating and adding to my own."

"What's so painful, then?" Hunger, I bet. Nobody on TV ever mentions what they eat. Far as I know, no bugger's actually been gobbled by a Blighter, neither, no matter how close up they get. Funny, that.

"The gravity of our world is far lesser than yours. There, we were able to spread our wings. We could burst through the atmosphere, when it was our time to leave. Here, we are pulled down to the Earth and unable to move. I would not have the strength to unfold my wings, even if I were free of this stone prison. Every moment is a punishment. I am suffering."

Well. Aren't we all?

"Why did you leave your cushy old world in the first place, then?" I say.

"Our planet fractured. The tectonic shifts became so extreme that first the land became inaccessible, then the atmosphere poisonous. We did not grieve our world, however. Its time was at an end. We simply launched ourselves away in the hope of finding a home."

"You picked a shitty spot."

"It is unfortunate. But I understand that your people do not wish to harm us."

That's probably going a bit far. It probably never heard about the bombings last summer, before the governments thought better of it. Bits of Blighter meat chucked up all over the beaches. Even when scientists figured out all the stuff about the 'circle of calm' around each Blighter, and how bloody lovely it was to stand in it, all people did was fight over their Blighters and then hide them away to stop *other* people fighting over them.

I suppose now's the time to find out what that's all about.

I do my best Louis Theroux impression. "So tell me this... Why do you make everyone all gooey-eyed when they come close?"

The Blighter's mouth opens even more and drool sprays onto my face. If it weren't for the last of the giggly buzz, I'd chuck my guts up right there and then.

Gail's voice says, "An inadvertent side-effect. It is a defence mechanism that has served us well in the past. Here, the calming effect appears to be amplified, against our wishes. It has rendered us unable to speak to your people. Until now."

I always wanted to be somebody special. And now I am and I don't like it one bit.

"But it don't last forever, does it? Your happy-clappy buzz, it runs out. Why can't you just have your chat after people come back down from their high?"

The Blighter goes quiet. Its mouth twitches. I look back at Gail and her mouth's doing the exact same thing. I'm half-thinking about giving either one of them a prod when the Blighter starts talking again, in Gail's tinkly little voice.

"You have witnessed this? A failure of our defence mechanism?"

"On TV. Yeah. In fact, most of you've ended up that way. All worn out."

Gail sighs. "It is more than that. If the defence mechanism has failed, that can mean only one thing. It signals the stoppage of brain activity. Those of my kind affected in such a manner are now simply catatonic. Effectively dead."

I don't know what to say to that.

"I sensed a lessening of the pain," Gail whispers. "Not my own, but that of my brethren. Now I understand. They suffer less because they are dying. Perhaps that is the only way."

It might be a fuck-ugly slug, but it's proper tugging at my heartstrings all the same. Something else pops into my head and I can't decide whether saying it will make the Blighter feel better or worse.

"They're not all going ga-ga like that," I say. "Some of them are just getting blown up and suchlike."

It's hard to figure out how the Blighter takes that. It goes all quiet, having a good old think. "Under what circumstances?"

"What do you mean, under what circumstances? Getting shot circumstances, that's what. One of you got the chop just last night. Caught in the crossfire between two countries who were basically pals right before that. A no-score draw."

That massive mouth twitches again. Looks almost like a smile.

"I understand. It is a source of no pride to me, but I

understand. Rather than suppress their defence mechanism, my brethren have elected to amplify it. They have engendered love to such a degree that humans cannot tolerate the thought of no longer possessing them. When more than one faction is affected in such a way, war can be the only outcome. And war must end in destruction."

"So... you Blighters are committing suicide?"

"Suicide. Yes."

I suck in a deep breath and then the stink makes me wish I hadn't. "Fuck. I'm, well. I'm sorry. I really, really am."

And I ain't lying. I reach out towards its shiny snout. It shudders under my hand, even before I touch it. It's warm, which I guess I didn't expect. And even though it's wet as a dog's tennis ball, the slime isn't so bad. It's not sticky or gooey or anything, for all that shine. Once at primary school we got to touch a snake and nobody could believe it was dry, and this is easily as weird as that.

"What about you, then?" I say. "You've been cranking out the love yourself. People go all cross-eyed when they get up close."

"I have performed no amplification. My defence mechanism is simply more powerful by default, a consequence of my seniority. My role is to lead my family. And I have failed."

I pull my hand away. "Family. So you're saying you're like their dad?"

The Blighter doesn't answer. Gail lets out a quiet moan.

"I don't know what to do," I say. "This ain't your fault, I know. But it's unreal how much you've fucked things up around here. My friend would still be my friend if not for you. My Auntie Alice would still be my Auntie Alice."

I rub at my eyes with my free hand. No time for tears.

"What is it you actually want?" I say. I can feel anger bubbling up, pushing out the last of the Blighter love.

The Blighter don't say nothing.

"So I'm special, and we can have our heart-to-heart, and that's proper lovely and all," I say. "But what next? You want to talk to the big guys? Get NASA to fire you all up into space again, right? I'll just get Ten Downing Street on the phone for you, shall I?"

Gail makes a ragged, raspy sound and the Blighter shudders again.

"I understand your meaning, if not your words. You are mocking me. But the answer to each of these questions is 'No.' All of these things, if they were achievable, would take time. I do not have time. And I have lost hope for my brethren. I am ashamed, but it is the truth. I care only for myself, now."

Slime runs off its sides in dollops because of all the wriggling.

Gail's voice starts getting shakier and shakier. "I do not believe I have the capacity to wait. Even if you were to alert others in the region about my presence, even if I were able to inspire war between rival groups, with my own destruction as the ultimate aim... It would take too much time."

"So."

The Blighter's whole body lurches. It's nodding.

"The pain is too much," it says in Gail's voice. "I beg you. Kill me."

I step back and put both my hands up to my face. I don't care about the slime. I don't care about me right now, all that much. I'm shivering and shivering and shivering.

Pull yourself together, Becky Stone.

I force myself to look straight at it. If I'm going to do what it wants, I need it to know I'm doing it because I understand. And say what you want about Blighters, but everything it's said makes a shitload of sense.

I look back at Gail. I think about her all hopeless and crying, back at the flat. Now, even though the words coming out of her mouth are sad as anything I've ever heard in my life, Gail's slack mouth—the expression on her face—makes her look like she's having an endless orgasm. There's no way she'll be able to forget this happy feeling, now she's had a full-on taste of it. She'll do whatever it takes to keep coming back, if she can.

Killing the Blighter is a plan I can get on board with.

15

THE BLIGHTER HAS the bright idea of making the circle of calm bigger, just for now. If there's anyone out here waiting in the cold, it don't hardly matter no more. Even so, I check around all over before I walk out of the bothy. Sure enough, there's a couple of cops up there on the ridge. Arms up in the air, like a surrender or a prayer.

I can see something else, too, something I half-saw the first time I came here with Gail. A way away from the bothy doors, there's a load of soil that's been like dug up or something. Before, I thought it was the Blighter's crash-landing site, but no. It's different. It's not like something's landed here, but more like something's been ferreting around, like a mole or a dog looking for bones. The soil's been yanked up in clumps still with the grass on top. Underneath there's the glint of hard rock.

It means something, I know it. But right now I got things that need doing.

After a while I start running, not so much because of the cops but because I don't want to go slow enough to see Auntie Alice's mashed-up body.

Just like I expected, in the boot of Auntie Alice's Volvo, there's a plastic canister of weedkiller and a coil of hosepipe from her gardening side job. Just like before, with Dad.

It's like she left it all there for me. Like she wants me to do this. Except she don't know what I'm up to, because she's over there stone cold dead. And the thing is, it's not how it was back in 1999, either. Auntie Alice didn't know. She weren't part of any of this, then or now. It weren't her fault.

I tip out the weedkiller. The smell catches in my throat, much worse than the Blighter stink. Makes me feel all faint.

"Have a drink, darling," is maybe what Dad says, back then, to Mum. "Let's talk this whole thing through."

I'm not the same as him.

Dad lifts his slipper and whacks and whacks. Woozy wasps smeared all over the lino.

I'm not the same as him.

This is different.

Wasps aren't people and neither's Blighters. So it isn't murder, but that's not what this is about, anyway. It's about the reasons behind the killing. Dad killed them wasps just because he could. Same with Mum. And then the only way out of the mess was to do himself in, too.

The reasons I'm doing what I'm doing aren't nothing like Dad's reasons.

I'm better than him.

I open up the petrol cap and stick in the end of the hose. I suck until petrol starts pouring out and into the canister.

It's getting colder and colder out here, but as soon as I get back inside the circle of calm I can't hardly feel it no more.

I try not to look properly at the Blighter while I'm spraying the petrol all around. It's still shuddering, but it don't speak. It's tricky squeezing past it to get all the way around inside the bothy. When I get back to its front end my jeans and jumper are covered in its slime.

Gail don't move a muscle when I rummage around in her pockets for her Zippo.

She just says, "I thank you, human."

I turn and face the Blighter full on.

I shrug.

"You made a mistake," I say.

I push Gail away from the doors of the bothy. All that love I had for her should have turned into hate the moment she bumped off Auntie Alice, I know, but all I got right now is sadness and more sadness. And one thing I know for certain is, I ain't going to burn her up.

Her mouth twitches and twitches even though she's still grinning. The real Gail—my Gail—is in there, still. And I know for sure she don't feel just sad the way I feel. She hates me already for what I'm about to do.

I light the lighter and chuck it inside the bothy.

16

WHAT DO YOU expect? Gail didn't forgive me for all that. Didn't have a word to say to me once she came round and realised her precious Blighter was cooked. She blinked and blinked and then she saw that burning building and the cops all racing towards it and then I dragged her away and she just bawled. I wish I could say she was feeling guilty about Auntie Alice, even just a tiny bit, but I know there ain't no way. Gail was selfish through and through.

Dropping her off back at her house was all sorts of weird, after everything that happened that day, but I don't know what else I could have done. She sure as hell wasn't getting back into my flat. And I figured that the only people that knew Gail was ever part of all this were already dead.

Maybe she just carried on with her normal life, but who knows? I never went into the Beast again. I don't know if Ralphie ever showed up.

So that's that.

To be honest, I don't even think about Gail all that much. Auntie Alice neither, even though her story's way, way sadder, because it had so much less going on in it.

I got too many other thoughts whizzing around, see.

I met this bloke once. He shot a kid who burgled his shop. Self-defence, more or less. Said he never got over the feeling of killing another human. So how do you think I feel, then? A Blighter's tons bigger than a human.

I bet you Dad never fretted for a second about them wasps. I know they're smaller, but the point still stands.

I try not to think about it. I keep moving.

At first I figured I was looking for something. Another Gail, or at least somewhere to live. But it's hard picking somewhere. I can cash Dad's cheques from banks in any town in the country.

So I keep moving.

Took me months before I worked out what I was actually doing.

The more you look, the more you listen, the more you hear the rumours. Everyone knows about San Francisco and Lisbon and Hamburg and Saskatchewan and them other famous ones. But then somebody will drop a hint about some farm on some Scottish island, where two families got a Blighter to themselves. And someone else tells you about one that wriggled way down into a cave in Snowdonia.

I go from town to town and village to village. I don't stay in one place more than a couple of nights.

In each new place I head straight to the local pub, even though I've stopped drinking.

Because that's where you see the clues.

You see the huddled groups. You see the suspicious looks. They're all sizing you up.

I swear them Blighters are everywhere.

So there you go. I'm looking for Blighters. But I know that still don't explain why. The first few months I told myself it's a fresh taste of the happy calm I want. Later I told myself I want to help because them Blighters are in pain just like me.

But it's not any of that.

That word 'help.' It's got a nasty ring to it. You don't help things by killing them.

And I'm not totally sure I killed that bothy Blighter because I wanted to help, anyway. I killed it because it had a hold on Gail and because it was sad and because it asked me nicely to do it, which made actually doing it a whole lot easier.

It gets worse.

I *enjoyed* killing it. Just like Dad enjoyed killing them wasps.

I'm my father's daughter. That chews me up.

At night, when all them bad thoughts whizz around, I tell myself one thing over and over. I tell myself why it was that I enjoyed killing that Blighter.

I enjoyed killing it because killing it stopped people from cheating. Gail, them farmers and the cops, too. If I had my way, every one of them Blighters would fly off into space right this second, just like they was supposed to.

Everyone's got nasty dark stuff in their heads, see. Everyone's a victim. But you've got to stand and face it. Blighter calm's not real calm. It's cheating.

I know what you're thinking. I'm a cheat too, just in a different way. But the more I travel round the country, the more I'm sure I'm not actually running away from anything. I got my sad past and that's what got me here. And now I know where I'm going.

The last few weeks I've been hearing this new kind of rumour. A new idea. Get people talking enough and they tell you things. They tell you about Blighters that got lucky and landed on softer ground. Blighters who were able to push down with their ugly snouts, pushing and pushing until maybe they got all the way properly underground.

I hear more rumours about Blighters than most folks do, and who knows which ones are right. But then I think about that big old hole outside the bothy at Tarn Crag. Maybe that Blighter—*my* Blighter—really was digging away, before any farmer found it. Digging and digging and digging and hoping the pull of its heavy-as-hell body would take it down, down, down.

Getting away from us. Away from people.

You couldn't blame them for trying.

They say there's only one way to tell if that type of underground Blighter's really there. If you happen to wander where a Blighter dug itself down and got itself buried far below, you'll feel it. Just a taste, enough to know you're near it, nothing that'll give you much of a buzz. But those places stay calm for good, for real.

Once I heard that rumour, I stuck to tramping around in more out-of-the-way parts. I'm a countryside lass, these days. First I stayed inland, maybe thinking of Sadgill and the like. But now I've noticed I'm shifting further and further out, without really planning it.

So.

I'm my father's daughter, alright, but I'm my mother's daughter too.

When I get tired of being on the move I'm heading to the coast.

I'll find me a proper calm spot and I'll face out to sea.

ABOUT
THE AUTHOR

Tim Major's time-travel thriller novel, *You Don't Belong Here,* was published by Snowbooks. His first novella, *Carus & Mitch*, was shortlisted for a *This Is Horror* Award and his short stories have featured in *Interzone, Perihelion, Every Day Fiction* and numerous anthologies. He is the Editor of the SF magazine, *The Singularity.*

cosycatastrophes.wordpress.com

RAGS, BONES AND TEA LEAVES

JULIAN BENSON

PART ONE

1

Leeds, 1967

THE DOOR SWUNG open with a shove, and Eli backed into the small flat, his hands full with two large boxes. Hal stepped past him, his eyes on the carton in his own hands.

"Musty," said Hal's mum, sniffing the air as she entered. "Mr Foster said it hasn't been lived in for months."

"At least it's clean." Eli set down the boxes to prop the door open. He put his hands on her shoulders. "It's nice. You'll like it more when it's filled with your things. Hal, let's get some more stuff out the van."

Hal ignored him and opened the box he'd been carrying. He lifted out the photo of his father and placed it on the mantelpiece, looking out at the drab living room.

"Oh, not there," Hal's mum said.

Hal left the picture where it was and went down to get more boxes out of the van. He walked quickly, staying ahead of Eli so he couldn't talk to him. When he came back, the picture was still up and his mother was in the kitchen cleaning the countertops.

They spent the morning unpacking, finding places for all their things. When they weren't looking, Hal would spy on Eli and his mum out of the corner of his eye. The man was forever near her, giving a helping hand, finding excuses to touch her arm or back. At every touch Hal would feel a small flash of irritation. Even when he wasn't looking, Eli made Hal angry; overhearing him suggest places for their things, the way he'd laugh at his mum's jokes, or talk to her in soft tones.

Eventually, unable to hide his temper, Hal took a box of his things and went to his new room.

IT WAS SMALL and dimly lit. The one window looked out onto the estate, and the identical homes opposite. Each one a two-bedroom concrete allotment. The Quarry Hill estate was a swarm of flats—nearly a thousand of them, according to the welcome brochure, 'offering modern living for its 3,000 residents.' It made Hal feel small and trapped.

"Hal?" A knock at his door. "Are you in there, Hal?"

Eli opened the door and came in. "I've got something for you, Hal. It's your father's, but he didn't want it, so I held onto it for him."

Hal turned, but didn't say anything.

Eli held up a shoebox. "It's photos of him, and some other things from the war."

Hal felt the prickle of goosebumps. They had almost never talked about the war in Hal's old house. Anytime it came up, Hal's father would become angry; or worse, he would go silent, sometimes for days.

Taking a seat at the end of Hal's bed, Eli opened the box and took out a small stack of photos. "This is one from our old unit," he said, holding it out. Hal took it with care,

314

letting it lie lightly in his hands. "It was taken at the end of our training. You see your dad on one knee in the front row? That's me stood behind him, look. Right from the beginning, we were together." Hal barely recognised his father, he wasn't thin, his hair was neatly trimmed, and there was a warmth to his expression. He wasn't smiling, but he looked… lively.

Eli offered Hal another photo. "Here we're on the boat to Cherbourg. It was a holiday to us, no one in our unit had left England before and here we were heading to a hero's welcome in France. The Germans hadn't yet crossed the border, and most of us thought they never would." In the photo, Hal's father lay out on the deck of the transport, dozing in the sun. Hal stared at the picture, unable to fully understand it. He saw his dad, but he didn't recognise him, he looked so at peace. Ill-fitting, overlapping visions of his father—the man he knew and this man he saw—butted in his mind, raising a curling discomfort within him.

"We're not in this photo," Eli continued, unaware of the turmoil. "This is the camp we were kept in. This was taken after the war, but you can see our bunk hut—"

Hal knew of the camp, but only through overheard half-started stories and unfinished sentences. Eli was pointing out details in the photo and talking, but Hal wasn't hearing him anymore. He stared at the photo, his eyes running along the huts, the fences, the fields, trying to picture the three years his dad was held there. Trying to picture the things that turned him from the young man dozing in the sun to the man Hal had known.

"Your father refused to take this," Eli was talking to Hal, something clasped in his hand. "He wouldn't even look at it. I went to the major after I heard and promised to hold onto it for him, to give it to him when he was ready. Now, I can at least give it to you."

Eli opened his hand to reveal a silver cross in his palm, a medal. At the end of each of the arms of the cross were little crowns, and in the centre were the letters *GRI*. Fixed to the top of the cross was a white-and-purple ribbon that draped over the back of Eli's hand. Hal took the medal from Eli, feeling the cold weight of it in his fingers.

"He was given that for what he did—"

All Hal's life, the war had been a cloud over his family, darkening his dad's mood, upsetting his mum. It could cause weeks of tension in their home. Dad would shout at them, or ignore them, or leave without explanation. He'd come home days later, or they would have to go to the police station to get him after he had been picked up for trespassing. It had driven his parents to move to the country, where his mum hoped the peace would help calm his father's mind.

"—run the seven miles to the next camp and straight into—"

The move had left them isolated and friendless. And after years of it—all of Hal's life—he still did *that* to himself. As he stared at the medal in his hands, Hal grew angrier and angrier. The war had stolen his father from him, and now Eli was trying to tell him *stories* about it?

"—saved fifteen men—"

"Shut up!"

Eli fell silent, stunned.

Hal's whole body was tense, his hands in tight fists. The walls of his new room felt suffocatingly close. He had to get out. He wrenched the door open and ran through the living room and out the front door, his mum's confused shouts fading behind him as he fled from the flat. He threw himself down the three flights of stairs at the end of the hallway and out into the courtyard, and kept running until his lungs burned.

Panting for air, Hal came to a stop. His cheeks were wet with tears—he hadn't noticed he'd been crying. As he caught his breath, he became aware of a pain in his hand and looked down at the white and purple ribbon trailing from his closed fist. He'd been gripping the medal so tight it had left deep welts. Sick of the sight of it, he threw it away as far as he could.

As his heart slowed and the adrenaline drained from his body, Hal turned on the spot, taking in his surroundings. All around him were blocks of identical concrete flats, lined with identical windows, and identical concrete lattices. Everything was uniform: four floors high, an interior staircase every four flats, heavy-looking doors opening into the courtyard at regular intervals. Nothing but concrete in every direction except the sky above.

Hal was lost. All these flats looked the same and he had no idea which was his. A chill prickled the back of his neck.

An odd noise cut through his anxious thoughts. There it was again: a click, followed by a grinding noise. He looked around for the source of the sound; it seemed to come from the block of flats to his left.

There it was again. He looked up and saw a flash of movement on the fourth-floor balcony.

Hal dashed to the stairwell of the block and took the stairs two at a time, hearing someone coming down from the floors above, fast. He collided with the figure on the second-floor landing, knocking them to the ground: a boy, thirteen maybe, no older than Hal. As he scrambled to get up, Hal pinned him to the floor, both his hands on the boy's shoulders and a knee on his chest. The boy's hands went to a camera hanging from his neck, covering it protectively.

"Why were you taking photos of me?" Hal spat.

The boy looked nervous, tightening his grip on his camera.

"I wasn't—I mean," the boy started, his voice cracking, "I was waiting to take pictures of the Rag and Bone Man when you came sprinting into the courtyard. I didn't mean—I just photograph things I find interesting."

Hal eased back, letting go of the boy's sweater, and got to his feet. "What's your name?"

"Shahid," the boy said.

"Do you know how to get to Jackson House?"

ON THE WAY back to Hal's block, Shahid pointed out details of the estate, calling out the names of the houses as they passed them: Savile, Thoresby, York, Moynihan, Lupton. Each block looked the same to Hal, but to Shahid they were unique. Moynihan House, he said, was full of empty flats that, if you knew the trick, you could break into without anyone knowing. Over the summer different gangs of children would take over a flat and build a base—"Though you want to mind yourself, there's a man on the ground floor who I swear watches us from behind his curtains," he said, pointing to a window. He told Hal to avoid York House because that's where the rougher families lived—he'd been beaten up by the Hayes brothers who lived on the first floor and didn't want repeat the experience. As they approached Lupton House, where Shahid lived with his mum and dad, Hal recognised Eli's van still parked outside of Jackson House. He grabbed Shahid's sleeve—"Let's keep going. Can you show me the rest of the estate?"

Shahid was happy to show someone around; Hal got the impression he didn't have many friends. Whenever they passed other children playing on the estate he'd look at the ground, trying to avoid their attention.

The Quarry Hill estate was like a great concrete fist in

the centre of Leeds. Surrounded by main roads on all sides and ringed by an unbroken sweep of flats, the estate was its own island. Within the perimeter, along with more housing blocks, was everything the 3,000 strong community would need: greengrocers, a bakery, a wash house, even two restaurants and a chippy. There were 13 different houses in all, Shahid told Hal, each named after a different figure in Leeds' history. Lupton House, for instance, was named after a well-to-do family who'd owned a lot of the city's wool industry. Hal's House, he learned, was named after William Jackson, a Leeds politician who became a baron.

Shahid pointed out where the foundations for a community hall were laid but never built on, and where the shell of a building that was supposed to become a swimming pool was erected but never completed; "They made the boiler room for it, though," the boy said, pointing out a slug of a building off to one side of the unfinished pool, away from any of the houses. "They burn all the estate's waste to heat the boiler. It smells awful around here in winter." Shahid pulled Hal's arm, leading him towards one of the housing blocks. "I'm going to show you a secret you can't show to anyone."

Shahid went into Moynihan House and motioned Hal to be quiet. The two boys went up to the top floor and along the rows of doors to No. 52, where Shahid showed Hal how the lock could be jimmied open. Inside and with the door shut, Shahid broke the silence, saying, "I found this a few months ago. A lot of the flats here have never been lived in since the building opened in the '30s."

The layout was the same as the flat Hal had moved into that morning. The walls were stained with damp, mould creeping across the carpet in the living room. The air was thick with an acrid smell. "Mice, I think," Shahid said, seeing Hal's nose wrinkle.

"What I really wanted to show you was this," he continued, going through to the bathroom and opening the window wide. "You have to trust me, this is worth it." He climbed out onto the sill and began to climb. Hal watched through the window as Shahid's legs kicked for a moment and then rose out of view.

Hal rushed to the window and put his head out to look up. Nothing. Just the edge of the roof above. Then Shahid poked his head over the edge. "Come on! You can get your foot on the drainpipe and use the window frame to climb up."

Hal started climbing before his nerves got the better of him, and Shahid helped pull him onto the roof. They lay on the concrete roof, panting and looking up at the bright sky.

"No one else comes up here," Shahid said, getting up with his arms outstretched, free from the eyes that watched from behind closed curtains. "With a rope, we could make a harness and pull up chairs and a basket with food. This could be *our* den over the summer."

Hal pictured what it could look like, as Shahid walked to the edge of the roof, saying, "You can see over the whole of Quarry Hill from here, too." He pointed out the pool and the other landmarks he'd shown Hal earlier. "See that pipe there." He indicated a large, concrete-ringed opening on the far side of the playing fields. "That goes into a stream you can follow all the way to Meanwood. Last month the beck was full of frogspawn. It was grim, but if you go now, there are hundreds of little hopping frogs."

The boys spent all the afternoon on the roof, throwing stones at each other, pulling up loose concrete slabs and building towers, all the while talking about themselves. Shahid told Hal how his parents had moved to Leeds from Pakistan in the '40s. His uncle had come over first and started a corner shop. His father did the books for him and other Pakistani businesses—"It's not easy for us to get an English accountant"—he has an older sister at university and a brother living in Pakistan.

Shahid's mum worked as a housekeeper in a number of the flats around Quarry Hill. He'd overhear her and his father talking gossip some nights when they thought he was asleep in bed. "There's one story they still talk about now, though it happened years ago." Drawing closer to Hal, he began to talk in a whisper "In 1953, in that flat over there, No. 26"— he pointed to a flat in York House—"there was a murder. A woman called Sarah Williams lived there, mum used to clean for her. One morning mum went to clean and found the door open. She found Sarah in the living room, a great wound in her belly. She says she'd been stabbed so deep there was a hole in the back of the armchair. They caught the man who did it two days later—Simon Calvin. He was her boyfriend, my mum says. They'd had an argument and he attacked her, the police say."

Hal stared at the flat. It looked no different from those next to it, no sign of its grisly past. "No one's lived there since. It's sat empty for fourteen years. Mum still talks it through with dad. She's not sure Simon's guilty. She says the two were so lovely together."

"Who does she think it was?"

Shahid scanned the estate from their perch. "Him," Shahid said. He gripped Hal's shoulder and led him to the low wall surrounding the roof. "See that man in the coat?"

Hal's eyes followed Shahid's pointing finger. The man was tall, over six foot, and walked with a stoop. Despite the heat, he wore a heavy wax coat over a thick woollen jumper. Gloves covered his hands and black wellington boots went up to his thighs. He wore his collar up and a flat cap; Hal couldn't get a look at his face from their high vantage point.

He pushed a two-wheeled cart in front of him with some half-filled sacks heaped in it.

"That's the Rag and Bone Man," Shahid said. "He goes around the estate taking away people's old clothes and waste metal. He can get money for them at the scrap yards. Here, use my camera, see if you can't get a look at his face."

Hal put his eye to the viewfinder and twisted the lens to get a closer look at the man. He couldn't work out quite what he was seeing—the angle was bad and the flat cap obscured his view—but the man's face looked lifeless and frozen in place. His complexion, too, was off; it looked painted on, like a china doll. With a jerk the man turned and stared straight at Hal, his gaze seemed to pierce straight through the lens. Hal fell back away from the wall.

"He saw me!"

"No, he didn't," Shahid said.

"He looked right at me."

"Didn't you see?" Shahid said. "He can't see you, he doesn't have a face."

Then it clicked for Hal, what he had been looking at. The man wore a china mask, the kind people who had come back from the war disfigured by shrapnel wore.

"It felt like he looked right at me," Hal insisted.

"Did you at least get a picture? I've been trying to get a good picture of him since I got the camera for my birthday."

"Your mum thinks he killed the woman at No. 26?"

"Look, no one knows who he is, really. He's been hanging around the estate for years, I don't even know if he lives here. My mum's sure he has something to do with it, though. See, he doesn't just collect scrap, some of the women on the estate pay him to tell their futures. Don't look at me like that. People say he knows how to read tea leaves. Anyway, it doesn't matter if I believe them, Ms Williams did, my mum says. He was round her flat every week, sometimes more, telling her what he could see."

"That's crazy."

"I've not told you all of it yet. No one on the estate talks about, it but it's no secret: her old flat, it's haunted."

"Bollocks."

"Honest. Everyone knows it. Ever since she was murdered, there have been nights when her ghost can be heard weeping inside the flat. No one's lived in the place since. It's never sold. The flats next door have been empty for years, too. The families moved out after the murder and no one's moved in."

2

THE CEILING LOOKED like a rotten pudding, the plaster soft and cream-coloured. Bloated with moisture. The edges browned, rivulets of copper-coloured water running down the walls to a peeling checkerboard lino floor.

Hal turned from the ugly scene and rose from the bathtub. First testing the wet floor with his bare feet, he stood, letting the hems of his pyjama trousers touch the damp lino. He could hear confused muffled sounds in the flat and walked to the door, opening it to the living room.

Mould dusted the beige furniture like moss on a country wall. The walls wept with great brown streaks of damp. The rot didn't bother the figures in the room, nor did Hal's presence.

Sat in the mouldy chair was Sarah Williams, tea cup and saucer in one hand, the other gripping the chair's arm. Looming over her was a creature in a wax coat. Hal watched as it leant down and bit into her throat, the chair tilting back from the weight and violence of the attack.

* * *

HAL'S EYES SNAPPED awake, woken by a sharp pain—he'd bitten his tongue in his sleep. The panic slowly ebbed from him as he swallowed down the metallic taste of blood. His copy of *Dracula* lay open on his chest.

Lying in his bed, turning over his dream and the man he saw earlier that day, Hal gave up on sleep and quietly got out of bed. He put on his dad's jacket over his pyjamas and left the flat, descending the stairs to the courtyard below. Outside it was cold and dark, the only light from the lamppost in the courtyard. He heard nothing in the night, the sounds of the city blocked by the wall of flats.

Keeping to the edge of the courtyard, he walked to Moynihan house, praying not to be heard. The block was an imposing sight in the dark; looking up, he couldn't see where the building ended and the sky began. Pressing firmly against the door to the stairwell until it slowly opened, he slipped inside and closed it quietly behind him.

The lamppost outside gave enough light for him to make out the impression of the bottom step, but as he climbed to the first floor the stairwell became pitch black and he had to duck onto all fours to feel for the stairs as he ascended. Reaching the landing, Hal felt for the door into the hallway. His hands found a light switch, but didn't dare press it.

Working from the memory of the identical hallway in Jackson House, Hal crept down the hall, the fingers of this right hand lightly tracing the wall, feeling for the doorframes and counting them out in his head. When he reached No. 26 he hesitated, feeling silly for having believed Shahid's ghost story. Still, he had to know.

He pressed his ear to the door.

The blood drained from him as he heard the sounds of weeping through the thin plywood. It was muffled, but he could hear the sharp intakes of breath and trickles of high-pitched moaning. He kept his ear to the door, hooked by the sound's familiarity—he'd heard the same from his mum's room in the months after his dad's death. He hadn't *seen* her cry since she found his body; in front of him, she always tried to stay collected, busy, and pragmatic. He had tried to do the same.

A sound within the room brought Hal back to himself. The weeping had stopped. He heard heavy footsteps approaching the door. There wasn't time to get to the stairs, so Hal stepped back, pressing himself against the door of the flat opposite, making himself as small as he could and holding his breath. Hal heard the door of No. 26 swing inwards. He stood fixed in place, fearing that even the sound of his beating heart would betray him. The door clicked shut as whoever it was left the flat and Hal listened to their footsteps walking away, down the corridor towards the stairwell. Only when he heard the door to the stairs close did he let out his breath.

Hal's legs felt weak, but he had to know for sure who had been in that flat. Moving quickly, he snuck down the hallway and the stairs to the door looking out from Moynihan House onto the courtyard. Hal scanned the dark, but he couldn't see anyone. Then movement caught his eye: skirting the edge of the court, keeping to the shadows was a tall figure in a wax coat.

His quarry sighted, Hal let himself sink to the floor of the stairwell where the cool concrete calmed his nerves. He dared not follow the Rag and Bone Man on his own.

3

THE NEXT MORNING, the boys met outside Shahid's flat. Hal hurried Shahid down to the playing fields; when he was sure there was no one around who could hear them, he told him what had happened the night before.

"I *told* you. I told you he was suspicious. My mum's been worrying about him for years. We have to find out more."

"Shouldn't we tell your mum or someone?"

"We've nothing to tell them. Not yet. You say you heard someone crying in a flat and then, later, you saw a person in a coat. I know what it means, you know what it means, but the adults won't listen." Shahid thought for a moment. "We have to learn more. We have to catch him doing something illegal."

"And we need proof, too," Hal said. "Something we can show an adult."

"We should follow him. If we can find out more about him—where he lives, what he looks like, and if there's anyone suspicious who talks to him"—Shahid held up his camera—"we've got him."

Sticking together, the boys walked through the estate's linked courtyards, searching for their mark.

They heard his shout before they saw him—"Any old scrap?"—calling up to the women hanging washing on the lines between Victoria House and Wright House. The boys kept low and hidden, peeking round the corner of Wright House. A few women came down to sell him rags and food cans, which he stuffed in a sack hanging from a belt inside his coat; despite the hot sun, he wore the same heavy clothing he wore the day before. When his work was completed, the man set off away from the boys, round the corner from Victoria House towards Thoresby and the football pitch the boys in York House had painted onto the concrete. Keeping their distance, the boys followed. They cautiously poked their heads round the turn the man had just taken, but saw nothing. The man was nowhere to be seen. They walked the length of the building and peered round the next turn. Again, nothing.

"He must have gone inside," Hal said.

"Quick! You go to that corner and see if he comes out the front of Thoresby and I'll watch the back."

The boys split up and sprinted to their watch points. Hal waited and watched. Five minutes passed, then ten. No one came out. He turned to check if Shahid had seen anything, and saw Shahid looking back. Both boys shrugged, and Shahid came to join Hal.

"Either he's still inside or we've missed him somehow," Hal said. "You stay here and watch the front. I'll go up and check each floor." Before Shahid could protest, Hal broke from cover and ran up the stairs.

Hal checked on each floor and found nothing, and trudged back down to the ground floor to find Shahid was gone. He looked round the side of the building, round the back, down the row of blocks and couldn't see him. Panic rose in his gullet as he ran to the front of the house; he swallowed it down when, up the row, he spied Shahid waving to him. He sprinted over.

"He's over there," Shahid said, pointing ahead to the distant Rag and Bone Man now talking to the women huddled outside Priestley House.

"How'd he get past us?"

"No idea, but if you watch from here I'll circle round and watch from the other side. That way, whichever direction he leaves, we should be able to follow. Just don't let him see you if he comes this way."

Hal nodded and watched Shahid jog down the side of Savile House.

Ten minutes later, his sack full, the Rag and Bone Man set off in Shahid's direction. Hal lost sight of him when he went into the Savile courtyard—he had to hold back with no cover to hide him—and as he rounded the corner he came across an exasperated Shahid. "Did you see him?" Shahid asked. "He passed right by me, then the fruit cart came through and I lost sight of him."

All afternoon the boys would spot the Rag and Bone Man and then lose him, never quite managing to get a good look at him. They continued the chase the next day, and the day after. Each day their plans became more elaborate: one time Shahid climbed onto Jackson House's roof and directed Hal from there, pointing out the direction the Rag and Bone Man had taken, waving his arms like a conductor. But as always, the man got away. Neither boy wanted to admit it, but they'd both realised their mission to uncover a murderer had become something of a game, and they kept up the search because it filled the long summer days.

On the evening of the third day, after saying goodbye to Shahid, Hal came home to find his mum waiting for him.

"I had a visit today from Mr Foster, head of the estate's housing board," she said sternly.

Hal's blood ran cold.

"He tells me you've been hounding the rag and bone man. What have you got to say for yourself?"

Hal stood dumbly in the doorway.

"We've not even lived here a week. One week. And already I've had a complaint about you. Didn't you think once about the poor man? Three *days* you chased him, and just because he looks different. Just so you could get a look at his scars. Yes, Mr Foster told me about that. It's not the first time boys have taken an interest in the rag and bone man. But never— never, he says—have they followed him with a camera."

"I didn't—" Hal began.

"Didn't what?" she interrupted. "Is Mr Foster lying? Did my son and his friend not chase a man burned in the war to try and get a photo of his scars?"

"It wasn't that—It was a game—" Hal mumbled. His stomach felt heavy, like it was full of lead.

Hal's mum sent him to his room, saying she needed time to think of an appropriate punishment. He lay curled up in his bed as the shame washed over him, thinking of what he and Shahid had done to the man.

4

HAL WAS WOKEN by a knock at his door. His eyes flicked open, registering the dawn light, a moment of confused awakening before remembering the night before.

"You're coming with me to the university today," Hal's mum shouted through the closed door. "Get dressed." Hal could picture her firm expression.

He dressed and joined his mum for a silent breakfast. He couldn't meet her eye. After breakfast, she checked herself in the mirror by the door and then ushered Hal out of the flat.

The sun was rising as they walked the length of the estate and out through the great archway that cut through Oastler House, the entrance gate to the city they had driven through in Eli's van earlier that week. Hal's mum walked quickly, eyes ahead, not checking to see if Hal was keeping up—the surety of a parent leading a guilty child. The two exchanged no words.

Outside, where the main road ringed the estate like an asphalt moat, was a bus stop already busy with a queue of men and women waiting for a ride into the city. They joined the end of the line. Hal stared at his feet.

The bus came and they took their seats. Hal looked out the window, watching people going to work. Leeds was coming to life, shopfront shutters rising and pavement signs coming out.

The bus took them through the heart of the city, down the Headrow, packed with its department stores, and up towards the university.

Hal felt a tug at his sleeve—they were getting off here.

The bus left them right outside the Parkinson Building, the university's main entrance. It was an impressive sight, a great classically-styled building made of white stone that stretched off in both directions, longer even than Moynihan House. A sweeping flight of stairs led to three sets of vast oak doors framed by columns. Reaching up to the sky overhead was a great clock tower with squared sides.

"Hurry or I'll be late," Hal's mum called to him, already halfway up the steps. Hal raced to catch up.

The heavy doors opened into a hall big enough to house one of the blocks at Quarry Hill. The cool air of the place gave Hal goosebumps. He expected it to be quiet, especially this early in the day, but students and professors crisscrossed the stone floor to and from lectures, seminars, and libraries. The noise of their footsteps on the floor and their conversations were amplified by the space, making a confusing clamour.

Ahead of Hal, in the centre of the hall, stood a circular desk, a ring of brown oak in the stone chamber. Three receptionists manned the desk, poised to answer questions from visitors.

Hal's mum offered them a quick "Hello" as she marched him past and towards a staircase down to the basement. The change was stark: the lower floor of the Parkinson was a rabbit warren of tight corridors, seminar rooms, toilets, and, finally, a staffroom.

Hal's mum shepherded him inside and stood in the doorway.

"You're to stay in here and clean the place up," she said. "The PhD students have been messing up the staffroom for all of us and everyone will appreciate you giving it a thorough clean."

Hal surveyed the messy room. It was actually quite a large space, made to feel cramped by the cheap sofas and armchairs crowding the floor under the low ceiling and artificial light. Strewn about the tables were half-empty cups of tea and coffee, plates of unfinished meals, and ashtrays piled with cigarette butts and ash. Hal could barely make out the floor, it was so covered with newspapers—as though, somewhere under all this, he might find an animal being toilet trained. Hal's heart sank when he spied the small kitchenette in the corner of the room, and the mountain of crockery in the sink and on the counter.

"But—"

"I'll be back in a few hours," Hal's mum interrupted. "And I don't want to hear you've been bothering anyone."

She closed the door behind her before Hal could finish his protest. As she left, Hal felt the nagging shame dissipate, replaced with the dawning despair of the Herculean task ahead of him. He hardly knew where to start.

Hal rummaged through the cupboards of the kitchenette and found some sponges, a tea towel, and soap. He set to work gathering up the crockery, assembling it into precarious towers beside the sink, fitting them in around the mess already there. He found mess within mess—in the cups of half-finished teas and coffees, were cigarette butts, doused out by students heading off to lectures; a ritual of the rushed. Plates, too, held grubby secrets. Packed between the stacked crockery, like mortar between bricks, was leftover food pressed down by the weight of the plate above.

The day gave Hal a new and deeper understanding of the word 'pigsty.'

As the hours ticked by and he washed crockery, upending dregs and butts into the bin, the door to the staff room would sporadically swing open, announcing the arrival of a new group of PhD students. The groups would always be deep in discussion, trying to upstage each other in their knowledge of a granular subject. They barely noticed Hal as they made themselves teas and coffees—spilling them when the debate was most animated, Hal noted. Other times a single student would enter, poring over a book or a paper. Again, Hal made little impact on their morning—though, when they'd tap out ash on the sofa, missing the tray they'd balanced on the arm, they'd impact his. There was one student who came in, spotted Hal and, thrown by the presence of a child, immediately backed out of the room. Simply because he did nothing to add to the mess, Hal kept him off the rapidly growing list of students who he felt had crossed him.

By lunchtime, he had started to make some headway. The bulk of the crockery was washed and drying by the side of the sink. He had managed to clear a path through the newspapers, folding and piling them on a table in the corner of the room. He had even managed to clean the coffee tables of all but the most persistent stains. Hal's mum couldn't hide her approval when she came to collect him for lunch.

She took him to the café in the hall above. Over sandwiches and cups of tea, the silence of the morning thawed. They talked about the students he'd seen, and his mum tried to identify them from their different manners. The one she sure of was the timid man who had backed out of the room; he was studying a PhD in architecture.

"A sharp man," she said. "But terribly shy. That's not a great problem among academics, but it has been an issue with the seminars he leads."

It wasn't just the iciness of the morning that was breaking down, Hal realised. There had been a gloom between him and his mum for months now. In their last house, they'd been the whole world; she'd walked him to and from school, played with him in the garden, kept him away from his dad on his darker days. Clouds had formed in the weeks after his death. She'd become detached, often not leaving her room until the evening. Then there was Eli, who had arrived so suddenly in their lives.

After lunch, she walked him back down to the staff room, where any kindly thoughts on the last months were banished at the sight of what had become of his morning's work. He stood in the doorway and stared in despair at how the piled newspapers had been plundered and strewn about the sofas and coffee tables. The plates and cups he had left drying by the sink had been largely used by a horde of hungry students for hurried lunches. Those that hadn't been used were speckled with ash from a smoking sandwich maker.

A gentle push on his back from his mum sent him back to work. She left with a grin on her face.

His afternoon was spent undoing the damage of the lunchtime rush and continuing his work from the morning. Head down, scrubbing dishes, he was surprised by a voice behind him.

"Well, aren't you a marvel." Hal turned to see a woman in her twenties looking around the room in exaggerated surprise. "No, not a marvel. A godsend. You've even managed to get the tables clean! I heard that Patricia Ward's son was down here working wonders, but I couldn't believe a single person could clean this place up, and that it wasn't a team of cleaners with hoses and bottles of bleach."

Hal smiled, taken aback.

"I'm Rose," the woman said, proffering a hand. "Your mum's done us a great favour conscripting you to our cause."

"Hal," he said, taking her hand.

"How did she do it? Offers of jewels? Grand days out on the town?"

Hal hesitated. "It's actually a punishment."

"Ah, hard labour. I think I'd prefer to break rocks than deal with this mess. Should I be looking through the papers to hear tell of your crime? Must have been severe to land you in this brig of academia."

Hal told her about following the Rag and Bone Man, emphasising how it had become a sort of game, that they'd not meant to be cruel. Rose empathised; her curiosity had got her in trouble at times, too. She told him how she earned a little money working in the university's main library, the Brotherton, and had been told off for accessing the special collection without supervision. "One day I'll get a look at Shakespeare's First Folio," she said with a gleam in her eyes, explaining that it was kept under lock and key.

Rose stayed for a tea and helped Hal clear away the clean crockery before going back to her work.

Hal had finished cleaning the staffroom by four and spent the last few hours leafing through the newspapers and filling in the crosswords. The hours without work crawled by slowly. He welcomed his mum's return, and the bus ride back to the estate.

* * *

BACK AT THE estate, Hal found out it could have been worse.

"Dad sent me to count all the stock in uncle's shop," Shahid told Hal with a sigh. "I finished after lunch and then my uncle sent me to his friend's shop two streets over. I'm doing stock in every shop in the community."

5

THE REST OF the week followed the same routine. Hal's mum would wake him in the morning, they would take the bus to the university, and he'd spend the day fighting the tide of mess. After the first day, Hal learned to take a book with him, and he would spend the last hours of the day reading *Frankenstein*.

Each day he'd look forward to a visit from Rose in the afternoon. She would tell him about the university and he would get her up to speed on what had happened in *Frankenstein*.

After four days, it had stopped being such a chore, though he was aware of the summer holiday ticking away with each passing day and not being able to spend time up on the roof with Shahid.

On the Friday, after lunch, Hal's mum said he had been punished enough and could go back to the estate. He was almost sad to go.

Almost.

*   *   *

THE SUN WAS all out when Hal got back to Quarry Hill, bathing the estate in its warm glow. He knocked on Shahid's door, but no one answered; it appeared his sentence hadn't been waived like Hal's.

Stopping home long enough to get a flask of water, Hal went to the top floor of Moynihan House. He checked he was definitely alone, then jimmied the lock to No. 52 and slipped inside. He walked through the empty flat to the bathroom, opened the window, and climbed out onto the windowsill.

It hadn't seemed so high to him when he had climbed to the roof with Shahid—company brings courage, particularly between 13-year-old boys. He stuffed the water flask into his pocket, freeing up his hands, and found the lip of the window's concrete surround with one hand and one of the brackets holding the drainpipe in place with the other; the rusty metal bit into his fingers as he pulled himself up. He had a hairy moment when his foot slipped on the narrow bracket, but he kicked out and found the handle of the bathroom window, pushing himself up until he reached the edge of the roof. With a final heave, he scrambled up the wall and rolled over onto his back, breathing deeply and looking up at the golden summer sky. Baked by the day's sun, the roof gave off a gentle warmth.

Once he had his breath back, Hal rose to his feet and surveyed his reward. From the roof of Moynihan, he could see over all of Leeds. Close by, to the south, was St Peter's Church, splayed like a cross with a great 140ft tall tower for a head. From the ground it was a daunting sight, taller and darker than anything else around it, but from the roof it seemed no bigger than the warehouses in the distance. Working clockwise, Hal picked out Kirkgate Market and the train station. He squinted into the sun at the town hall to the west, its domed clock tower dripping gold. He could just make out the top of the Parkinson Building's rectangular tower, looking like a white brick stood on its end.

To the north and east was a sea of brown and red brick terraced houses as far as he could see. An image of his father flashed into Hal's mind; another summer day, years ago, before his dad had got sick. They were at the beach. His dad was raking the sand to clear away any stones before laying the towels for Hal and his mum. The rake carved a trail of uniformly-spaced shallow trenches, which had fascinated Hal. Seeing his son's interest, Hal's dad kept raking the sand even after the towels were laid. He went from raking straight lines to drawing great swirling patterns, all of them made up of the same even rows. Looking now at the terraced houses, Hal's mind swam.

He turned away from the city.

HAL SAT UP on the roof for hours, reading his book, taking occasional sips from his water flask. He had wanted to spend the day with Shahid, but he was glad he had had the roof to himself today. It was the first time since moving into Jackson House that he felt his time was his own. Between moving into the flat, meeting Shahid, spying on the Rag and Bone Man, and his days at the university, the last two weeks had rushed by him in a blur.

When Hal looked up from his book, the sun was much lower in the sky, casting long shadows over the rooftop. He had to get back before his mum realised where he was. Hal lowered himself down from the roof, his feet searching for the drainpipe bracket and the top of the window. His shirt slid up as he went down and the stone scratched his chest as he slipped lower. He couldn't look down, so he kicked for the pipe and found the bracket, letting him shift his weight to his foot. He reached with one hand to find the window's concrete border; his foot found the window handle and he laid his weight onto the grip. A shock ran through him as he felt the handle turn and give beneath him. Hal slipped and lost his footing on the drain bracket, suddenly dangling by one hand from the roof. He heard a bang from somewhere on the rooftop.

He was going to fall.

Hal felt a crushing pain in his wrist and the world dropped away. Images ran through his head like a stuttering projector: He was

—*looking down at the ground from the roof*—

—*watching a circle of dancing shadows*—

—*looking down the lens of a camera*—

—*staring into dark water holding a stone*—

—*a dark tunnel*—

—*a muddy field*—

They became a blur, indecipherable.

Then, finally, black.

LIGHT CREPT IN at the sides of Hal's vision. He was looking up at the sky. A figure stood above him pulling on a glove.

"You are safe."

The Rag and Bone Man. This close, Hal saw how the man's skin was bleached white, giving his thin mouth the look of a scar carved into stone.

"Don't be afraid, I have saved you," the man said, again. "You slipped—"

"I saw—It was so clear—"

"—You have questions, but now is not the time. Your

mother is coming and I will not be seen. Be happy, my Ward: you have broken from fate."

The figure departed, using the service stairs to the top floor. The bang Hal had heard must have been the Rag and Bone Man charging the door to the roof.

Shakily, Hal stood, adrenaline still ebbing from his system. His ears beat with the throb of pumping blood. He tried to make sense of what had happened, what he had seen. He should have stopped the man from leaving, he thought. How did he know where he was? That he needed help?

Out of the confusion, one of the things the figure had said rose to the surface: *Your mother is coming*. Too late, Hal realised the beating in his ears was the sound of footsteps sprinting up the staircases of Moynihan building.

Hal's mother marched out onto the rooftop and slapped him across the face, tears streaming from her eyes.

"What were you thinking?" She managed to get out, striking him again. "You stupid, stupid boy."

Before Hal could answer, she had pulled him into her bosom, clutching him as though she were afraid he'd fall through the floor.

"You stupid boy," she kept saying as she rocked him in her arms.

6

VISIONS HAUNTED HAL'S dreams that night. Dark water and lightning storms collided and confused him as he fitfully woke and fell back into sleep. Through them all, a man of stone with a china face loomed over him, his fingers piercing Hal's wrists like nails.

Hal woke with the dawning light to find his bed sheets soaked through with sweat and a hot fever scratching at his skull. A wave of nausea overwhelmed him and he vomited down the side of his bed.

PEOPLE WERE MOVING Hal like a puppet, lifting his arms, opening his mouth, raising him up to a sitting position— he felt cold spots on his back—he couldn't make sense of himself as he felt himself lowered back to bed.

IT WAS NIGHTTIME. A figure sat sleeping in an armchair opposite Hal's bed. Hal reached for the glass of water on his bedside table. His exhausted arm failed him and he knocked the glass to the floor.

* * *

MORE PRODDING AND pushing from cold hands. Hal looked up at the old man gently turning and pressing his wrist. Hal stared at his arm, trying to make his eyes focus on the fingertip-sized welts on his wrist.

The man lay Hal's arm back down on the bed covers and turned away from him to talk to two blurred silhouettes in the distance. The doctor's voice was like a croaking toad; no words, just a bass rumble.

Hal tried to listen to what the doctor was saying, but it was too much. He closed his eyes and let sleep overtake him.

THE STONE MAN with the china face loomed over Hal in the dark.

"Rest up, my Ward." The words slithered out of his slit of a mouth. "Come find me when you're well. I have great plans for you. Great plans. First I'll need to teach you to see, but then—great plans."

When Hal woke the next morning, he was certain it had been a dream.

AFTER WHAT FELT like days trapped in his cocooned senses, Hal began to see and hear more clearly again, like a curtain of fog was slowly rising. His mum comforted him, explaining he had an infection.

"You're going to be okay."

Hal tried to smile. He still couldn't lift his arms or raise his head, but it felt good to be out of the confused isolation of the past few days.

That night, despite his exhaustion—or perhaps because of

it—he couldn't sleep. He tossed in bed, weakly kicking at his covers. His skin felt like it was being lightly punctured with a thousand hot needles. The itching pain was all over, but it seemed to centre on his wrist and forehead, where rashes had broken out in the day.

Someone spent the night replacing cold flannels on his forehead, keeping his fever down.

As the light of the sun rose in the morning and Hal finally found himself able to drift off, he made out the figure of Eli dozing in the armchair opposite him.

ON THE DAYS Hal was more alert, Eli would read him stories from a book of Jewish fables. "My father read these to me as a boy when I was ill."

Hal heard stories of a rabbi whose wife turned him into a wolf, and how the wolf roamed the forest eating any hunter who came for him. One day, when the King came to the forest, the wolf was able to befriend him and communicate to him the fate that had befallen him. The King went to the rabbi's town and stole from the wife the ring the rabbi needed to turn back into a man.

Another story was about a rabbi who protected the Jews of a city by making a guardian out of clay, breathing life into it with a prayer. The clay man did the rabbi's bidding and saved the Jewish people from an evil priest who wanted to harm them. Eventually, though, the creation turned on its master and its life had to be taken from it, returning it to a statue.

A lot of the stories confused Hal—they didn't build to an ending or have a clear point—but he grew to like them simply because of the way Eli told them. He brought every character to life, with different voices and mannerisms; when he recounted a story, it was like something he had heard from a friend, not something written in a book. Hal hung on every word, and his exhaustion would fall away.

In the evenings, Hal's mum would sit with him and they'd listen to the radio. He would often fall asleep like this.

WHEN THE FEVER finally broke, it left Hal diminished, sapped of energy. The doctor told his mum Hal would need his rest over the next few weeks, warning that any major exertion could make him ill again.

HAL AWOKE TO noises from the living room. His mum was talking to someone in hushed tones. Keeping the light off, he slipped out of bed and crept to the door; his mum had been leaving it ajar to stop his room from getting musty. He peered through the crack.

The living room was dark except for the light over the dining table. Hal's mother sat at the table with a saucer and cup of tea in her hands. Although he could only see the back of him, Hal recognised the Rag and Bone Man immediately.

"The others told you about my gift, yes? But they won't have told you what I told them, only that I read in the leaves things they didn't know of themselves. Things that have happened, things that will."

Hal could see the edge of the man's face, outlined in shadow. In the daylight, it blended into his skin; but in this light, to Hal, it looked like the mask covered a black void.

"Why has Hal been talking about you in his sleep?" she asked. "Had you two spoken?"

The Rag and Bone Man held his hands before him, holding an imaginary cup and saucer. He twisted his wrist, bidding Hal's mum to finish her tea. She drank it down quickly and he took the saucer, firmly tugging it from her grip. He raised the cup in the air, placed the saucer over it like a lid and set it on the tabletop.

"How—if you don't mind my asking, do you—you can't *see*, can you?" Hal's mum said, putting her fingers to the bridge of her nose to indicate his mask.

"You're sceptical. You think your friends are gullible—or worse, that they've lied to you. I don't need eyes to see. I don't need eyes to know, for instance, that the war killed your husband."

"He didn't die in the war," Hal's mum whispered, then louder. "He didn't die in the war."

"I didn't say that," the Rag Man said, a hint of annoyance in his voice. "He died in his noose, but the war is what killed him."

Hal's mum was taken aback. "Hal told you that?"

"The boy said nothing. The boy *says* nothing, you know that. You write about it in your diary."

"How—?"

"I don't need eyes to see these things. You trust that now, yes? This is why the others swear by me, but don't share what I tell them. Come, it's not all bad, your new life. You are in the grip of love. It's a comfort, a new ear to empty worries into."

"That's enough," Hal's mum said, rising from her chair. "We're finished."

With a flourish, the Rag Man lifted the cup from the saucer.

"Be calm. The worst is over," he said, tilting the saucer towards her, showing her the tea leaves. "The worst *is* over. There is a little more pain to come, but not your pain, and then the man has a gift for you: a ring, yes, but also a family, a home."

Slowly sitting, "And Hal? What about Hal?"

"It's not his future I'm reading, and I wouldn't dream of sharing it while he's watching." The Rag Man turned to face Hal's door, his eyeless mask staring straight at him. Hal fell back as if struck and scrabbled back into his bed.

He heard his door open slightly, but he shut his eyes, feigning sleep in the gloomy darkness. After a moment it closed again, this time shut.

"I think that's enough for today," Hal heard through the door. Then the sound of the front door.

"IT's HARDER GETTING up there now, my mum's on my case since your mum told her you nearly fell off the roof," Shahid said, miming Hal's fall with the piece of cake in his hand. "Still, I've managed to get a sheet up there to make a sun shade. And I didn't tell you: my uncle's got two folding sun loungers out the back of the shop that he says we can have if I work the weekend. If we can get some rope, we'll be able to haul them up through the bathroom window, no trouble."

"My mum'll actually kill me if she catches me up there again," Hal said. "I'm lucky I got ill right after or I think she might have wrung my neck. She still might, when I get better."

"It's what you get for going up there without me."

"You just said you'd been up there to build a shade."

"Yeah, I'm allowed to, I found that roof first. And it's not like I should be waiting around for you to get your bed rest. School starts up again in three weeks. Besides, you still haven't told me what happened. I've been hearing rumours around the estate that you were pushed."

Hal frowned at Shahid, confused.

"You know, by the Rag and Bone Man."

"He didn't push me, he saved me," Hal said. "And there's more to it than that, besides."

Hal told Shahid the whole story of it, how the Rag and Bone Man had somehow known Hal was going to fall and was right there when he needed to catch him, about the strange visions that Hal had had when the man grabbed his wrist—he showed Shahid the marks on his wrist—"and he knew, he knew that my mum was coming up the stairs."

"There's something going on with him."

"That's not all of it. He was here, in my flat, doing that thing with the tea leaves for my mum. He knew loads about her, stuff I didn't even know."

"What a creep!"

"I'm going to get answers as soon as I get out of bed."

"When's that?"

"The doctor says two weeks, but my mum's going back to work tomorrow, so... tomorrow."

Shahid's face was the picture of disappointment. He had to work in his uncle's shop tomorrow. Hal promised him he'd tell him everything that happened when they met up in the evening.

7

"MY WARD, YOU have come," the Rag and Bone Man said as Hal approached, walking weakly through the courtyard. The tall figure beckoned Hal closer.

"I—I think you told me to come."

"And now you can help me with my work. Show me your arm." Hal pulled up his sleeve to show the scars on his wrist. "Good, it's healing well."

"When you grabbed me, I saw things. Images."

"You saw what I see," the Rag and Bone Man put two fingers to his mask, pressing them against his china eyes. "Though you won't be able to make sense of it on your own."

"What did they mean?"

"You will need to help me in return." He pointed to his cart of rags and scraps. "For now, you will push this."

Sapped of his strength by the fever, Hal struggled to keep up with the Rag and Bone Man, but the strange man gave him no help.

*   *   *

As THEY WENT about the estate collecting scrap, Hal asked the Rag and Bone Man all the questions swirling around his head: what were the visions he'd seen? How had the man known he was going to fall? How he could get about the estate so easily without being able to see?

The Rag and Bone Man ignored every question. Instead, the man talked about objects.

"You must stop looking at them as inanimate things," he said, plucking an old shawl from the cart. "Every object is alive with as much of a destiny as you. It has a history and a future and as much a say in both as you do. We are only ever seeing it at a point in its path." He trailed the shawl through the air like a comet crossing the sky. "Like people, some objects have richer lives than others. This shawl has had a long life, but a common existence." He held it before him in both hands, stroking the fabric between his fingers. "It's made from cotton Mrs King bought at the market. She dyed it blue in her sink, staining the enamel. She used to wear it most weeks as she went to work as a clerk at the bank. She was wearing it the day she heard her son had been in a car accident and when she rushed to the hospital to see him. She kept it in a drawer ever since—see how even she is touched by the object's history, even though she does not see things as I do?—After leaving it seven years in a drawer, she finally decided to be rid of it, so it ended up in my cart.

"That is this shawl's history. But its life is far from over, I will give it to Mrs Bell. She will wear it around the estate, and whenever Mrs King sees it, she will be reminded of her son. Eventually, she will snatch it from Mrs Bell and tear it in two. A common life."

Hal attended every word, not sure if he believed any of it.

"So... fate is fixed?"

"There are many fates, but some are more likely than others."

At the day's end, the Rag and Bone Man took the cart from Hal and told him to find him again tomorrow.

LYING IN BED that night, Hal looked about his room, trying to hear the stories his belongings could tell. He wondered about the people who had owned his books before him and why they had given them up. His eyes came to rest on his dad's coat hanging from the back of his door. He had found it in the attic when they'd been packing up the house, hidden at the bottom of a box in an old broken wardrobe: his dad's old Army coat.

He got out of bed and slipped it on. It was too big for him, but he'd taken to wearing it after the funeral. It was comforting in the way it enveloped him, the sleeves extending past the end of his hands. It used to smell of his father, but that had faded now—he had to press his nose into the collar and breathe in deeply to catch a hint of it. He brushed the woollen coat down with his hands, savouring the rough sensation on his fingertips. What stories could this coat tell him?

Out of the dark of his memory shot the image of his father's medal, hitting him with a great wave of guilt. He hadn't thought of it since he'd thrown it away in anger.

Wrapped in his father's coat, he sobbed at the stupid loss.

THE NEXT MORNING Hal retraced his steps of that first day, looking for the place he'd thrown the medal. It was hopeless, he thought; he couldn't remember where it had landed, nor see anywhere it could have lain undisturbed all these weeks. He checked the gutters and all along the edges of the courtyard. Someone must have taken it. He could picture it now, hidden away in someone's drawer, like Mrs King's shawl, an anchor of history lost to him.

With his shoulders slumped and his mood low, he went in search of the Rag and Bone Man.

"Don't say a word," the Rag and Bone Man said as they stood in the hallway on the third floor of York House. "Just watch and listen."

He knocked on the door of one of the flats. It was opened by a woman in her 40s, who stepped aside to let the Rag and Bone Man enter. The whole thing was done with an air of ceremony. Hal followed him in before she closed the door.

A single candle lit the living room, casting a flickering glow over everything, giving the scene a sense of something cultish and medieval. In daylight, it must have seemed a depressingly normal living room: family pictures hung on the wall, floral-patterned cushions adorned the sofas, and a copy of *Queen* with Julie Christie on the cover sat on the coffee table.

"I've brought my Ward with me today, Mrs Bell," the Rag and Bone Man said. "He's learning the ways of my family. Do not worry, he has been sworn to secrecy."

Mrs Bell looked at Hal, noticing him for the first time. "Well, take your shoes off and sit over there."

Hal did as she bid, picking a shadowy spot out of the way.

Mrs Bell sat at the table, closed her eyes and began to measure her breathing, like she was meditating. The Rag and Bone Man went to the kitchen, feeling his way with his hands. Hal watched through the doorway as he filled a kettle with water and began boiling it on the stove. He came back with a teacup and saucer, which he placed on the table in front of Mrs Bell.

When the kettle started to whistle, he didn't immediately take it off the stove, waiting until the piercing whistle caused Mrs Bell's nose to wrinkle. He poured the boiling water into her cup, not spilling a drop, then retrieved a small hessian pouch from inside his coat, loosened the neck, and took out a pinch of tea leaves, sprinkling them into the cup. He stirred the liquid once and sat down on the chair opposite Mrs Bell, the candle and the tea between them.

They all sat in silence, Mrs Bell with her eyes closed, the Rag and Bone Man motionless, hands resting in his lap. Hal watched them both. He realised they were waiting for the tea to cool.

"Let us begin," the Rag and Bone Man said, breaking the uncomfortable silence after a full five minutes. Mrs Bell wriggled in her chair, settling herself. "Last time I read the leaves I told you your son would get sick. Is he better?"

"Oh, yes, I got the doctor round as soon as he got a fever," Mrs Bell said eagerly. "His chickenpox cleared up in a week."

"And the disruptive storm I said was coming?"

"Yes, well, I took that to mean my James' mother, my mother-in-law. She came unannounced for the weekend. I'm sure that's what you were seeing. Every time she comes, everything gets thrown—"

"The tea should be ready," the Rag and Bone Man interrupted.

She looked stung at the interruption, but took the cup in both hands like she was drinking from a goblet of communion wine. Lips pursed, she drank the whole thing in one go. The Rag and Bone Man took the cup and saucer from her and repeated the movements Hal had spied in his living room the week before. He placed the saucer on the table and raised the cup, and Mrs Bell leant forward to take a look.

The Rag and Bone Man beckoned Hal forward to take a look at the damp dregs.

"What do you see?" he asked Hal.

With a flicker of surprise at being asked, Hal stared at the tea leaves, trying to pick out a pattern.

"Weeds?"

"Don't be a dullard," Mrs Bell snapped. "It's clearly a crown. Yes?"

Despite his china face, Hal was sure the Rag and Bone Man gave them both a despairing look.

"What I see is that sadly Mrs Bell will lose a friendship and a loved possession, though she may be happier for it. The storm is returning and this time it will stay for longer than before, and be more turbulent. I am afraid, also, that your husband's having trouble at work."

Mrs Bell asked questions of the predictions and the Rag and Bone Man offered a little clarity, but kept the specifics, if he knew them, to himself. After a while, he signalled an end to the transaction by blowing out the candle.

On the doorstep, about to leave, the Rag and Bone Man turned and said, "Oh, Mrs Bell, I have a gift for you—" Out of a pocket, he drew the blue shawl he had shown Hal the day before.

"What a marvellous colour," she said, taking the shawl and holding it up to the light. "I'll wear it out with the girls later."

"I HADN'T REALISED there was such ceremony to everything," Hal said when they got down to the courtyard below. "You didn't do that yesterday when you told me about the shawl."

"The ritual is for them. Everyone I read for brings their own ideas of what it should be like. This"—taking the small sackcloth bag out of his coat—"is just PG Tips loose leaf. What did you see me do?"

Hal recounted what he'd seen, focusing on the Rag and Bone Man's actions. He had gone to the kitchen, boiled the water, brought back the crockery, brewed the tea, flipped the cup.

"Objects hold their owner's history, I told you this. Mrs Bell will lose a friend when she wears that shawl to see Mrs King later today."

"You said she'd be happier for it, though."

"Most people are happier without Mrs King in their lives."

"And her son, how is his being ill tied up in that cup's history?"

"When I was in the kitchen I didn't just pick out one cup and boil the kettle. I listened to a lot of stories. The whisky tumbler had a lot to say about Mr Bell's performance at work."

"This is crazy."

"Is it really so bizarre? Right now, your scientists are plotting the paths of satellites between the gravitational pulls of planets, based not on where the planets are now but where they will be years—decades—from now, when the satellites have travelled the millions of miles to reach them. My people have a gift for perception. What your people need a computer to do, our minds can do by focusing on a teacup."

"But—"

"Enough, we've more work for today."

HAL AND THE Rag and Bone Man went to more flats. Each time it was different, with the tenants bringing different rituals. One woman answered the door all in black, like she was dressed for a funeral. All the pictures were turned to face the wall or placed face down on shelves. In another, the man had lit incense and listened to his reading while lying on a chaise longue with the Rag and Bone Man sitting on a chair opposite him, like a psychiatrist.

Each time, Hal was asked to interpret the leaves, and each time he found himself looking at indecipherable mulch. Aside from 'weeds,' he said he saw a squid, spaghetti, and—when he was feeling a little more frustrated with the routine—a horse ridden by Death. None—particularly the last—seemed to be what the Rag and Bone Man was looking for.

"I DON'T GET it," Hal said, when they were back in the courtyard. "Why did you have me try to interpret the tea leaves?"

"That? That was for my own amusement."

Hal's face coloured.

"You say you can tell the future of an object just by touching it, and you're using that gift to convince people in a housing estate in Leeds that you can read tea leaves?"

"Yes."

"What a monumental waste."

"My Ward, you don't know how I came to be here, and you don't know my ways." The Rag and Bone Man bent so his face was only inches from Hal's. "Don't presume to tell me my duty. Even this small act is a violation, to my brothers and sisters who are happy to be stones in a stream. Go home. We're done for today."

Angry at being fobbed off again by an adult, Hal returned to the flat, a plan forming for how he could get answers to the questions the Rag and Bone Man was avoiding.

8

THE NEXT MORNING, after their parents had gone to work, Hal went over to Shahid's flat. Sitting on Shahid's bed, Hal told him everything that had happened over the past two days.

"There's a trick, there's got to be," Shahid said. "He's already lying to the people he's telling the future for—that whole thing with the tea leaves is an act—so what's to say he's telling you the truth?"

"But that doesn't explain how he found me on the roof," Hal said. "I've got an idea how we can get some answers, without going to the Rag and Bone Man. Remember when we got told off for following him around the estate? It wasn't him who told our parents, it was someone called Mr Foster."

"I know him, he's an old man living in Nielson House. He's been here as long as anyone; I think he actually moved in when the estate was first opened. He used to be the head of the neighbourhood association. My mum cleans his flat."

"Well, for some reason, he's doing jobs for the Rag and Bone Man. He might know something else about him, and I want to know everything we can about the Rag Man before trying to talk to him again."

* * *

SHAHID KNOCKED ON Mr Foster's door. It looked like all the others—the same concrete facade, the same plywood door with mottled glass—but the man who lived inside had tried to make it his own: a welcome mat and two standing plants framed the entrance.

Through the glass, the boys watched a figure approach the door slowly. They listened to the sound of locks clicking, before it swung inwards to reveal a man bent with age.

"You've come," he said in a rasping voice. "In. Come in." He beckoned them in.

The boys hesitated, but the man was already turning to go back into his flat. They followed.

"He said you would come, but not when. Never when. Find yourselves somewhere to sit." Mr Foster gestured at the sofa, threadbare with age. "I'll make us tea."

The boys sat close to each other, trying to take in every detail of the packed room. The walls were lined floor-to-ceiling with bookcases, every shelf stuffed. Looking over the spines revealed the mind of a polymath—plays sat next to histories, wedged between manuals on cosmology and volumes of poetry.

The only gap in the cases was filled by a desk littered with papers.

"You must tell me what it was like, what you saw," Mr Foster said, returning to the living room carrying a tray of cups and a pot of tea. He placed them on the table before the boys, pouring them all a cup before sitting in the chair by his desk. "He's never shown me, you see. I've been asking him for 30 years and then—you've been here, what? A month?"

Shahid looked at Hal.

"I don't know what I saw," said Hal.

"Your future. He showed you your future, boy."

"No, I mean the images didn't make sense—he can't really see the future—"

"—the tea leaves are an act," Shahid interrupted.

"Yes, they're an act," Mr Foster said. "He doesn't need the leaves, but what he sees is prophecy. He touches objects and he does see their future." He turned to face Hal. "You know this, you've seen him do it."

The boys sat silently, not sure what to say to Mr Foster's certainty.

"You"—pointing at Hal—"you he touched directly. He's always so careful not to brush against someone. His gloves, coat, it's all to cover him. Years he's come to my flat and he's never even taken off his cap. He's told me things, yes, but never shown me, not like he showed you."

Hal frowned.

"Why did you tell our mums we were following him?" Shahid asked.

"He came to me and told me who you were and what I had to do. We had to set you on the path."

"The path to what?" asked Hal.

"Please, tell me what you saw," Mr Foster said, leaning forwards in his chair, his eyes fixed intently on Hal. "When he touched you, what did you see?"

"I—I don't know. There was water. Lightning, I think. Dancing shadows, and a candle on a table? The images were only flashes and they were all over so quickly."

"It must have been overwhelming," Mr Foster said, leaning back in his chair with a look of disappointment. "Goan was born with this ability, and has had a lifetime to understand it. It may just be too much for the human brain."

Mr Foster twisted in his chair and picked up a notepad and pen from his desk, starting to make notes.

"What—" Shahid started. "What did you mean by that?"

"He's not like us," Mr Foster was excited, animated. "No, not at all." Leaning in again, he added, conspiratorially, "He's not from here."

"Where is he from, then?" Shahid asked.

"I don't know, but it's not Earth."

"Bollocks," the boys said in unison.

"What's an *alien* doing in a housing estate in Leeds?" Hal said.

"They're hiding."

The boys waited for Mr Foster to continue.

"From their war," he eventually added.

"'They'?" asked Shahid.

"I don't know it all—or I did, but I lost it. Things go missing around them, memories. It's why I write it all down, now—I've been trying to piece it together for years." The old man indicated his piles of papers. "Their people were being eradicated. It seems being able to see the path of things is a dangerous talent, wherever you come from. Goan, he led a group of refugees here."

"To Leeds?" Shahid said incredulously.

"No, not to Leeds," Mr Foster said with annoyance. "They were transported here—I don't know where from."

"How many are there?"

"Never been sure. Not many. Twenty, maybe."

"Where?" Shahid said cynically. "I've lived on this estate all my life, and you're saying I've had twenty aliens as my neighbours?"

"You don't understand. Why *would* you know? Goan has been walking about the estate your whole life and it never entered your mind. He's an odd figure, and that's all you need in this world to shield you from most people's curiosity. People stare at the strange, but they don't engage with them.

It took him reaching out to draw you in. As to the others, they aren't like Goan, they don't leave the boiler room, they hold up there like monks in their cell."

"Even so, how can they not have been found in 30 years?" Hal asked. "Thousands of people live in Quarry Hill. You can't keep a secret like that."

"You can if the right people are keeping it," Mr Foster said, leaning back in his chair. "The Farreter—that's what they call themselves—didn't just wander up to Leeds, they were planned for. This estate was built to keep them safe, at least in part.

"It was Jenkinson's idea, as far as I know; he was a priest here in Leeds, who looked after the people living in the slums. They were awful places to live, those old terraced houses. He and another man—can't remember his name, Lively or something—they were on the Council's housing association and the pair of them designed this place, but underneath their plan was a secret purpose—a sanctuary for these unique refugees."

"They've been here the whole time?" Shahid asked again.

"Yes!" Foster replied irritably. "Built into the foundations. When we moved in back in '38, a few of us were brought in on the scheme. Everyone on the housing committee helped. We didn't have to do much, they keep to themselves mostly, but if any of the residents started causing trouble, we'd solve the problem quietly, move people along—talking to the mothers of inquisitive boys, mostly. I still have the key to the boiler room, but I've not been down there in years; Goan gets them their food now. He only comes to see me to borrow books and talk with a human. I don't think he can stand his brothers' cloistered life."

"But, why here?" Hal asked.

"I don't think this was the long-term plan, but the war

changed things. Where could they go to, where people wouldn't ask questions? At least here they were settled in, and there were people in place to keep them safe. Now, though, most that knew about them are dead, or have moved away and forgotten about them."

"How could you forget about a thing like this?" Shahid asked.

"You'll see. It's something they do—or something our minds do to themselves. The Farreter slip from your memory, if you aren't careful."

THE BOYS SPENT all afternoon with Mr Foster, Shahid making them teas while they talked about what Hal might have seen— the old man was certain, with practice, a human could make sense of the visions. Hal tried to dig into the Farreter's history before Quarry Hill and find out why they were on Earth, but Mr Foster either didn't know or couldn't remember the details. Hal didn't realise how draining this was until they left and Shahid had to help him walk back to the flat.

Back home, Hal got into bed, making sure there was nothing to give away his excursion to his mum when she returned from work.

"Do you believe it?" Shahid asked Hal, sitting in the chair facing Hal's bed.

"I—I don't know," Hal replied. "It can't be true, can it? I mean, a secret plot to hide aliens that can see the future?"

"Well, tomorrow we can at least check out one part of Mr Foster's story." Shahid leant forward in his chair, extended his arm, and dangled a key in front of him. "The old man had his keys for the estate hanging from a cork board."

Shahid tossed the key to Hal who read the tag linked to the keyring: *Boiler room.*

9

THE BOILER ROOM sat like a pillar box guarding the football field, away from the housing blocks; a concrete slug with a single metal door. A strip of frosted glass along one wall was its only other feature. Using the key they'd taken from Mr Foster's flat, Hal unlocked the heavy door and heaved it inwards.

The door opened into a room full of plumbing. Six large tanks took up most of the space, hooked up to pipes running into the metal floor. The air was warm and thick, the smell of oil was overpowering. Nothing obviously moved, but a cacophony rose from the tanks: liquids flooding through the pipes and the clicks of burners turning on and off, maintaining a steady temperature in the tanks.

Shahid closed the door behind them, encasing themselves in the gloom. Hal flicked the switch by the door and strong lights flickered on overhead, washing the tanks in a harsh glow. A bolted hatch in the floor in front of them stood out; he drew the bolt and together they lifted the hatch to reveal a ladder to a concrete passage below. Hal climbed down into the darkness first.

"What do you see?" Shahid asked from above him.

"It's dark, but it looks like the corridor heads back to the estate, maybe towards the washroom," Hal replied.

Shahid climbed down into the dark corridor, leaving the hatch open for the little light it gave. It was too tight a passage to walk side by side, so Hal took the lead. The walls of the tunnel were lined with wide pipes radiating heat. He set off down the tunnel, plunging into total darkness after thirty feet or so. He held his hands out in front of him so as not to walk into anything blocking his way. Every few steps he'd graze one of the pipes with his arms or shoulder, scalding his skin on the hot iron.

As Hal walked into the dark, he began to hear singing on the thick air, growing louder as he walked. He couldn't make out the words, but the music was punctuated with rhythmic stamping and clapping.

"Do you hear that?" Hal whispered.

"Keep going, it's getting louder."

After sixty feet or so Hal's hands hit a metal door, and he stopped to feel for a handle. Shahid walked into his back and they stumbled forward, the door opening under their weight.

The door opened onto a large square room lined with beds and tables, its centre cleared of furniture but for a single table laden with candles. In a wide circle around the table were tall figures, singing and clapping. They moved in time with the music in a slow sidestepping circle, the candles casting flickering, bowing shadows on the walls. Bone effigies of birds and other small animals hung from the ceiling by fine threads. The strange talismans swung in slow circles, disturbed by the motion of the figures below. The flickering gave them a ghostly life.

One figure led the chanting song, bathed in candlelight. Hal stared at his face—it was featureless, besides a small, lipless mouth. No eyes, nose, or ears, like an unfinished marble sculpture.

The figures paid him no attention and continued their song. Hal tried to pick out the words, but the language was like nothing he'd heard. If there were individual words in the music, they ran into one another, rising and falling lyrically in one unbroken chain.

Shahid stood in wonder, taking in the scene.

"I'm looking for Goan."

The singing and dancing stopped.

"I'm looking for Goan," Hal repeated, louder than before.

"Goan?" the leader said, turning his head towards Hal to stare at him blindly. "That's what he calls himself now."

"My name is Hal, this is my friend Shahid. Goan's been teaching me to see like he does—like you do."

The figures closest to Hal parted, clearing the way for their leader.

"And what is it that we see?"

"The future," Hal said, hesitating.

"We are the channel, a stone fixed in the riverbed, aware of the current and the water, where it has come from and where it is going to. Whatever he has been teaching you, it is not that. You are a tribe that is carried by the current."

"You're wrong. I saw the future when Goan saved my life." Hal raised his arm and pulled down his sleeve to show the marks on his wrist. "He is teaching me to understand what I saw."

"Shande saved your life?" The leader turned to the other figures assembled around him. "Again our brother transgresses. How many violations must we allow this radical before another yeger is born?"

Shahid gripped Hal's wrist and whispered, "I think we should go."

Ignoring him, Hal asked, "What is it that he did wrong? He saved my life."

"What right do we have to manipulate the current? We are blessed to see the stream, but it is not for us to alter its course."

Shahid backed towards the door, tugging at Hal's arm to have him follow.

"You're criticising him? Do you even know what the world is like above you? You've lived in a concrete bunker for three decades."

The leader strode towards Hal, raising his voice. "It is *not* for you to tell us our duty, Golem! If you can't find Shande, then he did not mean to meet you. Now *leave* us, before we fix his change in fate."

Hal backed away, letting Shahid pull him towards the door and into the corridor. The creature slammed the door shut, and Hal heard the sound of a metal bar being slid home, locking it in place. Left in the dark, Hal seethed.

"They're real. They're really real," Shahid said. "Did you see their faces? What were they singing?"

"'It is not for us to tell them their duty'? He wanted me to have *died*. Who does he think he is?"

"Please, Hal, let's get out of this tunnel," Shahid said.

Shahid set off ahead, head bowed, nearly running. Hal followed more slowly, his mind racing.

OUT IN THE light, the hatch bolted and the boiler room locked behind them, Hal could see how shaken Shahid was. His skin had gone pale; he was looking around to check they weren't being watched.

"I'm not going back in there, Hal."

"But we're finally finding something out."

"Did you see all the bones? The ceiling was strung up with them. I could recognise some of the animals, but their skeletons had been assembled all wrong."

"Shahid, we've found aliens. Real-life aliens."

"We found *monsters*, Hal."

10

THE BOYS WENT their separate ways, Shahid telling Hal to leave him out of his plans, at least for now.

That night over dinner, Hal pieced together what he'd learned and how he could find out more. He could try and ask the Rag and Bone Man—Goan, Shande, whatever his name was—but he'd likely just avoid his questions. Mr Foster didn't know anything more. He could try going into the basement of the boiler room again, but as much as he wanted to get answers, he didn't much like the prospect of going down there without Shahid. If he could just find out where the Farreter were before they came to Leeds, then maybe he might learn why they were here on Earth.

"What's going on with you?"

Hal looked up from his mashed potato. "Huh?"

"What's going on with you?" Hal's mum asked him again. "You've hardly said a word to me tonight."

Hal stared at her.

"Where have you been going all day? Yes, I know you've been leaving the flat, I'm not dim."

"I've been exploring with Shahid."

"If I find you've been up on that roof again—"

"No, no, he took me to meet a man called Mr Foster, who told me about the estate."

"Oh? That sounds... surprisingly wholesome. Did he have lots of stories?"

"Yeah, though he was muddled about things. He doesn't know much about how the estate was built."

"If that's something you want to know, you should come with me to the university when you're feeling better. I'm sure there's something in the archive under the Brotherton. Every newspaper published in Leeds is stored down there. There must be lots about Quarry Hill."

She carried on about how they would go when he was well, but Hal was already planning how he could get to the university without her knowing.

THAT NIGHT, LYING in bed, one thing ran round his head over and over. He was sure the leader had called him 'Golem.' Maybe it was coincidence and the word meant something different to the Farreter, but Hal recognised the word: it was the name of the monster in the story Eli had read to him when he was ill—the man made of clay that protected the Jews of Prague. Hal couldn't work out why the Farreter leader had called him that, or how he even knew the word. He tossed it around in his head before finally falling asleep.

HAL LAY AWAKE in bed the next morning, waiting for his mum to leave for work. After the click of the front door closing, he made himself a quick breakfast and headed down to the bus stop.

Just in case, when he reached the arch of Oastler House, he slowed his walk and crept through the tunnel, watching ahead to see if he could spot his mum still waiting for a bus into town. There was no queue at the stop; a bus must have just gone. He took a place at the stand, rattling the change in his pocket.

Despite the warmth of the day, Hal felt cold and clammy. When the bus came, he took his seat and focused on the city passing by outside the window to keep alert.

THE STEPS OF the Parkinson Building were dotted with clusters of students enjoying the sun —dozing, talking and smoking. None of them paid him any attention as he hurried up the steps and heaved open the heavy door.

Inside he saw his first obstacle: the receptionists' desk. He hadn't got familiar with them when he spent the week cleaning the staff room, but couldn't be sure they wouldn't recognise him.

Hal ducked behind one of the wide columns that lined the inside of the hall. The entrance to the Brotherton was directly opposite the doors, but if he walked across the lobby he'd be spotted for sure. He was scanning the room for a route out of sight of the receptionists' panopticon when the solution burst through the doors of the Parkinson, led by a student enthusiastically pointing out the particulars of the architecture. A tour of prospective undergrads.

Hal overheard snatches of the parents' hushed observations—"Isn't this grand?" "Can't you just picture yourself here?" "It's much nicer than Liverpool." Hal slipped from his hiding place as the group passed him, and wormed into the thick of the scrum.

"Construction of the Parkinson building began in 1938,"

the student tour guide shouted, struggling to make herself heard over the din. "Work stopped at the outbreak of the war, though, and it wasn't completed until 1951. The building is named after Leeds alumni Frank Parkinson, who donated funds to the building's construction."

The tour moved past the receptionists' post and towards the entrance to the library. Hal could see the library's front desk, staffed by one solitary librarian, barring the staircases to the collection from anyone lacking a library card.

"Ahead of us is the Brotherton Library. Opened in 1936, it housed all of the University of Leeds' books and manuscripts, except for the medical textbooks and Clothworkers' Collection. Unfortunately, we aren't able to go inside; we wouldn't want to disturb any students hard at work."

The librarian was looking down at something on the desk, and the tour group was turning away; this was his chance. Hal darted forwards, ducking below the lip of the desk. Keeping low, he shuffled round the curved wall of the desk and up the staircase.

Hal pushed through the doors and stopped. The library was like no building he had seen: two stories high, with a great domed roof, and ringed by slender columns. The walls and columns were pond-green, startling after the stark white of the Parkinson. The warm light slanting through the dome's curved windows gave the space a comforting feel, taking the edge off its cavernous size.

Looking back down, Hal was entranced by the desks and writing tables crossing the marble floor, radiating from the podium at the centre of the room. Students sat dotted around the tables, poring over their work, books spread before them like peacock's feathers in a display of quiet competition. There was no way they all actually needed quite so many books at a time.

Hallways led from the room to other collections, and staircases led to the upper gallery and the basements below.

From a floorplan on the wall, Hal learned that the newspaper archive was stored in the second basement. He quietly crossed the room to the stairs. Unlike the cacophony outside in the library, all was quiet and still. No one looked up from their books as he passed. It was like walking through a mannequin display in a clothes shop.

Down the stairs, the air became colder still. This was where the university archived its journals; the temperature was kept low and the air dry in order to preserve the pages. The basements were circular, like the library above, study rooms punctuating the curving corridor. The central chamber was filled with metal bookcases, each six foot tall at least, pressed together so you couldn't get in between them. Each case was marked with a metal plaque engraved with dates; over the plaques were metal wheels.

Hal walked the ringed corridor trying to work out where the newspapers were kept, and was startled by a hand on his shoulder.

"Hal?"

Hal felt his stomach go cold.

"It is you, isn't it?"

Hal turned around and his heart leapt: Rose.

"I'm sorry! I didn't mean to scare you," she said. "Only you've done two laps of the doughnut and you looked like you were searching for someone."

"Rose! Please, you can't tell anyone I was here."

Rose ducked low with theatrical stealth.

"Why ever not? Are you on a secret mission?"

"I'm trying to find something, but my mum can't know I'm here."

"What are you looking for?"

"She told me all the newspapers published in Leeds were down here, but I can't find *any* of them, let alone all."

"Newspapers? You know that one of the few original copies of Shakespeare's plays is upstairs?" Rose looked Hal up and down with mock despair. "Well, I don't know about *all* of the newspapers, but I think I know what she was talking about. Come on, I'll show you."

Rose led Hal by the hand to a set of shelves.

"When's your birthday, Hal?"

"May 4th, 1953."

"1953... 1953..." Rose said to herself as she traced a finger along the shelving plaques. "Ah-*hah*." She gripped the metal wheel on the end of one of the cases and began to turn. The whole bookcase moved sideways, opening up a gap in the block.

As Rose led Hal between the bookcases, she explained how each case was sorted by publication and date. Hal couldn't see any books or papers on the shelves, only rows and rows of plain white boxes, each with a label taped to one side. He had the eerie sensation that he'd been there before. Rose stopped in front of one shelf and started searching along it with her finger, muttering, "May 4th... May 4th..." She stopped in front of one of the boxes, plucked it from the shelf and gave it a gentle shake. "In here is the people's history of Leeds, Hal."

Rose set off down the hall, still talking to herself. "Now we just need a reader..." She walked back to the corridor and started peering through the windows of the study rooms. Eventually finding what she was looking for, she opened the door and ushered Hal inside.

Besides the desks and tables Hal expected, there was a strange machine against one wall. Rose flicked a switch on the front and a large panel on its face lit up with a yellow glow. She pulled out a tray below the glowing panel and opened the box she'd taken from the archive.

"This is called a 'microfilm,'" Rose said, handing the reel to Hal. "It's like the film reels at a cinema, but each frame is a photo of a page of a newspaper. Using this"—she pointed to the machine with her thumb—"you can blow it up to read it."

Taking the reel back from Hal, Rose fixed it to a pin next to the glass tray, unspooled the end of the film, and ran it under the glass tray to a spool on the other side. Hal watched with fascination as the glowing panel filled with a blurred newspaper image.

"Just need to focus it," Rose said, turning one of the wheels on the front of the microfilm reader. The page on the panel sharpened until Hal could make out the words *Yorkshire Evening Post* and above them *January 3rd, 1953*.

"You can use this wheel here to move through the pages," Rose said, pointing to another wheel.

Hal spun the wheel and watched the year's news flash by.

"Not so fast! Look, you're already in April. The tiniest turn is enough."

Hal gave the dial a careful turn, finding *May 4th, 1953*. The newspaper from the day he was born. It was a weird sensation: the day he was born was just like any other day, as far as the rest of the world was concerned.

"Look at that, *Experts See Comet Wreckage*," Rose said, pointing to a story halfway down the page. Then with a tone of disappointment, "Oh, it's only about a Comet Jet airliner. I hoped for a moment the *Post* would be covering a British Roswell."

Hal looked at Rose blankly.

"You know, the Roswell incident? When aliens supposedly crash-landed in New Mexico," Rose said, smiling. "I don't believe it really, but the rumour goes that aliens crashed in America in the '40s and the government tried to cover it up. It's nonsense, but a fun story. Anyway, I best get back to my work. If I show you how to take the microfilm off the reader, do you think you can put it back when you're done?"

Hal assured her he could.

HAL ONLY HAD a name and a date to work with: Jenkinson and 1938, the year Quarry Hill was opened. He wound up the microfilm Rose had found and took it back to its shelf, returning with boxes covering 1938. He loaded the most recent of the films into the machine and started working back.

It was slow going. Hal wasn't sure if the opening of the estate would make front page news, so tried to scan every page as it went by. He could feel himself getting hot and sweating under the coat, but his skin was clammy; his fever was coming back. But he wasn't sure when he'd get another chance to steal into the archive, so he carried on.

After an hour, the pages started to blur, but Hal was sure he was getting close. The letters pages in the July papers made mention of the estate, some people calling it a concrete monstrosity, others that it was modern and elegant. As he moved into June he found it: *First Residents Move into Quarry Hill Estate*.

The image heading the article was of a long queue of people carrying bundles and boxes, presumably waiting in line to be assigned their flats. Another image showed a group of people framed under the Oastler arch. Everyone in the group was dressed smartly; the man in the centre wore robes and a large ceremonial chain about his neck. To his left was a man in a black clerical gown and dog collar. Hal read their names in the caption: *Rev. Charles Jenkinson, Rowland Winn (Lord Mayor of Leeds), R. A. H. Livett (Architect)*.

That must be him, Hal thought, recognising the name Mr Foster couldn't remember: Livett. He was a lean man with a thin moustache, dressed in a sharp wool suit. Hal read through the article, but didn't find much that he didn't already know. One thing that stood out was a brief note about Livett, saying he 'often graced the *Yorkshire Evening Post*'s letter pages.'

Hal unwound the microfilm and returned it to its shelf in the archive. It was getting late; he had to get home before his mum missed him. On the way out, he knocked on the window of the study room where Rose was working and waved goodbye.

HAL GOT HOME an hour before his mum and went straight to bed. He could feel his fever returning, but he was set on going back to the archive the next day. He was close, he knew it. Somewhere in those newspapers, he'd learn where the Farreter came from.

THE NEXT DAY, Hal got up after his mum left for work and again made his way to the University. He worked back through the newspaper archive, picking through the years of the estate's construction, for stories about Quarry Hill's development and in the hope of finding one of Livett's letters. He read of delays to the project, the hopes of Leeds Housing Council; he found a letter of Jenkinson's talking about the poor conditions in the slums and the need for modern social housing. But nothing that answered his questions.

He returned the day after, and the day after that, sneaking

past the watchful receptionists and keen-eyed librarians each time. Sometimes he'd run into Rose, who took to calling Hal her 'little historian.' If he was entirely truthful with himself, he'd be getting through the archive faster if he spent less time talking to her.

In the second week of his search, as he was giving up hope of finding anything, he came across a letter of Livett's in 1933. Livett had recently been appointed Housing Director of Leeds (with the help of Rev. Jenkinson, according to other articles in the paper) and he talked about his plans to design estates to rehome thousands of Leeds' poorest people, taking them out of slum living and into the modern age. That wasn't what caught Hal's attention, though: according to the letter, Livett and Jenkinson had recently returned from a visit to the Karl-Marx-Hof housing estate in Vienna. This was it, Hal realised.

"Found anything interesting, little historian?" Rose asked from the door of the study room. He hadn't even heard her come in.

"I have," Hal began. Over the weeks he had told her a little about what he was up to. He'd left out the Farreter, of course, saying he was interested in his home and its history. "Quarry Hill's architect..."

"Livett?"

"Yeah, him. He travelled to Vienna. Apparently, the estate's inspired by something called the Karl-Marx-Hof."

"That's good?"

"It is, but I don't know. I want to know more about it, and I won't find that in these papers."

"Why don't you talk to someone who lived there?"

"How would I even begin to do that?" Hal asked.

"Hal, you're in a university. There are thousands of people above you, who between them have links to every major city in the world. One link to start you off, though: my boyfriend. Steve studies architecture here. He can ask a lecturer, if you want?"

Hal wasn't keen to include more people, but he agreed. He wrote a letter Steve could forward on, wording it carefully, saying he had met a member of the Farreter family here in Leeds and believed they had once lived in Vienna. He asked for any information about how they came to move to England. Hopefully it would mean nothing to the wrong recipient and everything to the right one. He folded the letter and left it with Rose.

11

HAL WAS WRETCHED. Since coming home from the archive, he'd been lying in bed with a fever. He didn't want his mum to come down on him—she already knew he'd been leaving the house—so he did his best to hide his illness from her.

He was woken on Sunday morning by a knock at his door. His mum stuck her head in, telling him to dress smartly, they were going to Eli's parents' home for lunch. Hal washed and dressed in his best shirt and trousers and come out of his room to find the flat smelled of baking; his mum had been up early to make a lemon drizzle cake to take with them. The sweet smell made Hal nauseous.

They took the bus north, out to Leylands, leaving the concrete city behind them as they travelled deep into the red brick terrace rows Hal had looked out over all those weeks ago. The terrace houses were all virtually identical in design, but didn't have the uniformity of the flats at the estate: the gardens were tended differently, with colourful flowerbeds or high hedges, and many were cleared altogether so families could hang out washing or sit out in sun loungers. Being a Sunday, many families were outdoors, gardening, relaxing, or talking to their neighbours over the thin fences.

Hal was mesmerised by the lively streets, only coming out of his stupor when his mum tugged at his arm to get off the bus. They walked up the road, his mum counting off the numbers. There was a nervous excitement to her that morning; she had straightened his collar twice already on the bus, and she kept readjusting her pastel green dress.

At length, she led Hal up to a house with a blue door. She knocked, turning to check Hal's shirt a third time.

Eli opened the door and greeted Hal's mum with a warm embrace. "Patricia, you're right on time." Turning to Hal, he said, "Let me take that," and took the cake from Hal's hands. He ushered them both to go inside, a hand on Hal's back.

The doorway led into a narrow hallway, where Eli's parents were waiting to be introduced. "Patricia, Hal, these are my mum and dad, Ruth and Daniel," Eli said. Ruth and Daniel embraced Hal's mum, Daniel kissing her on each cheek.

"So wonderful to meet you," Daniel said and, to Hal, "My son tells me you've been up to all sorts of mischief." A great smile broke over his face. "I heartily approve."

Hal and his mum were led into the living room, where the adults quickly got into small talk about how Hal's mum was finding Leeds, the new flat, and her job at the university. Hal listened to the conversation, but his mind drifted off to thoughts of the Karl-Marx-Hof and hopes for his letter. No one seemed to notice; the focus was all on his mum.

Over lunch, Hal continued to turn over plans for his next steps. He was close to learning the origins of the Farreter, but he still wanted to talk to Goan and find out what he had done wrong in saving his life—why the leader had called Goan a 'radical.'

"My son tells me you like his stories. I read them to him when he was a boy."

Hal looked up at Eli's father, Daniel.

"Which is your favourite?"

Hal was surprised at the direct question, but didn't hesitate. "The Golem."

"Ah, I think that may be the favourite of every Jewish boy across the world. I know it was mine, and I remember Eli pretending to be a golem when he was younger than you."

"Is it... is it real?" Hal asked.

"No one can say for sure; no one living, at least," Daniel replied. "I'll tell you this, though. It is said that after the Golem in Prague had done its duty and protected the Jews from the blood libel, Rabbi Liva ordered the creature to climb the ladder into the attic of the Old New Synagogue. He then ordered the creature to lay down and sleep while he, his son, and his student undid the spell they had cast to animate its clay body. Since that day, no one has been allowed up there. Some believe that the Golem is still there, waiting to wake and protect the Jews when it is needed again."

"And no one has been up since?"

"Well, there are stories that during the war a Nazi agent climbed up the ladder to the attic. Nobody knows why; maybe they were looking for valuables, or they had heard the legend of the Golem and wanted to see if it existed. The story goes that his body was found in the street before the temple with its skull bashed in."

"The Golem?"

"No one knows. What I do know is that the Old New Synagogue is still there today and people are still not allowed to go into the attic."

Sitting on his mind was what the leader of the Farreter had called him in the room under Quarry Hill.

"Are all golems made out of clay?"

"An interesting question." He turned to look up the table.

"Eli, we may have a khokem in our midst." Turning back to Hal, he continued, "In all the stories I have read, a golem is made of mud or clay. But there are also writings that suggest Adam was a golem, before God breathed life into him. Either this is because he was formed of clay and changed into flesh, or that any man without a soul is a golem. The word itself simply means 'raw' or 'unfinished.' Though now, it has become something of a cruel term—meaning someone is stupid or doesn't think for themselves."

Hal and Daniel spent all of the lunch talking about Jewish myths, even Eli joined in to point out Jewish creatures in modern books and films. "Frankenstein's monster is like a golem," he said. "Though it's a perversion of the story: the raw creature Frankenstein creates becomes murderous and self-commanding." He claimed also that *The Wolf Man*, a horror film released in the '40s, was in part based on the werewolf story he had read Hal when he was ill. "In that, the victims of the creature are marked with a star," he added.

When Hal wasn't lost in conversation, he sat back in his chair and looked around the table. Ruth would keep adding food to their plates; Eli would try and stop her, but she would always find a moment when he wasn't looking to sneak him another potato. Daniel had clearly learned it was a futile fight and would offer up his plate whenever she caught his eye.

It was his mum he watched most intently. Here, with Eli, she looked *relaxed*; Hal tried to think of a better word for it, but he realised that for months—longer even, years, since before his father died—there had been a tension to his mum that he hadn't seen until now, when it was gone. It filled him with troubled joy; he was happy to see her like this, but it also made him recognise the same tension within himself.

12

HAL AND HIS mum were walking back to their flat. They had talked the whole bus journey home, recounting conversations from lunch, and she pointed out all the nice things about Eli's family home. Now, conversation spent, they walked in happy silence. Hal recognised that in this short month his feelings towards the new man in his mum's life had reversed.

They climbed the stairs to their floor and stepped into the hallway to their flat.

"Have you seen Shahid?"

Shahid's mum stood outside their door, tugging nervously at her dress.

"Please, tell me you were with him," she said desperately.

Hal's mum explained they hadn't.

"He's not come home. No one's seen him since he went out this morning." The panic rang in her words. "Is there anywhere the two of you go?"

"Have you been back on the roof?" Hal's mum asked him.

"I... I haven't, not since... he had been, I think."

The three of them went back to Shahid's flat. His father

pulled the door open as soon as he heard the key in the lock. "Shahid?"

Hal's mum offered to wait in their house while they went out looking, and Hal and Shahid's parents started searching the estate. They knocked on doors as they went, and other parents joined them in the search. It was dark now; many of them brought out flashlights. Hal woke up Mr Foster and got the keys to the roof from his kitchen; he and Shahid's father went to check, but he wasn't there.

From the top of Jackson House, they could see the different search parties sweeping the grounds by torchlight. Someone must have called the police; a pair of cars with blue lights flashing drove through the arch and through the estate towards them. The searchers cast long monstrous shadows in the chaotic light.

"They'll find him," Shahid's father was saying to himself. "They'll find him."

When Hal returned to the flat, a policeman was asking Shahid's mum questions.

"This is his friend, Hal. He may know," Shahid's mum said when Hal came in.

"Hal, is it?" The officer turned to him. "I've some questions for you. Don't worry, you won't be in trouble, but I need you to answer honestly. Is there anywhere the two of you go that you shouldn't? Your mum told us about the roof already."

Hal tried to think of everywhere the two of them had hung out over the summer. He told them Shahid knew how to get into unoccupied flats, and about the flat they'd climbed through to get to the room—their parents still thought they jimmied the roof access door. The only place he didn't dare mention was the boiler room, Shahid wouldn't go there, and he didn't know if the Farreter would be able to hide from a search.

"And is there anyone, *anyone* Shahid has mentioned that was suspicious?" the officer asked.

"Yes!" Shahid's mother exclaimed. "The rag and bone man."

"You bothered him," Hal's mum added. "You two followed him and he complained about you to Mr Foster."

Hal's heart sank as he saw the direction of the investigation turn.

"No," he said loudly. "No, we apologised to him." Then he remembered: "There was someone. On the first day we met, Shahid mentioned someone used to watch him from their flat in Moynihan house. I never saw them, but... maybe that's—"

"Which flat?" the officer asked, calling his partner over from the kitchen, where he had been talking to Shahid's father.

Hal didn't know the number, but Shahid had pointed out the window.

"Show us." Hal led the officers through the estate. As they neared Moynihan, he pointed to one of the ground floor windows overlooking the playground. They told him to stay where he was. Hal's mother stood behind him, her hands on his shoulders protectively.

The police sprinted over the courtyard and one of them beat on the door with his fist while the other flashed his light through the living room window. They shouted through the letterbox. No one answered.

It took an hour for the warrant to be signed and delivered. The police kicked in the door the moment it arrived. Hal later learned the flat was a squat. No furniture, and not much of anything else, although it seemed as though someone had packed in a hurry. Shahid wasn't in the flat, but they found his camera, the film missing.

When the officers told Shahid's parents, Hal could hear it across the courtyard. He listened to them wailing into the night, his room bathed in cold blue light from the police cars below, flashing with the regularity of a pulse.

At first, they hoped the man who lived at No. 12—Charles Taylor—had taken Shahid with him. A vile hope, but the alternative was worse.

But in the morning, police found Shahid's drowned body in Meanwood Beck, about a mile north of the estate.

THE DAYS FOLLOWING Shahid's murder were a confusion of activity and stillness. Hal was questioned and re-questioned by the police, who'd become a constant presence on the estate, but all other life in Quarry Hill seemed frozen. Parents kept their children inside and peeked out through the curtains to watch the officers. Hal's mum sat in the living room listening to the radio, and he stayed in his room trying to make sense of what had happened.

Hal tried to visit Shahid's parents. He didn't know what he wanted to say, but he felt he had to say something to them, explain he had no part in what had happened, even though it was clear already he hadn't. They never opened their door to him, though. Maybe they were out, but he hadn't seen them leave the flat in days and police officers would often go in.

The newspapers led with stories of the manhunt for Charles Taylor. Hal read them all, thinking about how they'd soon be printed on microfilm and stored down in the cold archive, the world's only recollection of his friend.

On the fifth day, the papers revealed that the police had finally found him, sleeping under an overpass outside Birmingham. Taylor—who the papers described as 'troubled,'—confessed to the murder, but the same article that pronounced his guilt convinced Hal it wasn't the right man.

It was a double-spread, charting the progress of the investigation. The papers had been using the same images for days, but there was one in this piece that Hal hadn't seen before. A policeman stood up to his thighs in the stream where they found Shahid's body. The photo was taken at night, the man framed by lights downstream of the crime scene. Hal stared at the image. He knew he had seen the place before. For months he'd been trying to picture this place, and now it finally fell into place: when Goan saved him from the fall. He had seen this stream, seen Goan's long white arms holding Shahid under the dark water.

Hal felt sick. Not only because he'd been so close to his friend's murderer, but because he didn't know what to do now he knew. The police had a man in custody who had confessed to the crime, they had evidence supporting the confession—evidence Hal was certain Goan had planted—and Hal's only evidence for them being wrong was a vision he had had when an alien touched his arm.

Worse, in the coming nights, the vision he had fought so hard to see before now wouldn't leave him. Every night he found himself watching his friend as he drowned. Sometimes he stood upstream of the murder, watching Goan hold Shahid under the water, other times he was Goan, pressing Shahid down into the silt, impassively watching as his struggles grew weaker.

HAL'S MUM WATCHED her son become paler each day. She knew he wasn't sleeping well, hearing the moans of his nightmares as she sat in the living room each night. They had to get out of Quarry Hill.

13

As the summer holiday drew to a close, Hal's mum and Eli married. It was more than convenience, Hal saw that, though the quickness of the arrangement was driven by the events of the summer. He knew his mother could no longer live at Quarry Hill

The ceremony was small, as neither had much family, and what family they did have didn't all approve of the match— "Whether it's because he's a Jew or I'm a widow, they would rather I was alone than happy," Hal's mum said to her son one night.

After the wedding, they moved in with Eli's parents in Leylands. There was no one to say goodbye to when they left. Shahid's family moved away after the funeral, Mr Foster had gone into care, and they hadn't lived on the estate long enough to make much of an impression on anyone else.

The evening after the move, they were all sat in the living room. Hal paid little attention to the conversation around him. As was increasingly the case now, he sat lost in thought.

He tried to unpick the other things he had seen, to recognise what was to come before it came. He wondered whether the other Farreter were aware of what Goan had done, had condoned it—they couldn't have, surely? Even if they had no care for human life, as they had made clear, they couldn't approve of Goan taking it, either. He had spent all summer trying to know these creatures, learn where they had come from, what they were capable of, and it hadn't taught him anything. It hadn't warned him.

"You are deep in thought, grandson."

Hal's eyes came back to the room, he had been staring without focus at the tea cup on the table before him.

"I seem always to be interrupting your introspection," Daniel said. "I suspect it is not golems today."

Hal shook his head.

"When I was your age, I had a friend, Isaac. When Eli told me about you and your friend climbing the roof, I was reminded of him. When we were your age, all this part of Leeds was terraced houses. I suppose to you it still is, but these houses were smaller, colder things. We lived with my mother's sister's family, all ten of us, in a place half this size. In a place like that, you need to get outside—I think you know this feeling well. My friend Isaac and I, we would spend all summer finding the secrets of our neighbourhood. We found that the baker left the window open in his basement to let the cool air in as he cooked. We slipped in there some mornings and took the custard slices while his back was turned. You never forget friends like those."

Hal's memories of his first days at Quarry Hill came flooding back, climbing onto the roof with Shahid, exploring the estate, sitting up in his room making plans for the summer. He felt himself well up.

"Come, come," said Daniel, leading Hal away from the

others, taking him to the kitchen. He sat Hal at the table, wiping a tear from the boy's cheek with his thumb and turning to search through drawers and rifle through boxes. "My son, Eli, told me about what happened to your friend. It is a truly ugly business." He came back to the table with a long thin candle, a silver candlestick and a box of matches. "You must not feel you have to hide away your feelings. I have lost many people in my lifetime, family and dear friends. It helps to *feel* those emotions when they come, not drive them down."

Daniel lit the candle and placed it on the kitchen table. Its light warmed the room. From his jacket, the old man took out a little black cap and placed it on his crown. Standing solemnly for a moment, he began to sing.

Hal didn't know what to do. Religion wasn't part of his life and this was, Hal was sure, a prayer. Whether it was for him or for Shahid, it struck Hal as strange. Shahid had been a Muslim and Hal, though his mum was Christian, had rarely been to church. He couldn't even understand the words.

But then he started to listen, drawn in by the strange words. They seemed to falter and flow like the jumping of the candlelight, sometimes rolling, sometimes flickering. He couldn't understand what was being said, but he was struck by the compassion of the act: here, in this strange kitchen, his new grandfather prayed for a boy he had never met. As the thought turned in Hal's mind, he began to weep. The long-pent-up turmoil of guilt and loss seemed to burst and pour from him. The confusion of the weeks since Shahid's death cleared and, for a moment, in that kitchen, listening to a song he didn't understand, Hal was able to mourn.

In time his tears ended, and Hal realised he had heard the language Daniel was singing in before. He didn't understand the words, but the sound and rhythm were so familiar.

He had heard it once, weeks ago, sung in the cloister beneath the boiler room at Quarry Hill.

When the prayer was finished and the candle extinguished, Hal embraced Daniel, holding him tightly in thanks. He cleared his throat and said, "I'd like to ask you something, but, please, you can't tell anyone about it."

"Of course," Eli's father said, gripping Hal's shoulder firmly.

"What language was that song? It sounded so familiar."

"Hebrew. It's the language of our people, used in all our ceremonies. I'm surprised you found it familiar, though."

"Is *goan* a word in Hebrew?"

"Goan?" Daniel said, his eyes narrowed. "It means pride, but it is more than that. It is a mark of respect. The greatest rabbi and teachers are called goan. The wise men."

"And, what about *shande*?"

"That's not Hebrew, that's Yiddish. It means 'shame.' Hal, how did you learn these words?"

"Please, one more," Hal said. "*Farreter*?"

"That is also Yiddish. It means 'traitors.'"

Hal sat at the kitchen table, staring. He finally knew something about the creatures under Quarry Hill, and yet he felt like he was back at the beginning, knowing nothing at all.

14

Daniel tried to probe his grandson, but Hal remained firm, saying he couldn't say where he had learned the words. The old man stopped asking after a while, but Hal couldn't imagine he'd forgotten.

Since the prayer in the kitchen, Hal began to sleep more soundly. He still grieved for his friend, but it felt like he had loosened himself from the images that had haunted him. His mum put it down to them being away from the estate. She put him to work in Ruth and Daniel's garden each day, while she went to work at the University and Eli was at the family shop.

One day when Hal was working in the front garden, she returned from the university looking perturbed.

"Hal," she said, "Rose Wheldon came to me today with this for you." She withdrew a thick envelope from her handbag and handed it to Hal. "When did you two become such firm friends?"

Hal didn't even make an excuse. He tore open the envelope, which had a Viennese postmark, and walked into the house, reading the first page of the bundle of papers as he climbed the stairs to his room.

To Another Who Knows,

Your letter was forwarded to me by Claus Struker, who was the building manager in our block of the Karl-Marx-Hof when my family lived there in the '30s. He knew of the building's secret, but it was my late father who was its author. I suspect that is why he's asked that I share its story.

My family moved into Block C, Flat 15 on September 16th, 1931. It was a big moment for our family; we had always lived in shared homes, my father's work at the university brought in only a little money. The Karl-Marx-Hof meant we could have a place of our own. It was the same for many of the city's Jews.

My father was to continue at the university, but he had secured a place in the apartment block by offering to work at the synagogue after it finished construction. I swear the building manager was a chachem attick, everyone in our building got on the housing list by making deals with him. The Karl-Marx-Hof became something of a commune for Viennese Jews. Many of those that would become his congregation had flats in the estate. Each Friday we would gather in the community hall where he would hold Shabbat. I remember we would turn off all the lights and he would light candles, their warm glow lighting the faces of the assembled people. He would lead the prayers and we would all join in for the songs.

That first winter there was brutally cold. All new buildings have problems, but the Karl-Marx-Hof was one of the largest housing projects in Europe, and many of its innovations were untested. Those cold nights revealed all their flaws. The boiler would fail, gaps in the roofing and window fittings would whistle with wind and drip with water. Many nights we would climb into our parents' bed for warmth, my brother, my three sisters and I.

One of the nights we'd taken to sleeping with our parents in January, we were woken by banging on the door. My father answered. I remember lying there and hearing him talk in whispered Yiddish. He and the guest made much noise as they gathered up all of my family's coats and spare blankets, taking them from our beds, leaving only those we slept under in his room. They boiled water and filled the flasks we took with us when we skied in spring. Loaded up, he and the men at the door left the flat. It was the dead of night, and he said nothing of where he was going.

I remember my sister Helen and I were playing with toy soldiers in the living room when my father returned the next morning, long after the sun had risen. He didn't say a word to us, just took our mother into their bedroom and shut the door. We could hear a muffled conversation, but nothing of what was said.

When they emerged, my father kissed us goodbye and left immediately without taking breakfast. My mother began writing a list, which she gave to my oldest sister, Mila, and sent us to market. Helen and Danka stayed with mother and began baking.

Mila, my brother Poldek and I went to the market with the list and the money she gave us. It was food enough for an army; it looked like we were to prepare a feast for half the Jews in Karl-Marx-Hof.

When we returned I could see all the bread my mother and sisters had prepared. There were loaves cooling on the counter, more in the oven, and fresh dough waiting its turn on the table. We asked what this was all, for but my mother wouldn't say; only something about unexpected guests and a long journey.

Poldek and I were told to go to the other Jewish families in Block C and ask for spare clothes: shirts, trousers, coats, enough for twenty-seven. It became something of a game to us, we would go to each flat and say, "Have you anything for the guests," and we'd be handed clothes and blankets. Sometimes, too, there were treats, sweets and candied fruits. We took everything back to our home and separated it into piles, folded all the clothing and linen. Packed the bread into baskets. Helen and I even put our tin soldiers in one of the baskets, a gift for the guests.

Early that afternoon my father returned with three men who also lived in the building. He beckoned over Poldek and me and told us to pick up as many bundles as we could carry and to follow him downstairs. We carried our bundles with great ceremony, I remember, proud we had a responsibility not afforded to my sisters.

Father led us downstairs and directed us to go through to the basement. We had never seen this part of the building before; the doorway was hidden beneath the staircase.

I still remember the smell. The day had built an excitement in us that left me wholly by the last step of the staircase. The sickly-sweet smell of rotting flesh was overpowering. It took all I had not to vomit. The basement had been turned into a makeshift medical ward. Everywhere were men lying prone, horrible sores on their flesh. The sight was overwhelming. I remember realising slowly that the sick weren't *people, that beneath their wounds I could see their faces lacked eyes, noses, ears. Their bodies were too slim, their limbs too long.*

I focused on placing the bundles so I didn't have to look at the ill. They were taller than any man I'd seen, and what unblemished skin I could see was as white as ivory. Men from the building attended the sick. Two of the men I knew were doctors, the other was our butcher. They were cleaning and bandaging wounds, and from the bucket by the boiler I could see they had had to amputate more than one limb. More than the smell, the sense that stays with me is the silence. None of the creatures made a sound through all this suffering.

My father bid us go along the rows of patients and collect up used, dirty bandages. The doctors showed us how to clean the creatures without touching their wounds. On closer inspection, I could see that besides the sores, which looked like frostbite, many of the guests had other wounds. Some had holes punched into their flesh, others had been slashed, leaving deep trenches in their bodies. We filled cups with water and held them to their lips when they wanted to drink. We cleaned the floors, soaked the bandages, and delivered a bundle of clothes to each, making sure each of them had a set to dress himself in.

After hours of this, my father took us aside and said we were to tell no one what we had seen, no one outside our family. We returned to our flat and he went to sleep, promising he would answer our questions when he had rested.

That evening, we sat around our table, the whole family, and he told us how Mr Dresner, the night watchman over the synagogue construction site, had heard a great clatter after midnight. "Like fireworks under water," he said. Well, Dresner investigated and came across these injured creatures huddled in the foundations. Most bore injuries like gunshots and sabre slashes. Dresner rushed here and woke father, who sent Dresner to get the doctors, the butcher, the coats and blankets.

They took the butcher's van to the building site. It couldn't have been more than an hour since Dresner left, but already frostbite had set in—these creatures are far more susceptible to the cold than us. Those that couldn't walk were loaded into the van and brought back with the doctors. My father and the night watchman led back the twenty or so that could walk. My father said how one of the guests walked with him at the front. He was an uncanny scout, motioning for his brethren to clear the street almost before the car or nightwalker would appear.

When the group reached the Karl-Marx-Hof, father led them to the basement where they'd be hidden and warmest. The rest of the night they did what they could to treat the guests' injuries.

Father told us the guests would be staying until they could find a safer place and find out why they were here. No one could know outside our community, he told us. 'The world isn't a safe place right now for those that are different.' I didn't recognise the truth in those words at the time.

Each day my brother, my father, and I would tend to the guests. Their wounds healed quickly, though they left terrible scars. I noticed that as they healed, the guests slipped off their clothes. It was strange; I would catch them shivering as if they were cold, and they would cluster around the boiler for warmth, but still they would not wear our clothes. It was as if they could not bear to.

There were many intriguing things among our guests, but what surprised my father the most was their Yiddish. The creatures picked the language up in weeks simply from listening to us talk. They even took on names for themselves, choosing words from our languages. Their leader chose to call himself Rikhter, meaning 'Judge,' which I always thought suited him, he was unbending in his beliefs. We didn't approve of all their names, they started to refer to their group as 'Farreter.' We explained this meant 'Traitors,' but they did not change it. There was also one of their number who sat apart from them, excluded. It was him who aided my father in leading the group back to the flats on that first night. They called him 'Shande,' shame. We were never told why he was called this but there was a particular bitterness between him and Rikhter.

The creatures mostly kept to themselves, but Shande would speak with me. Whereas the others seemed to actively avoid contact with us, he would seek out conversation. He wanted to know about our world. I would tell him stories and history, filling him up with cultures alien to him. He had a peculiar fascination with the story of the Golem, a creature created to protect Jews.

Shande and the others told us bits about themselves, but the history was only ever piecemeal, to be assembled in night-time conversations by us, their carers. They had fled a conflict—their people were hunted for their prophetic abilities. An insular people, *they weren't trusted or understood. Nor did those who dealt with them ever wholly trust them; their insights bred envy.*

In time, through little suggestions at first, we started to become aware of something our guests could see but weren't telling. They aren't a talkative people—you doubtless know this—but when it comes to sharing talk of the future, they are especially cautious. I think it was when they realised they were trapped without our help that they talked. They saw something, something coming, a danger that would eradicate them if they could not escape that basement.

In 1934, we thought the coming danger had arrived. Insurgents fighting in the Civil War barricaded themselves in the building. We all hid in the basement with our guests when the men holed up in the apartments. Not that there weren't supporters for their cause in our community, but we didn't want to be caught in any fighting should the army try to force them out. We shouldn't have given them so much credit: they didn't send troops in, they fired on the apartments with light artillery. More than a hundred of us hid in the basement with our guests.

During the siege they would calm us, saying they could see we would be safe. When the shelling was at its worst one of the guests placed his hand on a child to calm him, show he wouldn't be harmed by the shells. The boy did settle, briefly, but the guest laid his hand on him too long. The boy saw beyond the war and onto something else. What he saw terrified him. He wept and screamed, but could not say what had horrified him. I often think of that boy, now that I know what he could see.

When the shelling ended and still our guests warned of a coming danger, my father began planning their escape. My father contacted a rabbi he had trained with, who had moved to England after becoming ordained. He was able to put my father in touch with a Reverend Jenkinson. His thinking was that an English priest was able to move more freely and with less suspicion than an Austrian Jew in those days (and today, too, I suppose). My father begged him to visit and see if he could arrange a safe passage for some 'desperate refugees,' as my father called them.

I met this Jenkinson when he came. He ate dinner with us the night he met our guests. He said nothing about it over the meal, but shared stories of Leeds and England. After dinner, though, he and father discussed plans. Soon they would load the guests onto trucks bound for Jewish shops throughout Europe, relaying their cargo between different businesses. Before this could happen, he needed to talk to a man named Livett back in England. Jenkinson returned to Vienna once more with Livett, this time under the auspices of inspecting the building which was to form the basis of a housing project in Leeds—I believe you know it well.

In 1938, it was clear to even those without prophetic powers that they had to leave then or never. One night, packed into trucks loaded with spices, they left. Within a month German troops marched into Austria. Had they stayed any longer, they would have suffered the same fate as my family.

You will know more than I what happened to them when they reached England. My father had plans to maintain contact with Jenkinson and the guests, but the war changed everything.

I have often wondered how much those we cared for knew of what was coming. They gave us no warning, other than how it threatened them. I do not hate them for it, I have seen how fear can make men act.

Take care of them, Hal: they are scared, and can never return home.

One who knows,

Ignaz Mitsrayim.

PART TWO

15

Leeds, 1977

HAL AWOKE GROGGILY. He'd gone to bed long after midnight, having stayed late at the *Yorkshire Evening Post*'s offices. He always stayed late on the days he filed copy; he'd sit with the subeditors until they told him to stop looming.

He'd wanted to be sure his article on the impending demolition of Quarry Hill wasn't passed over or missed out by some accident. It had never happened before, but he couldn't bring himself to leave until he saw his article filed along with the others.

It was still night time, he realised. Something must have woken him up.

Then he heard it, a light knock at the front door. Hal slipped downstairs to see who it was before their knocking woke up everyone in the house.

Stood in the garden was a Farreter.

"I must speak with you, golem," the creature said.

Hal stood in the doorway, knuckles white on the handle. He had not seen any of the Farreter since being driven from

413

their bunker a decade ago. He had tried to wipe them from his mind, but still, there were nights when he woke up from nightmares of seeing through Goan's eyes.

"You come to my house?" Hal hissed.

"You must speak with us. We are in desperate need."

"I have nothing to say to you."

"Please, we have nowhere else to go."

As Hal's eyes grew accustomed to the dark he saw that the creature's skin was covered in sores and burns. His resolve weakened. Stepping aside, he ushered the creature into the house and down the hall to the kitchen.

In the light of the kitchen, Hal realised he recognised the Farreter as Rikhter, the leader of the group, the one who had driven him and Shahid from the bunker.

"Why are you here?"

"I am so sorry, Golem. We didn't know."

"Why do you keep calling me Golem?"

"Because that is what he called you. It's what he meant you to be. You were fated to die on that roof and he saved your life; you were to become inanimate, but he imbued you with a new purpose. To protect him, to protect us."

"I am not his. Did you know he was a killer? That he killed my friend, a defenceless child?"

Rikhter shook his head. "We didn't know. He hid it from us. Our brother has always been difficult, complicating us. We didn't look closely. You must understand, he saved us and shamed us in the same moment. We have never forgiven him and it made us blind."

"What do you mean?"

"Before we came here, to your world, our people have always been observers. It was our way for centuries. Many travellers wanted to use our sight, but we vowed neutrality. We believed this would make us safe, but it made us

414

enemies—we were blamed for our inaction. In time they came to eradicate us. Many thousands of our people were killed, more were enslaved.

"When the yeger came for our tribe, we were prepared to accept our fate as we had been taught; all of us except for Shande. Using his foresight and their technologies, he was able to bring us here, to your planet. We thought he had delivered us to hell. We arrived to a world of blind, feral whiteness. The cold air blistered and burned our skin. We believed we were being punished for our flight, for interfering with the channel. But we were sheltered from the storm by a kind people. It's hard to explain what it was to survive. That was a new idea for my people. In our culture you die when you are appointed to die. That is the way of things. It is your time because you saw it to be so. Shande isn't the first to act as he has, but radicals like him were exiled on our world; even speaking of them was forbidden. Trapped in that basement, we couldn't escape what he had done, couldn't escape that we had benefitted from his transgression. We pinned that shame on him and did what we could to ignore him. Not that we could escape him in our bunker."

"He killed people, innocent people."

"He kept that hidden from us."

"How? You see everything."

"No." Rikhter paused. "We closed ourselves to him. We knew he was a radical. We were with him when he talked to those who found us first. He told them about our people and they told him about theirs. We were present during those transgressions. But in this second home we locked the door to our bunker and didn't see what he did outside—we didn't care to. That is our crime."

Hal closed his fists, not trusting himself to speak.

"You don't know what it's like. That bunker, our constant cell, it screams its future at us. When we lie in our beds, we see the roof caving in, when we sit at our tables for meals the floors and walls tell us it will become a tomb. It started as a whisper that we could ignore when we first arrived, but now, with the demolition coming closer and closer, we cannot escape what we see. We know what it is to survive now, and this constant knowledge of our fate is a torture to us."

"How did you find out he was a murderer?"

"It was Novi who discovered them. He couldn't take the visions anymore. He felt like he was suffocating. He unbolted the door to the bunker and fled, he got as far as the boiler room before his panic subsided. He couldn't bring himself to go outside—there are too many unknowns in your world. As he calmed down he started to hear something calling to him. He located a bundle hidden in the boiler room that contained tokens: a knife, a watch. And this—" Rikhter placed a small silver medal on the table.

Hal snatched it up, inspecting it closely, turning it over in his hands. It was his father's medal, he was sure of it. Rage flamed in Hal. All these years, it hadn't been lost, it had been kept from him.

"He kept them from us, Golem," Rikhter said. "He meant for us never to find them."

"What do they show you?"

"Ugly crimes. He cut short the fates of two people, changing the direction of the channel. We don't know why."

"Two people?"

"Yes, your friend, and many years ago, a woman."

"Sarah Williams," Hal said. Shahid had been right from the first. "Why have you come here?"

"Please, you must help us escape Quarry Hill."

"Why would I do that? You did nothing to help the people who took you in in Vienna. You've done nothing but hide under the estate for forty years. And you've sat by and let your brother murder two innocent people."

"We fled a war created by an envy of our sight. It wasn't right, but lending our knowledge to strangers, even caring ones, that was too great a risk."

"Why should I help you?" Hal repeated.

"Because you can," Hal heard from behind him. He turned to the doorway and saw Daniel watching them both.

"Who is this man forming a puddle in my kitchen, Hal?" Daniel asked, walking into the room. He stopped when he saw Rikhter's eyeless, skinless face. He showed neither fear nor even shock, but simply took it for what it was. He was silent for a moment.

"Something tells me I'm about to hear how my grandson came to learn Hebrew."

THE THREE OF them sat in the kitchen for an hour. Hal told his grandfather everything: how Goan had saved him, how he and Shahid had discovered all they could about the strange figure, what they had found in the boiler room. Hal read them both the letter he had received from Vienna. Daniel listened patiently, asking only a few questions.

When Hal was finished, Daniel turned to Rikhter and asked, "How long do the Farreter have?"

"We do not see beyond this week."

"Then we must act soon. You will stay here today, and tomorrow night we'll have a plan. Hal, show our guest to your bed and come back downstairs."

When Hal returned, Daniel was still at the table, watching the morning light through the window.

"It is not for us to decide who is worthy of help," Hal's grandfather said into the stillness. "The Farreter could have helped, and yet did nothing; that was wrong. But now *we* can help, and if we choose to do nothing, we are no better."

He told Hal to start preparing the kitchen for a meeting, and then took his coat and left.

16

As the sun rose, men began appearing at the house. Hal invited them into the kitchen and served them coffee. Hal had seen them all in Eli's home over the years, often for Shabbat. They owned shops and businesses in the area. As the kitchen filled, the conversation grew louder; they spoke as old friends, discussing the past, the future, their families.

The noise brought down the other people in the house. Hal's mum asked what was going on and he just said that Daniel would explain when he got back.

Shortly after the nearby church's bell rang, Daniel returned, bringing with him the last guest.

"Thank you for coming," Daniel said, quieting the room. "I invited you here because we need your help." Turning to Hal he said, "Go get your guest."

Hal went upstairs, finding Rikhter awake, standing at Hal's desk, running his hands over the photos of Hal's father.

"It's time," Hal said, leading Rikhter to the kitchen. The room was silent with expectation.

"My grandson will explain," Daniel announced.

Hal looked to Daniel and back, momentarily afraid of

addressing the room. Eli gave him a supportive nod from the back of the kitchen. He took a breath and, for the second time that night, explained all he knew of the Farreter: who they were, where they were from, how they'd come to be here. The men stood impassively throughout.

"—their part of the estate will be demolished within the week, so we must act now to save them," he eventually finished.

The room was quiet for a moment. Some of the men stared at Rikhter, looking for proof of the strange story they had heard.

They began to speak all at once, talking over each other—

"—We could split them up, keep them in the community—"

"—We should use them. What can they tell us about the coming year?—"

"—Why should *we* help?—"

"—They left good Jews to die—"

Hal raised a hand to get their attention and said, "They are not a resource to be exploited. Their race was nearly wiped out because of that sort of thinking. Sharing their knowledge goes against everything they believe in; we must respect that.

"We need to get them out of the city. Quarry Hill began as a sanctuary, but it has become a prison. They can't leave their bunker out of fear of discovery. Many of them have not seen the sky in forty years. They need somewhere open, somewhere private where they can be safe. And we need to keep them together. They are a family, they move as one; and splitting them up increases the risks."

"Each year we celebrate Pesach," Daniel said. "We tell stories of the Jews fleeing from the horrors of Egypt to find a safe home, a sanctuary away from persecution. Can any of you in good faith do that again if you turn down the chance to help these people?"

One arm rose at the back of the room: a man in his 50s who Hal recognised from the nearby bakery.

"I know a place. A place they may be safe. My cousin lives in Argyll in Scotland. There's a farming community up there who may be able to take them in."

"That could work," Hal said. "Next we need to sort out transport. Who has a van we can use?"

Over the next hour, with little dissent, they fleshed out a plan. The group had to act fast, deciding to move that night.

IT BEGAN RAINING that afternoon. By night it had become a constant, heavy downpour. The mechanical rubbery squeak of the windscreen wipers filled the cabin of Eli's van, and for a half-second after every swipe, Hal caught a watery glimpse of the sleeping city. The headlights barely cut into the darkness and near-impenetrable rain, but from what Hal could see there was no one on the streets.

As the convoy of vans circled the estate, driving towards the Oastler arch, Hal saw the demolition work had already begun, workmen breaking the buildings apart with machinery. It had the look of a half-finished dissection, flayed walls exposing gutted homes. Jackson House, Hal's old home, was already gone, a pile of rubble marking the block's final rest. Even the still-untouched buildings were ruinous, their walls cracked and crumbling, the metal frame exposed, visible on the surface like varicose veins. The narrow arch through Kitson House was blocked with rubble. In the darkness, the tunnel looked like a mouth, the rusting iron its fangs.

The vans entered the estate through the Oastler arch, driving past silent machinery. It was an eerie sight. There was no light on the estate; the shattered buildings still blocked out the city lights, and the courtyard's lamps had been disconnected when the last residents moved out.

The vans parked near the playing fields, not wanting to get stuck in the mud. The men got out of the vans and formed a huddle. They all dressed in raincoats and carried torches.

"Rikhter and I will go in first," Hal shouted over the rain. "The tunnel is narrow, so we'll have to go single file. You three"—Hal pointed at some of the drivers—"will stay with Eli in the vans. If anyone comes, sound your horns and drive away. There's no good excuse for being here, and no need to get in trouble. Daniel, you'll stay in the boiler room; if the vans leave, sound the warning to us and join us in the bunker. Joseph"—the bakery owner—"you're with me. Finally, everyone: if you see a man wearing a china mask, do not approach him. Warn us and then leave."

"I'm coming with you," Eli said. "If you and Dad are going to be in the bunker, that's where I need to be."

Hal didn't argue. His step-father's company would be reassuring.

Hal led the way across the field, lighting the way with his torch, Rikhter at his side. The creature wrapped itself tightly in Hal's father's coat, trying to keep out the cold and the rain. The rainfall had turned the field into mud, and they had to keep moving as the waterlogged ground tried to trip them or suck them down. Hal retrieved the boiler room key from his pocket—he'd kept it all these years—and let them inside, out of the rain.

The boiler room was cold and silent, the machines now still. The smell of oil remained, but Hal could now smell a coppery quality to it, a suggestion of blood. He felt like he'd stepped into a mausoleum.

Daniel took up his post at the door and Hal unlocked the

hatch into the tunnel. Rikhter led the way, Hal lighting the tunnel ahead. Eli and Joseph followed.

Rikhter knocked on the metal door. He had ordered for it to be bolted behind him after he left. There was no answer, and Rikhter knocked again. Joseph turned to shine his torch back the way they had come. Rikhter knocked again, louder this time. Hal could feel the tension in the group as they waited. Finally, they heard the sound of the bolt being drawn.

"Novi," Rikhter said when the door opened. "I have brought the golem."

It's hard to read the face of the Farreter, but Hal thought he saw Novi's relax at the sight of them. The Farreter guard opened the door wider and let them inside.

The bunker was a lot smaller than it had seemed, those years ago. The candlelight and dancing shadows had hidden how tight a space it really was. It was a grim cage for twenty-seven creatures to spend so long inside.

"We didn't know it was you," Novi said, explaining the delay. "Since you left, we heard noises in the tunnel. Something was banging on the pipes and pacing the length of it."

The Farreter were not used to uncertainty, Hal realised. Their sight gave them confidence, but they so relied on it so heavily they weren't aware of the things they were blind to.

"You must gather your things," Hal shouted to the room. "We have vans waiting to take you to a safer place. You will never be able to return here, so do not leave anything you can't live without." The Farreter went to their bunks and started stashing things into their pillowcases. "We will leave in groups, each with an escort."

Hal watched the Farreter stuff their sacks with bones, scraps of clothing, and other strange trinkets. "Rikhter, why are they packing those things?"

"They are memory aids," Rikhter explained. "If we like an object's history, then we sometimes like to keep a token of it." Hal remembered the way Shande had caressed Mrs King's blue shawl.

The creatures assembled at the bunker's entrance as soon as they were packed. Hal, Eli, and Joseph began leading groups of three to the waiting vans. They had to keep moving the Farreter along: despite the harsh cold, which must have hurt them, they seemed to revel in the sensation of rain and the feeling of walking in soft mud.

The evacuation became confused as the Farreter started to meet them at the boiler room instead of waiting in the bunker, and the groups started drifting on the walk to the van. Some of the creatures left without an escort and had to be herded towards the waiting vehicles.

When it appeared all the Farreter were assembled, Hal did a headcount to be sure: twenty-six. They were all there.

The group had agreed to leave Shande to his fate. They were not killers, and they couldn't bring him to justice without revealing the existence of the other Farreter. Eli and Joseph took their places in the vans and Hal waved two torches over his head, the signal for Daniel to join them. Hal could see his flashlight in the boiler room, but it didn't move, so Hal signalled again. He signalled a third time as he started to walk over the field, worry starting to build in his gut. Rikhter followed close behind.

Hal broke into a jog. He felt crunching underfoot and pointed the torch at the ground to see bits of broken china— the all-too-familiar mask, now in pieces. He began to sprint towards the open door, Rikhter picking up pace behind him. Hal heard the sound of van doors opening as the other men saw something was wrong and came to help.

Daniel's torch lay abandoned on the floor of the boiler

room but Hal saw no sign of his grandfather. The hatch lay open, a terrible invitation. Hal shone his torch through the gap, checking the tunnel below, before climbing down.

Hal sprinted down the tunnel; the only sounds he could hear were his heavy breathing and Rikhter's footfalls as he kept pace behind.

Hal slowed at the bunker. The lights were off and he couldn't see anything when he shone his light through the doorway. He motioned to Rikhter to follow him inside, crossed the threshold and swept his torch beam from side to side. As he turned, he felt something heavy connect with the side of his head. He saw

—himself stumble sideways into one of the bunk beds, dropping his torch—

He heard the metal door slam shut behind them, the bolt sliding home. Banging and shouting from the tunnel began a moment later.

"No one move," a voice said in the dark. The only light was the beam from Hal's torch as it rolled across the concrete floor.

"Brother, we're leaving," Hal heard Rikhter say.

"He's got a knife," another voice said.

"Daniel?" Hal shouted. "Are you okay?"

"Nothing permanent," he grunted. "I'm sorry, grandson, he looked like all the others."

"Brother—" Rikhter began.

"Brother? Not Shande?"

"We must leave here, brother."

"I saved you all and you said I shamed you."

"We were wrong—"

"So faithful you all are, I thought. I transgressed by escaping death, I acted in bad faith. I shamed my brothers by pulling them away from their fate."

Hal tried to locate the voice in the dark as he edged towards the door.

"You, you faithful—My Ward, if you keep moving I'll cut your grandfather open—Here was a perfect test of your faith, brother. If you accepted death, all you had to do was stay here, stay in this bunker."

"You showed us we didn't have to, you showed us we could survive—"

"And you named me 'shame,'" Shande shouted. There was a sudden movement in the dark and Rikhter stumbled into the light, clutching at his chest, blood on his hands.

"I didn't want to kill *any* of you," shouted Shande. "I wouldn't *have* to, if you'd just lived up to the ideals you attacked me with."

"What about Shahid?" Hal shouted into the dark. His eyes were adjusting to the light; he made out the outline of a tall figure in the gloom.

"He was going to tell the world about us. He was going to *expose* us. He had my photo. For months he'd tried, but after you two met my brothers, he hounded me. He did it behind your back. My mask slipped once—just once— and he was waiting. I had to protect my brothers." Shande stepped and leant over Rikhter's writhing body. "I made myself *monstrous* for you!"

"And Sarah Williams?" Hal asked, seeing Shande's shadow move closer as he talked. "Was she going to expose you?"

"I trusted her," Shande said, circling back into the dark. "I read her future every day. I told her more than the others. I cared for her; I thought she could help us. I thought she was good. But when I touched this knife"—the figure gestured— "I saw the knife would stab me. I acted, I attacked her before she could attack me. I thought she must have blinded me somehow, her future had said nothing of this danger. As she died, I saw that I was wrong, she hadn't wanted to kill me at all."

"What about me? What did you have planned for me?"

"I wanted to make you our protector."

Hal could see Shande step towards him in the dark. He tensed in preparation.

"You were supposed to die on that roof, but I broke your fate. I gave you new purpose. I thought I could teach you about us, tie you to us. You could prot—"

Hal dove forwards, tackling Shande to the ground. As soon as Hal touched Shande's skin his head filled with visions. He saw

—himself lying on the ground being punched—

Hal felt the blows on his face as he struggled to get on top of Shande. He swung his fist and caught the creature on side of the head, knocking Shande off him. Hal's head cleared and he could see again.

Shande rose to his feet in the harsh light of the torch, half in light and half in shadow, knife in hand. He lunged at Hal with the blade and Hal managed to step aside just in time. Shande swung at Hal's neck and he ducked; he stepped forward with another lunge and Hal tripped and fell backwards. Shande was on him in a moment. He pressed Hal's head into the concrete. Hal saw

—Shande gripping his hair and smacking Hal's head onto the ground—

Something strange was happening to Hal. He was seeing visions from Shande's eyes as before, but now through his own eyes, too. With this double-vision he saw Rikhter behind Shande, holding back his knife arm, keeping him from stabbing Hal. The vision in Hal's head was moving beyond the present

—Shande crawling towards the bunker door—

Hal pulled at the knife in Shande's hand
—*Shande pulling himself along the tunnel floor*—
Hal stabbed the knife up, driving it deep into Shande's side
—*the tunnel collapsing on Shande*—
Shande let go of Hal's head and pressed his hand to the knife wound in his side. Hal scrambled out from under him and ran to the door, throwing back the bolt and turning on the lights.

"Don't touch Shande," Hal shouted as Eli and Joseph burst in.

Eli checked Hal was okay and ran to Daniel, who was lying injured on one of the bunks. Hal and Joe dragged Rikhter by the coat away from the writhing Shande. They fled together down the tunnel and up into the night.

"What about Shande?" Eli asked.

"I saw," Hal said. "He doesn't escape."

HAL SAT IN the back of Eli's van beside Rikhter, who lay on the floor, blood soaking into Hal's father's coat. They had bandaged him as soon as they got into the car, but he was looking weak. They couldn't do any more for him at the moment, so the convoy had decided to set off for Scotland as planned.

"You protected us," Rikhter said. "Just as he meant you to."

Hal sat in silence.

"Hal, if you could see the things I see wearing this." He indicated Hal's father's coat. "You're just like he was, before he went away."

"I don't even know that man," Hal said quietly. "He abandoned us."

"He saved people, too."

They sat in a long silence.

"Come, let me show you," Rickter offered Hal his hand.

Hal stared at it for several long seconds, then reached out.

He saw.

He saw his father, from the moment he first wore that coat, through that long war.

He saw his father find a group of soldiers lost in a snowstorm and he saw him lead them home.

He also saw things that broke him, left his father a shadow of himself.

Worst, he saw how it crushed his father to see Hal and his mum and not to be able to feel joy.

Hal saw further.

Hal saw

—*the trucks arriving at the farm*—

—*the home the Farreter make*—

—*he stays with them*—

—*watching over them*—

—*as Goan had planned.*

ACKNOWLEDGEMENTS

This book wouldn't have happened without the help of two people in particular: Cassandra Khaw and David Moore. Cass pushed me to pitch a story, introduced me to David, and chased me when I dragged my feet. David found the story within the manuscript, trimming away wasteful words and giving what I'd written new life. Most of all, he didn't once point out that at the start of all this he asked me for an alien invasion story.

Matt Zitron gave invaluable help, correcting my use of Hebrew and Yiddish terms, and offering incisive notes to improve the whole story.

A great help, too, was Jonathan Oliver, who took the last pass over the manuscript, slicing away the last of my repetitions.

Then there are Adam and Barney who put up with weeks of me walking around the flat at night, talking to myself and making coffee. And, then, after all that, reading my early drafts with fresh eyes and pointing out muddles and mistakes.

Mum and Dad, too, for reading through my drafts and then submitting to long phone calls where I asked them endless questions about what they'd read. Though, Dad, giving me notes about suggested puns when I was one night before deadline is less helpful than you would imagine.

Julian Benson

ABOUT
THE AUTHOR

Julian Benson is the deputy editor at PCGamesN, a website about video games, their makers, and the people who devote their lives to them. Tired of concerned family members suggesting the low wages of video games journalism wouldn't be enough to support himself, he has started to write sci-fi novellas, where he is positive he will make his millions (Right, David?). He once interviewed the space pope of an online universe and he won't shut up about it.